Praise for *The Life You Longed For*

"A fiery and modern-day version of the witch hunt, *The Life You Longed For* is the story of how a mother can be accused of the worst offense by any doctor, friend, or neighbor. But this is no dark tale. *The Life You Longed For* is beautifully written and filled with characters that are fallible, utterly human, and completely compelling. It is a novel brimming with joy, heartbreak, and the power of love."

—Colleen Curran, author of *Whores on the Hill*

"Crammed full of fascinating historical and scientific detail, this novel is a perfect book-group selection."

—*Library Journal*

"The agonizing truths about losing a child while still longing for 'a life beyond the one you were living' come through clearly."

—*Publishers Weekly*

"A gripping novel, weaving several storylines together in a satisfying and thought-provoking way."

—*Tampa Tribune*

"Grace is as vigilant, astonishing, and brave as she is exhausted and imperfect. Simply put, she is a mother. In intimate and achingly lyrical language, Maribeth Fischer tackles the question: How do we love in the face of inevitable loss? The answer she gives us is, fiercely, completely."

—Marisa de los Santos, author of *Love Walked In*

ALSO BY MARIBETH FISCHER

The Language of Goodbye

THE LIFE

YOU

LONGED FOR

MARIBETH FISCHER

A TOUCHSTONE BOOK
Published by Simon & Schuster
New York · London · Toronto · Sydney

TOUCHSTONE
A Division of Simon & Schuster, Inc.
1230 Avenue of the Americas
New York, NY 10020

First Touchstone trade paperback edition March 2008

TOUCHSTONE and colophon are registered trademarks
of Simon & Schuster, Inc.

For information regarding special discounts for bulk purchases,
please contact Simon & Schuster Special Sales at 1-800-456-6798
or business@simonandschuster.com.

Designed by Lauren Simonetti

Manufactured in the United States of America

1   3   5   7   9   10   8   6   4   2

Library of Congress Cataloging-in-Publication Data
Fischer, Maribeth.
The life you longed for / Maribeth Fischer.
p. cm.
1. Munchausen syndrome by proxy—Fiction. I. Title.
PS3556.17628L54 2007
813'.6—dc22   2006051125

ISBN-13: 978-0-7432-9328-0
ISBN-10:   0-7432-9328-2
ISBN-13: 978-0-7432-9331-0 (pbk)
ISBN-10:   0-7432-9331-2 (pbk)

In Memory of "My Goose"

She had always thought there would be time enough—that you could lead a certain life and then, when it faded, exchange it for the one you'd always longed for . . .

—Andrew Sean Greer, *The Path of Minor Planets*

PART I

Desire

There are two tragedies in life.
One is to lose your heart's desire.
The other is to gain it.

—George Bernard Shaw

ONE

*C*hristmas Eve, 2000.

The gray-hued landscape of the Pine Barrens blurred by as Grace drove, dark spindly trunks of pine trees dissolving into thin gray branches, sienna-tinged against the colorless sky. She was supposed to be last-minute Christmas shopping but had realized the night before that she was finished. And the house was clean, the presents were wrapped, her mother had already agreed to babysit. Which meant that Grace was free. For the entire day, if she wanted. And she did.

The two-lane road was nearly empty, nothing on either side of it but straggly scrubland, interrupted now and then by a sagging farmhouse. Wind buffeted the car, wrenching the steering wheel that Grace held in one hand. The other held her Starbucks coffee—and not just coffee, but a venti cappuccino, because with the whole day, she'd had time for this too. She exhaled a long breath and smiled, regarding her reflection in the rearview mirror: gray eyes, thick shoulder-length auburn hair, and today, for Noah, lipstick. "Coral spice" or "spicy coral" or . . . she glanced again at her reflection, felt her heart cartwheel in her chest. People told her that she didn't look thirty-seven. And today, with all this time—no doctor appointments for Jack or driving Max to hockey practice or Erin to the Y for swim lessons—Grace didn't feel anywhere close to thirty-seven. More like seventeen, she thought, the age she had been the summer she met Noah.

"Do you ever wonder why this happened?" she asked him a few weeks ago. *This:* their meeting again after twenty years, falling in love.

"Coincidence?"

"That's it?" Already something in her was retreating, burrowing away from him.

He squeezed her tighter against his chest. "Hey you, get back here."

Hey you. She tilted her head up to look at him. His face was backlit by gold winter light. Through the windows behind them, the sun was setting over the bay.

"So, you think it was fate?" he teased. "The will of the gods?"

She leaned up on one elbow to look at him. "Why is fate any more far-fetched than coincidence?"

"It's not." He moved his finger around the outline of her lips and pretended to draw a smile. "But does it really matter? Call it anything you want, Grace Martin, as long as you don't disappear this time."

Grace Martin. She hadn't been Grace Martin in fourteen years.

Ahead of her loomed the sign for the Atlantic City Expressway. She flicked on her turn signal, then slowed for the tollbooth. She had phoned Noah earlier to make sure he'd be in his office today. It was Christmas Eve, and though the Cape May Bird Observatory stayed open through the holidays, Noah was flying home to Ann Arbor tonight. He had sounded rushed, his voice excited, and she thought it was because of his trip, until he explained: There had been two sightings of a brown pelican at the Observatory that morning. Unconfirmed, but *still.* "Brown pelicans are rare anytime, but God, Grace, *here*? And at this time of the season!" He was headed to Higbie's Beach, he told her. "Can I call you around ten-thirty? I should be back in the office by then."

"Ten-thirty's perfect." She was smiling. With luck she'd be *in* his office by 10:30. She'd almost added, "I'll see you then," but he hung up—thank God—before she could. Even as a child, she was always the one to inadvertently slip and ruin a surprise or blurt out a secret and then, too late, clap her hand to her mouth. She shook her head, wondering, as she had so often these past eleven months, how she had held the secret of Noah within her all this time. But you hold onto what you have to, she knew, thinking of how certain desert cacti can hoard a single drop of rainwater for decades, of how a virus lies dormant until conditions are exactly right for it to replicate, of how birds carry in their genes maps to places they've never been. And people with their secrets? They were no different, she believed, preserving them at enormous costs because sometimes, like water or instinct, their secrets were all that allowed them to survive.

Grace's affair with Noah felt like this sometimes: a matter of survival. It sounded so melodramatic, so Emma Bovary, so Anna Karenina, and if she had dared to voice such a thought to her best friend, Jenn, Jenn would have scoffed and asked Grace how she could even think something like this—*survival?*—when she had a child who was literally struggling to survive every day of his life. You want to talk about survival, Jenn would have said, then spend a day in the Pediatric ER. And Jenn would have been right, which is why Grace hadn't confided in her best friend, hadn't confided in anyone.

Snow flurries flew against the windshield and dissolved like tiny comets into silvery streaks. It still amazed her—the pulse of electricity that rushed straight through her whenever she thought of Noah. How was it even possible that someone's name—the *thought* of his name—could cause such a physical reaction? And after twenty years.

Twenty years.

Grace first met Noah at a church picnic along Lake Erie while visiting her grandparents. His long braid of red-gold hair was falling down his back as a loud swarm of kids pushed and pulled him toward the water, intent on throwing him in. She could tell he was letting them, though he pretended otherwise. "Hey, ya little protozoan," he yelled, or "Man, you are *such* an amoeba." Then he glanced up, caught her eye. "Hey you, how about a little help, here?"

Hey you.

She had ended up in the lake with a bunch of kids chanting, "*He likes you; he likes you,*" and Noah blushing and saying, "Cut it out, ya protons."

Noah tutored inner-city Detroit kids in science and by the end of

the day he had talked Grace into volunteering as well. The job would
look good on college applications, she told her parents; it was great
experience. She convinced them to let her stay for the summer. And
so, she spent two months teaching kids to make baking soda–pow-
ered rockets; to eliminate the foam from root beer; to write invisible
messages on acid-free paper with lemon juice, then decode them
with Windex. Years later, doing similar experiments at the kitchen
table with her son, Max, memories of that summer would return to
her in sharp-edged fragments: the cement walls and uneven floor-
boards of the church classroom where they taught; one of the kids
sneaking up on her and putting an ice cube down her shirt; a paper
airplane sailing across the room, an invisible lemon-scented "I love
you" on one of the wings.

Grace pressed her foot to the accelerator, casting up a silent prayer
that the police were tied up with holiday traffic near the malls.
Clouds of white spray from the damp road swirled around the car
like steam. Only when the speedometer pushed toward eighty did
she ease her foot from the gas pedal. "Not in a hurry today, are we?"
she teased herself, glancing up and once again catching her reflection
in the rearview mirror: the same wide gray eyes and bright lipsticked
smile, but in this light she now saw the beginnings of crow's-feet
when she smiled, and something gaunt in the way her cheek bones
protruded in her face. Strands of gray in her hair. Twenty years.
Something sharp pushed against the walls of her chest. Twenty years.
How does it happen, she wondered, the person you thought you
were just disappearing beneath your life the way the road was disappearing beneath the wheels of her SUV?

Twice that summer Noah arrived at her grandparents' door with his
face painted blue and white, the home colors of the Detroit Tigers, to
take her to a game. He *loved* the Tigers, he explained as the team went
extra innings against the Toronto Blue Jays. Baseball united people
across class, race, and religion as even religion couldn't. A few weeks
later, they watched a no-name pitcher miraculously beat the Boston

Red Sox, 3–0. A Sunday afternoon. David defeating Goliath. Who needed church? Noah asked, his voice hoarse from cheering.

He was strange and smart—as a junior in college he'd already been accepted to Princeton's PhD program in biology—and he didn't care what anyone thought of him, and he made Grace laugh, and when she was with him, she didn't care about what people thought of her either. But home in New Jersey that fall, she felt ashamed when she tried to describe him to her popular field hockey–playing girlfriends. He sounded weird, they said, which wasn't the reaction Grace had imagined. Noah was older, after all; he was in college. And he wanted *her*. Loved *her*. She had thought her friends would see her differently, respect her maybe, but instead they only rolled their eyes when she showed them photos. "Well, of course, he's in love with you, Grace. You're probably the most normal person he's ever dated." Shallow, high-school-girl comments, but Grace had listened to them so that, sometimes, on the nights when Noah phoned, she found herself seeing him through their eyes. And so, although she would watch the Tigers win the World Series four years later, she stopped returning Noah's phone calls that first autumn. Eventually, he stopped phoning. She graduated from high school and went to college, then grad school—a master's in epidemiology from Penn. She fell in love with Stephen, married him in a huge traditional church wedding, had Max a year later, Erin seven years after that, and then, finally, Jack.

Grace found Noah's salt-crusted, bumper sticker–laden Volvo in the deserted parking lot at the Hawk Watch Platform. Even the die-hard bird watchers were absent today. Home with their families, no doubt, getting ready for the holiday. Her stomach sank with guilt. "Damn it," she whispered. For a moment she sat, unmoving, the engine running, holding her cell phone in her lap. She should be home, she thought. With her kids. It was Christmas Eve. She was a mother. What was she doing?

She stared at the white totals board at the base of the Hawk Watch Platform listing the number of sightings to date for each type of raptor: Cooper's hawk, red-tailed hawk, Swainson's. The counts were down, Noah had told her, the numbers for peregrine falcons half of what they'd been three years ago. Something like grief on his face when he talked about it. It made no sense to her. Not when there were wars and genocide and people dying of AIDS and cancer. Not when her own child was dying of a genetic disease few scientists understood. Noah had told her how over a thousand biologists and volunteers from ten nations had convened at the International Piping Plover census of 1991, created to increase the breeding population of the endangered species. She had been sickened. For a *bird*, she kept thinking. A bird.

She sat for what seemed a long time, staring up at the soft gray clouds pulsing overhead. The sky a sonogram of winter. And then resolutely, she punched in her home phone number on the cell. "You're *sure* everything's okay?" she asked her mother. *With Jack,* she meant. "I can come home." She held her breath, not aware that she was doing so until her mother reassured her: everything was fine, Max was out with his friends, she and Erin were baking cookies; Jack was taking a nap.

"Did you remember to check—"

"His blood pressure was fine, honey."

Grace slipped the phone into the pocket of her field coat and leaned her forehead against the steering wheel and slowly exhaled. It sounded like a sob—of gratitude and guilt and relief, but mostly, she thought, of gratitude.

The minute she crossed over the dunes, it was like entering another world, the wind shrieking, the waves crashing onto the beach—one every five seconds, Noah had told her, fourteen thousand a day. The air smelled of salt and rotting wood and distance and longing, and yet for the first time in weeks, she felt as if she could breathe, actually take in a full breath without a tight band of sadness constricting her lungs.

This was why she had come here. This was her Christmas present to herself. And yes, of course, she felt guilty, but she also knew that if she didn't get away from the kids and Stephen and even her mother for a few hours, she would simply shatter inside. And if one more person asked if she was happy that Jack was home for the holiday or suggested that she be grateful to have this Christmas with him; if one more person told her that she "was such an inspiration," or she was "a saint," or the worst, that Jack reminded them of the *real* meaning of Christmas . . .

Why? she felt like asking. Because he's *dying*? *That's* what you need to remind you what the holiday is about?

Noah was down the beach a couple hundred yards. She shouted to him, but the wind lifted her sounds like a flimsy hat and flung them in the opposite direction.

She started walking into the wind, chin tucked to her chest, squinting against the blowing sand and snow. It was like treading through a current of fast-moving water. Spume lifted and blew in the gusts of wind. And then she heard a wild yell, and when she glanced up, he was running, sprinting, leaping—what exactly *was* it?—toward her.

No, not running. Charging. Stampeding. Open-armed, holding the binoculars away from his chest, the wind pushing him down the beach. She laughed out loud. Who was this man? He crushed her to his chest in a bear hug, swung her up in his arms. "Stop." She was laughing. "Put me down, you'll hurt yourself."

"I don't care," he said, holding her more tightly. "I can't believe this! What the hell are you doing here?"

"I'm not sure," she laughed into his ear. "I just needed to see you. Is that okay?"

"Okay? Are you kidding me? *Okay?*" He set her down, scanning her face with that inscrutable scientist's gaze of his. "It's wonderful, it's fantastic, it's—come here, you," and he was tugging on her coat collar, pulling her face close to his, then kissing her. Tears pricked her eyes. My child is dying, she thought, and I'm happy, I'm so goddamn happy to see this man and to just be here with him on this beach for an hour.

When he let her go, she turned to face the water, and he stood behind her, enveloping her in his bearlike warmth. A row of sander-lings lined up at the water's edge, standing one-legged to preserve heat. Foam blew sideways against the gray background of sky, the waves moving forward, then retreating. He pressed his chin to her shoulder, his face cold against hers. It had started to snow for real, a faint layer of it sticking to the broken shells and eelgrass along the wrack line.

"So, how long do you have?" Noah asked after a minute.

"An hour and a half—maybe."

"What do you want to do? Eat, get coffee, walk?"

"Walk, then maybe coffee?"

He offered her his arm. "Shall we?

She linked her arm in his. "We shall."

She was home in time to get Jack from his nap. "Snowing!" he cried when Grace opened his bedroom door. He was standing in his crib, pointing to the huge powdery flakes falling past his window.

"You like the snow?" she asked, scooping him up. He wriggled in her arms like a little fish. He was soaked with sweat. Her breath tumbled unevenly through her chest. Don't get sick, she willed silently. Please. They had an appointment the day after Christmas with the cardiac transplant team at Johns Hopkins. A heart transplant was Jack's last hope

"You see snow, Mama?" Jack asked as she laid him in the bassinet by the window. Even without taking his pulse, she could feel that his heart rate was high. Her own heart seemed to slow as if to compen-sate. "What's going on with you?" she asked him, as she held her fin-gers to the pulse in his wrist. She stared at the second hand on her watch and counted. After ten seconds, she stopped, calculated the number and closed her eyes in relief. His heart rate wasn't as bad as it had seemed. 120. High, but not terrible.

"Mama see snow?" Jack asked again.

She smiled at him, holding his face in her palms. His eyelids were droopy—one of the symptoms of the disease, the muscles in his eyes so weak that he had difficulty focusing. She'd gotten in the habit of holding his chin, lifting his gaze up to meet hers. "Yes, Mama sees snow."

"I see snow too?" he asked.

"I don't know. Do you?"

"I do!" he laughed. She placed the thermometer under his arm for a basal temperature, then held his hand close to his side.

"Why you taking temperature?" he asked.

"I'm just checking," she said. "Is that okay?"

"Why?"

"So I can make sure you aren't sick."

He placed his free hand against his forehead. "I not," he informed her seriously.

"Good! You better not be."

"Why?"

"Because it's Christmas, Silly Goose." She pulled the thermometer from his arm. 97.8. No fever. She exhaled slowly, an ache in her lungs left over from the frigid ocean air.

A fat snowflake plopped against the window like a bug on a windshield and Jack smacked the glass, laughing as he squirmed away from her. And then, "Max see snow too?" he asked as she tugged off his wet clothes and lifted his tiny bird legs to slide a diaper beneath him.

"Max might be out *in* the snow." Playing hockey with the kids two streets over.

"Why?" Jack asked.

"Because he likes it."

"Why he likes it?"

"Hmmm." Grace pretended to ponder this. "I'm not sure. What do you think?"

He shrugged. "I don't know." And then, "Erin see snowing too? And Daddy?"

Grace glanced at him, his damp curly hair sticking up like the down of a newly hatched chick's. Where had this come from, she wondered, this recent need that everyone see or feel or do the same thing? She had read in Elisabeth Kübler-Ross's *On Children and Death* that even very young children somehow sense when their deaths are imminent, and it occurred to her that maybe this was Jack's way of holding onto them, anchoring himself to their world.

Grace tugged Jack up so that he was sitting. She pulled a clean red turtleneck from the bottom drawer of his bureau and slid it over his head. "Oh no! Where did Jack go?" she teased. "Where could he be?" But her voice caught. After he was gone, these were the words that would break her heart.

TWO

The story of mitochondrial disease begins with the story of the mitochondria themselves, those minuscule organisms in our cells that convert food and oxygen into the energy we need to live. Like most stories, this is a story about desire, a word that stems from the Latin sidus, or "star," referring to those distant suns whose light often touches us only after the stars have died. Desire is similar, is it not? Its target is like a star's glow, something we reach for but can never hold. Or is the equation backwards? Maybe it is because we desire something that it begins to die, altered by the force of our want.

The story of mitochondria is also a story of suffering. Ordinary, everyday suffering. A virus. An infection. For it was as a virus that the mitochondria first invaded our cells billions of years ago. A symbiotic relationship soon formed. A marriage, you might say. Our cells provided food and shelter; in return, the mitochondria produced energy in the form of ATP, or adenosine triphosphate, without which we cannot survive.

This too is a common story, perhaps the most common of all: the one about how desire becomes necessity. Scientists infecting amoebas with bacteria then breeding the survivors, for instance, have found that after five years, the amoebas can't grow at all without that bacteria. So it is with the mitochondria: These long-ago viruses are accustomed now to living within us; we are accustomed to having them there. We can no longer survive without each other. One tenth of our cells is made up of mitochondria—one tenth of us. In fact, if you were to lay all the mitochondria in a single human body end to end, they would circle the earth two hundred times.

Think of it: an entire planet, circumnavigated by desire.

Still, it is DNA, that famous double helix—and not mitochondria—that garners the attention. At the end of the twentieth century, photos of computer-generated models of DNA made the covers of national magazines, and DNA was mentioned in the headlines of major newspapers. "The decoding of the human genome," the president declared to a flock of reporters on the White House lawn, "is without a doubt the most important, most wondrous map ever produced by mankind." And yet, without the energy provided by mitochondria, organelles so tiny that a billion of them fit inside a grain of sand, even the unraveling and replicating of DNA would not be possible.

No wonder mitochondrial diseases are so devastating. For all movement—a heartbeat, a breath, the blink of an eye, the splitting of a cell, the firing of a nerve signal—is fueled by ATP, by the mitochondria. And movement too is about desire, isn't it? Aren't we always moving toward what we want even when it feels as if we are running away?

THREE

$\mathcal{G}$race arched her neck, her weight on her elbows, and tilted her head back into the jet of hot water, rinsing the shampoo from her hair. The bottom of the tub was gritty with sand. She could feel it each time she moved. It had been in her socks and ears and hair and under her fingernails; she'd had to empty her shoes over the toilet.

Before she left Cape May, she had told Noah, "I know I wouldn't have seen you over the holidays, but I miss you more—*if* that's even possible—when you're in Michigan."

He nodded. "Like quarks."

"Quarks?" She grinned. He was *always* doing this—one of the things she loved.

"Quantum physics. The farther two quarks move away from each other, the more fiercely they're pulled back together."

"Ahhh," she smiled. "So that's what happened to us?"

She pushed herself into a sitting position and turned off the water. From downstairs came the sound of Burl Ives singing "Santa Claus Is Coming to Town." *He knows when you've been bad or good . . .* She stood, her legs red from the heat, and lifted a towel from the hook on the door. The mirror was fogged with steam. She couldn't see her face but knew it was wind-burned. Even the cotton towel felt scratchy against her skin.

"Mama!" Jack called from the family room the minute she came downstairs. Despite sweatpants, turtleneck, cardigan, and big socks, Grace felt chilled, the ends of her hair still damp. "What, Goose?" she asked Jack. "Was your movie good?" She hit the eject button on the VCR as she passed it. The Christmas tree was on, its colored lights glowing in the reflection of the windows.

"Max called Santa a turkey," Jack said.

"He *what*?" She made a face at her oldest son who lay sprawled across the couch, feet dangling over one end. *"Max."*

"I said he was *in* Turkey, Mom. Erin asked where I thought he was, and I was showing her on the globe."

"He was, Mama," Erin said without looking up from her drawing.

Grace leaned down to plant a kiss on the top of Erin's head, then handed Jack the video they'd just watched. "Here, silly, put this on the shelf and stop trying to get your brother into trouble." She squeezed Max's ankle. "Sorry."

He nodded without lifting his eyes from his *Sports Illustrated*.

The globe was the same turquoise sphere with pastel-colored countries, many of them no longer in existence, that she'd had as a child and on which *her* father had mapped Santa's route for *her*. A commercial pilot, her father factored in headwinds and tailwinds, turbulence, and cold fronts. "Now, with those winds coming down from Canada, it might get a little bumpy coming across the Atlantic," he'd tell her. Or, "You know, Gracie, you might want to hit the sack a little early, because with that tailwind, I have a feeling Santa's going to arrive ahead of schedule this year."

In the kitchen, Grace flipped on the light over the sink and filled the coffeepot with water. On the counter sat a stack of mail—Christmas cards mostly, along with the plate of peanut butter cookies Erin and Grace's mom had made earlier. Grace broke the edge off one and ate it as she opened the first envelope. It was from Jenn, she knew, recognizing her friend's handwriting. The gurgling of the coffeemaker filled the room as she scanned the note. She hadn't seen Jenn in nearly a year. She stared at the enclosed photo of Jenn's three boys, the oldest already a sophomore in high school. All of them were tall and dark-eyed like their mom. The Barbarian family, Jenn would laugh. The boys had her great smile.

Grace had met Jenn, who had been in the nursing program at Penn, in a graduate seminar on Children and Disease. Grace still had the texts from that class: David Morris's *Illness and Culture*, Leavitt and Numbers' *Sickness and Health in America,* Batshaw's *Children with Disabilities.* The diseases sounded like law firms, Jenn said: Wolf-Hirschhorn; McCune-Albright; Beckwith-Wiedemann; Borjesson-Forssman-Lehmann. She and Grace would drill each other over cosmopolitans at the Ruby Lounge during Friday-night happy hour: Maple Syrup Urine Disease, characterized by syrupy-smelling urine; Cri-du-chat syndrome, so named because of the catlike cry infants often made. The diseases were trivia then, possible quiz questions. They hadn't connected these illnesses to real children yet, to the parents of those children. Young and single, neither could have imagined that one of them would one day have a child with such a disease. Back then, mitochondrial disease—Jack's disease—wasn't even in the medical literature.

Grace set Jenn's card down and opened the next. It was from Kent, one of the guys in the beach house in Rehoboth, Delaware, she and Stephen used to belong to. He and Ciera had decided to divorce. Grace reread the words, shaking her head. Kent and Ciera. Of all the couples, and there'd been five, they were the last couple Grace would have imagined getting divorced. She thought of all those beach-house mornings, walking onto the back porch and hearing the thrumming of the outdoor shower, Kent and Ciera laughing and murmuring while the rest of them slumped at the picnic table sipping coffee in hungover silence and irritation. Eventually, Kent would emerge from the shower wrapped in a towel, all but beating his chest. Ciera behind him, flushed and defiant. Tarzan and Jane.

Now, Grace skimmed over the generic phrases: "Comes as a shock," "grown apart," "for the best," before setting the card aside. Outside snow lofted down over the spherical shapes of the pine trees. She crossed her arms over her chest as if she were still cold, feeling pensive and sad. Did anyone ever know what was happening with anyone else? Ever *really* know? She thought of how easily she had just disappeared from her own life for a few hours and of how easily she had simply returned, standing here now in sweatpants, reading the mail, nibbling one of her daughter's cookies. How no one who knew her would ever guess, not just *where* she had been, but *who*. Someone else. She closed her eyes, pictured Noah lifting her in a bear hug, and felt an ache settle in her chest.

"Mama, did you try the cookies me and Grandma made?" Erin leaned her elbows on the counter and propped her chin in her hands. No one had combed her hair today, and she'd lost another tooth last week. She looked like a waif.

"Your cookies are absolutely great, honey-bunny." She cupped Erin's face in her hands, pushing her curly hair from her eyes. "Are you leaving some for Santa tonight?"

Erin nodded. "That's what Grandma asked me."

"What'd Grandma ask?" Max slouched into a chair at the table.

Grace glanced at him. "You look tired, honey. How was hockey today?"

"*Bad*. I *really* need new skates, mom." The Bauer 400s in the back of her SUV.

"Well, did you ask Santa?

"*Mom.*"

She grinned. "*Max.*"

From the next room came the shudder of the automatic garage opening. "Daddy's home! Daddy's home! Daddy's home!" Jack shouted, hurrying for the door, yanking his mini suitcase on wheels—his oxygen canister—behind him.

"Mama, why is your face so red?" Erin asked.

Grace lifted her palm to the side of her windburned face. "Is it?"

"If you could be any animal, what would you be?" Stephen read the question from the rectangle of colored paper Jack had pulled from the glass candy jar. The jar was filled with similar questions written on scraps of colored paper and folded into squares; *If you could change the sky to any color besides blue, what color would you choose? If you could re-live one day of your life, what day would that be?*

"This is so stupid," Max said now around a bite of cheesesteak.

"Anytime you want to write your own questions," Grace said.

"*No, Mama*," Erin whined. "He'll just write things about hockey."

The question jar was a gift from one of Grace's mother's friends who was a creative writer. They took turns picking the questions each night.

Stephen grabbed a handful of potato chips. "What animal would you be, Erin?"

Erin cocked her head to the side, thinking. Grace caught Stephen's eye and smiled. He'd come home with Philly cheesesteaks—extra hot peppers for him, onions for Grace—their Christmas Eve tradition. And now a glass of Merlot, the snow falling . . . This is enough, she thought, guiltily thinking of Noah. This is more than enough.

"I'd be a polar bear," Erin announced.

"You mean a Teddy bear?" Max laughed.

"Mama," Erin whined. "Why does he *always* make fun of my answers?"

"He's teasing," Grace said. "Tell us why you would be a bear." She leaned forward and took another bite of cheesesteak. Sautéed onions dripped onto her plate.

" 'Cause I could play in the snow all day and not get cold." She glared at Max, who rolled his eyes and muttered, "I'd be anything that lives alone."

"Like a snake?" Erin said.

"No, not like a snake," Max mimicked.

Jack laughed. "Max is snake, Mama!"

Grace pointed at him. "*You* are a little instigator."

"No, *you* gator, Mama."

Erin giggled. "Not *alli*gator, silly."

"I'd be a bird," Grace said. *A brown pelican. At this time of the season!* Noah had once traced his finger over her sternum and told her, "If you were a bird, this is where the flight muscles would be attached— here, to the bone protecting the heart."

"Alligator!" Jack insisted.

"A bird," Grace laughed. "Maybe a goose like you. Or a swan."

"They mate for life, don't they?" Stephen asked. "I guess that settles it for me. I'd have to be a swan too."

Max groaned. "Gross, you guys, I'm trying to eat."

"Mama, what does 'mate for life' mean?" Erin asked.

"It means that you stay with one person that you really love for your whole life."

"Like you and Daddy?"

Something fluttered in Grace's chest. A bird taking flight. "Yes," she agreed. "Like me and Daddy."

"Can I be a swan too, Mama, so I can stay with you and Daddy my whole life?"

Max snickered. Grace warned him with a look. "Of course, you can be a swan."

"I swan too?" Jack asked.

Grace laughed. "Yes, you too." He looked so good, she thought. If it weren't for the nasal cannula and the raspy hiss of his oxygen, you almost wouldn't know he was sick. For a moment, she couldn't swallow, her throat tight. Please let him live, she thought.

Everything was done: stockings filled, presents placed under the tree, a note from Santa thanking Erin for the cookies. Stephen was bringing in firewood for the morning. Grace was checking her e-mail, most of the messages from the women in her mitochondrial support group. She often felt closer to these women than to anyone, including Jenn, her mother, even at times, Stephen. She hadn't even met most of them, yet they had pictures of each other's kids on their refrigerators, knew the kids' birthdays and what complex of mitochondrial disease they had, what their symptoms and prognosis were. They knew the same specialists, had been to the same hospitals: the Cleveland Clinic, Scottish Rite in Atlanta, both Children's and St. Christopher's in Philadelphia, the University of California, San Diego, a handful of others. It was a small world.

As she sat at the computer now, waiting for the e-mails to download, she couldn't help but smile, despite the edge of sadness that had been pushing at her all night. Most of the messages would be from

the women in the support group, wishing one another happy holidays, sending prayers for whoever's child wasn't doing well, maybe
sharing a joke. Like the string theory of the universe, which held that
the world was composed of billions of invisible threadlike strings,
constantly moving, vibrating, holding the universe together. The support group was similar, Grace thought. All these woman reaching
across vast distances to seek or offer consolation, encouragement,
support. Kempley in North Carolina, Anne Marie in Seattle, the
woman in Australia whose five-year-old daughter had just died from
mitochondrial-related complications, another mother from Japan,
Beth from Pittsburgh. Hundreds of invisible messages, tiny strings of
words, moving across states, entire continents. Holding up the world.

Mostly, the women listened to one another vent and grieve—and
laugh, which they had to do, and which no one who didn't have children as ill as theirs could begin to understand. They traded medical
articles and advice. It was Kempley who insisted that Jack's muscle
biopsy had to be redone if Grace wanted any chance of locating the
exact mutation in the mitochondrial DNA. Kempley who explained
to Grace the difference between a fresh and a frozen muscle biopsy.
Kempley who explained why it mattered.

And Kempley, of everyone in Grace's life, in whom she imagined
confiding about Noah. Kempley, who maybe wouldn't approve, but
who wouldn't judge her, wouldn't think she was a bad mother, a bad
person. In Grace's mind, they were the same thing.

Of course, there was no message from Noah tonight. He was in
Ann Arbor by now. He wouldn't have access to his e-mail, refused to
travel with a computer. It was one of the first things she'd learned
when she found him last January.

Found.

As if he'd been lost.

Actually, finding Noah had been Max's doing. He had been writing a
report for school on John James Audubon and ended up on the Web
site for the Cape May Bird Observatory. Grace was helping him. And

there was Noah's name under "Director." A prickly feeling in her throat. "Wait, Max, I think I know this guy."

Her first e-mail had been brief: "Noah, is that you?"

She had wondered if he was married, if his hair was still long, if he'd remained loyal to the Tigers. He was still twenty-two in her mind, writing secret messages on acid-free paper with lemon juice, showing ten-year-olds how to make sandwich-baggie bombs, trying to explain to her why a baseball stadium was more necessary to a community than a church, especially in Detroit.

"You'll never believe who I found." She had paced into the kitchen where Stephen was finishing the dishes. She didn't wait for him to ask. "Noah McIntyre."

"Who?"

"Noah, from my grandparents' church. The guy who went to Princeton. I taught science with him that one summer. The Tigers' fan?"

"The guy whose heart you broke?"

"Yeah, him."

The first two days after she contacted him, Grace found herself checking her e-mail constantly. First thing in the morning, coffee-deprived and groggy; or rushing in from one of Jack's therapy appointments at the hospital, still in her coat and shoes, purse tossed wherever, telling Jack, "Wait just one minute, Goose, Mama has to check something." She drove to and from the hospital on automatic pilot, imagining the conversations she and Noah would have, trying to explain why she'd treated him so badly twenty years before, asking questions, answering his, telling him about her kids, her life. Already, she was different in those conversations—easier, lighter, more animated. She gestured to the windshield, to the empty passenger seat next to her. Sitting in traffic one morning, shaking her head and waving her hand in chagrin at something she imagined Noah saying, she found a group of teenagers in the next car pointing to her in unison, then rotating their index fingers in a circular motion at their foreheads: *You're crazy*. She laughed and threw her hands up in a "What can I say" gesture. They were right.

After three days without a reply, she was irritated. And disappointed, though she couldn't say why, exactly. Maybe it wasn't her Noah, she told herself, but she didn't believe it. And then she got mad. Was he holding a grudge after all this time? *Grow up,* she thought.

The next day she found his response. One question. Capital letters. "WHERE ARE YOU?"

Later he would explain that he didn't respond immediately because he'd been away at a conference, that he never took a laptop when he traveled, that he had panicked when he saw her e-mail (at two in the morning) and realized that five days had passed since she'd sent it. He laughed. "Never mind the twenty years that had gone by." She heard something in his voice, like when a button pops loose of whatever holds it in place.

Stephen paused in the entrance to the family room, his arms loaded with firewood, breathing heavily.

"You okay?" she asked.

"God, it's cold out there." He set the logs in the wrought iron basket on the hearth behind her, then stood, brushing wood chips from his sweater. "This is obscene," he laughed after a minute as he stared at the Christmas tree.

And it was obscene. Presents crammed up under the branches and spilling along the back wall and halfway into the room. It didn't take a psychologist to figure it out. This might be Jack's last Christmas, and Grace wanted him to have every possible thing he could ever want. Since October, she had been telling herself to just stop, she had enough presents for him, but then she'd see something that he'd like—a LEGO space station that Max could help him put together, sneakers that flashed colored lights whenever he moved—and it seemed so utterly stupid *not* to get it. So what if she was going overboard, so what if she was spending a fortune? It might be her last chance.

She leaned back in her chair. "We overdid it a little, huh?"

"*We?*"

She shrugged. "Okay, *I*." She glanced again at her e-mail. Stephen stood behind her and massaged her shoulders, his hands cold through her sweater.

Without turning around she said, "Anne Marie, from Seattle, the one whose daughter also has dilated cardiomyopathy, was at Hopkins last week, and I was wondering if she'd heard anything."

"Do you realize it's already Christmas?" He leaned forward and kissed the back of her neck. His face was as cold as his hands.

She glanced at the clock in the corner of the computer screen. Just past midnight. Outside it was still snowing. She thought of that man in Vermont who had photographed thousands of different snowflakes against black velvet in the instant before they dissolved. Sometimes she felt that this was what they were doing with Jack—trying to hold onto something fragile and transitory before it disappeared forever from their lives.

"Jack looked good tonight, didn't he?" she said softly, still staring at the snow.

"He really did. I can't remember the last time he looked this great."

"It sounds stupid, but I keep thinking that there must be a mistake."

"I know." He squeezed her shoulder. "No one who sees him can believe he's as sick as he is."

She nodded, suddenly exhausted and sadder than she could bear to feel right now. She glanced once more at the computer screen, ready to call it a night. But "We're on the list!" she saw in the subject heading next to Anne Marie's name. The list. UNOS: United Network for Organ Sharing. She felt something tilt inside of her.

"They accepted Anne Marie's little girl," she said. It meant the team at Hopkins had deemed Bryn a suitable candidate for a heart. Grace's voice felt detached from her body. "I should congratulate them." But her hands were in her lap. There was no way to process this. Anne Marie's little girl would get a chance, and Jack—Jack probably wouldn't. It was a long shot at best. She knew this.

Stephen knelt down and gathered Grace against his chest. He smelled of firewood. "Oh Grace, I'm sorry, baby," he whispered.

"No—" She lifted her head, pulling away from him. "God, Stephen, don't be sorry; it's good, it's—I'm happy for them, really, it's just—" Her face crumpled. "I don't know how I'll ever live without him."

FOUR ·

race sat on the couch, her feet tucked up under her, a book open-faced in her lap. The tree lights were turned off, the kids' opened presents stacked now in neat piles—Max's on one side of the tree, Erin's another, Jack's near his toy box. From upstairs she could hear Stephen moving back and forth from Jack's room to the bathroom, changing him and giving him his eleven p.m. medications. She stared at the book in her lap. *An ice game known as* Kolven *was popular in Holland in the seventeenth century.* Max's Christmas present to her: *Hockey for Dummies.* She was trying to understand this game her son was so passionate about. *Later on, the game really took hold in England.* It was a struggle to concentrate, though. Sentences slid out from under her like wet leaves.

She closed the book, set it on the coffee table, and stood. A rectangle of yellow light fell into the hallway from the stairwell. She paused at the foot of the stairs, listening to make sure everything was all right, then walked into what used to be Stephen's office. The antique rolltop desk his mother had given him for his college graduation was covered with boxes of plastic tubing and nasal canulae, latex gloves, disposable syringes. Stacks of xeroxed medical articles were piled on the leather armchair and ottoman. Grace stood in front of the bookshelves, head tilted sideways, scanning the titles in the light from the hallway. She found the book she was looking for, pulled it from the shelf, and, still in the near-darkness, turned to the chapter on heart transplants.

"So what did you think of Mandy?" Stephen said from the doorway.

Grace looked up from the book in her lap. "I think your brother's smitten." Mandy was his older brother Jeff's girlfriend. "It's been what, almost a year now? Isn't that a record for him?"

"I guess. I just wish he'd find someone his own age. Twenty-three. It's embarrassing." Stephan sank onto the sofa next to Grace, handing her his glass of eggnog.

"At least she's not like the last one. God, all those metal studs in her tongue and nose and eyebrows, and I don't even want to think about where else." She took a sip, then handed it back to him. "Mandy was actually very sweet. Asking a lot about Jack. And Erin loved her."

"Well, they're practically the same age."

"Oh, stop. Your brother's happy." She leaned against Stephen's shoulder. "He's . . . I don't know, different with her. More gentle or something. It's nice to see."

"I suppose." He handed her the eggnog again and nodded at the *Hockey for Dummies* sitting on the coffee table. "What? You give up already?"

"*Excuse* me?" Grace grinned and began reciting from memory: "The word *hockey* comes from a French term meaning 'bent stick'; there are five face-off zones in a hockey rink, one in each—"

"Never mind." Stephen laughed. "I should know better." He nudged her shoulder, trying to get a glimpse of the book in her lap. "So, what are you reading now?"

She turned the book so that he could see the title. *Parents' Guide to Heart Disease in Children.*

He looked at her. "Worried about tomorrow?" They were leaving at five in the morning to drive to Hopkins. Max and Erin were spending the night at Grace's parents.

"Can I read you just one thing?" Grace asked.

"Go ahead." Stephen leaned his head against the couch back and closed his eyes.

"*Children who have been bedridden for years with severe cardiac failure often become asymptomatic, returning to normal activities within days of successful cardiac transplantation.*" She glanced at Stephen. "*Survival rates are over 90 percent if the child was reasonably well at the time of the transplant,*" she continued. "*Results were poor, however, when the child was in the ICU directly prior to the procedure.*" She closed the book, though she kept her finger on the page, holding her place.

"So you think because Jack's doing better than he was in—when was it? October?—the team at Hopkins is going to having a different assessment?"

"I'm not sure. It's just *'kids that are bedridden for years'* you know? And he's still so active, Stephen. I mean, look at how he was today." She glanced at the stockings that hung from the mantel. It was crowded with photos of the kids, a disproportionate number of Jack. Jack in denim overalls toddling blurrily towards the camera, holding a football. Jack on Santa's lap. Jack sitting between Erin's legs at the top of the bright yellow slide. The ache Grace had felt all day in the center of her chest spread to her stomach. "He's doing better than he was in November, I know that much. And his troponin levels are—"

"Hey—" Stephen laid his hand on her knee. "You don't have to convince anyone, Grace."

"I feel like I do, though." She turned sideways to face him, her long wool skirt twisting uncomfortably. She lifted herself for a moment, then settled again. "I keep thinking that Anne Marie's little girl was *much* sicker than Jack and now—" She stopped. "I'm just so afraid of forgetting something that might help them decide. If he dies"—her voice cracked—"and there was something I didn't think of, some question I could have asked—"

"But you have, Grace. Over and over." He reached for her hand and pressed it against his chest. He was wearing a faded red Lambda Chi Alpha T-shirt that had shrunk so that it fit tight across his shoulders. It was the same T-shirt he'd worn the night she met him sixteen years before at a party in grad school. Stephen had been in charge of the blender and because Grace didn't know anyone, she feigned interest in observing him as he emptied a bottle of dark rum into the pitcher filled with ice. He was good-looking, she thought, but she'd already dismissed him because of the T-shirt. A fraternity boy.

Once—and only once—after one of those parties, Grace had gone back to her apartment and sat Indian-style on her narrow bed, the phone cradled in her lap and she'd dialed information for Princeton, New Jersey, for McIntyre, Noah. She was a little drunk. It had been over four years since they had spoken, though she looked for him at her grandparents' church every time she visited them in Ann Arbor. But there was no listing for a "McIntyre, Noah" in the Princeton area, the operator told her. Grace wondered if maybe he hadn't gone to Princeton, if maybe he had stayed in the Midwest, and if, maybe, it had anything to do with her, with all those autumn afternoons after their one summer together when he'd phone her in New Jersey, and she'd tell him breathlessly, "I've got to go; I'll call you tomorrow"— and never did.

Of course, she dismissed the idea almost as quickly as she had dismissed Stephen the first time she met him. She and Noah had been a high school romance. Puppy love; infatuation. She'd been seventeen, he barely twenty. They had been too young to comprehend what love was, what it meant. It was silly to think that it would have altered his life in any significant way. Silly to imagine that it would ever alter hers.

"Do you honestly believe Jack's better than he was two months ago?" Stephen asked, and she felt her shoulders slump in defeat. No, Jack wasn't that much better, a little, maybe but . . . She shook her head. It's just that she had been so wrong about such important things in her life—both Stephen and Noah. It terrified her now to think that she might just as easily dismiss something crucial about Jack's illness.

She pulled her finger from the page she had been marking and set the *Parents' Guide to Heart Disease in Children* on the coffee table next to *Hockey for Dummies*. "You're right. I don't know why I'm doing this," she admitted. Stephen lifted his arm around her shoulders and she snuggled into his side. Jack hadn't even been able to wear the elastic-waist pants she'd bought him for church today, his belly so swollen with fluid that his weakened heart couldn't rid his body of, despite increased doses of his diuretics. And he was self-protecting, unconsciously tensing his stomach muscles whenever she picked him up. His fingers and feet were icy from poor circulation, and he'd been coughing more—just a cold, she hoped, though this too was another symptom of heart failure.

"So did he go right to sleep?" she asked after a minute.

"Out like a light."

She smiled. "He *was* something today, wasn't he?"

"I didn't tell you, but he's sleeping with his new race cars."

Grace laughed. "And Max liked his skates, huh?"

"*Like?* Did you see his face when he thought he'd opened all his presents and he hadn't gotten them?"

"Oh, he knew. He had to." She paused. "Did you know he was getting me *Hockey for Dummies?*"

"Yeah."

"He accused me of not caring about him as much as I cared about Jack."

"He's just at that age."

"I do focus too much on Jack, though." She shook her head. "And poor Erin."

"Erin's fine, Grace. Come on. You're being too hard on yourself." He pulled her closer and she lay her head against his chest and closed her eyes, tired suddenly. After a few minutes he said quietly, "We're doing okay, aren't we?"

"With the kids?"

"With each other."

"Yes, of course." She sat up to look at him. "Come on, Stephen. I've been running like crazy trying to get ready for the holiday and—"

"Hey, I know. That wasn't an accusation. I just miss you, okay?"

She nodded, unable to tell him that she missed him too.

He grazed her cheek with the back of her hand. "You really did get one hell of a windburn the other day didn't you?"

She forced a smile. "I told you that mall parking lot was brutal. Like crossing the great tundra—"

"And all for Max's skates?" He shook his head. "See, if only he knew the lengths you go to for him."

She couldn't meet his eyes and so stared at his shirt, the fabric faded to a dusky pink. She remembered another time she had watched him in that shirt, making drinks for their friends at the beach house in Rehoboth. Everyone crowded into the kitchen, getting ice, slicing tomatoes for a salad, carrying dishes to the picnic table out back. A Cuban CD was playing. There was no air conditioning in the house. Grace was sitting in the dining room nursing Max, trying to stay cool. Ciera sauntered into the kitchen in a bikini top and a bright Mexican wrap tied in a knot at her waist. Sweat glistened on her collar bones. She lifted her hair atop her head and someone whistled a cat call. The kitchen smelled of fresh mint from the *mojitos* they were making. Rum and dark brown sugar and lime juice and mint. Lots of mint. Grace couldn't drink because she was nursing. She was angry and uncomfortable, and she felt fat, and she had looked at Stephen in that fraternity T-shirt and for a horrible minute she thought, what in God's name am I doing with *him*? With these people? But in the next instant, Stephen had looked up and winked at her—just that—and Ciera turned and smiled at Max with such love in her pretty dark face, and the moment was like a wave that curled in on itself. Grace had looked at her husband and felt suffused with happiness that Stephen loved her, that *this*—these friends and this house and her child at her breast—was her life. *Hers*.

"I can't believe it's over," Stephen said.

He meant the holiday, but for a second, it was almost as if he could read her mind and was referring to them, to the life they'd once had.

FIVE

*G*race turned to look at Jack, asleep in his car seat, his head lolling sideways. His swollen belly and chest rose and fell with effort. Still dark outside, his face was in shadow but for the headlights of the trucks passing in the opposite direction. She felt Stephen watching her as she watched him, her own heart feeling swollen and too full.

"You okay?" Stephen said.

She shook her head no as she settled back against her seat. After a moment, she said, "How can we *not* do this?" This: taking Jack to Hopkins; meeting with the Cardiac Transplant Team. "To not even try? I don't—" Her throat tightened.

Stephen put his hand on her knee. "Anju's a great doctor, Grace, but she's not his mother. You're doing the right thing."

The *you're* registered. Not *we're,* though she knew Stephen supported the decision to bring Jack here. When had he started leaving these choices solely up to her, though? She knew he trusted her to understand the medicine better than he, to know what was right for Jack. But she couldn't remember when it had started to feel so lonely.

A green road sign flashed by—BALTIMORE 57 MILES—and she felt her stomach clench. They'd be there in an hour. Johns Hopkins. No longer the best hospital in the world as it had been in the first half of the century when it single-handedly changed the way doctors were taught, when the pillars of modern medicine—William Osler, William Henry Welch, William Stewart Halsted, Howard Kelly—had reigned, but still: for the last ten years *U.S. News & World Report* had ranked it the #1 teaching hospital in the country; it was still the first choice medical school for students from all over the world; its doctors were still the recipients of more research grants from the National Institutes of Health than the doctors at any other teaching institute. Still the place where the first "Blue Baby" operation took place, which led to open heart surgery, which led to heart transplants. Grace held onto this knowledge. Ballast against the weight of Anju's question: "Why in God's name would you want to put him through this, Grace?"

The question had stunned her. After Stephen, Anju Mehta, Jack's primary doctor, was the first person Grace had phoned upon receiving news that the transplant team at Hopkins would consider Jack. "We have an appointment. December 26." Grace was nearly crying. "I feel like it's Christmas already, Anju. Just the fact that they're considering him means that it's not hopeless."

Silence. And then that question. *Why in God's name . . .*

Grace had felt as if the wind had been knocked out of her. "*Why?* What do you mean, *why.* Because what if it works, Anju? What if it buys him another year, another five years?" He would be eight then. *Eight.* It was a ridiculously small number, an unbearable joke of a number. As if eight—*eight,* for God's sake—could possibly be enough. "My God, Anju, what if they find a cure by then?" *What if.* The words seemed to contract and expand in her throat. She'd had to press the phone hard against her ear, trying to steady her shaking arm. She knew Anju thought she was clutching at straws, but straws were all she had and who knew—who could possibly *ever* know—what might happen in five years? Scientists had already learned how to successfully put a mechanical heart in a person's chest, clone animals—by the following summer experts predicted they would have decoded the human genome. She began to cry. "How—how can you even ask me *why*?"

"I'm sorry, Grace, but I can't support this," Anju told her. "And frankly, I'm appalled that any doctor would after looking at Jack's records . . ."

Ahead of them, the sun popped over the tree line, and Jack whimpered, the sudden light full-force on his face. Grace turned, positioning her body so as to shield his eyes. "Shush," she whispered, brushing his hair from his forehead. "Is Mr. Sun trying to wake you up?"

He squinted at her, rubbing his eyes, then began to cry. "I don't want new hospital," he said.

Why would you want to put him through this, Grace?

"I know, Goose, but what if the doctors at the new hospital can make you all better?" *What if.*

"You mean I don't need oxygen anymore and I be just like Max and Erin?"

She nodded, her heart leaden in her chest. It would never be that simple for Jack. Even with a transplant, which would buy him at most five years.

She stared at the surgeon's fingers as he spoke, his words coming to her in fragments. *Adrenal failure. Fifteen percent chance of survival. I'm sorry.* His fingers were long. Like a pianist's, she thought.

"You've got a happy little boy here," the surgeon was saying, and she turned to look at Jack, lying on his side on the carpet, obliviously playing with his Matchbox cars. "And as long we manage his pain, he's got pretty good quality of life . . ."

Quality. She bit the inside of her lip to keep from crying. Did anyone really believe that *quality* could compensate for *quantity* when you were talking about a child's life? She'd trade quality for quantity in a heartbeat. Give Jack another year and she'd give up the hours of cuddling with him on the sofa after the kids were in school; give him two years and she'd stop standing over his crib at night, smelling the back of his neck, touching his hand curled loosely in sleep, whispering, "I love you, Goose." Give him five years and hell, she'd hire a nanny to watch him, she'd go back to work full-time. She'd said this once to her mother, and her mother had said something motherly and appropriate like, "Oh, but you wouldn't really would you?" And Grace had wanted to hit her. *Oh course, I would. If he could live? Of course!* How could anyone think that quality was more important than quantity?

• • •

It rained on the ride home. A downpour, at times, so that it seemed they were on a ship, plowing through heavy water, the world blurry, swollen looking. Rain smashed sideways into the windshield, the wind howling and abusive, pummeling the sky. Stephen leaned forward, face grim, straining to see in the oddly bright light. Her own eyes ached, as if she'd stared into the sun too long, dared to look up at an eclipse. A sick, punched-in-the-gut feeling in her stomach. *Quality of life.* As opposed to *quantity.* She wanted to sob like a little girl, throw a tantrum. She didn't want *quality.* Not at this cost. And what mother did? Anju's words spun through her mind. *Why in God's name would you want to put him through this?* And Jenn: *Oh, Grace, are you sure?*

"No, I'm not sure!" she had exploded. "But it's all I goddamn have, Jenn." They'd been on the phone. She had wanted to weep. "I don't get to be sure," she added furiously. "I don't have that luxury."

Now, she leaned back against the seat, the pounding rain relentless, tears seeping from beneath her closed eyes. You don't realize how much hope you have until it's gone, she thought, remembering the title of a book she'd seen on Noah's dresser. *Hope Is the Thing with Feathers: A Personal Chronicle of Vanished Birds.* The title had come from a poem by Emily Dickinson, he'd told her. Outside the car, rain pinged on the roof and windshield. She couldn't remember the words of the poem, but she knew, as maybe she never had before, that hope is not light and feathery and birdlike at all. She thought of that doctor who'd done all those experiments weighing the body before and after the moment of death in an effort to prove that the soul had weight, that the body was significantly lighter after the soul departed, and she knew that if someone weighed her right now, she too would have lost pounds since the morning. Hope.

By the time they got home, the storm had stopped. The world seemed wounded, lifting itself slowly. Midafternoon, and Max was at hockey practice still, Erin was at Grace's mom's. At home, she helped Stephen get Jack into his crib. "Why are you so sleepy today?" she asked him. Another symptom of heart failure and she thought of the term "easy death," which the surgeon had used today, and she knew that nothing about her child's death would ever, in the slightest way, be easy.

In their bedroom Stephen was sitting on the edge of the bed, elbows on his knees, rubbing his eyes with the heels of his hands. A flicker of Stephen twenty years ago, sitting on the edge of the bed in the beach house, hung over, skinny, rubbing his eyes just like this. Grace kicked off her shoes, climbed up on the bed behind him, put her arms around his shoulders, and pressed her face to the back of his neck. "I'm so sorry I got your hopes up," she whispered into his skin.

He squeezed her arm. "Don't ever be sorry for that." His voice was raspy. "It just feels so real all of a sudden. Jesus Christ." He punched the bed next to him with his free hand. "Jesus fucking Christ, Grace. I mean what the hell are we supposed to do now. Just wait? Just wait for him to—"

She turned his head to hers and pressed her mouth over his before he could finish, and suddenly he was tearing furiously at her blouse and yanking off his shirt without lifting his mouth from hers, and she was moaning, clutching at him as she hadn't in years and years and years, she thought. He let go only to push her backwards onto the bed, to help ease her pants from her legs as he undid his own. And then he was in her, and his mouth was on hers again, kissing her so hard that her lips felt bruised. Grief sex, she thought. Not so much a coming together as a tearing apart. She wanted Stephen to hurt her, wanted him to yank her to the edge of the bed—as he did, then slam into her over and over and over.

Afterward, they lay side by side across the bed, wide awake, panting like exhausted swimmers. "I'm sorry," he said after a minute. He reached for her hand. "This isn't how I want us to make love. I don't want—"

"Why?" she asked gently. "I mean, why not if it helps?"

She thought of how in times of stress, colonies of bacteria will begin to mutate wildly so as to increase the chances that a few cells, a few mutations, would somehow have whatever was needed to survive the disaster of the new conditions, and she imagined this "grief sex" was similar—a frantic fight against all they were about to lose.

SIX

Stephen walked into their bedroom the night after their trip to Hopkins, still wearing his leather jacket, his shoes leaving wet tracks in the pale carpet. Grace opened her mouth to say something, but stopped. She noticed his face first, then his cut hand, his bruised swollen knuckles. My God, what had happened? Her eyes flew back to his face. Something damaged in his expression. He wouldn't look at her. She felt the blood drain from her face. Oh God, she thought. He knows about Noah.

She became aware that the heating pad against her back was too hot, that she should get some ice for Stephen's hand. She pushed back the blankets and swung her legs over the side of the bed. "I'll get ice," she said in a calm voice. Her hands were shaking.

"No," he said. "Wait a minute." He didn't sound angry. Tired, maybe. Or numb. He sat in the rocking chair by the window. Still wearing his coat. Still refusing to look at her. From one of the houses across the lake, red Christmas lights blinked intermittently, on, then off. On again. Off. The night was like the inside of a heart, she thought, filling with blood, then emptying.

Don't let him have found out about Noah, she was thinking. *Please*.

But he must have. This was why his brother had phoned earlier, asking Stephen to stop by the bakery Jeff owned. It was important, Jeff had said; he couldn't get into it over the phone. *It*. What else could *it* be? Grace massaged her fingers to her temples, head bowed, as if she had a pounding headache. How had Noah's presence in her life become so normal that she'd forgotten to be afraid? she wondered helplessly. But it was *because* their affair had somehow become normal that it had continued at all. What else was survival but this? Adapting even to what makes no sense? And it didn't. Make sense—

despite her rationalizations. How, *how*, could she have been so stupid? It didn't matter who Noah was or what he'd once meant to her or how happy he made her now or—any of it. So what if she was in love with him? It didn't matter. Why had she thought it did?

She stared at her hands, trying to calm herself, trying to stop shaking. I don't want to lose you, Stephen, she thought desperately. She couldn't imagine her life without him. She didn't *have* a life without him. The kids, the house, everything—even the pile of laundry in the clothes basket by the door. How, *how*, had this happened?

The first time she saw Noah again Max was with her. They had driven to Cape May so Max could interview Noah for his report on endangered birds. Grace saw the Tigers bumper sticker on the battered Volvo station wagon as soon as they pulled into the parking lot. "That's his car," she told Max. "He was a Detroit Tigers nut." She told Max about the games they'd gone to, Noah's face painted orange and white.

"You? At a baseball game?" He grinned. "That must have been rich."

She laughed. "I didn't say I understood any of it."

"Is that why he dumped you?"

"Excuse me? Who says *he* dumped *me*?"

"So you dumped him?"

"I'm not sure anyone *dumped* anyone," she said. "The summer ended—I told you this, that I met him at your grandfather's church—I had to go back to New Jersey." She shook her head. "God, that was a long time ago."

He looked at her uncertainly. "But did you love him?"

His question caught her off guard. "Well, I guess I thought I did." She reached to tousle his hair, but he ducked away from her. An old habit of hers that only in the last year he had stopped appreciating. "Sorry, I keep forgetting." She looked at him a moment, brow furrowed. "You aren't worried about him, are you?" She bit her lip to keep from smiling, trying to remember how serious it had all seemed to *her* at thirteen.

"Nah, I'm just wondering. Why didn't you marry him?"

"Oh, gosh, Max, I wasn't even in college yet."

"So?"

"*So*, I was way too young, thank God. If I'd married him I never would have met your dad."

She had rehearsed half-a-dozen things she would say when she first saw him, practiced making her voice casual. "I can't believe it's you!" or "Noah McIntyre with short hair!" or "You look so different without long hair!" Except he didn't. When he stepped from the office onto the gravel drive, she stopped short. He wore a flannel shirt and jeans, a down vest, hiking boots. She shook her head in disbelief. "You still look like you," she said.

"Liar." He smiled. "*You* look fantastic. I can't believe this is your *son*." He offered his hand to Max. "Hey, Max, I'm Noah."

"Wait—" Grace laughed. "This is too strange. My high school boyfriend meeting my son." Her chest felt tight with something she couldn't name, and her eyes welled with tears.

"Oh, no you don't—" Noah wagged his finger at her. "Don't you dare." To Max he said, "So she still cries at the drop of a hat, huh?"

Max grinned. "She was like that way back then too?"

"Way back then?" Noah laughed again and opened his arms to Grace. "He thinks we're *really* old," he whispered. He was trembling. She could feel his heart hammering against the walls of his chest. Later he would tell her, "I thought I was going to pass out. You looked so goddamn gorgeous. I felt like a kid, and you seemed so calm."

"Are you kidding me? I was a wreck."

How had this happened?

Stephen was staring past her at the framed print of David Hockney's "The Swimmer." A rectangle of pale blue water was stippled with white and intersected by a lemon-yellow diving board. A line of purple shadow and beyond that, another rectangle of blurred green trees. Every day before work Stephen swam at the Y, a mile and a quarter: forty laps. On weekends when Grace took Erin and Jack to the baby pool, she would sit on the warm tiles and dangle Jack between her legs and watch Stephen through the glass partition. All shoulders and arms. His eyes were uncomprehending behind goggles. He couldn't imagine not being able to swim, he once told her. That feeling of weightlessness, of inhabiting another world. He even breathed differently, concentrating on each breath, timing it perfectly. Like playing a complicated piano toccata, she thought, every note held, then released just so.

She wished there were some way to explain how being with Noah—talking to him on the phone, getting his e-mails, lying in his bed in the middle of the afternoon, walking with him along the wrack line of the ocean, watching cormorants dive into the slate-colored water—was *her* way of becoming weightless, of escaping to another landscape where, for a little while, what mattered most seemed as simple and as primal as breathing.

She closed her eyes. You don't compare swimming laps to cheating on your husband. Like it's just some hobby. She sighed. She heard how it sounded to even try to explain.

They had walked to the beach that first meeting. It was low tide. Fist-sized birds the color of wet sand scurried after retreating waves, then scampered back up the beach as the next one rolled in.

"What are they?" Max asked politely.

"*Calidris alba.* Common name, sanderlings." Noah lifted his binoculars over his head and handed them to Max. "Go ahead. Tell me what you see." Sunlight flashed on the water, glinted on the wet sand. Everything was silver and gold but the sky—a bright turquoise blue.

After a few seconds, Max lowered the binoculars. "Was I supposed to like, notice something specific or . . . I mean, they look pretty normal."

"Exactly. Sanderlings are found on almost every beach in the world. Or at least they used to be."

Noah took the binoculars from Max and handed them to Grace. "They're searching for food, by the way, which is why they're chasing the surf." He pointed. "You ever hunt for sand crabs, wait for a wave to retreat, then dig real fast where a tiny airhole appears? That's basically what the birds are doing."

"Cool."

"They're like toddlers playing keep-away," Grace commented.

"The amazing thing about sanderlings is that every year they fly nearly eight thousand miles to get to their wintering ground. Eight thousand miles. When they arrive in the Artic—that's where they go—they're nothing but hollow bones and feathers. Most of their body weight is taken up by their hearts."

Like Jack, Grace thought, but didn't say it.

"So what happened after Princeton?" They were still walking, Max between them with the binoculars. Noah had taken off his shoes and rolled up the cuffs of his jeans, damp now with surf. Their shadows stretched in front of them as they walked.

"I went to London. A fellowship at Oxford. But it's my turn now. Tell me about you. Epidemiology, huh?"

"I loved it. I was always interested in medicine—"

"I remember."

"You do?" She turned to look at him, not sure why this surprised her.

"I figured you'd end up in pediatrics, though. You were great with those kids."

"Yeah, but dealing one on one with children in pain—too hard. My best friend in graduate school—Jenn—was a nurse and she'd tell these stories about the kids she saw in the ER." Grace shook her head. "Anyway, epidemiology let me have my cake and eat it too. I got to deal with the scientific aspect of medicine, which always fascinated me, and I didn't have to get too close to the actual individuals in pain." She felt Noah's eyes on her. "Cowardice, I guess." It surprised her to admit it—she'd never even told Stephen this. Or Jenn. And if Max hadn't been here, she thought, she would have told Noah more, how every time she gave this spiel—and that's what it had become over the years, about having no stomach for the pain or blood—a part of her knew it was all a lie, that what she really had no stomach for was the intimacy, that sometimes she thought she'd never been truly intimate with anyone again after the summer with Noah twenty years before, never really been herself as she'd been that summer, uncon-cerned about appearances or pretenses; happy, goofy; unafraid. Maybe everyone was this way at seventeen, but after she came home and stopped taking Noah's calls, something in her just shut down.

"So you think you'll ever go back to epidemiology?" Noah was asking.

After Jack, she thought, but she wouldn't think about that. Not now. "That's your second question," she teased instead. "It's my turn. Tell me about London."

"What are those?" Max interrupted, lowering the binoculars. He nodded towards the tiny birds scampering madly just above the wrack line.

"I thought they were sanderlings," Grace said.

"No, Max is right. How can you tell, Max?"

"The beaks are shorter?"

"Nice observation. Anything else?"

"The legs are orange."

Noah grinned, then held out his hand for Max to slap five. "Okay, that's a semipalmated—which means its toes are partially webbed—plover, or *Charadrius semipalmatus*. Notice how they stay a little higher up the beach"—he pointed—"than the sanderlings?"

They went to the Drift In and Sea Café for lunch and so that Max could interview Noah. There were wooden booths, large laminated menus, and fishing nets strung with white lights drooping from the ceiling. An assortment of faded beach chairs hung from pegs on the back wall. French fries came served in paper-lined plastic beach toys.

Max had a list of questions: "So, like, what exactly do ornithologists do?" and "How did you get interested in ornithology?" and "What ornithologists inspired you?"

He liked Noah, Grace could tell. It shouldn't have surprised her. Noah had always been great with kids—of any age.

"Our teacher told us that, like, ninety-nine percent of all the species that ever lived are extinct now," Max said, "so isn't extinction just, you know, like, a part of things?"

"Sure, it is. But not at the rate it's happening today." Noah stabbed the last of his French fries into a puddle of ketchup. "An estimated million species will be lost in the next twenty-five years. That's eighty species a day. Thirty thousand a year."

"But, like"—Max glanced at his notebook—"four hundred thousand people die every day of starvation and malnutrition, so, I mean, isn't that more important than birds?"

"Why should people care, you're asking?" Noah pushed his empty plate aside, his eyes solemn, almost angry.

"Don't make any sudden movements," Grace whispered to Max. "He might be dangerous."

Noah looked at her and smiled. "Cute," he said. And then, "You still hungry, Max? Want to split another bucket of fries?"

"Do you *always* eat like this?" Grace asked.

"Like what?"

Like someone who hadn't eaten in a long time—which was partially true. He wouldn't tell Grace until later that he lost twenty-two pounds in the five weeks since she'd sent the first e-mail, that he'd been living on protein shakes and salad ever since. He told himself he wanted to look good for her, that he'd been meaning to lose the extra weight for a couple of years now, but the truth was that after that first e-mail, he was afraid almost to *let* himself feel full, as if he needed to get used to emptiness again.

"So 'why should people care about birds?' That's what you're asking?"

"I guess." Max nodded. "Kind of."

Noah grinned. "Okay, then. I've already told you about the sanderlings. Eight thousand miles, a bird the size of—" he glanced around, then pushed the small plastic salt shaker toward Max. "Smaller than this. Another bird, the blackpoll warbler, flies nonstop over water from Northern Canada to South America. It takes four days. That's ninety hours, Max, *nonstop*. It's comparable to a man running a four-minute mile for eighty hours straight." He took a sip of coffee. "Then you've got the arctic tern, *Sterna paradisaea*: twenty-five thousand miles round-trip from the South Pole to the Machias Seal Islands. Or the American golden plover." He waited for Max to finish writing, then continued. "They fly from Newfoundland to Brazil, two thousand miles, again over open sea the whole way. Or ruby-throated hummingbirds: they weigh less than an eighth of an ounce and fly five hundred miles across the Gulf of Mexico, wings beating fifty times a second."

Noah let out a breath, drummed his fingers on the table top. "What else?" He and Max were both grinning now. "You've heard of Houdini, right? The great escape artist?"

Max nodded.

"Okay, amazing feats of escape? In the 1950s, scientists took a bird, the manx shearwater, from its nest on an island off the coast of Wales, flew the bird to America, then released it. Twelve and a half days and thirty-one hundred miles later, the bird's back in its nest. Or frigate birds—entire flocks get swept up in hurricane gales and are carried hundreds, *thousands*, of miles, then dumped in some other country, and they fly back to their original destination."

"*How?*" Max asked.

Noah held up his index finger—*wait*—and kept going. It was like watching a performance. A juggler or a knife-thrower, hurling the sharp blades of his facts, a fortune-teller slapping down her cards. "*Vermivora peregrina*, the Tennessee warbler, travels three thousand miles and returns to the same exact tree. And penguins. They can't even fly, and yet when transplanted twenty-four hundred miles from their nesting ground, they swam—*swam*—home. Half a mile an hour. It took ten months."

His eyes rested on hers, those blue, blue eyes, and Grace felt a tiny click in her brain, like a tape recorder shutting off. She glanced away, feeling flustered and lost and strangely happy all at once. When she looked up again, he was still watching her, a sad, sweet smile on his lips. She noticed the laugh lines at the corners of his eyes.

"How about songs?" Noah shifted his attention back to Max as he beat another drumroll on the wooden table. He was loving this. "The male red-eyed vireo, *Vireo olivaceus*, can sing up to twenty-two thousand songs in a single day." Their waitress set down the second bucket of fries they'd ordered. Noah nudged it towards Max, then asked, "How long did that just take?" He glanced at his watch. "Fifteen minutes, you figure?" He didn't wait for Max to respond. "Another species just went extinct." He squirted a dollop of ketchup onto his plate. His hands were chapped and dry, his knuckles nicked and scraped. It was in his hands that he had aged the most, Grace thought.

"You ask why people should care," he said gently, "and I almost don't know where to begin, Max. Take the whole miracle of flight. Sure, it's a cliché, but for a man to fly, to do what birds do so simply *every day*, his wingspan would have to be a hundred and forty feet long. Or take the fact that birds are our only modern link to dinosaurs or that every great thinker—Aristotle, Plato, da Vinci, Darwin, you name him—mentioned birds, that every important piece of literature we know—and I'm talking the Bible, the Quran, Shakespeare's and Confucius's works—mentions birds. In classical mythology, the entrance to the underworld was marked by a birdless lake. Hell, in other words, was—and still is, if you ask me—a place without birds."

He picked up a French fry, then set it down. "See, the problem is that when people talk about saving an endangered species, it's too abstract. They talk about biodiversity and ecological systems and the food chain, and there's nothing wrong with any of that, except it's not about the actual birds. You name any single bird, though, and I will tell you something absolutely fascinating and unique about that bird: Asian tailor birds literally sew their nests together. Or *Sturnus vulgaris*—starlings: Did you know that Mozart based the closing variations of one of his best-known compositions, his Piano Concerto in G, on a starling's song? Ostriches on the African plains, the largest birds alive, can outrun a lion. I mean, I can't even imagine. And that's what angers me, or maybe *saddens* is the better word. How can people be so willing to relinquish something, whatever it is—a bird, a plant, a relationship—" His eyes found Grace's. "Before they even bother to learn what the hell it is that they're losing?"

Stephen was saying something about Child Protective Services. "Wait—" Her throat felt dry. What did Child Protective Services have to do with Noah? "What did you just say?" He moved from the rocking chair to sit next to her on the bed. Still wearing his coat.

"You knew Mandy worked for Child Protective Services, right?" Mandy? Jeff's girlfriend. Yes—well, no. She knew Mandy had been in school for social work, but she hadn't known where Mandy worked. Or she'd forgotten. But she nodded.

"Did you hear what I said?" Stephen asked.

"I'm sorry, tell me again."

But even when he repeated it, the words kept spinning away from her. Her first reaction was relief—this wasn't about Noah at all. And then she wanted to laugh because what Stephen was telling her was so utterly preposterous that there wasn't anything else to do *except* laugh. "You've got to be kidding me, Stephen. *Munchausen's?*" It was ridiculous. Munchausen Syndrome by Proxy was that disease where mothers made their children sick on purpose—injected urine into their kids' IVs, gave them ipecac to induce vomiting, smothered them with pillows, then rushed hysterically to the hospital, sobbing for help—all ploys for attention. Like the firefighter who becomes an arsonist so that he can look like a hero. And, according to Jeff's very young, albeit very sweet, girlfriend, someone had accused Grace of this?

She couldn't make the leap. Couldn't jump from the very real, very possible threat that Stephen had somehow found out about Noah to this abstract *theory* based on what? A twenty-something-year-old girl *thinking* she'd seen Grace's name in some file?

She shook her head. "God, Stephen, do you have any idea how

much you scared me when you walked in here?" She looked at him, but he wouldn't meet her eyes, wouldn't smile. "Come *on*. This is crazy. I can't believe you punched a wall."

"Look, I laughed too when Jeff first told me, but—"

"Are we even sure that Mandy saw *my* name? I mean, I like her, I told you that, but she's a child who's in love with a forty-year-old man who's never had a relationship last longer than six months." She would just keep talking until Stephen realized how silly he was being. "I love your brother, Stephen, but he's not the smartest choice, so you have to question Mandy a little, don't you think?"

"Look," he sighed. "All I know is that Jeff was really upset about this, I guess because Mandy was—"

"Oh, please. Don't tell me she thinks this is true?" A wave of anger washed over her. "So *that* was the reason for all her questions about Jack the other night? How dare—"

"Wait a minute, Grace. She had the decency to tell Jeff about this, so I doubt she thinks it's true. She's just worried, and I guess she thinks we should be too. Apparently, there was a big Munchausen's case in Philadelphia a couple of years ago that made national news, and ever since then—"

"Wait a minute. Marie Noe? Is that the case?"

Stephen looked up. "You've heard of her?"

Grace nodded. Of course, she'd heard of Marie Noe. Everyone in Philadelphia had heard of Marie Noe, anyone with a sick child had heard of Marie Noe. Marie Noe, now in her seventies, had been charged, arrested, and eventually convicted on eight counts of murder for the deaths of her own children some thirty years before. The week of her arrest, the nurses on the sixth floor of Children's talked of nothing *but* Marie Noe. Grace had asked Rebecca, Jack's favorite nurse, if she'd ever had a patient whose mother was guilty of Munchausen Syndrome by Proxy, and Rebecca had told her that it made her sick to even think about, but she probably had. Only it was impossible to tell, she said, because the Munchausen mothers were often the nicest ones, notorious for becoming friends with the staff and bringing gifts for the nurses. Grace had joked, "Well, remind me not to be nice to you guys anymore," but now she recalled that even then, two years ago, she had felt a stab of fear.

She wanted to laugh this off too, but her face felt stiff and rubbery. How could anyone think that she—my God, Marie Noe was a monster. All *ten* of her children had died. *Ten*. And Marie Noe had *confessed*.

Grace felt as if she were going to throw up. "Did Mandy also tell Jeff that Marie Noe's lawyer tried to prove that the children had a rare metabolic disease?"

"Are you serious? A mitochondrial disease?"

"I don't know." She couldn't stop shaking. "I can't believe this, though. I can't believe anyone would think—do you have any idea what Munchausen mothers do to their kids? They suffocate them with Saran Wrap. They inject their own menstrual blood into their kids' IV lines. They starve them. I mean, what do they think I'm doing? Do they think I'm putting something into Jack's blood samples, do they think—"

"No, no, Grace, come on, stop. Come here." He reached to hold her, but she pushed him away.

"I don't want comfort," she snapped. "I want to know who said this."

"Obviously someone who doesn't know you very well."

"But *who*?" Her voice cracked.

"I don't know." He raked his hand through his hair.

She felt herself crumpling. Stephen reached again to hold her, but she couldn't be held. She moved to the window across the room, as far from him, from that word—*Munchausen*—as possible. Tree branches held their wrists up to the sky. There was no moon. She stared at the Christmas lights from the house across the lake: on, then off; on, then off—and felt her own heart beating in tandem with them. She heard Stephen get up from the bed and cross the room to wrap his arms around her from behind as Noah had three days ago as they stood on the beach. She began to cry. How could she have thought for a minute that losing Noah—or even Stephen finding out about him—was the worst thing that could happen?

"Come on, Grace," Stephen whispered. He smelled of leather from his coat and homemade bread from Jeff's bakery.

"I just want to know how this could happen," she whispered.

"I don't know, but the investigation—"

She jerked away from him. *"Investigation?"*

"Well, whatever it was. Mandy said it was initiated last March, but obviously no one found anything, and hell, for all we know, the 'investigation' might have been nothing more than one call to Dr. Mehta and that was the end of it."

Grace felt herself go cold again. "Anju knew about this?"

"No, I don't know . . . I was simply—"

"Why wouldn't she have told us?" Grace was crying again. She had trusted Anju. She had—she still did—consider Anju to be a part of their family. She thought of the morning, the second or third that Jack had been in the ICU last year, when she woke after a few restless hours of sleep to find an exhausted-looking Anju standing over Jack's bed. "Is he okay?" Grace asked before she even sat up.

Anju smiled. "Our boy is doing much better," she whispered, without taking her eyes from Jack. *Our* boy. When Jack was in the hospital, Grace often felt as if Anju was his other parent.

Grace couldn't stop crying now. Anju was also the only person, the *only* person—not even Stephen—with whom Grace had ever discussed, seriously discussed, a DNR order. *Do Not Resuscitate.* How do you explain to anyone what it is like to determine the exact scenario in which you will no longer fight for your child's life? How do you possibly convey what it feels like in your bones and in the back of your throat to not only *imagine* that scenario but to *plan* for it the way you would plan for you child's first day of school? Not something that *might* happen. Something that *would.* And Anju was the only person in her life who knew what this had been like.

Stephen turned her around, forced her to look at him. "Baby, listen to me. I have no idea if Anju knows or not, but if she does, and she didn't say anything to us, it's because she thought this whole thing was bullshit, which it is."

She nodded bleakly. "But is that what *you* thought—" She paused. "I mean, when Jeff first told you, did you think—"

He pulled away from her. "Think *what*, Grace?" His voice was angry, but she saw that his eyes were terrified. Terrified because he *had* thought it, maybe for only an instant, less than that even. But he had thought it. She felt herself dissolving. She wanted to hate him, but she knew that had the tables been turned and someone told her that Stephen had been accused of Munchausen's, she would have vehemently denied it, but it wouldn't have erased that nanosecond of doubt, that silent *could he have?* And maybe a part of her would have even hoped—for only a second, she promised herself now, but still, *hoped*—that the accusation was true. Because if it was, it would mean that Jack wasn't really as sick as everyone thought. It would mean that he would live.

"I know you don't think that now, but just at first, Stephen, for a second—"

"No."

"Would you tell me if you had? If you ever—"

"Goddamnit." He turned away from her. "How can you ask me this? You are the reason Jack is alive."

She began crying again. "What if they take him away from us, Stephen?"

"They can't, Grace."

"Yes, they can, Stephen. You don't know."

"You haven't done anything wrong!" he bellowed. "You are torturing yourself with this, Grace." He lowered his voice. "Please. Nothing is going to happen."

She wondered if he really believed this. She thought of Noah telling her how along rural airport runways that were plagued by flocks of birds, loudspeakers played recordings of distress calls made by crows in an effort to ward the birds off. She thought that Stephen's voice was like that now, as if the sound of his anger alone could push this horrible accusation away.

From the doorway of the walk-in closet, Stephen tossed his shirt onto the pile of dirty clothes by the bathroom door. Grace stared at Stephen's arms and chest and thought what a beautiful man he was and how she didn't deserve him. "We're an open book, Grace," he said as he yanked a worn T-shirt over his head and flicked off the closet lights. "Let them investigate us all they want." He climbed into bed, handing her the pint of Häagen-Dazs that he had picked up on the way home. She thought of how in Stephen's family they always ate ice cream when they were upset, as if to numb themselves from the inside out. They'd eaten it for dinner the July night Stephen's dad walked out on his wife and sons for a woman young enough to be his daughter; they'd eaten it when their mother announced that she was remarrying a man neither Stephen nor Jeff could stand; and they ate it again when she left that man for another.

Years later, the night Grace and Stephen finally—after how many experts, how many trips to different hospitals—received the diagnosis for Jack, they sat at the kitchen table, wordlessly passing a pint of butter pecan ice cream back and forth to each other. And only yesterday, sitting in the family room after the trip to Baltimore, they'd played the scene out again.

Now tonight. Grace imagined that this was the taste of betrayal: cold and rich and so achingly sweet that for a moment—*maybe*—you forget how much you are about to lose.

SEVEN

Grace sat straight against the passenger seat, her shoulders pushed back, her hands in her lap. Knees pressed together beneath her gray skirt. It was like being in Catholic school again: obeying rules that made no sense.

She stared out the window at the city blurring by. How ugly it was here: miles of squat round oil refineries, trash heaps, and high-rise parking garages. And then the airport, planes suturing the sky. The large black letters of the word PREGNANT? glared from a shabby billboard followed by a 1-800 number. Grace dropped her eyes back to her lap. Did it not count for anything that she had wanted each of her children? Stephen reached from the steering wheel and squeezed her hand. "I know," he said. "It's not fair." She nodded, feeling both grateful and guilty. She didn't deserve him. She squeezed his hand in return. Like a coma patient, she thought, and this was the only way to communicate.

They were on their way to a lawyer's.

Grace had spent the last two days terrified to let the kids out of her sight. She didn't go out, didn't get dressed, didn't answer the phone. She couldn't stop crying. She canceled Jack's therapy appointments. She didn't trust anyone. She didn't want him near the hospital. She sat at the computer in her robe and a pair of Stephen's sweat socks, reading the Munchausen by Proxy Home Page, which had a database of over four hundred articles about the disorder. She'd had no idea the disease was this prevalent, that so many women were capable of devising such horrible ways to hurt their children. The titles of the articles themselves had read like advertisements for horror movies:

"Salvage or Sabotage: Munchausen's and the Chronically Ill Child."

"The Bacteriologically Battered Baby: Another Case of Munchausen by Proxy."

"Supermom or Super Monster."

Even the names of the journals in which the articles had been published seemed ominous: *Archives of Disease in Childhood, Journal of Forensic Sciences, Journal of Child Abuse and Neglect.* She couldn't erase from her mind the description of the four children so severely abused by their mother that they were dwarfed. Locked in closets for weeks and months at a time and slowly starved. A sixteen-year-old boy had the height of an eight-year-old; an eight-year-old girl had a bone age of three years. She pictured bonsai trees, their roots constantly cut beneath the surface of dark soil, abused into minuscule perfection.

None of it made sense.

They were nicknamed "helicopter mothers" because they were always hovering over their distressed child. She thought of how she had never left Jack alone in the hospital. People told her all the time: "I don't know how you do it, Grace" or "You're a saint," or "I've never met a parent as devoted as you."

Supermom or Child Abuser. The words echoed.

She couldn't sleep, couldn't eat. *In cases of Munchausen by Proxy, termination of parental rights is the only absolute way of ensuring the victim's safety.* Erin and Jack watched videos, one after the other, though normally the rule was no more than one hour of TV a day. She imagined that years from now she would remember little of this time except for the odd lines of high-pitched Disney dialogue: *I have come to seek the hand of the Princess Jasmine. . . . Take my advice, kid . . . Hakuna Matata.*

"Please don't argue with me," she had begged Max this morning, after reneging on her promise to let him go to the hockey rink with a bunch of kids from his team. "I wouldn't ask you to stay home if it wasn't important."

"You *said* I could go, Mom."

"*Please*, Max." She was sitting on the stairs in her bathrobe. She was exhausted, and she needed a shower and the house was a mess. Uno cards lay scattered on the hallway floor. A puzzle piece. One of

Jack's socks. Already she felt defeated. "I can't explain it to you right now, but—"

"It's not fair!" Max exploded. "You always do this! Why'd you even buy me new skates if I can't use them?"

Stephen had intervened from the kitchen. "Max, you yell at your mother one more time and you can forget the rink altogether." He strode into the hallway, a dishtowel over his shoulder, and told Max to go empty the dishwasher, swatting him with the towel as Max stomped off. Stephen squatted in front of Grace then. He hadn't shaved in two days, and she knew he was exhausted too. He'd been doing everything—all of Jack's medications, the cooking, laundry. "We can't keep him in all week," he said gently.

"I'm just so afraid," she sobbed.

She could feel Stephen watching her as he drove, though her eyes were closed. "What?" she asked without opening them.

"You look beautiful," he said.

She clenched her jaw against the irritation she felt. "I thought the whole point of this suit was to *not* look beautiful." Tears pricked her eyes. "I feel ridiculous." She wished she could have laughed at herself—trying on and discarding clothes for nearly an hour this morning, as if to prove to the lawyer that—*what?* Being a good mother was a matter of wearing the right costume? It was ludicrous.

But nothing Grace had tried on was right: her good clothes—high-necked sleeveless sweaters and long slim-fitting skirts; an impossibly small LBD, Little Black Dress, that Stephen bought her a few years ago—were too formal, too sexy. And you couldn't be sexy if you were accused of harming your children, could you? And no bright colors. Nothing that would attract attention. Munchausen mothers were *desperate* for this, after all. She had needed neutral shades: grays, off-white, beige. *Pastels*, she thought bitterly; a flower-print Sunday school dress. Below the knee, of course. She thought of how the nuns used to make the girls genuflect before leaving homeroom to confirm that their hems touched the floor.

She'd borrowed the gray suit from her mother. Nothing of her own was right. *She* wasn't right.

"Jack's blood pressure was still high when we left," Grace said as they passed the exit for South Street, the exit she usually took to Children's.

Stephen glanced at her. "I know, but we didn't give him the clonidine until almost one-thirty."

She shook her head. "I'm not taking him to the hospital until we get this straightened out, Stephen." Her voice rose. "I can't."

"Let's just see what the lawyer says."

They crossed the Schuylkill River, the pale yellow dome of the art museum off to the right along with the boathouses framed in white Christmas lights. The gray sky and gray river and gray trees reminded Grace of a faded photograph, of a time before color.

"Hey." Stephen reached for her hand and she gave it to him. "We're in this together, Grace. I mean that."

She turned to look at him—the high cheekbones that Max had inherited, the long-lashed eyes that Jack had. She loved that Stephen was handsome, that he was one of those men who grew better-looking with age, although except for the gray in his hair and the lines fanning out from his eyes, he didn't look all that different than he had fifteen years ago. The same short haircut and clothes: khakis, loafers, button-down oxfords, sleeves rolled casually a quarter of the way up his arm. Polo shirts in the spring and summer. A blue blazer on a hanger in the back of his car, "just in case." She smiled. He was wearing the Eeyore tie the kids had given him for Christmas. "Thank you," she said quietly.

He frowned. "For what?"

"Just being here." Her voice cracked. "For loving me."

"I hope you don't really think that's something to thank me—" A white Lexus cut in front of them, and he slammed his foot to the brakes. "Asshole," he muttered. "Didn't even look, never even saw me."

She rested her head against the seat back.

He glanced at her. "Did you see that thing on the news last night about driving?"

"Every two miles the average driver makes something like four hundred observations, forty decisions, and one mistake, which might or might not lead to an accident." She glanced at him. "Every two miles. Can you imagine?"

"Jesus, how do you remember this stuff?"

"*Why* do I remember it?" She turned back to the window, wondering how many decisions that equaled in a day, a week, a life? And how many mistakes? And how could you *ever* possibly know all the things you'd done wrong? She closed her eyes, her chest weighted with fear again. What had she done to make someone think she would harm Jack? And who would think this? The word echoed. *Who, who, who,* like the character of Mr. Owl in one of Jack's picture books.

She had been through everyone—Jack's doctors, his nurses, Noah, Jenn, even someone from the mito group. She was so honest with them. Had she said something that was misconstrued? The time Jack had the nasogastric tube in his nose, and she joked that he looked like a little elephant man. The jokes about him being an alcoholic because of the broken capillaries—*spider telangiectasias*—in his cheeks, caused by his malfunctioning liver. Or that time she and Andrea, one of his night nurses, were watching him sleep, up on his knees and elbows, which he did to protect his swollen stomach, and Andrea commented that he looked uncomfortable, and Grace laughed and said that at least if she needed to give him a suppository in the middle of the night for his blood pressure, he was in a good position. Andrea had laughed. She squeezed Grace's arm and whispered, "Isn't it awful? You really do start thinking like that after a while, don't you?"

She wondered if her mother might have said something, without meaning to. That Grace seemed consumed with Jack's illness or that she was overprotective. Grace had questioned Stephen even, and found herself watching him watching her and wondering what he was thinking.

• • •

"What are you *doing*?" She grabbed Jack from Stephen's back where he'd been clinging like a little barnacle. Stephen was pinning Max to the floor, and Erin was trying to tickle Stephen enough that he'd release Max. They were all laughing, trying to pull each others' socks off, the goal of the wrestling match.

Jack started howling the minute Grace pulled him away. "Do you not get it?" Grace said furiously to Stephen. "Are you trying to kill him?"

Erin started to explain: "We were just—"

"I'm talking to your father," Grace snapped. "Here—" She put Jack down. "Take Jack. Go do something, all of you."

They waited until the kids were out of the room.

"Trying to *kill* him, Grace?" Stephen was livid.

"Oh, please. You know I didn't mean that, but my God, he's in heart failure, Stephen."

"He was *laughing*!" Stephen yelled. "He was having fun, for crying out loud. Or have you forgotten what that's like?"

"Go to hell," she said. "You think I *like* being this way? You think I don't want my child to be happy?"

He didn't say anything. They were standing in the middle of the living room, facing off like boxers, both of them breathing heavily. Couch pillows were strewn on the floor, toys were everywhere. "I mean it," she pressed. "Is that what you think?"

He stared at her coldly "You're so wrapped up in the medical stuff—"

"I have to be," she said. "I have to be because *you* won't, Stephen."

"*Won't*, Grace?"

"Fine, *can't*. Whatever. You were still wrestling with a child in end-stage heart disease. I mean, how stupid—"

"*Stupid?* Jack was laughing. *Laughing*." His voice cracked. "God damn you," he said, and walked away from her to the fireplace, where he spread his arms like someone under arrest and bowed his head, shoulders heaving.

When he turned to look at her, he was crying. "Jack having fun like any other child," he said, "that's what I'm going to have to hold onto, and how dare you, how dare you try—" but he was sobbing then, and there was nothing to do but go to him and promise that it would be okay. She resented it, though; she resented a lot, she had realized these past few days, and she couldn't help but wonder how deeply he resented her too.

EIGHT

Grace stared at the row of black-and-white photographs of the four main bridges connecting Philadelphia to New Jersey that hung on the wall to her right. Bennett Marsh, the lawyer, sat across from them in a leather wing chair, a tall floor lamp just behind him.

Stephen filled Bennett in on what they knew: someone had called Child Protective Services last spring accusing Grace of making Jack sick—Munchausen Syndrome by Proxy. No one had informed Grace or Stephen of this. They had only discovered the accusation two days ago. Stephen's brother's girlfriend was a social worker who had happened upon the file with Grace's name.

The only sound in the dimly lit office was the scratch of Bennett's fountain pen across the legal pad. He asked basic questions: what they did for a living, where they worked, the names and ages of their kids, the name of Jack's illness, in what hospital he was being treated. "Have you ever had problems with Child Protective Services before?"

Grace glanced up. Never.

"Any arrests?"

She shook her head. Of course not. Her throat ached. She knew he had to ask. He was simply doing his job. Stephen squeezed her hand. Actually, *he'd* had a DUI when he was nineteen, he said. But that was twenty years ago.

"You'd be surprised what comes up in these files," Bennett said.

Noah grinned. "With my luck, I'll have some bumbling Matlock-type lawyer."

"And he'll wear those seersucker suits in the courtroom." Grace was laughing. "*What?* Don't give me that look. Doesn't Matlock wear seersucker?"

"You actually *watch* that show?"

They were sitting on the beach talking about the Philadelphia lawyer who had been missing for months; the judge she'd been having an affair with was now being investigated. Noah had joked that if either of them ever met an unforseen death, the other would automatically be suspect.

"Neither of us would have alibis, of course." Grace reached for a pretzel from the bag he held. "You'd have been out on your own trying to save a bird—or so you'd say."

"You'd insist you were driving to the hospital and got stuck in traffic. They'd search your car, though, and find beach sand beneath the floor mats."

"*And* in my hair." She laughed. "*And* my shoes. *And* under my fingernails." She folded her arms over her upraised knees and rested her head on them, watching him. His eyelashes were gold in the sunlight. "So what would the prosecution say my motivation was?"

"Oh, the usual. You discovered I was in love with another woman and became insanely jealous." He grinned to show he was joking, but the words had sharp edges.

"Is that what you want?" she asked quietly. "For me to be jealous?"

He squinted at her as if he wasn't sure. "Yeah, sometimes," he said. "Are *you*?"

"Jealous of you and Stephen?"

She nodded.

"All the time." He was staring towards the surf when he said this. She could no longer see his face.

Bennett looked up from the typed summary of Jack's medical record that Grace had handed him. "He's on *all* these medications? Every day?"

There were eleven: ACE inhibitors, calcium channel blockers, diuretics, dioxin, thyroid hormone, potassium tablets, coenzyme Q10, prednisone. And morphine.

"I see the morphine is as needed. Which means what? How often?"

"Every day." Her voice cracked, though she'd joked about this too. My little druggie, our little addict. She swallowed hard. It's not that she thought it funny, that she didn't take it seriously. She joked because it was too devastating to face what Jack's dependence on morphine really meant.

"How do you determine 'as needed'?"

"Jack isn't ever without morphine anymore. We'd have to gradually wean him at this point to cut back. If he's in pain, though, I'll up the dose."

"And Jack can articulate when he's in pain?"

Grace glanced at Bennett helplessly. "He tells me his heart hurts." Her voice quavered. "And there are signs. He gets irritable. He becomes cyanotic—blue—around the mouth. He self-protects, holds himself stiffly when I pick him up." She spoke slowly, deliberately. She would not cry. She would not. Even though this man was looking at her and maybe wondering if she was capable of drugging her child with a narcotic. If he were a good lawyer, and he was, then he had to wonder, didn't he? She imagined Bennett knew already that there had to be reasons for this accusation, that nobody was as uncomplicated as they appeared. She imagined that he would somehow understand, forgive her for whatever she had done wrong, as if he were a priest, not a lawyer, as if it were in his power to absolve her.

She took a deep breath. "His heart rate goes up, his eyes become dilated."

Bennett was writing everything down. "How long has he been on the morphine?"

"Since the summer."

"So this wouldn't be connected to the accusation." He made another note, then set the summary on his lap and removed his wire-rimmed glasses. "Your little boy's been through a lot," he said quietly. "And you have as well." He sighed. "Munchausen's is an insidious accusation. I'm sorry you're being put through this." He leaned back, his fingers steepled before his face. He had beautiful eyes, she noticed. Very blue. And very kind, and again she had to steel herself against the rush of tears burning her eyes.

In 1962, *The Journal of the American Medical Association* published a landmark paper called "The Battered-child Syndrome." A Colorado pediatrician, alarmed at the number of abused children he was seeing, had written physicians and district attorneys across the country, asking for their observations. He presented the findings at a conference conducted by the American Academy of Pediatrics: An estimated sixty thousand children were being abused in the United States. Worse, the abusers could be anywhere; and they could be anyone: your next-door neighbor, your lawyer or tax accountant, the head of the PTA. You never knew. No child was safe, not even from his own parents. As if to bear this out, calls reporting more and more cases began pouring in.

It was an easy cause to triumph: saving children. It was politically safe. Money flowed into social service agencies to set up hotlines, conduct more surveys and symposiums, establish child protection teams, and educate the public. Within five years every state in the nation had passed legislation mandating that physicians and nurses report to Child Protective Services any suspected cases of abuse. To not do so was to risk being prosecuted on both civil and criminal charges. It was the most quickly passed legislation in the history of the United States.

Child abuse became its own field of study. National and international conferences, academic journals, and a new group of experts became devoted to the subject. The definition of abuse broadened to include sexual abuse, psychological abuse, and abuse by neglect. "Child abuse is so prevalent that it is now an 'American tradition,' " declared one politician. By 1990, it was considered a national emergency. But as the meaning of the term grew, it became more vague. None of the fifty states regarded spanking an abuse—a concession made to get the legislation passed to begin with. However, in Illinois, rapping a child on the knuckles with a fork constituted abuse while in Florida, it did not—unless bruises persisted for more than three days. Women were reported to Child Protective Services because their homes were in disrepair. A mother who could not afford to buy eyeglasses for her child was accused of neglect. The sixty thousand reported cases in 1962 rose to over three million by 1994, with nearly half a million children taken from their homes and placed into foster care each year.

Less well known was the fact that 65 percent of the reports alleging abuse were based on erroneous information. In one year, in the state of New York alone, 85,000 of the 456,000 calls to Child Protective Services were determined to be pranks, the majority of which had to be treated as genuine until proven otherwise. It didn't matter. What politician would dare suggest that funding be cut to Child Protective Services or that maybe every case *didn't* need to be investigated? "How dare a family complain about a little inconvenience when a child's life is at stake," one politician responded to the criticism that too many of the accusations were false. "I'd rather see a family disrupted than a bunch of dead children." As if to bear him out, the major newspapers were filled with stories of children who had slipped through the cracks.

Grace had read "The Battered-child Syndrome" in graduate school. Its main author, Henry Kempe, was regarded as a hero for his studies differentiating intended injuries and accidental ones. Jenn had seen real-life examples of this firsthand during her student rotation in the ER. She had told Grace of the little girl with the grid of a heating grate branded into the soles of her feet; had it been an accident, only one foot would have been burned before the child leaped off the vent. The toddler whose bottom was scalded from being submerged in hot water, the water line across his abdomen as straight as if it had been painted there. It meant he'd been held down so forcefully, he couldn't move. The burgundy U-shapes across a boy's back, the imprint of the looped belt recorded on his skin like fast-motion photography.

Until two nights ago when Stephen walked into their bedroom

and told her of the accusation, Grace would have been the first one to say that it didn't matter how many false accusations there were if even *one* of these injuries could have been prevented.

"Can either of you recall any run-ins, however trivial, with any of Jack's doctors, nurses, even family members who perhaps don't understand his medical condition?"

Jack had been sick for over a year before they got a diagnosis, so yes, there had been run-ins with plenty of doctors and nurses and yes, even family members. "You know too much," one gastroenterologist had told her. "You're an epidemiologist, right? You're probably imagining every horrible disease—we all do it. Welcome to the club."

"It's a phase. So he's a fussy eater," another doctor told her. But it was more than fussy. He had been born full-term. He was healthy for the first two months. And then something happened. He was too tired to eat and even when he did, he wasn't gaining weight. Failure to thrive. Her mother once asked, "Do you think maybe he's picking up on *your* tension, honey?"

They'd done the tests. A sweat test for cystic fibrosis. A whole GI workup. Nothing. At seven months she'd called the doctor in tears when she couldn't get Jack to eat, and they'd scheduled a swallow test, thinking maybe there was some sort of blockage and of course, the day of the test, he seemed fine and took his bottle perfectly.

She'd find him asleep in the middle of his toys. His hands and feet were freezing, his nail beds bluish, his heart racing. "It's not normal," she kept insisting. "I'm telling you something's wrong." They discovered a Grade III diastolic murmur, but "lots of kids have ventricular gallops," they told her. They sent him home with a Holter monitor. Eventually, the cardiologist stopped returning her calls, made no follow-up appointments. Grace had phoned in tears one afternoon, terrified after a morning of watching him struggle for breath.

"What exactly do you want Dr. Buford to do?" the receptionist asked her.

"I want him to care," Grace said wearily.

Silence from the other end.

"Look, I understand that he's frustrated," she tried again, but was interrupted.

"It sounds like *you're* the one who is frustrated, Mrs. Connolly; most parents would be thrilled to know that there's nothing wrong."

Most parents.

She'd hung up. And that's when she started writing letters. She'd log onto Medline and HealthWeb and read about Beckwith-Widemann Syndrome or glycogen storage disease of the heart or dilated cardiomyopathy, and she'd write to the doctors who had authored those articles, enclosing a copy of Jack's medical history. *If you have any ideas that might help us find an answer,* she wrote. It felt as futile as putting a note in a bottle and tossing it to sea in the hopes that it might reach someone on the other side of the world. But a doctor from the Cleveland Clinic had responded. Another from Johns Hopkins. Anju Mehta from Children's in Philadelphia. John Bartholomew from the University of California, San Diego. He'd been the first, offering to fly Jack out to his clinic for testing, then abruptly changing his mind. Grace looked up, her neck warm. What was it he said to her? Something accusatory. Something about how eager *she* seemed to have Jack undergo tests. Sentences from the Munchausen by Proxy Web site flashed into her mind: *"Munchausen by Proxy is a career pursued by supposedly wonderful mothers who use their children as sacrifices to win the attention of the powerful doctors whom the mother worships as a god."* Is that what John Bartholomew had thought? She *had* been so grateful when he first called. She couldn't stop thanking him.

Yes, there had been run-ins, she told Bennett.

"And this Mandy? Your brother's girlfriend, how long have you known her?"

"Technically a year, but we've only spent time with her—" Grace glanced at Stephen. "What? Two, three, times?"

"She just graduated last June, so she's only been with Child Protective Services a couple of months," Stephen added. "Apparently she saw Grace's name in the file a few weeks ago, but she was afraid to say anything."

"But then she spent Christmas with us, and I guess after seeing Jack, maybe she realized that he really was sick."

"Was anything unusual going on last January or February, right around the time you think the accusation was made? Anything: medical issues, personal issues, work-related issues even?"

The muscles in her arms went limp, and she realized for the first time since Stephen told her of the accusation how tightly she'd been clenching her fingers, how she had literally been holding on. January was when she sent that e-mail: *Noah, is that you?*

So was that it? Had someone, one of the nurses or doctors or maybe one of the parents she'd come to know from the hospital, seen her with Noah, found out she wasn't so wonderful, after all, and somehow made the leap to Munchausen's? And *was* it really a leap? Why wouldn't they wonder: If Grace could be so deceptive in one aspect of her life, what was to stop her from being just as deceitful in other aspects?

"So no rekindled sparks?" Stephen asked the day she and Max had gone to see Noah. She was undressing for bed, and she'd paused, holding her nightgown in front of her, thinking.

Honestly, no," she said after a minute. "I mean, I think we were both nervous at first, but it was actually just . . . *nice*." She'd meant it. And was glad. They hadn't even hugged goodbye, just shook hands.

"Let me know how the report turns out," Noah had said to Max before they drove off. And that was it.

She hadn't been able to sleep, though, her mind reeling, not about Noah so much as about stuff from the past. Trying to remember the name of the professor who'd taught the research methodologies class that she'd loved, wondering if he was still teaching and if she really would go back to work one day. *Do you think you'll ever get back to epi-*

demiology? She tossed and turned, her legs twitchy, probably from all the driving, and too much caffeine. *That's what angers me . . . how can people be so willing to relinquish something, whatever it is—a bird, a plant, a relationship—before they even bother to learn what the hell it is that they're losing?*

Finally, she gave up and went downstairs. She'd check her e-mail, type a quick thank-you to Noah for helping Max. No sooner had she sent the message, though, than she got one from him: Why are you up at two in the morning?

Her heartbeat quickened. Couldn't sleep, she wrote. What about you?

Why couldn't you sleep?

She felt like a girl, talking to her boyfriend on the phone late at night. Why, why, why? she typed. You're worse than my three-year-old.

He didn't respond right away, and she waited, curled in the comfortable desk chair, not moving, not responding to the other e-mails on her screen. It was a beautiful blue-black night, stars like bits of stones and shells washed upon it accidentally. She couldn't stop smiling.

And then his e-mail. "Are you happy, Grace? Or is it pointless to ask when you have a child as sick as Jack? But has your life turned out as you'd wanted it to? God, I have so many questions. Is vanilla still your favorite flavor of ice cream, and do you still prefer rainy days to sunny ones, and since when did you start painting your fingernails— since when did you even *have* fingernails, and what's it like to have a teenage son?".

She exhaled slowly. It felt as if she had glass in her lungs, as if something had broken inside her. She remembered Noah telling the kids he taught all those years ago that the true genius of men like Einstein and Newton lay *not* in the complexity of the questions they asked, but in the simplicity. It was the answers that were catastrophic.

I am happy, she responded. Most days. Which is enough. She paused, then added, But I've never stopped loving you. She didn't send it, just sat back, conscious suddenly that she was sitting in darkness, as if she'd known before she even began typing the danger of revealing too much. Her chest felt too full suddenly. *Not* because of how easily she had written those words, but because they felt so true. And how was that possible? She stood and paced to the sliding glass door across the room, that single sentence glowing on the dark screen like a comet from another time. She'd gone years without so much as thinking of him, hadn't she? But what did *that* mean? That she couldn't love him now? Or that she hadn't allowed herself to *until* now? She stared at the line of pine trees out back, at the dark shape of the swing set against the snow-covered ground, and she thought of the life not lived that everyone must have inside of them. She thought of how bacteria two million years old had been found living in stones buried miles beneath the earth, of how snow that had fallen tens of thousands of years ago was preserved beneath layers of arctic ice, and she thought, why not love? Why shouldn't it, too, survive?

She hugged herself in her thick robe, though she wasn't cold and pictured how Noah had looked that morning—youthful and happy—felt again how his heart had thudded against hers when they hugged, of the spark of electricity that had jumped between their skin when he handed her the binoculars. But so what? she admonished herself. It doesn't mean anything. This is foolish. You love Stephen, you're happy, you have a good life.

And yet.

She stood for a long time in front of the computer, staring at those words, *I've never stopped loving you*, until they blurred into a single orange streak, a star slowly dying. And then she hit send and told herself that it didn't change anything, that he had the right to know, that she owed him this much.

In the morning, she was horrified, and the minute Stephen left for work and the kids were off to school, she e-mailed a new message: I'm sorry. I shouldn't have written that. I know better than to EUI— e-mail under the influence. She hadn't been, but she didn't care. She just wanted the words back.

"Bullshit," he responded. "Did you read the e-mail I sent you?" She hadn't wanted to. *I've never stopped loving you either*, it said.

• • •

"*Anyone* could have made that phone call for *any* reason," Bennett was saying, "and by law, as I'm sure you know, Child Protective Services *has* to look into it. The fact is, though, that two-thirds of all accusations are never substantiated." He sighed. "The child protection system is a double-edged sword. On one hand, if two-thirds of the accusations are false, then child abuse is much less prevalent than we think. But as you're unfortunately discovering, a lot of people—a lot of families—get put through hell."

"And nothing happens to the people who make the claim, even when it's false?" Stephen asked.

"Not if the accusation is made in good faith." Bennett glanced at Grace. "And I think most are, believe it or not. I truly think most of these accusations are legitimate misunderstandings."

Misunderstandings. Please let it be that simple, Grace thought, though it seemed absurd that it could be. Misunderstandings were ordinary, everyday occurrences that eventually got straightened out with rueful apologies—*Oh my God, I can't believe I did that!* or *I am such an idiot. I am so sorry!* Misunderstandings ended with embarrassed laughter and hands clasped to mouths once the mistake was realized. Misunderstandings were the stuff of sitcoms and Hollywood love stories, but not, *not* accusations of child abuse.

Bennett glanced at Grace. "I'm hoping this is what happened in your case." He smiled and again, Grace was struck by the warmth in his eyes.

"Me too." She smiled shakily. "But until we know—" I'm afraid to let the kids out of my sight, she wanted to tell him. I'm afraid to take Jack to his therapy appointments. I'm afraid to let Erin and Max go back to school next week. I'm afraid to talk to my friends because I don't know if one of them was the one who reported me. She stared again at the photographs of the four bridges and thought of Stephen's grandfather who had helped repaint one of them during the Great Depression. Part of Roosevelt's WPA project. Strapped in a harness, swaying over traffic, a man so terrified of heights he wouldn't sleep on the second floor of his house. Her father told her once that pilots are often terrified of heights, that they overcome it by learning to love the very thing they feared.

"I know you're afraid," Bennett said gently. "Understandably. And I don't want to tell you not to be because until I get a copy of the report from Child Protective Services I don't know enough." He glanced at Stephen. "I don't think it would be a bad idea to keep the kids close for the next few days. I assume they're on holiday break anyway?"

Grace nodded.

"And as a precaution, Stephen, you should accompany Grace to Jack's doctor appointments." He turned back to Grace. "If Stephen can't go, take your mom or dad, a friend, someone you trust."

Tears pricked her eyes. She didn't trust anyone anymore.

"The fact you were never notified might be a good sign," Bennett said as they were walking out to their cars. Snow was falling again. The rush hour traffic was bumper to bumper. Horns sounded impatiently as the lights changed. "My hope—and this isn't out of the realm of possibility by any stretch—is that the accusation was so minor, so low on the list of priorities that, quite honestly, whoever was responsible forgot." They were at their car. Bennett shook Stephen's hand, then Grace's. "I know it's not much consolation," he told her, "but whoever made that call probably believed that he or she was truly doing what was best for Jack. I doubt it was malicious."

She nodded, shivering as the snow fell around them like consequences, those tiny fragile truths.

NINE

$\mathcal{G}$race pushed open the door to Jack's room. Immediately, she smelled the ammonialike odor of his urine. Light from the hallway glinted on the metal oxygen canister next to his bed. The CPAP machine that monitored the rate and flow of air whirred softly like a rewinding cassette tape. Grace leaned over Jack's crib, her palm against his back, and felt the dampness of his pajamas. At least the diuretic was working, but like everything connected to this illness it was a double-edged sword. He needed the diuretic to rid his lungs of the fluid that was backing up in them, but if he lost too much, his potassium levels would plummet, which in turn would raise his blood pressure.

She pulled off his soaked clothes, repositioning him away from the damp part of the sheet, which she covered with a cotton baby blanket. She slid one of Erin's old Sesame Street T-shirts over his head, easing it past the tangle of tubes. "No, Mama," he whimpered, angry at being disturbed.

"Mama's just going to check your blood pressure, Jack," Grace whispered, maneuvering the cuff over his arm. He began to cry, and she shushed him, stroking his damp hair. "It's okay. Mama's almost done." Across the room, the red numbers on his pulse oximeter flashed his heartrate and oxygen intake. His blood pressure was borderline. She'd check it again in a little bit. "I love you," she whispered. Jack stopped sucking on his pacifier to mumble, "Wuv too, Mama," and she understood again the sheer impossibility that she could ever harm him. Tears burned her eyes as she felt her lips shape the word, and then the phrase, *Munchausen Syndrome by Proxy*. The sound was like the snow falling outside, melting as soon as it touched anything substantial. It meant nothing next to her love for this child. Nothing.

• • •

Downstairs, the house felt chilly. She pulled the sash of her robe tight as if to somehow hold her fear inside.

Grace sat at the computer, waiting for it to connect to the internet. Her desk was covered with unread medical articles, one of Jack's Matchbox cars, a half-naked Barbie, a leatherbound edition of *Gray's Anatomy of the Human Body,* one of the few books she had read, beginning to end, purely for pleasure.

Even as a child, she had never liked stories as much as facts, regardless of how odd or fantastic those facts were. *The longest distance ever walked by hand: 870 miles. From Vienna to Paris; 1900. It took fifty-five days of ten-hour stints. The smallest church: located in Málaga, Spain, and measuring 2.1 square feet. On special occasions when Mass is held, there is room for only one person to pray in it at a time.* Her favorite book had been *Wonders of Nature: A Child's First Book About Our Wonderful World,* as if a part of her had always understood, even when she couldn't have been more than five or six, that nothing in her life would ever be as certain as those simple statements printed in bold ink: *The sun is 93 million miles from the earth. Sunlight takes eight minutes and twenty seconds to reach us. Snowflakes have six sides. A raindrop is shaped more like a doughnut than a pear.*

In high school, she excelled in science, but brought home Cs in English and history. It was her father who gave her the leather-bound edition of *Gray's Anatomy* for her sixteenth birthday. She was fascinated by it, the human body like a vast and foreign landscape with its intercoastal veins, Haversian Canal and Capsule of Tenon. Hensen's stripe, Cartilage of Wrisberg, Jacob's membrane.

Now, Grace tucked her feet onto the rung of the ladder-back chair and began typing. Munchausen's would be no different from any other disease, she told herself. There had to be causes and symptoms and treatments. Case studies and research. Etiology. Prevalence.

Facts, as unbreakable as stone.

She moved the cursor down the screen, the clicking of the mouse the only occasional sound. She scanned the sites: an investigator specializing in Munchausen by Proxy cases, the International Mun-

chausen by Proxy Network, National Center for the Prosecution of
Child Abusers, the Federal Bureau of Investigation. Goosebumps
rose on her arm. She hadn't seen this one before.

The site contained a "profile" of the typical Munchausen mother.
Grace read it quickly, then again, slowly. *"Mother-perpetrator 'doctor
shops' until given attention she is desperate to receive; consequently, child-victim
has often been to numerous care-givers . . ."*

She heard again Anju's words: *Why, in God's name, would you want
to put him through that, Grace?* And Jenn's: *Oh, Grace, are you sure?* And
her own, shouted amid sobs to Stephen the night they returned from
Hopkins: *I don't care about quality of life! I want quantity, Goddamnit! I
want him to live!*

Mother-perpetrator.

Child-victim.

It took a moment for the phrases to register. Was this how she and
Jack had been described in that Child Protective Services report that
Mandy had supposedly seen? *Mother-perpetrator. Child-victim.* The
words were like thieves, stealing into her life without her knowing it,
taking everything of value.

"Mother-perpetrator is willing to have child undergo numerous
procedures and tests that often come back normal."

Oh, Grace are you sure?

Why in God's name would you even consider . . .

"Mother-perpetrator is medically knowledgeable and typically has
a background in medicine."

You're so wrapped up in the medical stuff.

"Mother-perpetrator is unusually friendly with hospital staff and
other parents of sick children."

"Father is typically absent during the child-victim's hospitaliza-
tions."

"Child-victim's disease is often described as rare and multisymp-
tomed."

She sat back, holding her palm over her mouth. She fit the profile.
She tried to let that thought settle. It was like trying to balance a
bowling ball on a pin. She fit the profile. But it didn't make sense.

Because Jack's disease was rare? Because she, *not* Stephen, stayed with Jack in the hospital? Because she had a medical background? Had "doctor-shopped," when there wasn't a diagnosis? She thought again of all those letters she had sent to various experts, asking for help.

"What was I supposed to do?" Her voice sounded scratchy and out of place in the silence. She heard the furnace kick in, the rush of warm air from the heating vents fluttering the Christmas cards pinned to the bulletin board above her computer. Light caught in the metallic red letters of the "Season's Greetings" on one card. She glanced at it, her fingers stilled on the keyboard. She thought of robins, of red-winged blackbirds, of Noah.

It wasn't until March that they made love for the first time. She was a wreck the entire drive there, her turtleneck drenched with sweat beneath her sweater, her legs trembling. She must have applied her lipstick a dozen times in the rearview mirror. And then she was knocking on the door of his condo, and he was there, enveloping her in his arms, whispering into her hair, "Oh, thank God. I was afraid you would change your mind."

His mouth was on hers then, and her hands were in his hair and he was holding the back of her head, then lifting her off her feet, kicking the door closed behind him, carrying her inside. His hands were on her shoulders then, her hip bones, and it felt as if he were touching every part of her simultaneously, her nerve endings ringing, her entire body like a bell vibrating beneath his touch.

In his bedroom doorway, he lifted her sweater and turtleneck over her head and let them fall to the floor, as he led her to the bed. They didn't speak, didn't stop looking at each other. She lay down, still wearing her jeans and socks, and he knelt next to her, pinning her arms over her head, the sunlight falling across her like a crocheted blanket. He brushed his free hand down her arm, trailed his fingers over and around her breasts. And then, still pinning her arms, refusing to let her touch him—"Not yet," he whispered—he leaned over her, kissed her forehead as gently as she kissed her children's. And then her mouth and her chin and the place where her heart pulsed at her throat. With his tongue, he drew a slow line down her middle, cut her open, until he reached the hollow between her hip bones, just above the top of her low-rise jeans. "I want to taste every inch of you," he said, looking up. And then he rolled over next to her, pulling her with him so that she was lying on him now, her hair in his eyes and his mouth, his fingers brushing it away as he told her, "You are so beautiful, Grace. I had no idea you were this beautiful."

Later, after she came again and again, her entire body trembling with the force of it so that it felt almost as if she were sobbing, he'd rocked her in his arms and blown tiny breaths against her neck and her throat, cooling her off. And then she *was* sobbing for real, and when he asked what was wrong, she said, "Oh Noah, I haven't been this happy in so long."

Oh Noah, she thought now, but there was no thought after that. He was so far away. He had no idea what was happening in her life.

The acronym M.A.M.A. appeared now on the computer screen: *Mothers Against Munchausen Allegations*. The house felt cold again, and she held her robe closed at her chest with one hand as she clicked the computer mouse onto the site with her other.

A color photograph filled the screen. A blond woman was laughing and nuzzling her nose into her child's chubby face. The baby was laughing as well, a huge toothless grin. *[. . .] died a horrifying death . . . a false Munchausen by Proxy diagnosis. .* .

Grace scrolled down to the next page, to the Sears-type portrait of a brown-haired woman and her three preschool-age children, dressed in matching pale blue polo shirts and khakis. They looked happy. Normal. *Kelsey, Davis, and Bethany, confiscated from home by Broward County, Florida, Child Protective Services, July 13, 2000; 166 days.*

Her hands were shaking. Another photo of a young couple holding a blond girl with long braids. "Samantha Nicole, never forget that we love you. We are fighting every day to get you home." *Taken by*

Lancaster County, California, Department of Child and Family Services, March 10, 2000; 287 days.

She kept looking. Names, locations, and the number of days since they'd been taken. Not weeks or months. A refusal, Grace understood, to package the number into something smaller, less horrific, more manageable. Or maybe an inability.

Ryan Michael, taken by Mecklenburg County, North Carolina, Department of Social Services, January 21, 2000; 339 days.

Natasha, taken by Kenosha County, Wisconsin, Child Protective Services; 38 days.

Ashley and Megan, abducted by Jacksonville, Florida, Department of Child Protective Services; 104 days.

Alexander, Bucks County, Pennsylvania; 19 days.

Trevor, Henrico County, Virginia; 43 days.

Tucker, Jason, Anna. Ohio, New Jersey, Texas. Taken. Confiscated. Abducted.

My God, what had happened to Marie Noe? *That* was Munchausen's. Ten children in one family dying mysteriously. But this? These were normal families. Families with kids who were sick, maybe; families with mothers who were overprotective maybe; but not, *not* families who deserved to have their children taken, confiscated, *abducted*.

Grace flicked off the screen. A horrible panicked cry was coming from her mouth. And then she was standing, moving through the darkened kitchen, bumping her hip on the edge of the table, racing up the stairs.

She shook Stephen awake. She couldn't stop the horrible jerking sounds coming from her mouth. Stephen woke immediately. "What?" Then he was out of bed, racing into Jack's room before she could explain that Jack was okay. For some reason, this made her cry harder, painful sobs that felt as if they were being wrenched from deep inside her. She lay on her side, face in the pillow, rocking herself back and forth. How, *how,* could this have happened? How could she have let it? She would lose her children.

Taken. Confiscated. Abducted.

Stephen's hand was on her shoulder. "You scared the hell out of me," he said. He was out of breath. "I thought—" He stopped and sat next to her, pulled her head against his chest. "What? What happened?" She could feel his racing heartbeat.

She told him about the Web site. All those children taken.

"You aren't like those other women," he told her

"You don't know that," she sobbed. "They're normal mothers, Stephen."

"It doesn't matter if they are, Grace. Listen to me." He tugged her hands from her face, forced her to meet his gaze. "Children are *not* just taken from families for no reason. Maybe in some other country, but not here. There had to be something."

"But don't you see?" She lifted her head from his chest. "That's what people are going to say about me."

TEN

*J*ack tried forcing the misaligned puzzle piece into place.

"Turn it, honey." Grace leaned forward to show him, but he snatched his hand away.

"No," he whined. "You can't help me."

"Okay, but you have to turn it, or it won't fit."

"It will too," he said, trying again, dislodging other pieces.

"Yo, cut it out, Jack," Max said.

"No you cut out, Max," Jack laughed.

Grace sat back, letting them be. The four of them, Grace and the three kids, had been working on the Christmas puzzle since breakfast, trying to finish it by dusk, the time New Year's Eve officially began in their house. Jack was more hindrance than help, but none of them really cared. He was so thrilled to be included with the "big kids."

The jigsaw puzzle was a holiday tradition passed down through her dad's family: they started the thousand-piece jigsaw on Christmas Day and had to finish it by New Year's Eve.

When Grace was a child, she and her dad would stay up until two or three in the morning, working on the puzzle. Her father's parents came from Arizona to spend the holidays with them, and they stayed up as well, her grandfather drinking single-malt scotch in his old-fashioned striped pajamas, her grandmother, hair in rollers, trying not to yawn. Her dad attacked the puzzle as if in a battle. "Come on, now, get in there, you bastard," he'd say to a puzzle piece. Or "Gotcha, ya little devil!" Whenever Grace got a piece in, her grandfather would grin, as if she had accomplished something wonderful. Her dad would slap her five, and tell his parents, "I think our girl's got the puzzle gene."

The puzzle gene. Was there such a thing? She stared at this year's puzzle, a Norman Rockwell scene of Santa with his feet in a metal tub of hot water. She leaned forward and lifted a piece, part of Santa's white beard, and set it into place. And what would the puzzle gene mean, exactly? The ability to take something broken and piece it back together? She had wanted to believe that she'd done this with Noah, somehow fixed a part of herself that had been broken. And maybe she had, but at what cost? She felt her heart constrict, and tightened her grip on Jack, who only squirmed loose. "Mama, why you squeezing me?"

" 'Cause I love you, silly." How could she possibly explain the love she felt for this child? She'd abduct him herself, go into hiding, before she would let anyone take him. She'd kill someone who tried. Adrenaline raced through her at the thought, her heart racing, arms shaking. How, *how,* could anyone imagine that she would hurt Jack? She glanced at Max as he set another piece into place. If she was guilty of harming any of her kids, it was him, she thought, this huge boy who towered over both of his parents. Six foot three. Size thirteen shoe. Where did he come from? Grace often laughed to Stephen.

"I bet you don't know the name of a single player on the Flyers," Max had challenged her a few weeks ago. He had failed a science test, so Grace had grounded him: no hockey for three days.

"You can't!" he cried.

"But I can," she told him. "Hockey isn't everything, Max, and—"

"How would you even know!" he shouted. "You haven't even been to a single game this year!"

She looked at him hard. "And you are old enough to understand why." Jack was too immune-compromised to take into a crowded gymnasium, and finding a qualified home care nurse to come in for only a few hours was all but impossible. "I'm sorry it's hard on you, but—"

"I bet you don't know the name of a single player on the Flyers," he interrupted.

She sighed. "Eric somebody."

"I'm serious, Mom."

"So am I."

"'Eric somebody?' That's the best you can do?"

"Okay, Gag or Gage." She sighed again. "Something with a G."

"You don't even care, do you?

"If you want to talk about caring, then let's talk about your science test."

"Lindros, Mom. Eric Lindros. He's only one of the top scorers in the NHL, and—" His eyes filled. "Never mind."

"I'll tell you what," she said. "You bring home at least a B on your next science test, and I'll learn anything you want me to about hockey."

And so the book, *Hockey for Dummies,* for Christmas.

"Gotcha!" Max said now as he connected two large chunks of the puzzle. He held up his hand for Jack to slap him five. "Hit me, brother!"

"Okay, brother!" His fingers were blue-tinged from lack of circulation. He'd been on oxygen all day, the clear tubing from the nasal canula hooked over his ears to keep it in place.

"Wow, Max," Grace said. "You're going to finish before your dad gets back if you keep this up." Stephen was still at the Y.

The fire popped loudly, and Jack screamed in surprise, then burst out laughing at himself. "That scared me, Mama," he said. "It scare you too?"

"A little bit." She kissed the top of his head. He was sitting on her lap.

"It scare you, Max?"

"No." Max rolled his eyes.

"Why?" Jack furrowed his brows and turned to Grace. "Why it not scare Max?"

" 'Cause I'm not a chicken like you are," Max said, scanning the sea of puzzle pieces. He was wearing an old Tom and Jerry T-shirt and the faded sweats he'd slept in, his hair greasy and uncombed. He looked so young, Grace thought. He *was* so young. Thirteen. He'd only just this year started liking girls, talking in a low voice on the phone, secreting himself in his room for hours, reeking, a few times, of Stephen's cologne when he left for school in the morning. She smiled and felt her heart slow, overwhelmed suddenly with gratitude: for her children, for this day. The four of them together, snow falling outside, the house filled with the scent of the pumpkin bread she was baking for Max. *Maybe*, she allowed herself to think for the nth time since seeing Bennett, *maybe* the accusation would turn out to be nothing or, if not nothing, then no worse than a warning. *Please,* she prayed silently, promising, as she had from the first moment that she'd heard about the accusation, that she would break it off with Noah; she would devote herself once again, without regrets or long-ing, to what she had right here, right now—her children. Stephen. It was enough. It was more than enough. She swallowed hard. How could she not have known this?

"I'm tired of puzzles," Erin whined as she fell back into the couch, her arms and legs limp.

"I know you are, sweets. Come sit with me and Jack." Grace held out her free hand, gesturing for Erin to come over.

Erin rolled herself forward, dragged herself to her feet, then plopped heavily onto the carpet next to Grace, slumping against her shoulder.

"Tell me what you want to do," Grace said into her daughter's tan-gled hair.

"You want to play me cars, Erin?" Jack said.

"No," Erin mumbled.

Jack leaned forward to peer at his big sister, then stopped, wincing, hand on his swollen tummy. "Ouch," he said as if surprised. "That hurted me." He looked at Grace.

"Well, you have to be careful, Goose. Here . . ." She straightened her legs beneath the coffee table so that he could lean back more. "Is that better?"

"Uh-huh." He settled against her, then asked. "*You* want to play me cars, Mama?"

"No, Mama's going to play with Erin for a while."

"Don't worry, Jack." Max snapped another piece into place. "They're just going to do yucky girl stuff."

Jack laughed. "Yucky girl stuff!" He reached his hand back to touch Grace's face. "You hear that, Mama? Max says you and Erin doing—"

"Yes, I heard, Mister Smarty-pants." Grace kissed his hand, then leaned sideways and whispered to Erin, "What do you say we get out your new Barbie makeup case?"

Erin looked up, eyes wide. "Really?"

"Why not? We'll get all beautiful for Daddy." Grace gave Erin's bottom a little pat as she jumped up and raced towards the stairs, thumping back down a minute later with the glittery silver and pink case that she set on the carpet next to Grace.

"Can I do you first, Mama?" Erin asked as she unfolded the mirror trays with their little glass pots of sparkly eye shadow and nail polish and different flavored lip glosses.

"Sure," Grace said. "What should we start with?"

"Eyes." Erin said. "Do you want green or purple or blue?"

"Hmmm, how about purple?"

She watched Erin fiddle with the case, her brow furrowed as she tried to open it. Beyond the front window, the pines dipped and bowed, wind and snow swirling in gusts. *Maybe,* Grace thought again. The word lingered. A possibility. A hope. *Maybe* this would all be okay. She would make it up to them. She'd start cooking more, instead of re-lying on frozen pizzas and macaroni and cheese. She'd bake more with Erin, take more walks with Jack, go to Max's hockey games, finish *Hockey for Dummies.* Already, she'd read two more chapters. She now knew that Wayne Gretzky had scored more goals than any player in NHL history, that teams played eighty-two games a season, that when hockey first started, the referee had to *place* the puck between opposing players' sticks during face-offs, resulting in numerous cases of broken knuckles. And Stephen. A tight band wrapped itself around her chest. She would fall in love with her husband again.

• • •

"Did you really question that *I* might have accused you?" Stephen asked as he climbed into bed.

She looked at him. "Only for a second. Less than that."

"But what made you think it to begin with?"

She sighed. She knew his question was genuine, that he really didn't understand how she could have thought this about him. He was so good. Good the way people used to be good. He believed in volunteer work and helping people, he believed in community and trying to make a difference in people's lives, and he assumed that others were basically as good as he was. He was genuinely surprised, even hurt, to find out they weren't. She glanced at him and, for a moment, felt her love for him rise in her chest like something endangered and rare, something she needed to protect, to fight for, to save, but she didn't know how.

She held her mug of hot chocolate to her chest, hands cupped around it for warmth. "Please don't be hurt," she said. "You know I wasn't thinking right. I just—" She shrugged helplessly and stared down at her hands. After a moment, she said quietly, "You're such a good person, Stephen."

"Come on. We're both good, Grace. We do our best."

"But I'm so angry, Stephen. At everything. Everyone." Her voice trailed off.

"And everyone includes me?"

She glanced at him. "I don't mean to be." She wasn't sure this was true though. She'd gotten used to being angry—at him, at the insurance company, at the doctors from Hopkins. At least when she was angry, she felt strong and in control. Like gravity, it weighted her, held her in place. How could she explain that it was this rage that so often exerted the far greater pull on her, greater even than love, and that this rage was, at times, the only thing keeping her from whirling out of this orbit of her life into utter blackness?

"It's stupid to blame you, I know that, Stephen, I just—" She looked at him. "Don't you ever blame me?"

"*Why*? Jack is alive because of you. I know that. Hell, half the staff at Children's knows that, has come right out and said it. My God, the idea that I could blame you—"

"I'm not saying it's rational. But, I mean, didn't it occur to you that my causing his illness would have meant that he was okay?"

"That's a hell of a trade-off, Grace."

"But I would have thought it about you; a part of me would have *wanted* it to be true, I think."

"I know."

"And that doesn't hurt you?"

He shrugged. "A little, but it's also one of the reasons I *didn't* doubt you. I know that you would give anything, including your own life— or mine—for our kids."

"Okay, now look," Erin said, and Grace held up the pink plastic hand mirror to see her eyelids covered with lavender glitter. "Wow, lovey," she said. "That looks nice."

Max glanced at her. "Yeah, if you're going for the *Addams Family* look." He plunked in another puzzle piece next to where Jack was maneuvering his into place.

"Don't, Max!" Jack swatted his brother's arm, then immediately began coughing with the effort.

"Hey," Grace said, patting his back. "No hitting, mister."

"But he can't help me!"

"I wasn't, you little snot."

Grace looked at Max. "And no name-calling either."

Jack plucked out the piece Max had just set down, then put it back. "Ha ha!" he wheezed. "Look what *I* did." He crossed his arms over his chest defiantly.

Erin giggled. "He's so stubborn, isn't he, Mama?"

"Are you stubborn?" Grace asked him.

"Yeah, I am!" Jack laughed. He didn't have a clue what stubborn was, of course, and so they couldn't help but laugh with him.

• • •

Later, in the kitchen, Grace set the steaming pan of pumpkin bread on the cutting board, and stood for a minute, giving it a chance to set.

Rivulets of water from the melting snow streaked the window in front of the sink. She was hungry, but trying hold off for the snacks she'd set out shortly: nachos, steamed shrimp, mini Greek pizzas with spinach and feta, Christmas cookies—*of course*—and the pumpkin bread for Max. She pulled in a long breath, then let it out slowly as if to dissolve the knot of sadness lodged in her chest. She both loved and hated New Year's Eve, with its promises and regrets, its hellos and good-byes, all tangled into one. And this year, especially this year—with Noah in her life again, with Jack getting sicker every day—*the best thing we can do is make sure he's comfortable*—Grace loved and hated New Year's more than ever. She wanted to simply stand still, hold onto things just as they were—as they had been only a week ago. One week. *"What the hell are you doing here?"*

"I just needed to see you. Is that okay?"

"Okay? Are you kidding me? Okay?"

She stared towards the emptied lake, the landscape blurring into a wash of gray, as hidden as a secret. Like the history of the Pine Barrens itself: an entire history of secrets. Tories had hidden in these woods during the Revolutionary War. Later, smugglers stored sugar and molasses here; during Prohibition, it was the bootleggers. Even the landscape conspired toward silence, the largest freshwater aquifer in the country—seventeen trillion gallons—lying beneath the forest and swamps. Her own secret, her love of Noah, felt like this—liquid and huge, uncontainable under the surface of her life.

"She still fills my Christmas stocking with socks and deodorant and a roll of stamps." Noah grinned. "As if I were in college still."

"I always liked your mom. Does she still make those cinnamon rolls?"

"You remember those?" In his eyes she saw the sudden sadness she'd come to expect whenever they talked of that one summer twenty years ago. "She usually sends me home with a half a dozen or so."

Grace lifted her head from his chest. "And you *will* save me one."

"As many as you want." He squeezed her tight. "Besides, after a week at home, I'll be back to a liquid diet."

She lay her head back down, fingers tracing the bones of his ribs. "I still can't believe you were fat." His chest was hairless, like a boy's.

"*Fat*? Whoa, I don't recall *ever* saying *fat*, thank you very much." His voice was back to normal. "Ample, perhaps. Pleasantly plump. Renoiresque, *maybe*."

"*Renoiresque?*" She lifted herself up again to look at him. "Where do you come up with this stuff?"

He shook his head. And then, "God, I love you," he blurted.

She smiled. "You do? Really?" She still couldn't believe it some days. That she'd found him, that he loved her after all these years, that she loved him. She snuggled against him, burying her nose into his neck as if to breathe him in through his smells—salt and cinnamon and something briny that made her think of the beach in the rain.

"So, at some point, my mom will ask *the* question," he was saying.

"Let me guess . . . Have you met someone? Are you *ever* going to get married?"

"Close, but the actual words are 'Have you met the right *girl* yet? *Girl*." He chuckled. "How old am I?"

She kissed his shoulder. "Not a day over twenty-two." Then his neck. "So what will you tell her?"

"Oh, same thing I always say: I met the right *girl* twenty years ago, but she dumped me."

"You do *not* tell her that."

"Oh, I absolutely do."

"Those words?"

"Those words."

She wanted to tell him that she had met the right "boy" twenty years ago too. But had she? And if so, where did that leave Stephen? Her children?

"*Hey*." Noah shifted beneath her, nudging her chin up with his thumb. "What's up?"

She shook her head. "It's sad. And I guess I feel guilty, like you blame me, like I ruined your life." She sighed. "I was *seventeen*, Noah."

"I know that, Grace. Come on. I was a kid too." He pushed himself away from her. "I do tell my mom that you were *the* One. And yeah, my brothers, and now their wives, all tease me about how I never got over you, but it's all in fun. I mean, if anything, it's kind of flattering, isn't it?" He sounded angry now. "Christ, the last thing I'm trying to do is make you feel guilty."

He stared at her another minute, then leaned back into the pillows, arms crossed behind his head, staring at the ceiling. "It's not like I was a monk for the last twenty years," he said finally. "I didn't shun society and don sackcloth and spend my evenings reading your old letters by candlelight—"

She smiled. "*Only* because I never wrote you any letters."

"You didn't?" He grinned. "Must have been another woman I was remembering."

"It must be difficult keeping track of us all." She traced her index finger along the cords of his neck.

"I love your touch," he said sadly, as if already anticipating the time when it would be gone.

"I love touching you," she said. And then quietly, "I do hate that I hurt you, Noah. Even if it was twenty years ago."

"I know." He nodded. "But you said it, Grace; you were seventeen."

"But you weren't that much older, so why—"

"Why didn't I move on?" He shrugged. "I don't know, and after a while, it didn't really matter. Maybe I didn't want to get over you. Maybe it was a way of protecting myself from getting too close to anyone else. Maybe I only want what I can't have. There's a thousand reasons, but the bottom line is that you've always been right here." He placed her hand on his chest, and she felt his heart thudding in her palm. "And I *like* that. I *like* that you're a part of me that way. I like having conversations with you, even if half the time they're only in my mind. Who knows? Maybe it's that you were the first person I really loved. Maybe it's that you were the first person to really hurt me."

"Those are two pretty different maybes, though, Noah. How can it not matter which one it is?"

"Because knowing doesn't change the outcome, Grace. It doesn't alter the fact that I've thought of you every day, every goddamn day, for the last twenty years. I *like* that. I *like* that a lot. I *like* that I can imagine a future with you. Do you have any idea what that means? I've never, Grace, *never* been able to do that with anyone else."

She edged the bread knife along the contours of the pan she had just pulled from the oven. *Future*. She'd read somewhere that its Indo-European root had once meant "grow," which was why, she imagined now, when she thought of that word at all—*future*—it seemed ocean-like and terrifying, as if to venture too far into it was to fall off the edge of the world. In the future, Jack would be gone.

She set the bread knife on the counter, then flipped the loaf of pumpkin bread onto the wooden cutting board, releasing it from the pan. A cloud of steam wafted up, smelling of cloves and ginger. She set the emptied bread pan in the sink and turned on the warm water, then stood for a moment, letting the liquid heat pulse over her hands. *It's over with Noah*. The thought darted in front of her like a frightened animal, and she felt something in her wrench away from it. *Why?* another part of her cried. Nothing had changed. Stephen hadn't found out. And he wouldn't. She would be careful. More careful. And assuming the accusation was a mistake, a misunderstanding—

But no.

It was over.

It had to be. There was no future with Noah; there never had been. He was the past—who she might have been, the life she *might* have had, if she'd made another choice. Something so simple, returning a phone call twenty years ago, and everything could have been different.

But it wasn't.

Abruptly, she lowered her head to her hands, grief unstoppered inside of her. How was she going to leave him? Really leave him? *Again*. And what was she going to do without all that joy in her life, that laughter?

Outside, the sky had darkened. Her reflection in the lighted window shone back to her. She thought of birds crashing into glass, confused by their own reflection, and felt herself slam up against the pane of truth that Jack's illness had long ago forced her to confront: Love *isn't* enough sometimes, love *isn't* all you need, love *doesn't* make the world go around, because if any of those clichés were true—*any of them*—children would not die.

She closed her eyes, promising herself, *you're doing the right thing,* but she felt flayed open by the thought of losing Noah all over again. She had only just found him.

Two more days and he'd be home. *Home.* Her word, not his. For him, Michigan was still home, and at one time, it was for her too, despite living in New Jersey ever since she was a teenager. She had been born in the Midwest, her aunts and uncles and grandparents lived there. But the day Max was born, *home* forever shifted—no longer did it mean the place where she had grown up, but the place where her children would.

"So what made you end up in Cape May?" she asked once as they were walking along the beach.

"What do you think?"

"*Please.*" She swatted his arm. "You did *not* end up here because of me."

"Okay, you're right." He grinned. "Not *because* exactly, but you *were* a motivating factor."

She didn't know what to say. They walked in silence, hands in the pockets of their sweatshirts, the sun only a faint pulse against the womb of autumn sky. An older couple, their pants rolled above their ankles, crouched at the water's edge, searching for shells or sea glass or maybe the flint arrowheads left centuries before by the Lenni Lenape Indians, who had once inhabited the coast. Or, who knew, perhaps they were hunting for Captain Kidd's treasure cache, rumored to have been buried at Cape May Point back in 1699. She smiled sadly. So many people searching for lost artifacts from lives not their own.

As they were almost back to the observatory, she stopped. "You really knew I was here? All these years?"

"It wasn't a mystery, Grace. My parents and your grandparents are in the same church. You could have just as easily found out where I was." *Except you didn't.* The words stayed unspoken.

She resumed walking, hands still in the pockets of her sweatshirt, following the glint of light on the rusted skeleton of the concrete bunker that was visible only at low tide. "So why didn't you ever try to contact me?"

"You were married, Grace. You had a child."

"I still do."

"It's different."

"Why?"

"Because you found *me*."

She turned off the water, leaving the bread pan to soak, and carried her coffee mug to the table. She pushed her shoulders up and swallowed a gulp of coffee. Why had she sent that e-mail? What had she imagined would happen? She tugged a dried leaf from the poinsettia in the center of the table. It had curled in on itself like a tiny fetus. She thought about what she would say to Noah the next time they spoke and felt a dull ache in her chest at the thought. And yet, there was also a tiny barely perceptible flicker of hope that maybe—and there was that word again, *maybe,* like a splash of red against gray, a cardinal or a robin flitting across a winter sky—*maybe* this would somehow work out okay, *maybe* Noah would be able to move on, *maybe* it had been enough to have had what they'd had these past eleven months. *Maybe.*

ELEVEN

They clinked spoons against their glasses of eggnog as Grace helped Jack ceremoniously set the last puzzle piece into place. "I did it," he laughed. His voice was raspy, his face flushed from the effort, shiny with sweat.

"Of course, you did it," Grace said. To Max, she asked, "Don't you want to eat something besides pumpkin bread?"

"Why?" He reached for another piece. "Why can't we have this all the time?"

"It wouldn't be special then."

"Well, this is what I want for Christmas next year. Pumpkin bread every week."

"No, no, no," Stephen wailed, lowering his head to the coffee table in defeat. "*Please* tell me you are *not* already thinking about next Christmas."

And then Erin handed out paper and pens for them to write their resolutions, which Stephen would keep until the following New Year's. Grace wanted to write what she had wanted to write for the past three years: I will keep Jack alive; I will not let him die. Instead, she wrote that she would learn about hockey and make pumpkin bread more often and spend more time with Erin. And she would mail in the Make-A-Wish forms that had been sitting untouched on the kitchen counter since early November because she couldn't bear to actually fill them out. It felt too much like acceptance, a giving in, a giving up. Jack's wish was to see a real rocket, so they would go to Cape Canaveral.

• • •

The best part of the night was reading their resolutions from the previous year. Max had resolved to keep his room clean and to be nicer to Erin. They blew their party horns at him, since he'd failed on both counts. Grace had resolved to not lose her temper so much, which sent Max into paroxysms of hysteria, and to be on time, which resulted in all of them blowing their horns at her and laughing. Stephen too had failed. He'd resolved to be home before seven at least three times a week and to lower his cholesterol. Only Erin, who had resolved to learn how to swim, and to ride a bike without training wheels, both of which she'd accomplished, had been successful. She beamed with pleasure, a large crooked smile, both of her front teeth missing. Jack's resolution, which Grace had helped him write, was that he get potty-trained and again, they were all laughing and blowing their horns in his face while he huffed and puffed on his, unsuccessfully trying to blow back and succeeding instead only in spitting on them.

"Gross!" Erin shrieked.

"You are disgusting!" Max laughed, wiping his hand with a napkin.

"Stop," Grace laughed, "He is *not* disgusting, are you, Jack?" She nuzzled his neck, but he squirmed away.

"No, Mama, I *am* 'gusting!" he protested.

By ten Erin and Jack had fallen asleep on either end of the couch. Stephen and Max played video games. Grace curled up in the Queen Anne armchair and watched. Her husband. Her giant boy, his hands bigger than his father's. Her daughter. Her baby. She let her gaze rest on Jack, his mouth open in sleep as he struggled for breath.

All autumn, she had prayed, wished, hoped, bargained: Let Jack have a good holiday. Don't let him be in the hospital. Let us have this much together. But as she listened to the wheeze of his breath and the steady hum of the oxygen pump, she felt her own heart seize with regret. Now that her wish had been granted, it terrified her. My God, why hadn't she asked for more?

At midnight, they woke Jack and Erin and stood on the front porch. Grace held Jack to her chest, inside her coat. Max and Erin raced around the yard in their PJs and jackets and boots, making snow angels and shouting. Echoes of *Happy New Year!* echoed from across the emptied lake where someone was having a party. Stephen squeezed Grace's hand before letting go to usher Max and Erin inside.

It was 2001.

Jack was asleep as she carried him to his room. She didn't turn on the lights, but stood for a minute in the doorway, locating herself in the darkness—the painting of the Cow Jumping Over the Moon on the wall, the shape of her robe on his rocking chair, her coffee mug from morning atop his dresser. Jack didn't wake even when she laid him in the crib. She laid her hand on his back, feeling the rise and fall of his ribs.

Light from the hallway spilled onto the glossy book jacket of *Happy Birthday, Moon* that was lying on the floor where he'd probably tossed it that morning. It was a story about a bear that talks to the moon, believing the echo of his own voice is actually the moon responding to him. "Tomorrow is my birthday!" the bear shouts, and the moon echoes, "Tomorrow is my birthday!" The little bear is delighted and tells the moon, "That means we were born on the same day!" and of course, the moon answers, "That means we were born on the same day!"

Sometimes, when Grace read this story to Jack, she'd lift him to the window and he'd call to the moon and Erin would stand in the hallway and pretend to be the moon, echoing him. Sometimes too they'd hear him talking to the moon himself after they'd tucked him in. "You going sleep, moon?" he'd ask. And then, "Okay, me too."

Outside, the tree branches tapped a Morse code against the house. She moved to the window for a minute, hugging herself against the chill. Snow shimmered, luminescent beneath the full moon, the stars like ornaments in the tops of the trees. Scientists now believed that the moon had been formed when another planet sideswiped the Earth, dislodging huge chunks of its crust, which flew off into space and became the moon. She thought of Noah, of how in so many ways he was this to her, the part of her life that had broken off—the life not lived. Maybe those unused pieces of your past become their own entity. A moon. Another planet. A place without gravity or sound. A place without wind or rain or weathering or erosion, so that even the smallest surface markings, each one a kind of memory, stayed in place for years. And yet always it was there, the moon—the past—waxing and waning, exerting its force over the tides of the life you lived now.

She sighed wearily and turned to leave, leaning into Jack's crib once more to plant a kiss on his forehead, to inhale his warm baby scent. As she turned to go, she retrieved *Happy Birthday, Moon* from the floor and set it on the crowded bookshelf with his other moon books: *Owl Moon* and *When the Moon Broke Away* and *Cosmo's Moon* and *Papa, Please Get the Moon for Me*. In most stories about the moon, someone was always trying to catch it, to pull it back down to Earth: the man who sees it reflected in the water and tries to pick it up, only to have it slip from his grasp just when he thought he'd had it.

PART II

Belief

For what a man had rather were true he more readily believes, [and] numberless in short are the ways, and sometimes imperceptible, in which the affections color and infect the understanding.

—Francis Bacon, 1620

A credulous mind . . . finds most delight in believing strange things, and the stranger they are the easier they pass with him, but never regards those that are plain and feasible, for every man can believe such.

—Samuel Butler, *Characters*, 1667–1669

TWELVE

*O*utside the St. Louis courtroom, gray ice the same color as the gray sky floats on the Mississippi. On side streets automobiles sit abandoned along curbs, and heaps of dirty snow line the salt-crusted roads. Downtown, exhaust from cars and buses hangs in the frozen air. There have been days without sun, days with the temperature never climbing above freezing. In gas stations and convenience stores, shelves that are usually stocked with antifreeze lie empty. People keep extra bottles in the trunks of their cars.

"Don't try to understand why this mother poisoned her child by feeding him from a baby bottle laced with antifreeze," the prosecutor tells the jury. "The point is that she did it. Only she could have done it. Only she would have done it."

A seemingly healthy child, a five-month-old boy, died suddenly the summer before. Ethylene glycol, the active ingredient in antifreeze, was found in his blood. A bottle of antifreeze was found in his parents' garage.

"You might not want to believe that a mother could do such a thing," the prosecutor says, "but there's a name for this: Munchausen Syndrome by Proxy. It has been scientifically proven. It has been researched by some of the best physicians. The findings have been published in the world's top medical journals." Perhaps the prosecutor slaps some of these journals onto the table before him: The Lancet, The New England Journal of Medicine, The Journal of Pediatric Psychology. And then, he looks up and stares hard at the jury. "Don't speculate that this five-month-old child died of natural causes," he says. "You might as well speculate that some little man from Mars came down and shot him full of a mysterious bacteria."

Munchausen Syndrome by Proxy. Does the child's mother feel how those words move across the lower edge of her life like subtitles in a foreign film? Those words that are only an approximation, not even accurate? But if those words are all the jurors have, all her own husband sometimes has—she knows *this—to translate what is unfathomable—their child has died and there seems to be no reason—into that which is comprehensible.* Munchausen Syndrome by Proxy. *Could she have done it, she wonders, could she have put the antifreeze in his bottle, and she simply can't remember?* Munchausen Syndrome by Proxy. *In the absence of other reasons, it becomes easier to believe. And why not? Isn't it less terrifying to believe in a rare disorder afflicting otherwise normal mothers than to believe the truth: A child from one of the richest, most medically advanced countries in the world can die without apparent cause, and there is nothing,* nothing, *any of our science or medicine or money can do?*

Belief, psychologists now say, like our ability to speak or use tools, is a product of evolution, a biological necessity, crucial to our survival. Without belief in something beyond what we can know, the world becomes emptied of meaning. And so we construct these shimmering nets of words—these stories, these beliefs—and we fill the world with them the way ancient mapmakers once filled the vast terra incognita with angels and monsters. Think of Hartman Schedel's 1493 world map depicting lands inhabited by men whose feet pointed backwards and whose ears were as large as wings. In the accompanying text, Schedel described a country named India, where men had the heads of dogs and spoke by barking; and a place called Libya, inhabited by people who were male on one side of their body, female on the other. Think too of Johans Ruysch's 1507 map locating a pair of islands off the coast of Newfoundland on which evil spirits were said to dwell. The 1652 drawing of Africa that contains intricate diagrams of mountains, rivers, and lakes, none of which existed. Or Peter Apian's sixteenth-century map of the world drawn in the shape of a heart.

What is a map, after all, but a projection of what we both hope for and fear? And what is a belief but a map of how we want the world to look?

No wonder that to lose one's belief is to lose one's direction.

And no wonder that we believe most fervently when we are most lost, our beliefs, like water, conforming to the shape of whatever absence we struggle to fill. And when a child dies and there seems to be no reason, that absence swells into something so vast and terrifying that we must fill it with something—anything—no matter how illogical or far-fetched. Think of the Salem Witch Trials, which began with the unexplained illness of a child. Think of that courtroom in

St. Louis three hundred years later, of that mother who is being accused of murder because her child has died and there seems to be no cause.

It takes the jury only ten hours to find the child's mother guilty of first-degree murder. She will spend her life in prison without parole. The courtroom fills with the sound of her husband's sobbing. His wife is led away. She is pregnant with their second child, though neither she nor her husband is yet aware of this. It is January 31, 1991, the anniversary of the day seventeen years before when the Child Abuse Protection and Treatment Act was passed into law. Perhaps the prosecutor mentioned this in his closing argument.

Beyond the courthouse windows, the Missouri sky is empty.

Seven months later, still in prison, the woman gives birth to her second child. Another boy, seemingly healthy. Within months, however, he is diagnosed with a rare genetic disease affecting only one in 48,000 children. Methylamalonic academia: it causes a buildup of dangerous acids in the child's body, one of which could, in a routine lab test, be mistaken for ethylene glycol, the active ingredient in antifreeze.

THIRTEEN

At the annual United Mitochondrial Disease Foundation conference in Minneapolis two years before, Grace had shared a hotel room with Kempley Trapman. They had met through the mitochondrial Listserv and had been e-mailing almost daily for eight months, though they had never spoken. Kempley lived in Charlotte, North Carolina. Grace had been in the Charlotte airport once and remembered the rows of white rocking chairs in the terminal, with passengers sitting on them as if on the veranda of a great plantation. She had imagined Kempley would be Southern and blond and would preface the beginning of her sentences with "y'all." Instead she found a blue-eyed, dark-haired Yankee with a Boston accent. A history professor at Queens College.

On the last night of the three-day conference, a group of women from the mitochondrial e-mail group congregated in their hotel room, reviewing the talks they'd attended earlier: discussions about dietary and high-dose vitamin therapy, end-of-life care, long-term research goals, networking groups. There was another lecture at eight: Laboratory Evaluation for Disorders of Energy Metabolism.

"Let's skip it," Kempley said. "Do something fun."

"*Fun?* Is that some kind of enzyme or coefficient or something?" Grace said. "I don't believe I'm familiar with that term."

Anne Marie, who had come from Seattle, laughed. "Oh, God, me either."

"Exactly," Kempley said. "We've talked about nothing but mito disease for three days straight." Even late at night, sitting in the hotel's Jacuzzi and drinking cosmopolitans, they were still discussing what they had learned. A stranger overhearing them talk of "oxidative metabolism" and "acyl carnitine" and "complex IV deficiencies" would have thought *they* were the medical doctors.

"But that's why we're here," Lydia said. "To learn all we can about the disease." Lydia's six-year-old son was the most recently diagnosed of their kids. She took copious notes in the conference handbook, dominated the question-and-answer sessions, and couldn't stop telling the story of all she'd been through, of how devastated she was, to anyone who would listen. Her fingertips were wrapped in Band-Aids because she chewed the skin around her nails until it bled. None of the women liked her, in part, Grace knew, because Lydia reminded them too much of those months when each of them first found out that their children were sick—that panicked, unmoored feeling that they would never get beyond what this disorder, this mitochondrial disease, would do to their lives.

Outside their motel room, the sky was dark, illuminated by the neon signs of chain hotels, fast-food restaurants, and gas stations. A lighted hot pink bowling pin blinked from the bowling alley/roller-skating rink across the highway. Grace glanced at Kempley, then followed her friend's gaze to the flashing "Skate Here."

"Oh no," she laughed. "Absolutely not."

"Come on, " Kempley said. "We'll get some exercise."

Scholars of seventeenth-century American history, Grace had come to learn, were familiar with Kempley Trapman's name. Apparently, it took effort not to be. Kempley was the sort of academic who inspired both envy and admiration: a master's from Yale, a PhD from Columbia, regular articles even as a graduate student in *American Historical Review, Journal of Interdisciplinary History, American Quarterly.* By the time she was forty, she had written three books on the Salem Witch Trials. Critics referred to her work as gutsy, controversial, and thorough. It was the last adjective that mattered the most to her. Too often, Kempley believed, history was presented as the grand gesture, operatic in scale: a story of martyrs and tyrants and complicated plots set against elaborate stage sets. A drama that distorted by eclipsing—a word that once meant "abandon"—the ordinary choices made by ordinary people.

At the mito conference, Grace and Kempley had sat up late each night, drinking Sambuca and talking. It was then that Grace learned that Kempley had grown up in Salem, Massachusetts, where each October during Salem's month-long "Haunted Happenings" Kempley had witnessed her small town of only forty thousand people transform, swelling to accommodate more than a quarter million tourists and generating nearly fifty million dollars. In the summers she had worked in one of the town's numerous souvenir shops, selling broomsticks and stuffed black cats, coffee mugs shaped like cauldrons, pounds of coffee in bags marked "Witches Brew," T-shirts with slogans like "Stop by for a *spell* in Salem" or "Just *hanging* around in Salem" or "The top ten reasons to visit Salem: Reason #1: Your wife couldn't find a pointy enough hat at the mall . . ."

Kempley thought nothing of this until her senior class trip to Washington, D.C., when after a day of visiting the monuments and memorials along the Mall she realized there were no jokes and no T-shirts with David Letterman lists of top ten reasons. At the recently dedicated Vietnam Veterans Memorial, she observed men weeping as they touched the name of a friend, a brother, an uncle: *Daniel Piotrowski, Tommy Lee Hawkes, Harry Smith*. Who were these men who had died? she wondered as she surreptitiously studied the faces of those who had come to grieve for them. Even the little school kids were oddly silent as they stood in front of the dark wall, staring somberly at the reflections of their own faces juxtaposed over the names: *Clifford Jenkins, Frank DaVila, Ollie Sands*.

Watching the other tourists that day, Kempley thought of the fourteen women and five men who had been hanged in her hometown all those years before, of the mothers and wives, sisters, daughters, husbands, fathers. Of Giles Correy pressed to death by stones. And suddenly, it made no sense: Why had *that* tragedy become a joke?

Reason #2: Your wife has become overly attached to the broom.

Something wrenched inside Kempley then, she told Grace later, and she felt what she would later think of as her first true adult emotion—this grief that had nothing to do with her own small life. She wrote a paper about it for her AP history class, submitted it to a national essay contest, and won. "On History, Lies, and Laughter." Six years later, it evolved into her master's thesis, then her first book. It got people's attention. *"Would you laugh at a T-shirt with the slogan 'What's cooking in Auschwitz?'"* she dared to ask in the first sentence. In the second edition, she added, *"What about a bumper sticker that reads 'Got bombed last night in Oklahoma City?'"* She became an expert on public memorials, which was how she came to think of her books. Landscapes of remembrance. She wanted people to read her words and respond as those veterans and their families had responded to the Vietnam Veterans Memorial. With reverence or silence or a sense of loss or anger. With curiosity. With tears. But not humor. She wanted people to feel history, to care about it.

Kempley told Grace about the morning when, sitting in the Essex Institute in Salem on a gorgeous Saturday in May, paging through transcripts of the trials, she came across the testimony of Joanna Childin, who on June 2, 1692, testified against her neighbor, thirty-eight-year-old Sarah Goode. Joanna claimed that Sarah's specter had appeared to her in the night, along with Sarah's deceased child, who claimed Sarah had murdered her.

"It made no sense," Kempley said. "Why would Joanna, why would *any woman,* make such a preposterous claim against another woman, especially one who was poor, unkempt, had recently lost her child, and who *wasn't* in a position of power? I kept thinking that if I could just understand Joanna, I could understand the rest of it." She'd spent hours searching the transcripts for other references to Joanna, but found only one vague reference. "And then I realized it didn't matter," Kempley said. "Even if I could figure out this one woman, I still had no idea why all this had happened *then*, *that* winter of 1692 and not five years earlier or five years later. And I kept returning to two facts: one, the winter of 1691–1692 was unbearably bitter, which meant that the infant mortality rate for the tiny town would have been higher than usual, and two, at the time of Joanna's accusation, Sarah Goode was pregnant again."

So, Kempley wondered: Did Joanna have any children of her own, and had any of them died? And if so, was accusing another woman of murder the only way she could express her grief and rage? Because if her own child had died, Joanna would not have been allowed to grieve: this would have suggested that she was questioning *God's* plan, *God's* desire, and how *dare* she doubt *God's* wisdom? It would have made sense that Joanna needed someone to blame.

Or: maybe she didn't have children, couldn't have children, and wanted them more than anything. In this case, seeing Sarah Goode, who was pregnant again, might have struck Joanna with pain in her chest so sharp that it doubled her over. And maybe, because it was too terrifying to accept that these feelings stemmed from her own desire and jealousy, Joanna instead decided she had been cursed, and blamed it on the woman who had caused it simply by walking by.

Maybe.

Either way, this was the history Kempley sought to understand in her second book. And because the trials began with the unexplained illness of a child, and because over half of the indictments against witches involved the sickness or deaths of children, Kempley began by studying the effect of child-loss on a community. She interviewed women whose children had died, asking them how this loss had affected their friendships, their faith, their marriages, their sense of self. She talked, as well, to the friends and family of these women and tried to understand *their* guilt, *their* helplessness, *their* fear. Less than a year after finishing these studies, Kempley's twin daughters were diagnosed with mitochondrial disease, and Kempley would reflect bitterly that if she'd waited, she could have saved herself a lot of time and effort on research. Her own children were dying and in one lousy sickening car crash of a minute she knew more about how this felt than she ever wanted to, than three years of research and interviews ever could have told her. She didn't write for six months. She felt nothing but rage, self-pity, grief, and guilt.

And then by accident, reading an unrelated biography, she, who had been studying the trials for years and who had lived in Salem all her life, discovered that Cotton Mather, one of the ministers who had interrogated and condemned the accused of Salem, had fathered fifteen children, all but two of whom died young. Kempley had been sitting in her daughters' hospital room that day, in a strange rain-drenched city where they'd gone for tests and answers and hope, and reading that sentence, she felt as if a pane of glass had just cracked inside her. *All but two*. And one of the judges in the trials, Judge Sewell, had lost *all but three* of his fourteen children. She stared at the rain beading on the window, and she knew that the words altered everything. Why had this never been mentioned? How could it *not* have been? To lose one child was horrendous, but thirteen? Eleven? How could these men not have been furious, terrified, and desperate—above all desperate—to find a reason, something—or someone—to blame?

The book Kempley began writing again was a far different book from the one she'd originally intended. She understood, as perhaps no other historian of the Salem witch trials could, how losing a child so annihilates your sense of how the world should be that nothing— *nothing*—makes sense. There is no reason, no understanding, no rational explanation for why one child gets sick and dies and another does not, and in the absence of this fundamental logic, of this basic way of perceiving the world, the trials became understandable to Kempley. No longer was there even a pretense of objectivity in her writing. *Not* being objective was the whole point. It became her mantra. Nothing in history was irrelevant, she told her students, including their own.

Now, on the first day of her research seminars, she told Grace, she began by piling on her desk milk crates full of books about the trials. "This is only a fraction of what has been written," she would begin, "about an event that occurred over three centuries ago, lasted less than a year, and as one critic aptly said, 'had no long-term impact on the future of Puritan New England.' " She paused, reading her students' implacable faces, wanting them to be outraged by this, wanting them to care:

At most, though, all she might see was a flicker of surprise, a raised eyebrow. Still, it was a start.

"So two questions," she would continue: "One, why should yet another historian devote time and energy to this subject, and two, assuming you can answer that, what can *you* possibly add to what we know?"

She didn't wait for answers. "The most important questions you can ask yourself as a historian are: Who am I? and Why do I care?"

For many of Kempley's students these were the most difficult questions they had ever been asked. They were used to seeking answers outside of themselves. It was why they had chosen history to begin with, turning to the past in the same way that young men and women once turned to the convent or the monastery, not as an act of faith or passion but as a retreat from the painful present. Kempley told her students about her children then, about how it wasn't until she acknowledged the truth of what their death would do to her life that it became possible to apprehend what the childrens' illnesses in Salem might have done to their parents' lives.

The best students were those who weren't afraid of such truths or those whose own wounds lay close to the surface: the woman who struggled with seasonal affective disorder and who, sitting at her desk one winter afternoon, had looked outside at the low gray clouds and immediately understood how that unseasonably cold winter of 1692 had contributed to the accusations as well.

Most students didn't like Kempley. She was too exacting, they said. Never satisfied. Their carefully researched papers came back bloodied with red ink: *So what?* she'd write in the margins. Or *Why does this matter?* Or *These are just numbers. This has no heart.* They joked: After a class with her, you might start believing in witches again. She knew they said this, she admitted to Grace, and was stunned at how much it still hurt despite the fact that years—sometimes decades—later, a student she could barely recall would write her a thank-you note, saying that she was the one professor who had actually taught them something of value: to pay attention to everything. Because it all matters, and because that's how lives are lived, how history evolves: a moment, a choice at a time.

It was a truth the entire country would begin to know in the aftermath of September 11. Pausing to make a phone call, get a briefcase, taking this stairwell instead of that one, or taking a later train so you could photograph your child on his first day of school, stopping for gas, smoking a cigarette—these became the only differences between life and death. Choices that small. Everything mattered. Everything. It was an understanding borne out in the *New York Times'* "Portraits of Grief," those one or two paragraphs describing the individuals who had died in the attacks. Lives were defined by the ordinary details: the girl nicknamed Gap because she always shopped there; the man who dressed up as a dancing bear for his daughter's third birthday; the elevator operator who studied the architecture of lighthouses in Maine; the man whose last e-mail—the one he was in the midst of writing when the plane struck—was a reminder to his friends about getting fitted for tuxes for his upcoming wedding. Ordinary details. The same thing Kempley had sought to understand about those who were executed three hundred years before in Salem. Those people were more than the role history had assigned to them. They were individuals. They had argued and laughed and fallen in love and had favorite foods and favorite colors and habits and idiosyncrasies.

It was a similar understanding that Kempley sought to impart to her children's doctors. History and medicine were alike in this sense. *Explanations* of historical events overshadowed the lives of the very people who were altered by those events, just as in medicine the diagnosis often eclipsed the life of the individual being diagnosed.

The three of them, Kempley, Grace, and Anne Marie, ran into Lydia in the hotel lobby when they returned from skating, still laughing at the image of themselves doing the Hokey Pokey. "I wish you'd come with us," Kempley said. She looked beautiful, cheeks flushed from the cold, strands of dark hair tendriled around her face. But Lydia only glanced at them coldly and walked away. Grace felt her face grow warm, ashamed suddenly of her own laughter. What had she been thinking? Lydia was right. My God, roller-skating while their children were dying.

In their hotel room, Kempley had wordlessly pulled her suitcase from the closet and opened it across the bed. Her jaw was tight though her eyes glittered with tears. "I *hate* that she made me feel like this, that I let her," she said quietly. She stood, hands on her hips, for a moment. And then, "Shit, I've lost a child. She can judge me when she knows what that feels like."

Grace watched Kempley roll a pair of socks into a ball, then fold a sweatshirt into the suitcase. "I used to be just like Lydia," Kempley said softly. "So sure that if I lifted my focus from the girls, from mitochondrial disease, for even a minute, something horrible would happen. It was my way to be in control. As long as *I* was vigilant, I could save them, and God help anyone who tried to tell me differently. People, including my husband, were always telling me I should get out more, do something nice for myself. Why didn't I take a walk, they'd ask. Why didn't I go to a movie?" She shook her head. "A *movie*. God. Doug used to tell me all the time: Nothing's going to happen to the girls just because you enjoy myself for a little bit." She glanced at Grace. "There was this one night when he said that for the hundredth time, and I remember looking at him—we were sitting at the kitchen table, and I can still see exactly what he was wearing, the exact mug he was drinking his coffee from—and I hated his guts, Grace. I literally felt sick looking at him. 'He really doesn't get it,' I thought. Our girls are dying, and he's so stupid, he actually thinks I can enjoy myself." She shrugged sadly. "But he was right. Carrie died when I was right there with her. Doing everything I was supposed to be doing." Kempley set the T-shirt she'd just folded into the suitcase, and gently smoothed the creases from it. Grace imagined she was remembering tucking Carrie into her crib. Rubbing her back.

"Beating ourselves up, refusing to let ourselves feel happiness or joy—" She shook her head, tears leaking from her eyes. "It's not going to save them."

"You've heard of it then?" Grace asked Kempley over the phone. *It. Munchausen's*. Already—in less than a week—the word had become familiar.

"*Heard* of Munchausen's? Of course. But do I believe in it? Hell, no."

Grace stopped. "What do you mean? How do you not believe in it?"

"You just don't."

"But women have confessed, Kempley." Irritated, Grace resumed her pacing, pausing at the foot of the stairs and listening for Jack, then returning to the kitchen where she'd been sitting with coffee. The house was quiet. Stephen was at the Y, Max was out skating, Erin and Jack were taking naps.

"Well, I'd confess too if some shrink was telling me that it was the only way to get my child back," Kempley said. "Confess and you won't hang. It's what women accused of witchcraft were told. Then when they did confess, everyone said, 'See? It must be real.' "

Grace smiled. *Professor* Trapman, she thought. Except the Munchausen's accusation wasn't some obscure academic subject. It was about her and *her* children, and the truth was that she could care less about similarities to the witch trials or even whether Kempley believed Munchausen's was real. The *accusation* was real. That her kids could be taken from here was real. What else mattered?

"Come on, Grace, you're an epidemiologist," Kempley said now. "You know better than anyone all the ridiculous things people believed in the name of medicine, and every time, *every* time, it was a way to explain what no one understood. The Witch Trials started that way. A child was sick, and no one could figure it out. People were terrified."

"I know, Kempley, but this isn't 1600 or whenever it was, and Jack *has* a diagnosis." Exasperation leaked into her tone. "Besides, there are thousands of sick kids where no one knows what's wrong, and *their* parents haven't been accused. But *I* was."

"Exactly. So what sets you apart?"

"I don't know. I keep thinking—" *Someone must have found out about Noah*. She squeezed her eyes shut against the thought, one hand on the counter, as if to balance herself. Bennett's question from three days before fell through her like something dropped from a great height, gathering momentum and weight each time she remembered it anew. *Was there anything unusual going on in your life at the time the accusation was made?*

"Have you considered that maybe you've been accused because

you know more about mitochondrial disease than half of Jack's doctors?" Kempley's voice was gentle.

Grace shook her head wearily. She'd forgotten how dogmatic Kempley could be. It had been helpful at the conference where Kempley was able to elicit answers that others simply couldn't. But the last thing Grace wanted was to turn this into an *Us v. Them* kind of battle. Parents v. doctors. Especially because, with the exception of Dr. Buford, Jack's first cardiologist, and the doctor from San Diego who had responded to Grace's letter about Jack, it contradicted her experience. She liked Jack's doctors, his nurses, his therapists. She trusted them. She respected them.

Mother-perpetrator is unusually friendly with hospital staff.

Or at least, she *had* trusted them.

"Studies show that doctors tend to dislike patients whom they can't help," Kempley was saying. "Which makes sense, if you think about it. Kids like ours are constant reminders of everything the doctor doesn't know."

"So you think the doctors accuse the mothers? I don't buy it, Kempley. And not with our doctors. Anju Mehta is like family to us."

"I'm not saying it's conscious. Maybe the doctors are just more inclined to believe in Munchausen's if they already don't like the parent to begin with. And they probably feel guilty for feeling this way. I mean, how the hell can you dislike a parent whose child is dying?"

Grace thought of Lydia and knew it was easier than most people could imagine. "I don't know, Kempley, it seems—" she swallowed hard. "What if it's not that complicated? What if it's just—" She paced again to the foot of the stairs to listen for Jack or Erin, then to the front window, looking for Stephen's car. The street was empty. She paused in a block of wintry sunlight, but couldn't feel any warmth. "I met someone," she said quietly. "Actually, I knew him in high school, and—God, this sounds so stupid—"

Kempley was silent. And then she said, "It doesn't sound stupid at all."

"I'm married, Kempley."

"Yeah, and you're also human, Grace. You're not the first married woman to have an affair, you aren't even the first married woman with a terminally ill child to have an affair. It doesn't make you a monster."

"I know." Her eyes burned. "But it's wrong. Stephen is so good. He's not some insensitive jerk, he's not—" Her voice broke. She sat on the stairs, chest to her knees, as if to hide. "What if I *am* sick somehow? What if I really do need attention?"

"*Everyone* needs attention, Grace."

"But I've lied to be with him, Kempley. And I keep thinking of how the Munchausen mother seems so wonderful, but she's really a liar and a pretender—"

The acting skills of the mother-perpetrator can match those of a veteran performer . . .

"You're *not* Munchausen's, Grace."

She is a master of manipulation and deception . . .

"But how do you know?" She was crying now.

"I just do."

"You can't," she sobbed.

"My God, Grace, don't you see what's happening? You're not perfect, but that doesn't make you capable of harming your child. I can't believe you've been carrying this around by yourself, that you've been thinking this."

"I'm so afraid."

"I know, sweetie, but having an affair doesn't make you a bad person or a bad mother. And yes, it's wrong, but Jesus, who the hell has the right to judge *you*? Or anyone? For all you know, having this man in your life makes you a *better* mother right now. Maybe he gives you the energy you need to deal with what's happening with Jack."

It was true. He did. The realization only made her cry harder. "I could lose my kids," she whispered.

For a moment Kempley didn't say anything. And then, "This is exactly what happened in Salem, Grace. Exactly. Good, decent, church-going women were accused, and they weren't perfect— maybe they envied a neighbor or they were angry or, maybe, God forbid, they committed adultery, but either way, it shouldn't have mattered. It didn't make them witches. But a part of them believed—just as you do—that maybe, maybe because they'd done those other things that were wrong, a part of them really was evil." Kempley paused. "You aren't causing Jack's illness any more than I caused Kelly's or Carrie's. But I feel guilty too if for no other reason than because mitochondria are inherited one hundred percent from the mother. *I* gave this to my kids. *I* did."

"But you *know* that doesn't make sense."

"It doesn't have to. The one thing a mother is supposed to do is keep her children safe, and I failed. Hell, if someone had accused *me* of Munchausen's when Carrie died, I probably would have believed it. Which is what's so insidious about the allegation. It preys on a woman's worst fears about herself, that deep down she's selfish or she's a liar or she's not really as smart as everyone thinks or she's a bad mother or whatever. And yeah, it *should* be a huge leap from thinking you've made mistakes to thinking that you're capable of harming your own kid, but it's not because we've been blaming ourselves anyway and have been for years."

"I want to believe you," Grace said.

"Then do. Come on: Can you name one mom in the mito group who *doesn't* feel guilty because her child is sick? Who doesn't blame herself somehow, some way?"

Grace lifted the pot of boiling pasta from the stove and poured it into a colander in the sink. Steam fogged the window, momentarily erasing the world. "It was good to talk to her," she said over her shoulder to Stephen. "She was so rational."

"Well, you sound better."

She nodded. The kitchen was warm and smelled of tomato sauce and garlic bread. "Anyway, she seems to think the whole notion of Munchausen's is bogus."

"Bogus how?" Stephen handed her a glass of red wine.

She smiled and took a sip, then set the glass on the windowsill over the sink. Rain beaded against the dark glass, making it look swollen. Grace tried to sound casual, indifferent. "Oh, she was just comparing Munchausen's accusations to what happened during the Salem Witch Trials." She ran cold water onto the steaming noodles. "She thinks the accusation is a way to silence women who advocate for their kids." She shut off the water and glanced quickly towards his face, then away. Don't make fun of it, she thought. I know it's far-fetched, I know it doesn't change anything, but at least it's an answer, at least it's something.

He was smiling but not in mirth so much as in discomfort.

"Go ahead," she sighed, staring towards the lake, which the township had drained two weeks before for cleaning, something it did every five years. In its place was a hole the size of three football fields.

"Well, what do *you* think?" Stephen's voice was careful.

She shrugged. "It sort of made sense." She looked at him.

He raised one eyebrow. "Does Kempley know that you wear black all the time?"

"Ha ha," she tried to joke as she turned back to the sink. Her face was burning, and she felt like a fool. For wanting him to believe this, needing him to, maybe so that she could. And for feeling hurt that he didn't, when she knew, she *knew*, that if the accusation hadn't been directed at her, she would have been the one rolling her eyes and making fun of the whole idea.

"Hey." Stephen touched her shoulder. "Come on, baby. I'm not making fun of you."

"I know."

"It just seems kind of extreme, that's all."

More so than accusing otherwise normal women of making their kids sick *solely* to get attention? she wondered. But she didn't say anything.

FOURTEEN

S he couldn't see Stephen, only the shape of him. She knew he was lying on his back because he was snoring. Usually, she nudged him and he'd roll over and grow quiet. Tonight she simply watched him, his arms at his sides, the pale comforter pushed to the foot of the bed and only the sheet covering him. *The way you sleep reveals your true self,* she thought. He was so open. And how different from her, always curled into her own tight ball, clutching the heating pad to her chest for warmth, hoarding it like her secrets. She was selfish. She knew that. Was this why she'd been accused?

Now, in the kitchen, Grace filled a thick mug with boiling water, poured in the envelope of instant cocoa, then carried the mug with both hands to the butcher block. She held it up to her face and blew on the scalding liquid as she stood in the half-darkness, the tiled floor freezing against her bare feet. Soon the sky would begin to lighten. Noah had returned from Michigan late the night before. She hadn't slept, aware of each hour, rehearsing what she would say to him. *I can't see you anymore,* and *It's over,* and *I'm sorry.* Words. Tiny capsules filled with pain. She felt her chest constrict and thought of how a muscle can't contract halfway. To stop an action in its midst is simply to use different muscles. And the heart was no different. Another muscle. Contracting, then letting go. All or nothing.

He would phone her later in the day, she knew, all energy and manic eagerness, wanting to tell her about his Christmas and his mom's cooking and the late-night card games with his brothers, and how he'd "camped" in a sleeping bag on the dining room floor with his nieces and nephews, making "forts" beneath the table with his mother's Christmas linens. His joy would be like a fast-moving river washing over her before she could say what she had to. *I brought you cinnamon rolls,* he would tell her, *and when do I get to see you, and tell me everything—How's Jack and did Max like the skates and God, did I ask you already—did you answer? When do I get to see you?*

From upstairs she heard the staccato buzzer on Max's alarm clock. They'd kept the kids home from school for the past three days, but today they were going back. She and Stephen had met with the school principals and Stephen had talked to the kids last night. If any adults whom they didn't know tried to approach them, they were to go immediately to the principal's office and call either Grace or Stephen.

"*Why?*" Max demanded. "Who do you think is going to come to our schools?"

"Hopefully no one," Stephen said. "But there are some problems your mom and I are taking care of and until we do, we're just being careful."

Erin had started to cry. "I don't want to go to school."

"No, no, sweetie," Grace comforted her. "You love school, and Mrs. Turner is going to take good care of you."

"Can I still play hockey?" Max had asked.

"*If* you stay with the coach." Stephen looked at him hard. "I mean this, Max. No riding to games with friends or friends' parents. You stay on the team buses, you come straight home afterwards. If you need a ride, you ask your mother or me."

"But what if you can't?"

"Either we can or you don't go. It's not negotiable."

Outside, the January sky grew pink with morning light. Grace scanned the mail Stephen had left out for her, smiling when she saw the manila envelope from Queens College in Charlotte, North Carolina. Kempley. Grace set her mug down and inserted her thumbnail beneath the flap. A book. Arthur Miller's *The Crucible.* A yellow Post-it was stuck to the cover.

Just a loan—not a gift. Hope marginalia not <u>too</u> distracting. Feel free to add your own notes, underlines, etc. You won't be first.

K.

Grace opened the book to the first page, and began to read. The Reverend Parris is praying at his daughter Betty's bed. A child enters the sickroom to inform the Reverend that the doctor can't find a cure. "*He bid me come and tell you, Reverend Sir, that he cannot discover no medicine for it in his books.*"

"*Then he must search on.*"

"*Aye, sir, he have been searching his books since we left you, Sir. But he bid me tell you that you might look to unnatural things for the cause of it.*"

Unnatural things. Grace frowned and looked up from the book. The words echoed. She thought of that woman in Missouri she'd read about on the M.A.M.A. site. A sentence from one of the Munchausen's books she'd read flickered through her mind: "When cures cannot be found for a sick child or when the apparent disease does not follow the expected course, physicians must consider Munchausen by Proxy." Grace dog-eared the page and closed the book. She felt a scratching in her chest as if a tiny animal were trying to get out. Unnatural Things.

The phone was ringing when Grace walked in the door after dropping Erin off at school. Heart in her throat, already she was praying, *Please don't let anything be wrong, please let the kids be okay, please, please, please.* She unzipped Jack's coat, yanked off his hat, then left him sitting on the floor in the foyer in his red plastic fireman boots. Her own coat still on, she hopped over her purse to grab the phone before the answering machine picked up. "Hello?" she said breathlessly.

It was Bennett. He'd FedEx'd the report from Child Protective Services. A guaranteed ten o'clock delivery for today.

She sank into one of the kitchen chairs. "Was it what you expected?" she asked, turning to make a silly face at Jack.

He didn't answer right away. And then, "It's more serious than I thought, Grace."

Her smile froze. She turned towards the window, the bright sedative of sunlight, and leaned her head against the glass. "Are—are the kids in danger?" She bit her lip to keep from crying.

"Don't take them out of school, but I would keep them close for a while." His voice was gentle. Too gentle, she thought, trying to take deep breaths. Beyond the window, the pale branches of the oak trees stretched like severed nerve endings toward the amputated January sky.

After a moment, Bennett asked, "How's Jack?"

She swallowed hard. "Not great." She felt her voice fray with fear.

"I'm sorry to hear that." He paused. "We'll get this straightened out, Grace."

How? she wanted to ask, as she slowly hung up. *How can we possibly?*

Now, she moved her finger down the page like someone just learning to read. Case #12090509—twenty-four pages. An official-looking stamp in the top right corner of the first page: Philadelphia Department of Health and Human Services.

Jack lay on the couch with his silver race car, watching a Blue's Clues video. Grace sat at the table where she could keep an eye on him, the report spread out in front of her. She felt as she had years ago learning to water-ski: each time she'd stay up a little longer—ten seconds, fifteen, half a minute—before plunging into the frigid Lake Erie water. So it was reading the report. She struggled to hold on, to comprehend what exactly it meant. *Department unable to justify further investigation at this time. However, case should remain open* without *contacting family as contact could cause further harm to child, and CPS currently does not have enough basis to remove child from parental custody.* She kept going under at certain words and phrases, feeling as if she were going to drown: *cause further harm, remove child from parental custody. Criminal background check,* she read, and *county police notified.* A quote from Jack's neurologist: "extremely vigilant," he had described Grace. Was this bad? She no longer knew the meanings of basic words.

Mother appears quite angry. Constantly second-guessing medical staff. The name of whoever had said this was blacked out. Like wartime correspondence.

Mother refuses to consider family counseling.

Mother overly focused on technical/medical aspects of child's illness. Obsessive documentation of child's medical history.

She kept flipping through the report. It included a "Family Needs Assessment," a "Risk Assessment of Future Abuse." Two points against Grace for having "unrealistic expectations" of Jack. *Why in God's name would you want to put him through this?* And yet, MSBP was supposedly based on the fact that she *didn't* have expectations, *didn't* want him to get well. Two more points against her because she was female, two more because Jack had special needs. The names of Jack's doctors were included, the dates they'd been contacted: "3/17, 10:55 am: phone call, Dr. M.. 4/21: letter to Dr. M. requesting records."

Mother always well-groomed, one of the doctors had said; *extremely conscious of external appearance.* Was this good or bad? She felt as if she were hearing only one half of a conversation or staring at a photograph with the faces of certain people cut out.

At times mother displays inappropriate sense of humor.

She swallowed wrong and coughed. Everything was out of context. Her elbows on the table seemed sharp. She thought of how just this morning, as she walked naked across the bedroom to grab her robe, Stephen told her, "You're starting to get too thin, baby," and without missing a beat, she joked, "The Munchausen Accusation Diet. I don't think I've ever lost weight over the holidays before."

Inappropriate.

Or Sunday morning when Jack started howling after Erin accidentally stepped on his foot, and Grace leaned over to Stephen and whispered, "If anyone in the family fakes illness to get attention, it's this one." Stephen lifted Jack high over head, stopping him mid-bawl, and said, "What are you up to, you little Munchausen?"

It probably was inappropriate, but she—they—were simply trying to make something terrifying less so.

Mother refers to hospital as "home away from home." Grace leaned forward, holding onto herself, more hurt than she thought she could be. Why had Rebecca repeated this? Grace's chest felt tight, her heart siphoning the blood from the rest of her. It didn't matter that the name had been blocked out. She *had* said this to Rebecca last year after the surgery to implant a port into Jack's chest. Less than a day after his discharge, he spiked a fever and had to be readmitted, and Rebecca was teasing Grace about how she couldn't bear to stay away, and maybe the hospital should charge her rent, and yes, Grace had joked that the hospital was her "home away from home." But in the next breath, she also said, "What's sad is that it's starting to be true. I wish it were a joke." Why wasn't that in the report? Was Rebecca the one who had called CPS?

And then on page sixteen the word "adultery," followed by a question mark, girlish handwriting in the margin: *Check if adultery part of Munch profile.*

But by now the words were like rain. You're cold and you're soaked, and after a while it doesn't matter that you're wet, you can't feel it anymore. Grace knew her affair with Noah wasn't the sole reason for the accusation—there was too much else that was damning: her apparent love of hospital life, her *inappropriate* sense of humor. She wanted to cry. Did they think, did they really think that Jack's illness was a joke to her?

She tried to imagine what Stephen would think when he saw the word *adultery*, and felt a cold wave of fear wash over her, even though she knew he wouldn't believe it, wouldn't allow himself to even consider it. It wasn't in his nature. It would only make him that much more furious. "Jesus, do these people even have a fucking clue? Like you have time to breathe much less have an affair." His eyes would be hard and angry, and nothing, if she ended up confessing to him the truth, would allow him to understand or forgive. That wasn't in his nature either. He saw the world in black and white. And she'd long since given up trying to understand why. Perhaps it was connected to his dad's walking out. Perhaps it was connected to his job in finance—numbers were unequivocal. Either a client could pay off a loan or he couldn't. And maybe this was how it should be. Maybe morality was as unequivocal as arithmetic, and maybe there were some things that should never have to be understood. A child's dying. A wife's betrayal.

• • •

On the caller ID she saw the words *unknown caller*. A cell phone. She grabbed the receiver, her breath in her throat.

"God, I've missed you," Noah said the minute she said hello.

She felt herself crumple at the sound of his voice. She sank to the floor, back against the kitchen cabinets so Jack wouldn't see her. She was crying so hard it sounded as if she were choking. She couldn't speak.

"Grace, *what*? Shit, is it Jack? Is—Grace, honey, please, what happened?"

She shook her head, beside herself. "They—they think—" but she couldn't finish. "They think—"

"Think what, Grace? Who?"

She shook her head, crying harder. She couldn't say it.

"You're scaring me, Grace. I don't—is Jack okay?"

She nodded yes, sobbing. "I'm so sorry."

"There's no need, honey, come on, just talk to me."

She nodded, hiccupping, and tried again. "They think I'm—" She closed her eyes. "They think I'm—" Tears ran into her mouth, and she tasted salt. "They think I'm trying to kill him," she whispered finally.

For a moment Noah didn't say anything.

"Noah?" she sobbed.

"I'm here, baby, I'm here, but I don't understand. Someone thinks you're trying to kill who?"

"Jack," she whispered.

"*What?*"

Father arrested for DUI, she read, and again in the margin a note: *investigate re: alcohol abuse*. The same bubbly handwriting.

Mother has history of depression. Mother prescribed Zoloft but is noncompliant. Sentences like wartime trains, carrying away entire histories. Grace stood to pour herself more coffee, then dumped it out and filled the tea kettle instead. Tea—as if she were ill. She felt that way.

How could the report be so wrong *and* so horribly true all at once? Or was this the nature of all truths? Like light, both particle and wave. She bent over, her elbows on the edge of the sink. Yes, she had taken antidepressants after Jack was diagnosed, but that didn't constitute a *history* of depression. And yes, she had stopped taking the Zoloft after a few months because it kept her up at night, and the Trazadone the doctor gave to help her sleep made her groggy in the mornings, but mostly she stopped taking the antidepressant because she had gotten angry. *Of course* she was depressed and she *should* be depressed, and not allowing herself this depression started feeling like one more thing that was being taken from her; it started feeling like a betrayal of herself and Jack. He was a year old then—*one year*—and he'd been diagnosed with an incurable illness, and to somehow make that bearable was unfathomable, was, in itself, unbearable. She had wanted to feel grief, every goddamn ounce of it.

"I didn't mention the affair," she told Bennett when she phoned him back. "I just, I didn't think it had any bearing."

"Is the relationship over?" Bennett inquired gently.

"It will be."

"I think that's wise, Grace." He paused. "I'm not necessarily convinced that the infidelity has anything to do with why the accusation was made, but I'm not unconvinced either." He paused. "Until this is settled . . ."

"I know." She swallowed hard, eyes closed. "Is it—adultery"— the word *adultery* landed hard in the pit of her stomach—"is it a part of the profile?"

"In that it suggests an ongoing pattern of deception, yes, I'm afraid so."

"Can you come home?" she asked Stephen when he returned her call. She was in bed, Jack down for his nap. Harsh January sunlight slammed into the room like an accusation. Her eyes ached. She couldn't lie still, couldn't think, couldn't focus. "I can't—I need someone to pick up Erin. And Max has hockey, and can you call my mom to see if she can help? I can't talk to her, Stephen—I can't talk to anyone." She couldn't stop crying. "It's so much worse than we thought. They asked Anju if she'd ever checked for traces of ipecac poisoning in Jack's blood. They subpoenaed all of Jack's medical records, they notified the police—"

"Okay, okay, but think about it: They did the most thorough investigation possible and still don't have enough evidence. They found nothing, Grace. Nothing."

His words didn't help. He didn't understand. They'd found plenty. It just wasn't enough. Yet. And who was to say they wouldn't keep looking?

She lay on her side, the pillow damp, hugging the heating pad to her chest. Jack was still napping. Her mother was getting Erin. Late-afternoon light shone through the windows, illuminating the sheen of dust on top of the night tables and armoire. A heap of dirty clothes sat on a chair next to a stack of Christmas presents she still hadn't put away. She closed her eyes, trying to sleep, but felt her eyelids twitching, her mind racing with explanations. She hadn't *refused* family counseling when that psychologist suggested it; it was the first time he'd even met her, and she had explained that with all of their schedules—Stephen's work and Max's hockey and Erin's Brownie troop and swim lessons, not to mention all of Jack's appointments—she didn't think it was feasible.

And maybe she was *overly focused on the technical aspects of Jack's illness*, his creatine counts and iron levels, but how could anyone whose child had never been seriously sick understand? That if she didn't sometimes focus on those *technical* aspects of Jack's illness, she would fly apart in rage and grief at what her child was going through. Still, she felt nearly sick with doubt. What if her behavior wasn't normal? What if there was something wrong with her?

She heard her mother and Erin come in and move around the kitchen, then the creak of the wooden steps and Erin's timid knock on the door. "Mama?"

"Come in, sweets," Grace called, sitting up against the pillows. She held out her arms to Erin. "There's my girl. How was school today?"

Erin cuddled against her. "Fun," she said. "Mrs. Turner said I could go into the Tiger reading group today."

"The Tigers? Isn't that the group Samantha's in?"

Erin nodded. "And in art, we traced our bodies on these big pieces of paper and Miss Gail is going to cut them out for us and tomorrow we're going to decorate the insides with anything we want that tells about ourself."

Grace tilted Erin's chin up so she could look at her. "I bet you've already been thinking about that, haven't you?"

"Uh hmm," Erin said. And then, "Mama, can I watch a movie in bed with you?"

Something settled in Grace. "That's the best idea I've heard all day," she said. "Why don't you go pick out a movie, and . . ." She nuzzled her nose to Erin's and whispered, "I bet if you ask Grandma real nice, she'll make us a big bowl of . . ."

"*Popcorn?*" Erin sat back, a smile on her freckled face, then threw herself forward again, arms around Grace's neck. "This is the best day of my whole life!" she exclaimed. And then she hopped up and raced downstairs, already calling, "Guess what, Grandma . . . !"

They were halfway through *Beauty and the Beast* when Grace heard her mother go into Jack's room, followed by his exuberant "Grandma!" and the squeak of his crib as he pulled himself up by the bars. She listened to the hum of their voices, followed by her mother shushing him in the hallway, saying, "Mama's not feeling good."

"Why she not feeling good?"

"Mom, bring him in with us," Grace called.

Her mother pushed open the door, with Jack on her hip and the backpack holding his oxygen slung over her shoulder.

"Mama, why you not feeling—" Jack started to say, but then he put his hands on his head and shouted. "Erin, why *you* in Mama's bed? You not feeling good either?"

"No, silly, we're watching a movie," Erin laughed around a mouthful of popcorn. "You want to watch with us?"

"Grandma *too*?" he asked.

"Oh no," Ellen laughed as she settled Jack onto the bed next to Grace. "That would be a little crowded for me." She smiled at Grace. "You okay, honey?"

"Thanks Mom," Grace said, glancing at the kids. "This is exactly what I needed."

They snuggled, Erin on one side of her, Jack on the other. The bed was warm with all of them under the covers.

"Mama, why did that man want to hurt the beast?" Jack asked, pointing at the TV.

"You mean Gaston, Goose?" She swept her hand over Jack's furrowed little brow. "He's not being very nice is he?"

'But why he not nice?"

"Well, Gaston wants Belle all to himself."

"You mean, he doesn't want to share?"

"Nope."

"But why he not want to share?"

"Maybe he's afraid that if he shares Belle, the Beast will take her away."

Jack wrinkled his nose at her. "But the Beast wouldn't do that, right Mama?"

"That's right, Goose."

Jack turned back to the TV, his head solid and warm against her arm. Grace smiled. Her little scientist. Questions inside of questions inside of questions. She watched him, absorbed again in the movie, his face almost incandescent in the artificial glow from the screen. The last of the fading daylight had dissolved, the sky its own dark movie screen now, stars rolling up like credits at the end of the day. From the kitchen drifted the scent of sautéing onions and baking apples. A few minutes later, she heard the hum of the motorized garage opener, the thud of the back door, then Max clomping up the stairs, loaded down with hockey gear. The clatter of silverware, the squeak of the oven door, the low thrum of Stephen's voice. And then he was creeping into the darkened bedroom, still wearing the Burberry overcoat her parents had given him for Christmas.

"And *what* is going on in here?" He turned on the brass lamp near the door.

"We're watching a movie, Daddy!" Jack said.

"A movie? A *movie?* Who said you could watch a movie in MY BED?" Stephen wiggled his fingers at the kids as if to grab them, and they both started screaming, burrowing deeper under the covers, shouting, "Get him, Mama! Get him." Grace smiled at Stephen gratefully as he groped for the two wiggling bundles on either side of her. "Is this . . . is this a head I feel? A foot? Hey! Whose foot is this?"

And then Jack was tossing back the blankets. "It's me, Daddy!"

Stephen snuggled in next to Erin for the last ten minutes of the movie, then ushered the kids downstairs, telling Erin to take Jack's Spaceship backpack and to go ahead of him on the steps, helping him slide down on his bottom. Grace started crying as soon as Stephen shut the bedroom door behind them. "I'm so sorry," she sobbed.

He sat on the edge of the bed. "Oh, Grace, this whole thing—you are the last person who deserves this, and I promise, we'll get to the bottom of it."

It didn't help. She only cried harder.

"Do you want me to bring you up some dinner?"

She shook her head. "My mom made apple pie, didn't she?" Her favorite dessert.

"And meatloaf, mashed potatoes . . . Are you sure you don't want to come down? It might make you feel better."

It would. She knew this. Rarely had being with her children, simply being in the same room with them, not made her feel better. And yet she had the sense that this was the last time in the coming weeks when she would be able to simply give in to what this accusation had already done to her life. A part of her almost wanted—or needed, was that a better word?—to fall apart because she wouldn't be able to later, couldn't afford to after this night. Starting tomorrow there would be phone calls and meetings with Bennett and Anju and the rest of Jack's team: his therapists, respiratory techs, the head of the birth-to-three program. She would have to talk to Max's hockey coach. And in the midst of all of this, she would need, more than ever, to make her children's lives feel no different from they had always felt, to be *ordinary*. It was a word similar to *misunderstanding*, which when Grace thought of it now, was like those huge beautiful air balloons, a hundred feet in circumference, that the Japanese had sent across the ocean, nearly ten thousand of them, during the Second World War. *Misunderstanding* was like this, Grace thought, a huge, graceful word, weighted down with bombs, that floated, seemingly out of nowhere, across the surface of people's lives.

She glanced at Stephen. His jaw was scratchy when she reached to touch his face. If she hadn't been "a great pretender" before, if she hadn't been "an imposter mom"—*her skills could match those of a veteran actor*—she certainly would become this. But not tonight. Not just yet. "I know I'd probably feel better if I had dinner with you guys, but I just . . . The kids will be okay, won't they?"

Stephen leaned over and kissed her forehead. "The kids will be fine."

She dozed off and on to the sounds of her family talking in the kitchen. Tears leaked onto her pillow as she slept. She had read once that by age sixty-five, the body produces only 60 percent of the tears it did at twenty-five, and by age eighty only 30 percent—as if each person had a finite supply of tears. Shouldn't it have been the opposite, she wondered, the older you get the more there is to grieve? Or is it that you cry less about the small things? Maybe the later griefs simply can't ever hurt as badly as the first ones.

She woke when Stephen climbed into bed with the report and turned on the reading light, a martini on the night table next to him. She watched him, her eyes locked onto his face. Now and then, he reached to touch her cheek with the back of his hand, to squeeze her shoulder or stroke her hair. She watched as he took a sip of his martini, shaking his head in disgust, his brow furrowed. And then, abruptly, furiously, he flung the report across the room, the pages fluttering wildly like a wounded bird.

She sat up. "What?"

"This whole thing makes me sick. Jesus. I can't believe they brought up my DUI from twenty goddamn years ago. And this bullshit, this absolute bullshit, about you having an affair. No proof, no nothing. A goddamn guess."

She dug her fingernails into her palms, so afraid she could barely breathe. "I knew that would infuriate you." Her eyes were on his face.

"*That*? Hell, you think I'm upset about that?" He laughed bitterly, then slammed out of bed, stomped across the room and grabbed the report. "This," he said, turning the pages roughly. "This is unconscionable. Here—" He read out loud: " 'Copies of child's chest X-ray were sent to—' " He glanced up, furious. "The name's blacked out, but it was sent to some cardiologist who . . ." He read again from the report: " 'felt that a mitochondrial cardiomyopathy would be consistent with the level of deterioration. Case was also sent to"—he glanced at her—"another crossed out name, but a psychiatrist who is apparently an expert in Munchausen Syndrome by Proxy cases. 'Said expert reported that Mother doesn't fit typical Munchausen's profile. Expert cautioned, however, that 'this does not rule possibility out.'"

He looked up, breathing heavily. "What the hell does that mean? What *does* rule it out?" He climbed back into bed. "I'm starting to think your friend Kempley is right." He shook his head, and took another sip of his martini. "It's a goddamn witch hunt."

Without turning on the lights, she could see that the kitchen was immaculate. Moonlight edged the long arm of the faucet, the teakettle, a foil-covered plate. The countertops gleamed. She filled a glass with water and drank it in one long gulp as she stood before the open refrigerator. She'd sweated through her T-shirt. She filled the glass a second time, drank more slowly, then let the door fall shut. She thought of how, in the 1940s, mothers of autistic children were called "refrigerator mothers," their coldness, doctors said, was the cause of their children's retreat from the world.

In the laundry room, she pulled off her damp T-shirt and tossed it into the dryer, then sat, a towel draped around her shoulders, her back against the warm machine. Her shirt made a soft thumping sound. She had carried the cordless phone in from the kitchen and now she dialed Noah's number. It was after three. His voice was thick with sleep.

"Hey, you," she said, and could hear him smile.

"I was just dreaming about you," he whispered. "Are you okay?"

"No." She rested her chin on her knees. "Was it a good dream?"

"You were with me." She heard him roll onto his back. "What can I do, Grace?"

She shook her head. "I have to end this, Noah. I don't want to, but—"

"I know."

"You do?"

"Of course."

Her eyes filled. "I was afraid you'd hate me."

"*Hate* you? I'm going to miss you like crazy, Grace but *hate* you? Why would you even think that?"

"I'm leaving you again," she whispered.

"Oh, honey, it's not the same. I know you don't have any other choice right now."

Right now.

She closed her eyes and leaned her head against the dryer. Its steady thump was like a heartbeat.

"Grace?"

"I'm here," she whispered. Her name, he'd told her once, was his flight song. He was referring to the notes birds called across the sky as they were migrating. It had been a wintry morning, and they'd been walking along the ocean, the low sky puffy with clouds like a goose-down comforter. As if to prove his point, he'd handed her the thermos of coffee he'd been carrying, then cupped his hands to his mouth and shouted her name into the wind. Its echo carried across the gray sand: "Grace! Grace! Grace!" As if in answer, a Bonaparte gull lifted off from a nearby dune.

It was how the loss lifted inside of her now: suddenly, as if in answer to something. "I'm not going anywhere," he was saying. "I'll still be here in two weeks or two months or two years. Hell, I've waited twenty already—"

"Don't, Noah." *His* name: the first half of it was the word *no*. "I can't promise—I might—" she stopped.

"—not come back? I know."

"Do you?"

He didn't say anything. "I don't know," he said after a minute. "Maybe I don't really believe that. It seems crazy that after all this, we wouldn't end up together."

"I can't jeopardize my kids, Noah. Already . . . I'll never forgive myself if something happens." She started to cry. "This accusation isn't just going to go away, even if Bennett can get the case closed . . ."

"What're you telling me, Grace? Am I even going to see you again?"

She didn't answer.

"Jesus," he said.

"Please understand," she sobbed. "I never wanted—"

"Do you still love me?" he interrupted.

"Oh, Noah, my God, of course I love you."

"Shush. Then it's okay. I'll be okay."

"How?" She shook her head, listening to the rhythmic pulse of the dryer. "Because I'm not sure I will be." And again, she could *hear* him smile. Was that even possible? She thought of birds and of how they could hear surf crashing on a shore hundreds of miles from they where they were flying.

"I want to see you one more time, though." His voice cracked. "I think I deserve that much from you, Grace."

"Don't you think I want to see you too?" She was sobbing again. "But I can't, Noah. I can't take that chance. I was so stupid to think I ever could."

FIFTEEN

"Look—" Stephen sat forward on the edge of the sofa. "I understand the need to report suspected abuse, but you're telling me that anyone can say absolutely anything without proof or evidence, and we have no recourse? None?"

"If the report is made in good faith—"

"*Good faith?* What does a DUI from twenty years ago have to do with good faith? Or questions about Grace's humor?" He didn't mention the comment about her infidelity.

Bennett glanced sympathetically at Grace, but she couldn't meet his eyes.

"Unfortunately these accusations, at times, take on a life of their own." Bennett sighed. "I know it feels like a witch hunt, but it's important to keep this in perspective. The DUI, for example. I doubt anyone went looking for it, Stephen. And I agree, it's not relevant, but it was there. It's public record, it's a fact."

"Fine, but what about the comments—"

"Please," Grace interrupted. "I just want to know what happens next."

Nothing, Bennett explained. Even if the case was closed today, by law, it would remain in Child Protective Services records until ten years after the child—in this case, Jack—turned eighteen. Bennett had the grace to blush when he said this. Jack wouldn't ever be eighteen. The law had been named after six-year-old Eliza Izquierdo, who was beaten to death in New York in 1995. Prior to her death there were numerous accusations of her abuse, but because they were never substantiated, the records were destroyed. Had they not been, someone might have gotten to her in time.

"Believe me, I've tried before to get reports of an accusation expunged, and I've never succeeded. It's the same old reasoning—if the parent is innocent, nothing will come of the file anyway. If she isn't, that file might save a child's life."

Expunged. Grace thought of how a word, like a virus, is most lethal when first encountered and how, after a while, it becomes less virulent—or maybe we simply learn to accommodate it, altering our lives so that both can survive. Words like *terminal* and *end-stage*. Words like *mitochondrial disease.* And now, words like *mother-perpetrator* and *child-victim* and *expunged.*

But she thought too of how a word, like a virus, can live on long after the person it infected has died. Those women in Salem, nothing left of their lives but the words *witch* or *accused.*

Grace's name was listed now in a central registry of child abusers: "*Accused but unsubstantiated.*" Her name was there with men convicted of raping little girls, with the woman whose son had been covered with inexplicable sores that never seemed to heal—until it was discovered that she'd been scrubbing his back with oven cleaner. *Accused but unsubstantiated.* One day would these words be all that someone knew of her?

She thought of how plant fossils still carried traces of fungal infections, of how ancient jellyfish still bore signs of the parasites that had lived within them thousands of years before, of how in the bones of long-extinct mastodons and dinosaurs millions of years old there remained evidence of bacterial infection. And not long ago, in a nine-hundred-year-old Peruvian mummy, scientists found the DNA of tuberculosis. She thought of how after an organism dies, all that survives sometimes is the evidence of what it had suffered, what damaged it, what hurt—as if in the end, these were the things that mattered most.

Grace looked up, hands clenched so tightly in her lap that her knuckles were white. "What if they find something else?" Her voice broke. "Can they really take the kids?"

"They can. Which is why you need to have someone with you at doctor's appointments, why it would be helpful if you could get letters from friends and family members who have seen for themselves times when Jack was in pain and needed morphine and who have seen you give him morphine—" He looked up.

"*Why* is this happening?" Grace said. "I don't understand."

SIXTEEN

*I*t was the first thing Grace noticed when she found Jenn at the bar at City Scapes, already sipping a martini: the red cowboy boots.

"Are you serious?" Grace nodded at the boots and hugged her friend all at once. She had phoned her as soon as she got in the car after leaving Bennett's. "I need to talk to you," was all she said, afraid that if she spoke another word, she'd start crying. That had been two days ago.

Now Jenn stuck out her leg, showing off the boots. "Aren't they great?" She grinned, though her eyes were serious, scanning Grace's face. "Christmas present from Diane." Her partner of nearly fifteen years. Jenn laughed. "I swear, I feel like a teenager, like I could go lasso up some young lad . . ."

Grace rolled her eyes as she slid onto the high bar stool. "I don't think you wanted to lasso up the lads even when you were a teenager."

"It's horrible *and* wonderful all at once," Jenn was saying now. "It's the neatest thing in the world to watch your own child falling in love, but I can't bear how vulnerable he is. I'm terrified she'll hurt him." Tyler, Jenn's oldest boy, was in love for the first time.

"Do you like the girl?" asked Grace, trying to picture Max falling in love.

"She's great, but . . ." Jenn set down her drink. "Why are we talking about this, Grace? Come on. What's up?" She nodded at the Diet Coke Grace had ordered. "You're not—are you pregnant? Is that it?"

Grace glanced at her drink in surprise. "Oh, my God, no." She tried to laugh, but her eyes immediately filled. She'd been afraid to order a drink. What if someone was watching her? Could this be used against her too? She shook her head. "Give me a minute, okay?" She smiled shakily. "I just . . . I just want to talk about something normal first."

Jenn looked at her, then squeezed her hand. "Okay then," she said. "Tyler's girlfriend. She's smart, she's gorgeous, she's athletic, and it makes me crazy: they're *so* perfect for each other, but they're *sixteen*. Why couldn't he have met her ten years from now?"

"You think that would make a difference?"

"You don't?"

She'd asked Noah once, "So if we'd stayed together . . ."

"We probably wouldn't have—"

She looked at him in mock indignation. "What happened to 'you never got over me'? What happened to 'I was the love of your life'?"

"Simple." He grinned. "I wasn't the love of yours."

She stopped dead, a few feet away from him. As usual, they had been walking along the beach. "Why do you always do that?"

"Do what?" He reached for her, but she backed up.

"I'm serious. Why did you say that? That you weren't the love of my life?"

"Was I, Grace?"

She gave him a look, and he threw up his hands, still grinning, and said, "Okay then."

"No, not okay then." They started walking again, though she kept her distance. "It was twenty years ago, Noah. *Twenty* years. And I'm here now, aren't I?"

"Yes," he said. "You are. And I'm happy." He held out his hand to her. "Come on. Finish your question." They were trudging up the dunes to the observatory. " 'If we'd stayed together' . . . what?" He stopped and waited for her to complete the phrase. She had been going to ask if he thought they would have had kids together.

When she repeated the question, he responded, "Honestly? I don't know. I love kids, but full-time, twenty-four/seven?"

"You were right, then," she told him. She couldn't remember ever *not* wanting kids, even as a teenager. "We wouldn't have stayed to-gether."

"So whatever happened to your first love?" Grace asked Jenn. "Do I even know who it was?"

"Eileen Cunningham. Long, gorgeous red hair and lots of freckles. We backpacked all over Spain the summer before junior year in col-lege." Jenn smiled wistfully. "I *still* dream about her."

"What happened?"

"Oh, she decided she wasn't gay after all and got married."

"She *decided*?"

Jenn shrugged. "I actually went to the wedding. One of the worst days of my life."

"I can't believe you never told me this."

"Well, I'd already met Diane by the time you and I got close." She signaled the bartender for another drink. "And I'm not convinced that first loves *can* last. Sometimes I think their whole purpose is to give us something to dream about later."

"*That's* depressing."

Jenn glanced at her. "It is? Why?"

"The assumption that the person we end up with can't ever meas-ure up." But it's true, she thought with a sudden pang. Jenn was right.

Jenn tilted her head quizzically. "I never thought of it that way. It always seemed comforting, the idea of that one perfect love still out there somewhere. Didn't you ever imagine what life might have been like with what's-his-name?"

Sometimes I still do, Grace thought. She'd never told Jenn about the affair with Noah, only that she had run into him again. *Run into him.* As if it had been an accident.

"What *was* his name, anyway? Something biblical."

Grace smiled. "Noah." Heat rose to her face.

Jenn narrowed her eyes. "Wait! You saw him again, didn't you?"

Grace started to protest, then stopped. "I never stopped seeing him; I talk to him every day . . . or I did." Her voice broke.

Jenn sat back. "Are you in love with him?"

"Yes. No. I don't know, Jenn. It doesn't matter, though." She took another sip of her Coke, avoiding Jenn's stare, aware suddenly of how this secret, maybe any secret, can make a person disappear. The woman her parents and Stephen and Jenn all thought they knew had been replaced with this other woman who had a whole other life that none of them could fathom. "It's all such a mess," she said finally. "It's so much worse than you could ever imagine."

"I wondered when you said nothing had happened with Noah." Jenn lifted her martini glass in both hands, but paused before taking a sip. Light from the votive candle flickering on the bar between them caught in her dark eyes. "You were so nonchalant about your meeting him, and I kept thinking that I would have been devastated if I saw Eileen Cunningham after all these years and there was nothing there."

"Trust me, you would have been a lot more devastated if there was something there. I mean, think about it. What if you did run into Eileen after all these years and she *was* everything you'd imagined, everything that was lacking in you and Diane? Would you really want that choice?" Grace shook her head. "It would ruin everything."

Jenn looked at her. "Did Stephen find out? Is that it?"

"It's worse, Jenn." She inhaled sharply. "I feel so stupid and foolish and ashamed." She stared down as if to gather the words from a great depth. And then, "I've been accused of Munchausen's," she blurted.

"What?" Jenn's hand flew to her mouth. *"When? Who?"*

"I have no idea. I found out the day after we got back from Hopkins. The accusation was made sometime last February or March, though."

"And you think it's connected to Noah?"

Grace's face crumpled. "I don't know, but doesn't it seem odd that the accusation was made right when I started seeing him?"

"You don't think he was the one, do you?"

"No. And it's not that I didn't question it. I even asked him."

"And you're sure?"

"Absolutely." She pushed her fingers against her upper lip to keep from crying. "I don't think anyone . . ." She paused and glanced away, then continued. "I don't think anyone has ever loved me as much as this man, Jenn. But—" She swallowed hard. "But if I had thought for a second that this . . ." Her throat tightened and she had to look away again, afraid that if she let herself cry, really cry, she wouldn't be able to stop.

Jenn squeezed her hand. "I know." And she did. That being a mother was who Grace was and that no matter what she was doing or who she was with, she was never *not* a mother first. Even now. "So you don't know for sure that the accusation is connected to Noah, right?" she asked now.

"I don't know anything anymore." *Even prosecutors may lose sight of the discrepancy between the seemingly normal mother the defendant appears to be and the monster mother the prosecutor must ask the jury to believe exists.* She told Jenn that she didn't know how to act anymore, what to do with her hands, with her face; she didn't know what was *appropriate* and what wasn't, didn't know if it was good to be *normal* or if *appearing* normal was just one more reason for someone to question who she really was. And she was terrified to take Jack to his doctors: what if it was one of them who had accused her? She'd been panicked last week when she let Erin stay home from school because of a sore throat—would someone accuse Grace of overreacting? She was hyper-aware of the other parents when she picked Erin up—had one of them said something? And she was unsure how to respond when one of the moms asked about Jack. If she said that he'd been having trouble with his breathing or they'd found out a few months ago that a transplant wasn't an option, would she be guilty of using Jack's illness to get sympathy? If she said that they'd had a great holiday, and Jack was hanging in there, he was actually doing pretty well (when he clearly wasn't), would they accuse her of *acting* the role of the devoted mother who *seemed too good to be true,* and who, according to the books, *wasn't so good at all?*

The last few doctor visits she'd drilled Stephen about what to say and ask so that *she* could sit demurely by his side, a sweet, pained little smile on her face. And even when she did speak up, it was pathetic. *I'm sure I'm wrong about this, but . . .* or *I'm not sure I understand what you're saying . . . do you think you could explain what you mean about . . .* as if she didn't have a brain or an opinion or an advanced degree, for God's sake, in a *medical* discipline. As if she didn't know what she was talking about, as if she hadn't read every goddamn article on mitochondrial disease that was out there.

Her life felt like one of those Fabergé eggs, she told Jenn, beautiful on the outside maybe, but fragile, so fragile you didn't want to touch it, didn't want to breathe almost, because the slightest stir of air could cause an irreparable crack. *"The most striking aspect of the mother perpetrator is how normal she appears."*

She told Jenn too of how just yesterday when her mother was forty minutes late returning home after picking up Erin from school, Grace had simply fallen apart, pacing to the window and back, watching for her mother's car, chewing at her thumbnail. *Why wouldn't her mother have called?* She lifted the phone receiver and listened for the dial tone to make sure it was working. When a half-hour had passed, she was convinced that something had happened at school, that Child Protective Services had taken Erin away from her. It could—it *did*—happen every day. In one Munchausen's case, dozens of armed police and a SWAT team arrived to remove a child into protective custody. All it took was a school nurse or a teacher concerned about something a child had written or drawn or said that, out of context, might seem worrisome, and suddenly a social worker was involved, a social worker who, in this case, would see Grace's name in that CPS file, would see those words, *accused but unsubstantiated,* and think of six-year-old Eliza Izquierdo in New York and decide not to take any chances.

When Erin and her mom finally came in, their cheeks rosy, laughing, stamping the snow from their boots on the Oriental rug, bringing Grace a cappuccino from Starbucks, where they'd stopped on the way home for a snack, Grace fell apart. "Do you have any idea how worried I was?" she shouted at her mother after Erin had gone upstairs to change. "I thought something had—that someone—" and then she dissolved, sat on the stairs, head in her hands, the anger evaporating into a thick cloud of gray numbness that seemed to obliterate any possibility of seeing the world clearly. "I'm sorry," she sobbed.

Her mother didn't say anything, just sat next to Grace on the stairs, put her arm around her daughter, and pulled Grace's head onto her shoulder. "Shush," she whispered. "It's okay, honey. You're right. I should have called."

Jenn nodded as Grace talked, eyes wide, her hand over her mouth again as if to stop herself from crying. She looked so bereft that Grace almost wanted to comfort *her*. She thought of how Jenn had probably researched mitochondrial disease as much as Grace had; of how Jenn had done Internet searches, ordered articles from the hospital library that Grace couldn't get, had twice stayed in the hospital with Jack so that Grace could go home and take a bath. And Grace had been there for Jenn too—for the late-night calls when Tyler was a toddler and Blake just an infant and Jenn would be sobbing, saying, "How do I do this, Grace? I don't know anything about boys."

"I need you to write me a letter," Grace said now, "about how you've seen me give Jack morphine and—" She stared down at her Coke, the ice melted, then looked up again. "I can't believe I have to ask this, that we're even *having* this conversation."

"I know," Jenn said softly. "It's surreal almost. I mean, of all people." Idly, she stirred her own drink. "Does Anju know?" Jenn worked in the ER at Children's and so knew most of Jack's doctors.

"She's known," Grace said. "But she never said anything, and when I confronted her, she looked at me like I was nuts to even care because it was so ridiculous."

Jenn shook her head. "And aside from Noah, you have no idea why?"

"There's this profile that supposedly describes a typical Munchausen mom . . ."

"Yeah, I've seen it."

"You have?"

"After the Marie Noe case, we had a mandatory in-service on Munchausen's."

"Well, apparently, I fit the profile."

"How?"

"'Mother is overly friendly to nurses; mother always stays with the child in the hospital; mother has a background in medicine.'" Her voice felt thick.

Jenn simply leaned forward, elbows on the bar, listening as Grace ticked off the reasons. She didn't say anything. Her face was neutral.

"What?" Grace finally said. "You're being quiet."

"I'm just thinking." Jenn turned her martini glass in small circles on the bar. "I mean, let's say someone saw you with Noah. How does that translate into Munchausen's?"

"It's a pattern of deception." Grace's voice broke. "Oh God, Jenn, I could lose my kids." She started to cry. "I'm so fucking scared and Stephen just keeps insisting that there's nothing there, that we're an open book, and we're not or I'm not."

"But Jack has a legitimate diagnosis, Grace. It's not like no one knows what's wrong with him."

Grace blotted a cocktail napkin against her eyes. "You know that doesn't matter." *Presence of actual disease does not rule out the possibility of Munchausen's.*

Jenn shook her head. "There's got to be something else. The profile isn't enough, though I have to admit that it did help us identify a Munchausen mom who kept bringing her kid to the ER last year."

Grace felt her heart drop. She sat back. Let the words sink in. "Wait," she said. "You're *not* telling me that you actually believe this thing?"

"I've seen it, Grace," Jenn said gently.

"You've *seen* a Munchausen's victim?"

"You'd be amazed at what parents are—"

"I know what parents are capable of," Grace interrupted. "But you've seen it? Proven, bonified cases?"

Jenn sighed. "Look, Grace, you know as well as I do that you can't prove it half the time because the minute these mothers realize you're on to them, they drag their kid somewhere else. The percentage of Munchausen mothers who take their kids out of the hospital AMA is huge. Way above normal."

AMA: Against Medical Advice.

Her entire body was tense, almost brittle. "*That's* your proof?" She lowered her voice, trying to hold it steady, trying not to cry. "Has it never occurred to you that maybe the reason for the large number of AMAs is that these mothers have been falsely accused of something absolutely heinous, and they're scared out of their goddamned minds? I'd do the same damn thing. In fact, I don't want Jack anywhere near that hospital."

"But that's crazy. You haven't done anything."

"And what if someone doesn't believe that?" Her eyes filled. "I don't understand how you could buy into this."

"And I don't understand how you *can't*."

Neither of them said anything, the clatter of voices and silverware and dishes from the lounge area behind them suddenly growing louder. Grace stared at her left hand lying inert on the bar next to her drink. Her fingers no longer seemed connected to her, but to some other woman who had come in here tonight to talk with her best friend. She stared at the bar, at the shine of the wood, at the way the light hit Jenn's martini glass. "I wish I hadn't told you," she said quietly.

"Don't say that," Jenn pleaded. "I hate that this has happened to you, Grace. You are the last person who deserves this."

Grace looked at her bleakly. "Sometimes I think I'm getting exactly what I deserve." She looked at Jenn. "We should get the check."

"No, don't," Jenn said. "This is ridiculous. We hardly ever see each other, and I want to help. I'll go to the doctor with you or babysit or—or—I'm going to write you that letter and the kids are safe right now, aren't they?"

Grace nodded without looking up. She imagined those birds that take off from water—grebes, maybe, and loons—of how sometimes at night after a storm they would mistake the reflection of water on asphalt for a lake and become stranded when they landed and found that there was nothing soft or buoyant from which to lift themselves off again. It was how her own life felt lately: a shallow reflection of everything she had believed it to be.

"Besides," Jenn continued, "who knows, maybe in some weird way, the accusation could be sort of good, you know?"

Grace felt the room tilt, bottles sliding into one another, the buildings in the mural over the bar toppling on their sides. *"Good?"* she echoed. Her sweater felt too tight against her throat. She couldn't breathe. *"Good?"*

"No, I mean, not the accusation," Jenn rushed. "Just, maybe it's good if you're kind of forced to not focus so much on the medical stuff, you know?" She squeezed Grace's wrist. "You've done so much and the truth is there's probably not a lot left—" Her face crumpled. "This doesn't sound right."

"I need to go," Grace said. "I'm not mad, I'm just—" Tears spilled from her eyes, and she kept dabbing them with a napkin, but it didn't help. "I just—I know I'm defensive, but I can't do this right now." She didn't know what else to say. *Good?* The night felt broken, a pane of dark glass suddenly cracked across the center. She thought of how in the seventeenth century, one of the common symptoms of depression was something called the "glass delusion," whereby depressed people literally came to believe that they were made of glass, that to sit on a hard surface might shatter them, that to embrace another person would be dangerous.

"Look," Jenn said. "I'm not saying things right, but you know I would do anything for you—"

"Remember Dr. Stemple's class?" Grace interrupted. It was where she'd learned of the "glass delusion." Mythology and Medicine. Mondays and Wednesdays, 5:30 to 6:45.

"Stemple's Temple of the Mind." Jenn nodded. "I loved that class."

"What about all those diseases we studied that were supposedly so prevalent once—that nerve disorder found in slaves, remember?"

"Drapetomania." Jenn smiled. "The single symptom was the desire to escape slavery." She squinted at Grace. "Is that what you think Munchausen's is?"

"I don't know." And sometimes she truly didn't. "I know there are some awful people out there and I know that kids get abused all the time. But I think of all those mythological illnesses—hysteria and neurasthenia and masturbation—remember that? And God, homosexuality, Jenn." She glanced at her friend. "Every one of those diseases is about making certain types of people submissive or trying to shut them up or making them go away, and I know, *I know* it's far-fetched, but isn't it possible that Munchausen's is similar, a way to get rid of demanding mothers who really are intelligent and maybe *do* know something about medicine and, therefore, aren't afraid to ask questions or complain or find another doctor if they aren't happy?"

"Of course, it's possible," Jenn conceded. "But can I ask you something?"

Grace smiled sadly. "You will anyway."

"Why does it matter so much whether I believe Munchausen by Proxy exists if I know without a doubt—and I do—that you aren't guilty?"

"But how do you know without a doubt? I fit the profile."

"But I know *you*. I know what kind of a mother you are. I know that if you could trade your life for Jack's you would."

Grace shook her head. "Women like me are master manipulators, remember?" *Her theatrical skills are worthy of an Oscar. Her tall-tales rival those told by the Baron Munchausen himself.* "How do you know I haven't deceived you too? Look at how long I lied to you about Noah." His name a sharpness in her chest.

"I know you," Jenn's insisted. "Why can't that be enough?"

"Because if someone like you who is smart and knows medicine and knows all the bullshit things people have believed in the name of medicine can believe this whole Munchausen's thing, then anyone can. It terrifies me. Stephen gets mad when I compare this to the Salem witch trials, because it sounds hysterical, and he's right, it does, but it's not that different. Maybe those trials started with a bunch of hysterical girls, but they never would have continued if intelligent, respected people like you, people that everyone else trusted, hadn't believed those girls. And what were they saying? Exactly what they are now, that normal good women were purposely making children sick."

• • •

She drove home without the radio on and with the windows down despite the freezing temperatures. She needed the cold, needed it to somehow brace her against the fluidlike sensation that she was dissolving. It was a beautiful dark night, the city gold and black beneath the bright moon. Christmas lights were still strung along the span of the Ben Franklin, the bridge struts pulsed rhythmically beneath the wheels of her car.

"What's wrong?" Stephen asked when she walked into the bedroom, her coat still on. She was shivering with cold, her mouth and fingers numb. "What happened?" He immediately set his laptop on the night table and got out of bed, but she waved him away.

"No—don't. I—don't touch me." Her words were like individual cubes of ice.

His face blanched. "Jesus, Grace, what the hell happened?"

Her voice was flat. "I told her," she said. "She thinks maybe it's *good* that I was accused." *Good.* This was not a word that would ever freeze, she knew; this was not a word that would eventually melt away into nothing. This word was like barbed wire, impossible to climb over, go around, escape. "My best friend," she said, dropping her coat on the bed. She sat stiffly, then, and began tugging at her boots. Her hair fell in front of her face, and her nose was running. Stephen sat next to her, and gently put a hand on her arm, but she jumped up, one boot off, the other still on, nearly tripping over the end of her coat. "Don't touch me," she said icily. "I mean it."

"Honey, please. I don't know what happened, but Jenn would do anything for you." But it was like an avalanche breaking away from the face of whatever was solid in her life. She whirled to face him. "Don't you get it, Stephen? It *doesn't* matter! It doesn't help. Nothing does because our kids can still be taken, and there's nothing I can do to fix it or make it better and nothing our lawyer can do, which means that we just have to live like this, afraid of everything, and my best friend thinks maybe this is *good*?"

"Grace, would you just stop for a minute?"

"Why? So I'll calm down? I don't want to calm down!" She was crying now and she wanted to hit him, hurt him, though she wasn't sure why. "I feel like I was *raped*, like everything— No! Don't touch me or I swear to God I'll scream—*everything* good about me has been taken. I'm afraid to make a joke, I'm afraid to be friendly, I'm afraid to go into a doctor's office with my child—*my child*, Stephen, and—and—" She sank onto the bed, head in her hands, shoulders heaving. "I don't even know who did this or why," she sobbed. How could she explain? Her entire life felt expunged. *She* felt expunged. Unsubstantiated. "I don't even know who I am," she cried.

"Oh, Grace," Stephen said. "I had no idea."

She looked at him incredulously. "My *name* is in that file," she cried. "*My. Name.* It will always be in that file."

SEVENTEEN

S he felt as if she had some sort of virus or infection that January. All she wanted to do was sleep, though she never could. She shuffled bleary-eyed through the mornings, feeling almost drugged. Standing in the shower exhausted her. Getting dressed. Making a phone call, trying to summon the energy to talk. She'd lie on the couch watching *Blue's Clues* with Jack, the two of them snuggled under a blanket she'd dragged down from her unmade bed. She hadn't heard from Noah, except for one e-mail: "Are you okay?"

"No," she wrote back. She wanted to tell him that she missed him, that she loved him, but she was afraid of this too. She'd read on the Mothers Against Munchausen's Accusation Web site of a woman who had had her computer confiscated, her history of searching out medical sites used against her in court.

When Noah responded with "Can I see you?" she wrote "No" again, though she sat at the computer for over an hour, fingers hovering just above the keyboard, wanting to say so much more, wanting to soften the *no* into *not yet* or *not now* or *this is a busy time* or something to diminish the starkness of that no, which, when isolated in the white space of the computer screen, seemed so much darker and bigger than it really was.

The worst days that January were the sunny ones, rectangles of yellow light falling in geometric patterns across the walls and carpets and floors. Lying in bed while Jack took his nap, she'd stare numbly at the wash of sunlight on the white ceiling, and she would feel almost accosted by the brightness, the beauty. It made her feel worse.

She could only take in things slowly. The smallest choices—what to wear, what to make for dinner—suddenly seemed overwhelming. She found herself misreading words: the *insulated* cardboard sleeve on her Starbucks coffee she read as *insulted*. Instead of *sacred* statues on an advertisement for an exhibit at the museum, she saw *scared* statues. In a magazine profile of some British celebrity that she read while waiting for Erin at the dentist's—the phrase "she stepped from the *lift*" translated into "she stepped from the *life*," which was, of course, how Grace felt, as if she had stepped from her own life into emptiness, into air, with nothing to hold her up, nothing to keep her from falling.

She did better on the cold, gray days when trees lacerated the drenched sky, and the wind was howling and furious. It was how she felt. She mentioned this in passing on the phone to Kempley, who teased, "Ahh, the weather of witches—fair is foul and foul is fair. I'm surprised *that's* not in the profile."

"It probably is," Grace laughed. The sound of her own merriment took her by surprise. "Warning number thirteen: Mother-perpetrator takes strange delight in inclement weather."

"Mother-perpetrator owns numerous raincoats," Kempley added.

They were both laughing now. "Mother-perpetrator refuses to leave umbrella alone."

"Mother-perpetrator appears overly focused on weather channel!"

"Oh God, mother-perpetrator secretly lusts after—" Grace couldn't finish. "She secretly lusts after the—"

"—weatherman!" Kempley hooted. And then, "Oh sweetie, it's so good to hear you laughing again."

After she hung up, though, Grace sat on the sofa for a long time, the phone in her lap. *Mother displays inappropriate sense of humor.* The sunlight falling through the sliding glass door held no warmth. The world felt sharp, full of angles: the silver blades of leaves and spears of ice, the serrated edges of the trees. Everything, even laughter, felt dangerous now.

Only when she was with her kids did the murmur of fear just beneath the surface of her life grow quiet. Ordinary moments like perfect seashells, containing the sound of the ocean inside, evidence of the world as it once was: rubbing cherry Vaseline on Jack's perpetually chapped lips, teaching him his ABCs or singing nursery rhymes with him. Sitting at the kitchen table before school, a sleepy Erin standing before her as Grace tried to coax his flyaway hair into a ponytail or barrettes or a god-awful Barbie hairband that, despite Grace's best efforts, made Erin's ears stick straight out. Later, Grace and Jack would wait in the car in front of St. Joan's, competing to see who would spot Erin first. "I see her, I see her!" Jack would yell, and there she was, dashing across the front lawn, disheveled and happy, a clump of papers and art projects in one hand, book bag in the other. Or reheating Max's dinner after an away game and sitting with him while he ate, listening to him talk. "Oh, man, Brian iced this guy so bad. . . . You should have seen this goalie from Pemberton. . . . Coach Harper thinks I should try out for the A league."

Grace stood in the hallway adjacent to Noah's kitchen and pried the *Selected Journals and Other Writings* by John James Audubon from the bookshelf. "Is this any good?" She was wearing his robe; they were making breakfast despite the fact that it was already one in the afternoon. She'd hurried down after dropping Erin off at school. Jack was with her mom. She needed to be home in time for his nap

Noah looked up from the sizzle of scrapple in the frying pan to the book she was holding. "Jesus, don't read that unless you want a cure for insomnia."

"I thought you loved Audubon."

"Not that much, I don't."

She slid the book back into the shelf. "Okay, then, what should I read? Recommend something. I want to understand what you do."

He had been right about the journals, she thought now, her eyes heavy as she glanced up from the yellowed page.

Thursday, Dec. 28, 1820: Saw some mockingbirds and was assured that they remained during the winter here . . .

Monday, January 29 1821: Drawing all day the brown pelican, collecting my earnings, purchased a crate of Queensware for my Beloved wife.

It was already after two a.m., and she was bleary-eyed with exhaustion. Which was why, on a whim, she had borrowed the *Selected Journals and Other Writings* from the library. A cure for insomnia.

The pages smelled of cigarette smoke from whoever had borrowed the book before her. Someone else desperate for sleep, maybe? She read, sitting in bed, the book propped against her knees. Stephen lay asleep beside her, a pillow over his face because of the light. Sometimes she took the book with her into the bathtub, hoping the heat of the hot water would help her to sleep. The pages swelled with moisture. She tried to picture Audubon, thirty-five years old, leaving his wife and sons for months at a time in his efforts to study and sketch every known and unknown species of bird in North America. Mostly, she thought of Noah, walking the trails at Higbie's Beach before the sun had fully risen, binoculars around his neck, searching for a species he might never find. His breath white in the frigid air. The sun a faint heartbeat beneath the smudged ribs of sky.

None of it worked. No matter how drowsy she became, no matter how many times she dozed off only to be woken by the sudden weight of the book on her chest, as soon as she turned off the light, she was wide awake again, her thoughts swooping through her mind like dark birds. *Why had she been accused?* And, *What if it happened again?* And always, always, *Who?*

She stopped e-mailing the women in the mitochondrial support group, afraid to seem "overly focused" on Jack's disease. *Child's illness becomes mother-perpetrator's claim to fame.* But she also didn't have the heart, the energy. To continue researching new procedures or protocols, to continue fighting for Jack, was to maybe only put him further at risk: *mother-perpetrator is extremely willing to put child through endless tests, procedures, and protocols.* She heard from Kempley that Anne Marie and Bryn were still waiting for a heart at Hopkins; Lydia's son had died; Marta was pregnant again even though both of her boys already had mitochondrial disease. "You have to wonder about someone like that," Kempley commented. "How anyone can choose to bring a child into the world, knowing it's got a twenty-five percent chance of having a potentially fatal illness. I mean, you want to talk about abuse."

Grace didn't respond. It was unfathomable to imagine never having had Jack in her life, mitochondrial disease or not.

"Even Mr. Godfrey never heard of it," Max said between mouthfuls of pasta. He was talking about mitochondrial disease. His science class had just begun studying the structure of the cells. "I'm doing a report on it."

Grace felt her smile turn rubbery. "Was that your idea?"

Max nodded without looking up from his plate. He was hunched low, chin to the table's edge, shoveling his food right into his mouth rather than actually taking the time to lift the fork.

"Sit up and take a breath, would you, Max?" Stephen said. "Your mother asked you a question."

Max rolled his eyes and set down his fork. "Well, *duh*," he said, "since I just told you that Mr. Godfrey didn't have a clue, it had to be my idea."

"I'd like to read the report before you turn it in, if that's okay," Grace interrupted.

Stephen glanced at her, eyebrows raised.

"What?" Grace snapped.

"Nothing," Stephen sighed.

"No, not nothing." She pushed her plate away and sat back, "Why do you not get this, Stephen? I don't want just anyone having access—"

"Nobody even cares," Max said.

"*I* care." She glared at Stephen. "And I am so sick of you not taking this seriously." She stood and carried her dishes to the sink, then headed upstairs.

"Why you going, Mama?" Jack called after her.

Grace was already halfway up the stairs. "I'm taking a bath," she called.

"Oh, for crying out loud," Stephen said.

"Jeez, what's wrong with her?" she heard Max ask.

• • •

Sunday, February 25, 1821: Killed some green-backed white-bellied swallows,
Hirondo veridis—*extremely fat, the gizzards completely filled with the re-*
mains of winged insects—could not perceive any outward difference between the
sexes.

She glanced up from the book, exhausted. Four a.m.

Grace eyed the clock over the aquarium, then resolutely returned to
the magazine she was paging through. Jack sat on Stephen's lap on a
yellow beanbag chair staring at the *Teletubbies* on TV, his mouth open
as he breathed heavily, his astronaut backpack with the oxygen canister on the floor next to him. Anju was already thirty minutes late. In
the back of Grace's mind, a tiny spasm of fear.

She stared at the glossy pages of the magazine. *Self.* She'd had to
force herself to read this instead of the *American Journal of Cardiology*
that sat on the coffee table. *Mother-perpetrator overly focused on*
medical/technical aspects of child's disease.

"Pamper yourself!" she read now in elegant red script.

"Scatter evergreens across your table for a festive postholiday
centerpiece."

"Pull on your coziest sweater and sip hot cider in front of a fire."

"Make oatmeal brûlée: sprinkle sugar over oatmeal and broil until
brown!"

She looked up, her face warm, anger seeping into her throat. Is *this*
what she was supposed to do? Go shopping? Create centerpieces?
This was how she was supposed to act, what she was supposed to care
about? "Buy a killer pair of calf-length boots . . ."

Defeated, she turned the page.

An ad for antidepressants. *If you have experienced any of the following*
symptoms for a period longer than two weeks. . . She wearily scanned the
list: excessive sleep during normal waking hours, insomnia at night,
sudden weight gain or weight loss, lethargy, irritability, tears. "Talk to
your doctor," the ad said. "You don't have to suffer alone."

She closed the magazine and set it back onto the glass table next to her chair. She knew that she had all the classic signs of depression, but she was afraid to talk about it, afraid to get the prescription for Zoloft refilled. *Mother has history of depression.*

I can't win, she thought. But she didn't want to anymore. She just wanted the accusation to go away, the file to be closed. Which meant that she would continue to be demure and grateful at Jack's doctor appointments, and she'd let Stephen ask the questions, and if she read the medical journals, she'd do it secretly the way in sixth grade all the girls passed around Erica Jong's *Fear of Flying* tucked inside a textbook so they wouldn't be caught reading the sex scenes. She'd learn to speak like a regular mother, saying "he's been moody" instead of "he's had increased lability," and "his coordination is off" instead of "he's hypotaxic." She'd been a fool. Saying the wrong lines, upstaging the leads. Silly mother. Didn't she realize she had only a bit part in this play? The doctors were the heroes, not her! Or was it her delivery? Was that the problem? Fine. She'd halt, stumble, carry Kleenex with her everywhere. She'd wear mascara that wasn't waterproof so that everyone *knew* she cried. And she'd smile and be courageously upbeat and talk about how Jack was her special angel sent by God, and she'd wear pastel-colored sweats and let her hair go gray—was that it? She didn't have the right costume? How dare she color her hair when her child is dying? Or laugh! Joke! Shame on her! How dare she?

PART III

Betrayal

Betrayals, even your own, can take you by surprise. You find yourself capable of things.

—Lorrie Moore, *Anagrams*

EIGHTEEN

The nineteenth-century physician William Osler once observed that "every age gets the disease it deserves." He was right. Think of the diseases marking the start of the twenty-first century: Alzheimer's, heart failure, depression, mitochondrial myopathies. Are these diseases fitting because in a world that we have betrayed so thoroughly, all that remains to betray is ourselves? There was a time, after all, when the worst diseases came from elsewhere: polluted water or air, virus-carrying mosquitoes. Now, however, some of the worst damage comes from within. We are—literally—our own worst enemies.

At the beginning of this century, more than five million Americans had Alzheimer's. Each year 370,000 new cases are diagnosed. It is not memories that are lost, however, but the synapses between those memories. Synapse meaning "to clasp" or "hold tight." Scientists now tell us that each time we remember something specific—the man we once loved, the song we once danced to, the color of his shirt that first night, the color of the sky—the synapse "clasping" that memory grows stronger. Like a path through the woods that becomes more defined each time we walk it.

If this is true, though, what then does it mean to forget?

And heart failure. Every twenty seconds someone in the United States suffers a heart attack, and with each, the heart grows larger, emptier. Like the homes we now live in with their cathedral ceilings and cavernous rooms, all that space and absence, as if to compensate for our families having grown smaller, the bonds between us frayed with distance. Not too little oxygen, then, which results in these failures of the heart but, perhaps, too little love.

And maybe this is why depression is currently the fourth leading cause of disability worldwide, according to the World Health Organization; maybe this is why depression is the leading cause of disability in the United States, where

10 percent of the adult population takes antidepressants. How easily we forget that depression, with its symptoms of silence and withdrawal, is not merely chemical, but also a means of saving our energy when we have very little, of protecting ourselves when we are most fragile. Something has broken in us that medicine alone cannot cure.

We have grown so estranged from ourselves, however, that even our illnesses deceive us. Two-thirds of all heart attacks are silent, the person never suspecting that a part of him has died. Alzheimer's begins years before there are obvious symptoms. "A disease of insidious onset," doctors call it, meaning that it has no definitive starting point. And mitochondrial disease. Perhaps no other disease betrays us as well or as thoroughly as this.

"That notorious masquerader," one expert called it, for mitochondrial disease throws on the mask of any number of illnesses. First it manifests itself as liver failure, then heart disease, next asthma or arthritis, but it is none of those and so will not yield to diagnosis attempts, to the usual cures. And just when—if—it does reveal itself, the disease shape-shifts yet again: now blindness; now bone marrow disease. And this is not all. Cells with normal mitochondria lie next to those with dysfunctional mitochondrial. Patients with identical mutations have completely different symptoms. In some, the disease progresses slowly; in some, it remains stable for years. There is no understanding why. No cure.

Mitochondria. Upon discovery in the years between 1850 and 1890, these minuscule foreign organelles were alternately called by a plethora of names. Blepharoblasts, Interstitial bodies, Speroblasts. Imagine rockets hurtled into space and landing in otherworldly geographies, galactic and dark.

"Every Betrayal is a kind of flight," writes Aldo Carotenuto in To Love, To Betray.

So, of course, is every disease.

NINETEEN

$\mathcal{G}$race stood in the lobby of Children's, clutching her coat over her arm. She stared at the row of numbers atop the elevators as if her concentration alone would hurry them. The numbers lit up in descending order as the elevators returned to the lobby. *He's going to code if we don't—* She closed her eyes against the words of the ER doctor. An intern, a resident, had he even known what he was doing? She switched her coat to the other arm. What was taking so long with the elevators? They were glass on two sides so that you could peer out at the brightly lit lobby with its huge mobiles and interactive displays: colorful discs connected by huge pulleys and levers and slides—a model of the digestive system—or a light display that replicated the firing of neurons in the brain. There were funny mirrors and a McDonald's, and parents and kids would survey it all from the elevators as a means of distraction from whatever horror had brought them here. Grace used to do the same thing with Jack: *"Wow, Goose, look how high we are!"*

"Just like Mr. Moon, Mama!"

She didn't hear Anju say her name until the doctor touched her shoulder. She jumped, then immediately began backing away.

"No, no, he's okay," Anju said. "They're transferring him up right now." Up. The CICU on the sixth floor. Cardiac Intensive Care Unit.

Grace nodded, then fastened her stare back on the lighted numbers. Both elevators were stopped at the third floor, which housed the ECHO and Cath labs and cardiac intake units. The third floor was where she and Jack had spent most of their time this past year. He'd only been on the sixth floor once before. It had been horrible.

"Grace." Anju's voice was gentle. "I think we should talk."

Grace didn't turn. "Not if it's about the DNR." Do Not Resuscitate.

The phrase was like the white cue ball in a game of pool, slamming everything else into its dark pockets.

"These episodes will get worse, Grace, and they'll become more frightening for Jack, as well."

Episodes. Ventricular fibrillation.

The elevator chimed as the doors opened. Grace stepped inside. "He was in the grocery store with me, just this morning, laughing—" *Laughing*. The word registered, like a flash of light on water, before it spun out of reach. She pushed from her mind the image of the tube in Jack's throat, his chest heaving up and down from the pressure of the ventilator, *He's going to code if we—* "He was sitting in the cart and I was pretending to crash it into things and— Oh, God, Anju, I can't—" She stopped. This can't be it, she wanted to say. I'm not ready, I thought there would be more time, that we would know it was getting close, that he'd be sicker or at least not *laughing* in the grocery store one minute and in the next—"DNR is not an option," she said as the doors closed on Anju.

Grace sat in the rocking chair by the sixth-floor window overlooking the hospital parking lot. Jack lay against her chest, the trail of tubes and wires and IVs falling over her knees, like the threads of an unraveled quilt. Saline and electrolytes dripped through the IV in his wrist. He'd been asleep since the night before, drugged on morphine. But he was out of the CICU, off the ventilator, and his heart no longer felt as if it would gallop from his chest. She caressed his swollen, almost translucent cheek with the knuckle of her index finger. His eyelashes flickered, tiny shadows across his otherwise still features.

"Hey, I heard you guys were here," Rebecca said, rapping lightly on the door frame. "How is he?"

Rebecca was Jack's favorite nurse. She was beautiful: white-blond hair pulled into a ponytail, Nordic blue eyes, a ballerina's perfect posture. She worked the late shift because her husband, a jazz pianist, usually had a gig during these hours. Grace had seen him a few times when he stopped by the hospital on his way home. A tall man with dark circles under his eyes, his clothes smelling faintly of smoke from whatever bar he'd been playing in. "You're Jack's mom, right?" he said to her one night as they stood in the communal kitchen, Grace boiling water for tea, Colin heating up a container of take-out Chinese food. "Becca talks about you guys all the time. She really admires you."

Now Rebecca walked quietly into the room and leaned over Jack, taking one of his inert pudgy hands in hers. "Hey, buddy," she whispered, caressing the top of his wrist with her thumb. She smelled faintly of cloves. "He's really swollen," she said, glancing at his oxygen saturation numbers.

"And this is ten times better than he was."

Rebecca shook her head. "I'm so sorry," she said, her brows furrowed with concern. "How are *you* doing?"

Grace shrugged dismissively and glanced at Jack. If she said she was fine would Rebecca think she was *thriving* on the drama? She couldn't even look at Rebecca, feeling betrayed all over again. *Mother refers to hospital as home away from home.* Tears burned her eyes. Why did you talk to that social worker about me? she wanted to ask.

The sun fell in the window behind them, the orange light reflecting in the plastic bag of fluids that hung from his IV.

After Rebecca left, Grace rocked slowly, holding Jack and simply watching him, her heart heavy with the immensity of the love she felt for this child. She leaned her head against the chair, eyes closed, and prayed. She couldn't imagine her life without him, couldn't bear to think that she would have to. How did a parent ever survive? She glanced at him again, not wanting to waste a single moment, memorizing him. His damp curly hair, the long daggers of his eyelashes, his pale chapped lips. Without the bright overhead lights, the room was steeped in gray. His tiny heartbeat was visible through the yellow Big Bird hospital gown that made him look jaundiced and sicklier than he was.

"Sometimes when Jack was a little tiny baby," she whispered now into his ear, "his Mama would rock him and rock him and then rock him some more, until finally her arms got tired, and she would give

Jack to Daddy." This used to be his favorite story, the one where everybody took turns rocking him. A chain of arms. "And then Daddy would rock Jack in his arms and rock him and rock him some more until *his* arms got tired and he would give Jack to Max." The chair creaked. "And Max would rock Jack and rock him. . . ." On and on: Erin would rock him, and all four of his grandparents, and his Uncle Jeff, and Dr. Mehta and Rebecca and Aunt Jenn and then they'd start all over.

Now Jack lay still, eyes closed, though his ragged breathing sounded steadier. In graduate school she'd read Holt's *The Care and Feeding of Children,* one of the primary books on raising children in the late nineteenth century, responsible in large part for the replacing of cradles with cribs. Holt had asserted that rocking a child was a "vicious practice," encouraging a child's "unhealthy dependence on unnecessary stimulation."

"He was a silly, silly, man, wasn't he?" Grace whispered to Jack. He didn't stir. Her arm had fallen asleep. Her thoughts wandered to the accusation. Stephen would be here soon to spend the night. *Mother-perpetrator refuses to leave child alone in hospital.* Her heart sank at the thought. She had never left Jack for an entire night before, and it felt wrong, no matter what the reason, no matter that Stephen would be here instead. All those studies on animals who, when separated from their mothers and given surrogates—one made of wire that offered a bottle of milk, another made of soft padding that didn't offer the bottle—always chose the soft one, touch more vital to survival than food. Or those experiments on infant mice. Deprived of their mother's touch for a single day, their brain cells died at twice the rate of their steadily mothered counterparts. She stared at the bright yellow balloon one of the nurses had tied to the foot of Jack's bed. Even well into the twentieth century, the death rate for infants in foundling institutions in the U.S. was nearly 100 percent, *not* because of lack of medicine or nourishment, but because no one held them. Something that simple. And yet, *Mother refuses to leave child alone in hospital* was one of the warning signs of Munchausen's.

Of course mother refuses, Grace thought sadly, swallowing hard.

TWENTY

The phone woke her before dawn. She had been dreaming of Noah and everything she had felt in the fluid landscape of that dream—joy, mostly, but also something quieter, contentment maybe? peace?—rose with her out of sleep.

In her dream, there had been a flood. She was lying against the prow of a canoe. Noah was wading waist-deep in the water behind her, guiding the narrow boat through the rivered streets of an unfamiliar neighborhood. There was no danger, nobody hurt. He leaned forward, kissing her. Bright sunlight cast diamond patterns on the water.

The phone wouldn't stop ringing.

In the split second between waking and remembering that Jack was in the hospital, disappointment that it was no more than a dream surged through Grace. But a second later—no longer, she promised herself, a half a second maybe—she remembered and grabbed the receiver. Her bedroom was dark. It was too early for a phone call. "What?" she said breathlessly.

No answer. But in the background, Jack: "Why Mama not home, Daddy?"

She sat up immediately. "Jack!" she called. "Jack!"

And then he was on the phone, his tiny little voice. "You home, Mama?" And to Stephen: "She *is* home, Daddy!"

Grace laughed, tears filling her eyes. He was okay. Thank God. "What are you *doing*, Goose?" He was okay, he was okay, he was okay. "Are you all better?"

"I think so." His voice grew muffled. "Daddy, I all better?"

"Tell your mama you've been chattering nonstop since five."

She collapsed against the pile of pillows, grinning. "Are you being a chatty Cathy?" She swiped the tears from her eyes. He was okay.

He laughed. "I waked Daddy up!" And then, "Why *you* aren't here?"

"Because Daddy's with you."

"Why Daddy with me?"

"Good question, Goose. You want me to come and see you?"

He was okay, he was okay, he was okay.

She sat on the edge of Erin's bed, rubbing her back in slow circles. "Guess who just called us?" she whispered.

Erin opened her eyes. "Jack?"

Grace nodded. "He's better. You want Grandma to bring you to see him after school?"

"When can he come home?"

"Soon." Grace kissed Erin's nose, resting her forehead against her daughter's. "Umm," she smiled. "Someone smells like cinnamon toast." Her mother had given Erin a set of bubble baths for Christmas: root beer float, apple pie, butterscotch sundae, cinnamon toast. "You ready to get up now, Lovey? If you hurry, we could stop at Starbucks on the way to school." Coffee for Grace, hot chocolate for Erin. A celebration.

He was okay.

Stephen, shaved and dressed for work, was dozing in the rocking chair when Grace entered Jack's room. Jack was sitting up, still on oxygen, but noticeably less swollen. *Sesame Street* blared from the overhead TV. "What are you doing, silly boy?" Grace whispered in his ear, hugging him close to her as she reached for the remote and lowered the volume before moving around the hospital bed to Stephen. He startled as soon as she touched his shoulder. Grace handed him the latte she'd picked up for him. "You might need to nuke that," she apologized. He looked exhausted, his eyes bloodshot, a cut over his lip where he'd nicked himself shaving. "Did you sleep at all?"

He shook his head no, yawning.

"When did he wake up?"

"Around five." Stephen smiled wearily at Jack. "I heard this little bird chirping, 'Daddy, Daddy, Daddy.' "

"That wasn't a birdie, Daddy! That was me!" He started to laugh, but began coughing. "I waked Daddy up, Mama!" he choked.

She thumped him on the back. "I know you did, silly." She turned to Stephen. "Has Anju been in yet? She's not going to believe how good he looks."

"Not yet."

"Has anyone?"

He cocked an eyebrow. "Are you kidding? You mean besides the nurses, the blood lady, the chaplain, let's see, the dietician, Jenn—"

"Jenn's here? Is she working?"

"She left. But she's back on tonight. She said she'll stop by." He sipped the coffee. "Listen, I've got to run." He stood. "You'll call me?"

The kiss from her dream and the sensation of floating stayed with her all day. As did the shard of sadness she had felt upon wakening and realizing none of it was true. Noah was gone. She hadn't spoken to him in nearly a month, though she thought of him often, saw reminders everywhere: an article in the paper about a group of scientists searching the swamps in Louisiana for a bird thought to have become extinct half a century earlier. A schoolmate of Erin's with bright red hair. A man in line at Starbucks arranging airline tickets on his cell phone. He kept saying "flight," the word gusting through her, soft-winged against the sky of memories. *Your name is my flight song. What is trust but a long-distance flight over water?* And yet, more and more, Noah's absence was beginning to feel permanent. Is this what the dream was about, some part of her refusing to let go? But what did absence really mean? He'd been absent from her life for twenty years. She thought of how the body's cells are almost 90 percent empty space—90 percent absence; still, they comprised two-thirds of the body's weight.

Jack slept, propped at a thirty-degree angle to keep the fluid from accumulating in his lungs. One arm was curled around a battered rocket ship. His eyes moved beneath his lids and she thought of Noah telling her that only fledgling birds dream, silently rehearsing in their sleep the songs they need to survive. She thought of how people typically assume that dreams result from what they've done or thought about on any given day, the unconscious piecing together random bits of memory and information. But maybe we dream our lives first, Grace thought, and then we live them. Infants dream more than adults, after all; premature babies dream more than those born full-term. Fetuses dream constantly.

She thought too of how dreams increase a person's heart rate, and of how in the midst of dreams, good *and* bad, some hearts simply stop beating, and it occurred to her that maybe the heart, and not the mind, was the place from where most dreams truly began. She eyed the phone on the table next to Jack's bed, desperate suddenly to phone Noah, to tell him that she loved him still. The urge felt automatic, almost instinctual—the way you reach out to grab hold of something when you are falling. What if something had happened to him? What if he was hurt, and the dream was his way of telling her?

Do you remember Bell's Theorem?

She let herself think of him. She hadn't in so long. Like being on a diet, and finally giving in and eating everything rich and decadent that you'd been denied. I miss you, she thought, and wondered if he knew.

Grace retrieved Kempley's second book, *A New England Sorrow,* from her overnight bag and opened it to where she had left off three days ago. It felt like three weeks. She and Jack had gone grocery shopping; they were laughing; she kept pretending the cart—with him in it—was getting away from her. Back home, she started dinner while listening to NPR on the radio, Jack and Erin playing in the family room. And then Erin was screaming, "Something's wrong with Jack, Mama!" Erin was on her knees, rubbing his cheek, his skin ashen,

hands already clammy, heart seemingly thrashing around in his chest.
"I didn't mean anything," Erin sobbed. "We were just playing cars."

"Move, Erin, just move!" Grace yelled. "Get Max, call 911."

Even now, her heart raced, remembering.

She read a few paragraphs of Kempley's book. *Nothing is more psy-
chically devastating than losing a child. Nothing renders us more desperate and
determined to locate in a suddenly meaningless world some illusion of order.
How, then—and why—in even the most thorough accounts of the Salem
Witch Trials is there no mention of this unbearable grief? That of Cotton
Mather's fifteen children, only two survived him . . .*

Grace held the book in her lap and looked at Jack. To have your
child die was to have the future fall away. Which was what Noah was
really about, she knew: her own desperation to grab onto a time
when there existed so many different lives she might have chosen instead of the one she had. If she had picked a different college, not
gone to the party where she met Stephen, returned even one of
Noah's phone calls, Jack would not be dying. Something so simple
and she might have been a completely different person with a whole
other history: Someone whose child didn't have mitochondrial disease.

*It was the specters of their own unlived lives, the choices unmade, over which
the townspeople of Salem were so desperate to control.*

Grace closed her eyes and leaned back against the rocking chair.
She was in the canoe again. Sunlight. The afternoons in bed with
Noah had carried the same sensation of floating, of moving in slow
motion through liquid, the two of them drenched with sweat afterwards, as exhausted as swimmers. She couldn't shake the notion,
though, that the dream—the whole affair?—wasn't about Noah so
much as it was about a longing for her life to be different. The realization fell over her like a dark cloth. She had simply assumed that
Noah came into her life as a counterbalance to all she was about to
lose, that he was *her* reward for enduring what no mother should ever
have to. But what if the whole affair, *her* insistence that she'd never
stopped loving Noah, wasn't about Noah at all but about her own
desperate attempt to save what couldn't possibly survive?

She sat up abruptly, feeling a tightness in the back of her neck, as if she'd been reading in dim light. No, she thought, it wasn't that simple. She loved Noah. Why else had she been so sad upon waking this morning? Why else was she constantly thinking of him? She loved him. She glanced again at Kempley's book, the black-and-white photo of a New England meetinghouse on the cover, and felt her heart sink. Kempley was right: belief in religion or witches or aliens, even in the perfect love—they were all about the same illusion, weren't they? The possibility of a life beyond the one you were living.

Grace looked up from reading *Happy Birthday, Moon* to Jack and smiled at Dr. Mehta. "Can you believe our little miracle man?"

Anju entered the room, high heels clicking on the tile floor. She stopped when she saw Jack. "You are good as new!" She held out her hand for him to shake, then pretended to wince as he squeezed her fingers. Grace watched her face for the worry lines that appeared between her brows whenever she wasn't pleased. The handshake was part of her assessment of Jack, Grace knew. She was noting the color and temperature of his fingers and nail beds, gauging his strength, observing what happened when he laughed, whether he coughed or wheezed or his lips took on that dusky bluish tinge. No worry lines, but tonight, something else in Anju's expression: Irritation, maybe, or anger.

"What is it?" Grace asked

"Let me shut the door first," Anju said over her shoulder in her clipped British accent. As always she wore her glossy hair in an elegant knot, a silk dress beneath her white lab coat. It looked almost blue beneath the overhead florescent lights.

Wordlessly, Grace flicked on the TV, then handed the remote control to Jack. Anju closed their door and turned, hands in the pockets of her coat. "I just rang off the phone with Dr. Markind from psychiatry." Anju cocked an eyebrow at Grace. "He asked if I'd ever considered your role in Jack's V-Fibs."

Grace stared at Anju incredulously. "What?" She shook her head as if she'd heard wrong. "He's never met me. How—" She stopped, crossed her arms over her chest to stop them from trembling. "Why is he involved? Who the hell asked for a psych consult?"

"I did, Grace. Jack's close call the other day coupled with his prognosis, which is not hopeful—you know this, right?"

"Of course, I do, Anju, but what does that have—"

"I had hoped that Dr. Markind might have some insights in terms of how—"

Grace shook her head. "This is about the DNR, isn't it?"

"That is a part of my concern, yes, but it is not—"

"Yes it is." Grace clamped her mouth shut, trying to stay calm, but though she spoke quietly, her words lifted away into something frantic and uncontained. "Look at him! He *has* quality of life, Anju, he's happy, damn it! What more do you—" She shook her head. "When did Dr. Markind even see Jack?"

"He stopped by last evening, while Stephen was present."

Grace stared at Anju helplessly. "I can't believe this is happening again." Her legs felt rubbery. "What exactly did he say?"

"He finds it suspicious that Jack recovered so quickly." She sighed. "When you were not present."

Wordlessly, Grace moved the few feet from where she was standing to the back of the room, squatted before her overnight bag, and began packing. Jack was watching all of this, but she didn't have the energy to distract him right now. "I want him discharged, Anju." Her voice shook. "I don't trust this." Her tongue felt thick. She reached onto the window ledge where she'd set some of her things: a blow-dryer, a bottle of moisturizer.

"Grace," Anju said. "It is not even twenty-four hours that Jack has been—"

"Fine, we'll go AMA." Against Medical Advice. She didn't care. She wasn't going to just sit here. She glanced up at the ledge to see what else she needed and grabbed Kempley's book, her copy of *The Crucible*. Lightning branched across the night, an angiogram of the sky. She hadn't realized it was raining.

"I understand that you are panicked."

"Do you?" Grace asked, pressing her palms to her eyes. "I can't believe this," she said. "What did you tell him?"

"Dr. Markind? That he is completely off the track. I am confident that I have diffused this, Grace."

As if it were a bomb.

"*I* am not worried. I am telling you only because I promised I would if there were any further incidents."

Grace nodded, still squatting on the floor, energy draining through her. She swiped at her eyes, not wanting Jack to see her cry.

"If this little man remains stable—" Anju nodded at Jack, "We'll get you both out of here first thing tomorrow. A home-care nurse can take care of the IV antibiotics."

Please don't get sick. Please don't get sick. A whispered mantra. The same tempo as a heartbeat.

She watched the drops of water ticking against their sixth-floor window. Halos of light formed around the streetlights below. The neon Emergency sign cast a red sheen on the rain-soaked asphalt. She'd phoned Stephen as soon as Anju left. The call left her feeling more alone than ever. He'd asked if she wanted him to stay with Jack tonight. "Oh, right," she said. "That'll work. Look what your staying here one night did."

"Are you blaming me?"

"No, I just—what did you say to him, Stephen? What did he say to you? There must have been something." Jenn's words to her. It was too impossible to believe that such an accusation could happen without a reason.

"I told you, he asked how Jack was and how you and I were holding up and if Jack was in pain. He seemed like a decent guy. He wasn't here more than three minutes."

"I shouldn't have left." She closed her eyes. "Everything was fine, and God, if I'd just stayed—maybe they would have accused you." She meant it as a joke, but it wasn't.

After Jack fell asleep, Grace retrieved Kempley's copy of *The Crucible* from her bag. She and Stephen had rented the video of the movie version a few years ago—Winona Ryder, Daniel Day-Lewis—and she remembered liking it, though it had seemed impossible to believe it had really happened, so many women accused, lives ruined for no good reason: If a woman had kept a doll, a poppet, she might be accused. If she missed church one Sunday or read books, she might be accused. If she healed someone—accused. If she couldn't heal someone—accused. If her neighbor's cow didn't give milk, if a neighbor's butter didn't churn—accused. If she had too much pride or anger or didn't believe in witches—accused.

If she'd had an affair.

She opened the book and read: *Is the accuser always holy now?*

She stared at the yellowed pages of the text, the faint penciled notes in the margin, and forced herself to keep reading, trying to stay calm, despite the surge of panic spiraling through her. John Proctor was questioning the Reverend upon hearing that Rebecca Nurse had been accused and arrested. It made no sense. *How may such a woman murder children?* Proctor demanded. He then proceeded to organize the townspeople to sign a petition attesting to Rebecca Nurse's good character, her unwavering faith in God, her piety. But to no avail. *There is a misty plot afoot so subtle we should be criminal to cling to old respects and ancient friendships*, the Reverend warns.

Grace lowered the book and held it unopened as she rocked, not having the heart to read further. She understood for the first time that maybe the accuser *was* holy, if for no other reason than that he alone offered an answer, which was all people ever really wanted. Without the accuser, the illnesses of the children in Salem, the failure of the crops, Jack's confusing and often perplexing disease, seemed to make no sense.

Her throat tightened and she stood wearily, tucking the book back into her knapsack on the floor by her cot. Outside it was still raining. She tracked a raindrop down the window pane, watched it disappear. She wanted to believe Munchausen's was different from the witch trials, but more and more, she wasn't sure: If a mother owned too many medical textbooks, knew too much about her child's illness, called her child's nurses by first name, became too friendly with the other parents of sick children, she was suspect. If she was overprotective, "tuned into her child's indirect emotional signals," she was suspect. But if she wasn't tuned in, had a "flat effect," did not cry, break down, shatter like a teacup when the doctors gave her bad news, surely, this too meant she was suspect, that she was secretly enjoying the drama.

The parallels didn't help, didn't reassure her as Kempley wanted them to. They only terrified Grace more. And all *The Crucible* reminded her of was what the medical articles and books on Munchausen's with their scholarly diction and footnotes and statistics had obscured: how little any of this had to do with logic or reason. "In addition to Munchausen mothers being assertive and demanding with their children's caregivers," one of the books had said, "they can also be very ingratiating and complimentary, even adulatory." And "while many Munchausen mothers push for diagnostic procedures, these skilled actresses at times will be quite compliant." So too emotional, too unemotional, too aggressive, too compliant, too friendly, not friendly enough. Like a house of mirrors. No matter which way she turned she came up against her own distorted reflection.

The rain was falling harder. Lightning razored open the dark forensic sky, but there was no accompanying thunder, a silent tearing apart. Grace looked at Jack, her baby, her Goose, and felt frantic inside. She walked to his bed and stood over him, hand on his head, simply watching him, her heart booming so loudly with love or fear or both that it seemed impossible it hadn't awakened him.

After a while she flicked on the news, the volume barely audible. Nothing seemed like news: controversy over the use of DNA testing to solve the thirty-seven-year-old mystery of the Boston Strangler. Details about Robert Hansen, the devout Catholic, father of five FBI agent who'd been trading secrets with the Russians. "To his family, his church, his colleagues at the FBI, Robert Hansen was one thing," the reporter said. "To the Russians he was quite another." News that Jesse Jackson's affair took place while he was counseling ex-president Bill Clinton about Monica Lewinsky. All of it about betrayal. About nothing being what it appeared to be.

She slept fitfully, sitting in the rocking chair. A sentry, keeping watch. Rebecca came in at eleven. Grace feigned sleep, listening as Rebecca moved around Jack's bed, stepping carefully over the confusion of tubes and wires. Grace heard her attach the Velcro cuff on the blood pressure machine, and a minute later detach it. The rustle of blankets as she checked Jack's legs to see if he was retaining fluid in his extremities. The click of her pen, then the scratch against paper as she recorded his vital signs.

She came in again at three, moving silently through the watery darkness. The room was illuminated by the triangle of light from the partially open door, the small pen light. Jack must have opened his eyes and glanced at Grace's empty cot. He whimpered and Rebecca quieted him: "Shush, baby, Mama's right here in the rocking chair."

"Why rocking chair?" Jack murmured, already dropping back into sleep.

Grace watched as Rebecca tucked the cotton blanket over Jack's hands the way he liked. Her blond ponytail was like a line of light down her back. She turned and caught Grace watching her. "You are up," she whispered. "Don't you want to lie down? That chair can't be comfortable enough to sleep in."

Grace shook her head and nodded at Jack. "You're so good with him. Thanks."

Rebecca glanced over her shoulder at Jack. "It's easy. He's a doll." In the corridor outside a hushed laugh from one of the other nurses or aides. Jack's pulse oximeter flashed his SATS: 97, 96, 97, 98. "He's doing great," Rebecca whispered. "You really should sleep." She paused. "Is something wrong, Grace?"

"No," Grace said. "I'm just—" She faltered, close to tears, then blurted it out. "Do you think I'm hurting Jack, Rebecca?"

"What?" Rebecca pulled herself back an inch. "God, no."

"I don't mean on purpose, but maybe some signal I'm sending to him that I'm not aware of, that I want him to be sick or—" She shook her head. "I'm not sure, but—"

"No. Absolutely not. You're a great mom, Grace. Everyone on the floor knows how much you do for Jack."

Grace turned away, her eyes full. "If I'm such a great mom, then why—" She looked up. "Why—" The word split open, muffled sobs rising out of her.

Rebecca walked around the side of the crib, her rubber-soled clogs making a dull shuffling sound on the tile floor. She handed Grace a tissue, then wordlessly sat on the edge of Jack's bed. Her hand was on Grace's knee. "Why what?"

"Why did you talk to the social worker about me?"

"What? I've never—social worker? I'm not even—*when?*"

"Last spring? After Jack had the VAD put in." Ventricular Assist Device.

"I remember. We had to readmit him, what was it, a day later?"

"I made some stupid joke about the hospital being our home away from home."

"I don't remember, but okay."

"You didn't repeat that to someone from Child Protective Services?"

"No." Tears sprang into Rebecca's eyes. "Why would I? Why would they even care?" She shook her head. "I have no idea what's going on, Grace, but whatever it is, I am so, so sorry because you are a great mom." Her voice trembled. "I tell Colin all the time that when we have kids, *you* are the kind of parent I want to be."

TWENTY-ONE

Grace woke to the sound of voices, her neck stiff. Jack was lying back, zooming his race cars over his blankets and upraised knees.

"I'm racing you, Mama," he told her when he saw that she was awake.

She smiled sleepily. "Oh no, does that mean you're winning again?"

"Yup."

"What do you mean 'yup'? Who taught you to say yup instead of yes?"

"Max did," he laughed.

She stood unsteadily, still in the rumpled khakis, T-shirt, and jean shirt she'd worn yesterday. She heard Anju's voice in the hallway. "Has Dr. Mehta been in to see you?" she asked, leaning over the crib bars to kiss Jack's forehead. He shook his head no. She glanced at her watch—not the one she usually wore. She'd never bothered to change the time on this one after daylight savings, so it read ten after ten instead of ten after nine. She liked the sense of finding an extra hour.

". . . primary physician," Anju said angrily, followed by another voice and then "unacceptable . . . you have no business . . ." Jack started to say something. Grace held her finger to her mouth. Shush.

"Why I have to be quiet?" Jack asked loudly.

"I want to hear what Dr. Mehta is saying," Grace whispered.

"Why you want—"

She furrowed her brows at him, and he clapped both hands dramatically over his mouth. "Like this?" he whispered through his fingers.

"Perfect." She was smiling, and he smiled in return, her happy boy.

"Page Dr. Markind, please." Anju's voice was almost shrill.

Grace felt her smile slide from her face. "Play with your cars, Jack," she told him. "Mama will be right back."

The hallway smelled of waffles and maple syrup. Anju flashed Grace a warning look, before directing her gaze back to the woman she'd been speaking with. The woman, whose face Grace didn't see, was wearing a long wool coat and low heels. Two nurse's aides quickly averted their eyes when they saw Grace. She felt her face go warm. In the bright hallway, she felt grungy and unkempt and lifted one hand to push her tangled hair from her face. She saw the hospital security guard then, standing a few feet away, his legs spread, hands clasped behind his back, eyes focused ahead. She felt sick to her stomach.

"Dr. Mehta?" she said.

The woman in the coat turned and extended her hand. She was younger than Grace had expected. Limp brown hair, a sharp nose, a beautiful peaches and cream complexion. "Mrs. Connolly?" The woman smiled. Dimples.

Grace nodded, pulling her jean shirt more tightly to her ribs.

"I apologize, Grace," Anju interjected. "I have already paged Dr. Markind."

The woman introduced herself. Kate someone. From the Department of Child Protective Services. Somehow Grace knew that this was the same woman whose curly handwriting had been on the investigative report. The woman handed Grace her department ID, but Grace only saw the glare of light on plastic. "As I explained to Dr. Mehta," the woman said, "our decision no longer involves Dr. Markind." She smiled again. Those dimples.

"Decision?" Grace asked Anju. The elevator opened and a group of interns, holding Styrofoam cups of steaming coffee, got out, followed by a mom pushing a little girl with balloons tied to her wheelchair. "Hi, Dr. Mehta," the girl said breathlessly, and Anju turned, hands on her hips, pretending shock. "Balloons in a hospital? What is the meaning of this?"

"Perhaps we could discuss this somewhere more private?" Kate interjected. "Isn't there's a conference room at the other end of the floor?"

She knew the floor then, Grace thought. She'd done this before. "No. I don't want to leave Jack." Her voice was on the edge of shrill.

"How about the playroom?" Anju said. It was right across the hallway. Grace would be able to see Jack from the table where kids worked on puzzles and art projects.

"Is Rebecca still here—could she stay with Jack?" Grace asked.

"Absolutely." Anju touched Grace's arm. "I will page her."

"Could you ask her to call Stephen?"

The woman's words reached her as if from under water. Something about taking Jack into protective custody, an evidentiary hearing, forty-eight hours. Anju was still at the nurses' station. Grace and Kate were sitting in the children's playroom, a Mr. Potato Head on the chair next to Grace, books stacked in a pile on the table. *Uncle Elephant; Maxine, Maxine the Beach Party Queen; Journey Through Heartsongs*, the book written by the little boy with mitochondrial disease who had been on *Oprah* and *Larry King* and *The Today Show*. On the back was a small sticker: "Donated in loving memory of Carly Hopper. Born May 30, 1997; became an angel on November 5, 2000." Grace traced her finger over the sticker. "I don't understand how a doctor who's never even met me—"

"We treat all reports seriously, Mrs. Connolly."

"I know, and you should. But—" Grace looked at her. "You're talking about taking my child—" Her voice rose, and she stopped, fingernails dug into her palms. Don't get angry, she kept telling herself. You cannot alienate his woman. You have got to hold on until Stephen gets here.

"Unfortunately, this is the second accusation CPS has received in a year," the woman—Kate—said gently.

"I know." She tried to keep her tone nonconfrontational. "But the first accusation was—there wasn't enough evidence." She looked at Kate, trying to see her as just an ordinary woman doing her job. Not an enemy, but someone who really believed that she was helping, maybe saving, a child. She swallowed hard. *Please be a good person,* she thought, praying that if she could see Kate as an ordinary fallible woman who was doing her best and had simply made a mistake, then maybe Kate could see who Grace was too: an exhausted, frightened mother whose little boy was sick.

"If you've done nothing wrong, there's really nothing to fear, Mrs. Connolly."

Grace glanced at her incredulously. "You are taking my child," she repeated.

"There will be an evidentiary hearing within forty-eight hours. And your son will remain right where he is under Dr. Mehta's good care." Kate looked up from her papers. "Hopefully, this will be re-solved at that point."

"How?" Grace was trembling and wrapped her arms tighter around herself. "What is going to change in forty-eight hours?" She stood, crying. "You can't just—just come in here—" Her voice rose. "I mean, should I be hoping that my son goes into heart failure while I'm away so *you* can be satisfied that *I'm* not doing this to him? How else do I prove to you—" She stopped.

Kate pursed her lips, her eyes steely. "Hoping your child goes into cardiac arrest seems a strange way to resolve the problem, Mrs. Connolly."

She realized that it was the worst thing she could have said. "I didn't say I hoped," she said. "I'm frustrated and I'm terrified and—" She stared at the shelf of games to her right: *Sorry, Trouble, Risk, Life.* The room seemed to enlarge around them, the air charged. "I'm sorry," she said meekly, hating herself for being so weak. But she couldn't afford to get on Kate's bad side.

"My son, Jack . . ." There, she would give Kate his name, make Jack real to her. He was *not* just a case or a child-victim or— "Jack," she said again knotting her hands in her lap to stop their shaking. "He

nearly died forty-eight hours ago, as I'm sure you know, and now—"
She glanced up. "You're asking me to leave him for two days." She
would plead, beg, she didn't care. Her words were like rocks in a
stone wall, she thought, each one perfectly selected for its size and
shape, weight and balance.

"But you left your son the night before last, didn't you? Didn't
your husband stay?"

"Yes, but—" Does it matter to you that I have two other children
at home? she wanted to say. That they need me too, and that the few
times I've had to leave Jack alone in the hospital for a few hours because Erin had a Girl Scout function or Max was getting an award at
the school sports banquet, it was always, *always*, an untenable choice,
and it always hurt? Would it help if she explained to Kate that the *only*
reason she had left Jack two nights ago was because of this stupid
Munchausen's thing to begin with? Did anything she said matter
right now? She pressed her palms to her eyes. She felt deadened.
Numb.

The woman's face softened. "You may not believe this, but I truly
am sorry."

"Can my husband stay with him?" Grace forced herself to look at
Kate. "Please?"

The woman started to shake her head. "It's only forty-eight—"

"The child has a heart condition," Anju interrupted from the
doorway. "I don't want him agitated, which he will be if one of his
parents is not with him." She glanced at Grace. "I'm sorry I took so
long. I was trying to reach Dr. Markind."

Grace nodded, then turned to look again at Kate. "My husband
will abide by whatever rules you have. Please."

"The father is to have *no* contact with the mother," Kate said to
Anju.

"Fine."

"Not even over the phone."

"I said 'fine,' Ms. Helverson," Anju said.

Grace stared at the playhouse across the room, plastic flowers in the window box, bright red shutters. A play sink and refrigerator and a lawnmower that played music when you pushed it. Little kids with pacemakers and oxygen tanks and wheelchairs pretending to be moms and dads, cooking dinner and going to work and talking on plastic yellow cell phones. As if the future were so easy to imagine.

She forced a smile on her face before pushing open the door to Jack's room. Her chest felt crushed. She couldn't think. Walk across the room, she told herself. Get your purse. The security guard was waiting to escort her from the hospital. Stephen was on his way. Rebecca stood awkwardly. "I'll pull some extra shifts, so I can be with him, Grace. He'll be okay."

"Thanks," she said in a squeaky whisper.

"Where you going, Mama?"

"Home, Goose." She forced a smile. The sadness caught in her throat. "Daddy's going to play with you today."

"Why Daddy play with me today?"

"Come here, silly." She held her arms out to Jack, inhaling his stale yeasty smell. Behind him the numbers flashed on the pulse ox, the line of his heart steady.

"Just hold on," she kept repeating to herself as she walked down the hallway to the elevators. The security guard stood discreetly behind her. "You in the parking garage?" he asked when they stepped into the elevator. She nodded, swallowing hard. They stared up at the lighted numbers over the doors. "Some days I really hate my job," he said softly. She glanced at him and tried to smile. Her nose was running, and he handed her an ironed handkerchief. "It's clean. Go ahead. Take it."

"Thanks," she whispered hoarsely, holding the white square to her face. It smelled of cigarettes and the cheap Old Spice aftershave she used to give her dad for Christmas, and it seemed just then like the saddest smell in the world.

In the parking garage, Stephen was just getting out of his car. "Oh, God, Grace," he said, hurrying to her as soon as he saw her walking towards him.

She stopped him, leaned against a car. "I—I'm going to be sick—I can't—" She was doubled over, dry heaving. She hadn't eaten since lunch the day before, hadn't even had time for coffee. "They— they—" But words were impossible.

Stephen stopped her, hands on her arms. "Listen to me, Grace. I called the kids' schools and told them you'd be picking up the kids early. And I want you guys to stay with your parents tonight."

"Okay." She straightened slowly. It hurt to breathe as if the air itself had become thinner, less substantial. She couldn't stop crying.

"And I need you to go to Bennett's. He's waiting. I've written down directions." He handed her a torn envelope scrawled with writing. She took it, sobbing harder. He cupped her face in his palms. "Listen to me, Grace." He forced her gaze up to his. "I am *not* going to just roll over and allow this to happen. I don't care what it takes." His eyes filled. "Are you going to be okay to drive?"

"Just—I don't want him alone." She began crying again. "No matter what, you have to stay with him."

Only yesterday she was an ordinary woman. An ordinary woman in khakis, a white T-shirt, a loose jean shirt worn like a sweater. Only yesterday. She held onto the words. Only yesterday. Only yesterday. She tried to tell herself she was still that woman—she was even wearing the same clothes—but everything was different, and now she would never be an ordinary woman again.

She felt nothing, or felt too much. The result was the same in the end. Too much anger, too much grief, rage, fear, guilt, and shame, and it was like mixing too many different colors of paint together into a muddied nondistinct gray-brown, the color of wet sand. That was what she was, what she felt. Gray-brown. Her thoughts swirled, made no sense. A friend of her dad's, a retired pilot who lived in Florida, was cleaning out a swimming pond on his property a few years before, when he saw an alligator. "I was sick with fear," he said later, until the alligator suddenly turned, and rolled onto its side. Alligators do this after eating, he knew, when they are full. He could breathe again; he was not in danger. But then he glanced down. He saw that his arm was gone.

Grace thought of this as she drove numbly through the late morning traffic. She was in shock. At some point she would look down. She would realize that a part of her life, a part of her, had been amputated. It happened so quickly, before she even knew it.

TWENTY-TWO

The forty-eight hours before the evidentiary hearing were, for Grace, blurry and fragmented, so that later, trying to remember those two days, all that survived were small inexplicable moments that had somehow been salvaged. Memories, like bruises, marking the place of damage. Grace couldn't recall what Bennett had said to her when she arrived at his office, but she would see with perfect clarity those four black-and-white photographs of the bridges connecting Philadelphia to New Jersey. Perhaps she stared at them so intently that day because it was easier than looking at Bennett, this man who knew the most shameful things in her life: she'd been an unfaithful wife; she was now considered an unfit and abusive mother. Or maybe it was that the purpose of a bridge is to join what is otherwise separated, and it was how her life felt that day, separated, disconnected, cut off, as if she were standing across a river from everything she had once been. Or maybe, *maybe,* she stared at those photos for no better reason than that they were black and white, and she needed the illusion of order that the absence of color provided.

She wouldn't recall driving home afterward or talking to her mother on the phone, though she did, or what words she used to explain to her children's school principals why she needed to take her children home, and why they would be absent for the rest of the week. Hours would dissolve into nothing more than a handful of images: Max mumbling under his breath, "I wish they *would* keep you away from us!" and Erin crying, and her mother rushing, coatless, from the house, her face stricken with fear when Grace pulled up with the kids. The slant of light on the blond wooden floor in her parents' hallway, an empty hummingbird feeder swaying from a tree out back, her father, looking older than Grace could remember, his eyes like two dark holes in his face, hugging her tightly, and whispering, "That hospital isn't going to know what the hell hit it when I'm through, Gracie." And then, breaking down, crying in front of the kids. It felt as if Jack had already died, and she had to keep reminding herself that he hadn't.

She explained to Max and Erin that there had been a misunderstanding. Bennett's term. It had sounded preposterous a month earlier, but now she understood: there was simply nothing else to call it. *Misunderstanding*.

They were on their way to her parents' house from school. "You know how there are some people who don't understand mitochondrial disease?" she began. "Like how Jack's really sick one day, then all of a sudden he's fine?"

"That always happens, doesn't it, Mama?" Erin said. She was sitting in the passenger seat, her goose-bumped legs protruding from beneath a red-and-black plaid kilt. Grace reached over and rubbed her legs, stalling. "Silly girl," she teased Erin. "What were you thinking going to school with nothing on your legs?"

"I didn't think it would be so cold," Erin whined.

"It's okay, lovey. We'll be at Grandma's soon, and we'll get you all warmed up."

Erin beamed. "We're going to Grandma's?"

"Why?" Max demanded, slumping even further into the backseat. Arms crossed over his chest, furious at missing school on a game day.

Grace glanced at him in the rearview. "It's only for a few days."

"A few days!"

"Max, if you'd let me—"

He flicked his eyes at her coldly, then returned to stare out the window.

Grace opened her mouth to explain, then closed it, staring straight ahead. After a minute, she said, "Your dad and I think it would be better if we stayed with Grandma and Grandpa until this misunderstanding gets straightened out." She glanced at Max again, but he wouldn't meet her gaze. "There are some people who don't understand Jack's disease, and so they think maybe I'm doing something to make him sick." Her voice caught, and she stopped, biting the inside of her cheek to keep from crying. "Anyway," she continued, "these people want me to stay away from Jack for a few days to see if he gets better." She rolled her eyes at her daughter, emphasizing how ridiculous it was. "Seems kind of silly, huh?"

"That's way silly, Mama!" Erin agreed too enthusiastically, and Grace ached for her. When—*she was only six*—had Erin learned to do this? Pretend that everything was okay when it so clearly wasn't?

"Oh, yes, *way* silly," Max sneered.

"Come on, Max," Grace pleaded.

"Why?" he exploded. "I'm so sick of Jack's stupid disease ruining everything!"

"*Ruining?*" Grace pulled into the gravel drive of her parents' house. Stones crunched beneath the tires. "Since when is missing two, *maybe* three, days—"

"*Three?* No! I can't, Mom! We're playing Cherokee Friday!"

Grace shut off the car, and turned to face her son. "I'm sorry, honey. I really am."

"I wish they would keep you away from *me*," he mumbled.

"Just get out," she said wearily. "We'll talk when you aren't being so nasty."

"Fine. But I'm not as stupid as you think." He opened the door. "You probably are making him sick." He slammed the door.

"She is not!" Erin shouted through the closed window.

Max turned around and laughed at her.

"I hate you, Max!" she screamed.

"Shush, honey, it's okay." Grace hugged Erin to her chest. "He's just mad. He doesn't mean it."

Later that afternoon, the three of them took a walk in the woods, trampling through mud and soggy pine needles. Grace's dad, tired of Max's attitude, had forced him to go along. "If you're upset with your mom, you need to talk to her," he insisted.

"She doesn't listen to me!"

"Then try again."

Now Erin sprinted ahead, a little forest sprite in a pair of her grandmother's leggings, rolled up at the waist and cinched with a clothespin, a huge sweatshirt over that, falling nearly to her knees. They hadn't been back to their own house yet to get extra clothes. The weather had turned suddenly warm, enough so that Grace and Max could tie their jackets around their waists as they walked, though their faces still shone with cold. It felt to Grace as if an entire season had come and gone since the morning. Her chest ached with the thought of it. Sunlight flickered through the trees in splotches. It had a dizzying effect, as if the ground were moving beneath her. The sky was bright blue. What was the color? Teal almost. Or ultramarine. Swimming pool blue.

Max walked behind her, still not talking. Erin dashed back every few minutes, ebullient, breathless, pigtails askew, her skinny freckled face pink with cold. "Look what I found, Mama!" She would hand Grace a pinecone, a pretty leaf, a smooth stone.

"Maybe she'll be a scientist," Grace said, watching her run off again.

"Yeah, right."

Grace glanced at him "I really am sorry about your games," she said.

He didn't answer.

"Look, Max," she sighed, pushing a tree branch out of her way, then stopping to hold it back for Max. It felt like the most solid thing she had held all day. "I don't know what you think you know, but it might help to talk about it."

"Why? Are you doing it?" He ducked under the upheld branch and kept walking.

She jerked her head up. "Am I doing *what*?"

He kept walking and without thinking, she strode up behind him, grabbed his shirt—hard—by the back of the neck, and swung him around to face her. "Doing *what*?" Her breath hung in the air. She wanted to slap him. "Say it to my face, Max."

"God, Mom, lighten up." He shrugged from her grip. "I was kidding, okay? It was a joke." He started to turn around.

"Don't you dare turn away from me when I'm talking to you." Her voice shook.

He turned back, rolling his eyes.

She stared at him, jaw clenched, trying to calm down. "What is it that I'm doing, Max?" Panic settled in the pit of her stomach. "Am I making your brother sick, is that it? Do you think I'm trying to kill him?"

He dropped his eyes from hers. "No, okay? I don't think anything."

"Yeah? Because there's usually an edge of truth in the jokes people make, Max."

"You guys!" Erin called from up ahead. "Come on!"

"We're coming!" Grace called, then turned back to Max. "Don't you *ever* say that again, do you hear me? Don't you *ever* even suggest it. I don't care how mad you are, I don't care if you do think it is a joke." Her voice frayed, and she glanced away. She knew that she needed to explain to him why she was so upset; she knew that he didn't really understand the ramifications of what was going on. She pulled in a deep breath and tried to start over. "If someone ever heard you question, even as joke, that I would hurt your brother . . ." she swallowed hard. "They could, and they might even have the right, to take you and your sister away from us."

"But I was only—"

"Listen to me!" she yelled. Her voice echoed in the clear air.

His face went slack, though his eyes still challenged her.

"Max," she began again, "if any mother, *ever,* hurt a child on purpose or tried to make her child sick, she would deserve to lose her children. *I* would want her to lose her children. And if I ever intentionally hurt Jack or you or Erin, *I* would want you to be taken from me so that I couldn't do it again. Do you understand? This isn't an issue to joke about. It's like kidding around about guns when you're boarding an airplane. Nobody's going to care if you're joking. They're going to arrest you because they can't afford to take any risks. This is the same thing."

"Fine. I won't joke about it again."

"Thank you." She looked at him. "Why don't you go catch up with Erin? I'll be there in a minute."

But he didn't move. "I really was only joking," he said. "I was just mad."

"I know," she sighed. "But honey, you cannot use getting mad as an excuse to say or do whatever you want." He was staring at the ground, his long lashes casting shadows over his pale skin. Something in her tore. He was only thirteen. She had to keep reminding herself of this. Thirteen. "Come on," she said more gently. "Let's just walk," and she started forward, but he stayed put, head bowed, refusing to budge.

"Hey," she said, then saw the tears beading on his lashes. His nose was bright red, his mouth pinched with the effort not to cry. "Oh, Max," she said. "I know this is scary and I know we should have talked to you."

"I don't know why I even said it." Tears dripped onto his sweatshirt. "You're nothing like them." He was crying openly now. "You're not like them at all," he sobbed.

Her mouth went dry. "Hold it—not like *who*?"

"Those mothers on that Web site, that M.A.M.A. thing." He sniffled. "You didn't log off one day and so I looked at it. I just—I was scared, I kept hearing you and Dad fighting and you were crying all the time and I didn't know what Munchausen's was. I thought it was like, some kind of disease or something." He started sobbing, and she pulled him to her, crying now herself. "I thought you were going to die, like Jack," he sobbed.

Grace sat at the kitchen table, warm in a pair of flannel pajamas she'd borrowed from her mother, the house quiet around her. Like being in high school, she thought, coming home after field hockey, then studying, sitting here at one or two in the morning, long after her parents had gone to bed. This same table in this same kitchen. The same silhouette through the bay window of black trees against a milky black sky. Noah had been in her life then too, she thought, and the longing she'd suppressed all day—to phone him, to tell him what had happened, bubbled up in her throat. *They took him*. Three words and he'd get it, he'd understand how scared she was, how terrified that maybe it was connected to him, how guilty she felt. Three words.

She punched in eight of the nine numbers, hesitated, her heart slamming against her chest, hit the last number. *They took him*. Already she was crying again, and when she heard his voice, she began sobbing silently, afraid to wake her parents. *They took him*. There was nothing else to say.

She set aside the article she had just finished reading and turned to the next one: "Children, Pain and Parents: An Epidemiological Triangle." Eric Markind, M.D. An epigraph read: "Even now I wrap what's most fragile in the long gaze of science." *Me too*, Grace thought. Always she had used science, or tried to, as a barricade against her fears, tried to make her life safe by cushioning it with facts. The irony was that the Munchausen's accusation stemmed from the same longing to make comprehensible what wasn't, as if surrounding something with information was to somehow understand it.

"Effective management of pain," Markind had written, "involves treatment of psychological factors that aggravate physiological disturbances." Grace glanced up at the word "aggravate," a tiny alarm sounding in her chest.

"Child's mother and/or primary caregivers should be observed at length for a detailed assessment of familial interactions that aggravate child's perception of pain." *Aggravate*. The word calcified inside her. She continued to read: A Swedish study found that patients' perceptions of pain increased threefold when in the presence of their spouses. The pain itself, measured by changes in heart rate, skin conductivity, and rate of respiration didn't escalate; what escalated was the patient's *feeling* that he was in more pain. Perhaps, Markind proposed, in the presence of those who responded toward this "imagined" pain with greater affection and concern, the patient subconsciously dramatized his symptoms. Couldn't a similar effect occur in the pediatric population?

Grace closed her eyes and exhaled a breath she hadn't known she was holding. The idea that she could have done anything—*anything*—that might have increased Jack's pain sliced through her with so much force she thought she might be sick. How—*how*—could *anyone* who had dealt with a child in pain even consider that a parent's presence would make things worse? The entire structure of pediatric hospitals had been altered in the last fifty years to make it easier for parents to stay with their children.

She glanced again at the last page of the article which featured a black-and-white picture of Markind in his office, the wall behind him crowded with photographs of smiling children. "A small sampling of the patients Dr. Markind has helped," the caption said. Grace studied his photo: a youngish man with sad eyes despite the wide smile on his face. As she had with John Bartholomew, Grace wondered if Eric Markind had kids and if any of them had ever been as sick as Jack and if it mattered—and if it should. But how could it not?

She thought of that Salem judge who had lost eleven children, of Charles Darwin and of how it was *after* the death of his ten-year-old daughter, Anna, that he became obsessed with understanding what survived and what didn't. *The Origin of the Species*. The whole theory of evolution.

She stared bleakly out the bay window. Galileo, abandoned by his mother at birth, had spent his life struggling to understand the force by which two objects, separated by empty space, could continue to exert force upon one another. Maybe, Grace thought now, every important discovery, everything important that happened in the history of the world, stemmed from loss. The Rockefeller Institute was founded when the first grandson of J. D. Rockefeller died of polio at age three. F. Scott Fitzgerald named the death of his siblings, both of whom died before he was even born, as the greatest influences on his writing. Mary Shelley wrote *Frankenstein* after she lost her baby. It made sense. Maybe the dark energy that supposedly comprised 90 percent of the universe was nothing more than grief, the world pulling itself apart at exponentially faster rates.

She glanced again at Markind's photo, then sat back, recalling a story she'd heard on the news about jurors in a murder trial who became traumatized after being forced to watch a video depicting the victim's rape and torture. The jurors were sequestered for the duration of the trial, unable to discuss with anyone what they had seen. Grace wondered if it was like this for certain doctors who were forced in their own way to watch, day after day, children suffer. And if it was a child like Jack where the disease kept shifting and changing and incrementally getting worse, it might seem that there would be no end to the suffering, and perhaps the doctor became traumatized too. How do you not want to turn away, and how do you not hate the people, parents like her, who day after day force you to watch, demand that you account for this suffering, will not let you go?

"Even now I wrap what's most fragile in the long gaze of science." The phrase wedged itself into the space between her breaths. It hurt to inhale. *The long gaze of science,* she repeated, trying to calm herself. *The long gaze of science.* And then, suddenly, she got it and was pushing back her chair and moving through the unlit hallway to her father's study at the back of the house. *The long gaze of science.*

Of course.

She turned on the green banker's lamp on her father's desk, illuminating an airline flight map of the U.S. push-pinned to the wall overhead, then turned on the computer. As soon as she found the M.A.M.A. site, she began charting on a pad of legal paper the state where each woman had been accused. Her hands were still trembling from the phone call to Noah, her handwriting shaky, as if she were trying to write while in a car. A disproportionate number of accusations in Florida, California, Texas, Illinois, Georgia, and Pennsylvania. Grace sat forward, drumming her fingernails on the desk, heart pounding. How could she have missed this?

It was so basic. John Snow, father of epidemiology, had ended a two-year scourge of cholera in London by drawing a detailed "spot-map" of where the cases occurred. The majority were from a neighborhood located between two main thoroughfares: Broad and Cambridge streets. Further investigation, a more refined map, and Snow was able to determine that those who pumped their water from the Broad Street water pump came down with the plague, while those who got their water from the Cambridge pump did not. The Broad Street pump was closed; new cases of cholera disappeared.

Grace smiled, remembering: Dr. Kuhn's Science of Medical Inquiry class. Tuesdays and Thursdays, three to five. A wood-paneled classroom, rust-colored autumn light spilling through the windows. Snow's premise, which became the foundation of epidemiology, had been drummed into first-year graduate students ad nauseam. *Diseases do not exist in isolation, but result from a unique intersection of time, place, and people.* Expanding suburbs in the northeastern part of the United States in the late '70s significantly encroached upon land populated by white deer; hence, Lyme disease. Building the Aswan High Dam in Egypt in the 1960s expanded the habitat for snails hosting the flatworm *Schistosoma mansoni,* and fifteen years later the proportion of people in the Nile Valley with schistosomiasis had increased exponentially.

On the legal pad, Grace wrote the equation: *Late twentieth cent. + large Amer. cities + ? = msbp.* She stared at the list of states that she'd jotted down. The obvious connection was that some of largest cities—she scrawled these in the margin: New York, L.A., Chicago, Dallas, Philadelphia, Atlanta—were located in these states. And this would naturally translate into larger numbers of "troubled" families, single parents living in poverty with histories of substance abuse, violence, unemployment, and a lack of education, which typically equaled increased risk and prevalence of child abuse. She tapped her pencil against her notepad. The problem was that Munchausen's didn't occur in typical high-risk families, but in white, middle-class families with two parents, one or both of whom had a college education. *A medical background.* She stood, paced, sat again at the computer, feeling as if she were standing on the edge of some huge precipice and all she needed were the right words to pull her back. Atop the margin of her paper she scrawled *Why????*, followed by a series of dark question marks. She pictured Dr. Kuhn with her long skirts and lace-up flat boots and wide pretty face. Her thick German accent. *"It is not only important what disease a patient has but which patient the disease has."*—William Osler, the founder of modern scientific, research-based medicine. The words moved across her mind in dark formations like lines of migrating birds. She stood again, walked in slow circles, hands on her hips, head bowed. She returned to the computer, clicked to another site. She typed in keywords, skimmed articles, revised her search, narrowed it, refined her question, read yet more articles. *"To find the right answer, one must ask the right question."*

TWENTY-THREE

I owe you an apology." Jenn tilted her head back and squinted toward the tops of the pines. Light filtered through the trees and shimmered over the glossy surface of her leather jacket. She had driven over after her shift at the hospital, armed with the new *Sports Illustrated* for Max, paper dolls for Erin, a bag of M&M's for Grace.

Grace walked just ahead of her, sidestepping puddles. It had rained earlier. Water plunked softly from branches onto the dirt. Nearby a bird twittered, and she glanced up. *The farther two quarks are pulled away from each other, the more fiercely they are attracted.* The sky was empty. She inhaled sharply, the cold air like glass in her lungs.

"I didn't realize how jaded I'd become," Jenn was saying. "I can't believe how awful I was to you when you told me about this."

"You weren't awful." Grace glanced over her shoulder at her friend. "You were honest." Jenn was wearing a bright blue beret, and she looked beautiful despite her swollen, red-rimmed eyes. "I'm sorry," she had sobbed helplessly from behind wads of crumpled Kleenex when Grace's mother opened the door to her. "Stephen told me. I can't stop crying. I can't believe I even made it here . . ."

"You're just being nice," Jenn told Grace now, "but the truth is that *one* inconsistency in a parent's story or the slightest question about how a kid got hurt, and I immediately assume abuse." They walked side by side again, the path dry, curving uphill and away from the lake. Pockets of white snow surrounded the bases of trees. "Most of the time my instincts are probably right—God, I hope they are—but still." Jenn stopped and cupped her hands to her mouth, blowing into them for warmth. "I had a kid a couple of months ago with a dislocated shoulder," she said after a moment. "He'd been pitching a fit, and the mom yanked his arm so hard she dislocated it. She was hysterical when I told her I was calling CPS, kept insisting it was a mistake and that she hadn't meant to hurt him." Jenn glanced at Grace. "You know what I told her?"

Grace shook her head.

Jenn took a deep breath. "I told her, 'too bad.' No sympathy, no attempt to understand, just 'too bad.' She didn't get to make that kind of mistake with a child, I told her, and if she did, she wasn't going to get the chance to make it again." Jenn exhaled slowly, her breath like smoke. "As if I never made mistakes with my kids."

"You didn't dislocate their arms, Jenn."

"No, but remember that time I plunked Henry into the bath without checking the water, and it was too damn hot? What if someone in the ER had accused *me*? And they could have, *easily,* and I would have lost him." Her eyes filled. "Can you imagine?"

They started walking again, hands in their pockets. Twigs and broken branches crunched underfoot. Away from the sun, the air felt frigid. Lights flickered on in the houses across the lake. Her own house was dark. She and the kids had gone over earlier for clothes and books. The beds had been unmade, dishes filled the sink, chairs were pushed out from the kitchen table. The house had felt abandoned, like a house where something horrible had happened.

"I feel so stupid," Jenn said. Her nose was red with cold.

"Why?" Grace asked. "You care about kids, Jenn, and you see a lot of crap that would probably make me jaded too. And for all you know, you were right about that kid with the dislocated shoulder."

"But what if she was a good mom, Grace? What if CPS took the kid?"

Grace looked at her. "That's what scares me." She stepped over the rotting trunk of an oak. "Eric Markind probably believes he's doing the right thing too." She looked up, holding her face to the last of the setting sun. "How can I fault him for that?"

In front of them the lake glowed silver, the sky streaked pink and gold. "You have so much support, Grace, " Jenn said. "Every nurse on that floor is behind you."

"So they all know. I wondered how quickly it would get around."

"Everyone's pretty upset. They really care, Grace. It's just—" she stopped.

Grace looked at her. "Just *what*?"

"Nothing, I—"

"No. Just *what*, Jenn?"

Jenn stared at the ground. "It's just that he's doing so well."

"So how long has it been since we've seen you?" Grace's mother asked Jenn as she set the sugar bowl and creamer on the table.

Grace and Jenn looked at one another. "Seven years?" Grace said. "Erin's christening." Jenn was Erin's godmother. "You had the flu for Jack's, didn't you?"

"Seven years?" Jenn shook her head. "That's crazy."

Grace's dad smiled. "Goes like that, doesn't it?" He snapped his fingers. "And can you believe this one?" He nodded at Max. "Taller than all of us."

The coffeemaker gurgled on the counter behind them, steam rising from the pot, the kitchen filled now with the scent of hazelnut. They'd eaten early so that Jenn could join them. Daylight Saving was still a week away, though, and already the sky was dark.

Grace's mom handed Jenn a mug of coffee.

"Perfect," Jenn sighed after taking a sip. And then, "So what are all the little notes?" She nodded at the glass vase that sat on the lazy Susan in the center of the table.

Max looked up. "Nooooooo," he groaned.

Jenn cocked an eyebrow at him. "Love notes, Maxwell?"

"Worse," Max moaned.

"It's a Question Jar," Erin was explaining. She was wearing Jenn's beret, which kept falling over her eyes. "We have one at our house too." She leaned forward on her knees and spun the lazy Susan. "Can Aunt Jenn pick a question, Grandma?"

Max slumped forward as if he'd been shot. "No," he whispered. "I beg you."

"Not enough hockey questions," Grace's dad explained.

Her mother set a plate of brownies in front of her grandson. "Think one of these might ease the pain?" she teased as she sat down. She glanced at her husband. "We've had some great conversations out of some of those questions, haven't we, Paul?"

"We surely have." Her father smiled, and for a moment, the tiredness around his eyes disappeared. He passed the brownies to Jenn. "So what question did you pick?"

Before Jenn could answer, Max, in a breathy Marilyn Monroe voice, said, "If you could make the sky *any* color you wanted, what color would you choose?" He fluttered his eyelashes. "Just listen to your *feeeeeelings*."

"Don't listen to him," Grace's mother laughed. "It's not like that."

"It is too!" Max yelped, spewing crumbs. "Come on, Mom—Erin! Admit it! We had that question!"

"Sit," Grace laughed. "And yes, I admit it, we did."

"But it didn't tell us to listen to our *feeeeelings*!" Erin giggled.

Jenn grinned. "So I read this out loud?" She unfolded the square of paper.

Erin nodded. "And then we all take turns answering."

Jenn cleared her throat. "You listening, Max?" She winked at him. And then read: *"If you could teach everyone in the world one skill in which you yourself are adept, what would you teach and why?"*

"What's wrong with that?" Grace's mother asked Max. "That's a great question."

"I'd teach everyone CPR." Jenn folded the paper. "Does this go back in the jar?"

Ellen shook her head. "We'll throw it away."

"CPR, huh? Why not how to donate blood or . . . I don't know, something with greater impact?" Grace's dad asked. He glanced at Grace and shrugged slightly, as if to tell her that he knew how little any of this mattered right now.

"You can't imagine how many lives would be saved if people knew CPR." Jenn was saying. "And it's not complicated."

"Now, see, that's a good answer," Grace's mother said. "I'm not sure I'd have anything that worthwhile."

"Teach us to bake brownies." Jenn took another bite. "These are amazing, Ellen."

Paul smiled. "A lot of unrest in the world could be solved with these, honey."

Sadness flickered briefly in her mother's eyes. Grace watched her, wondering what it was about. Regret over her own choices not taken? And what were they? Grace realized she had no idea. "I should hope I have more to contribute than a recipe," her mother said, but she didn't say what, and turned instead to Max. "What about you?"

"And don't say hockey," Erin commanded.

"Hockey," he taunted.

They took turns choosing questions, reading them out loud. *If you had to choose an adjective to describe yourself, what adjective would you pick?* The night filled with the sound of their laughter, the scent of hazelnut coffee. *If you could be holding onto any object in the world right now, what would you be holding?* The tablecloth was littered with brownie crumbs and colored scraps of paper. *If you had to be lost somewhere, where would you be lost?* Grace kept fighting the urge to weep, not with sadness, but with gratitude: for her parents, her kids, Jenn. I will never take them for granted again, she promised, staring at their reflection in the dark glass of the window.

If there was one invention you could uninvent what would it be? E-mail, Grace thought. It made it too easy to say what shouldn't be said. There was no time between thinking the words and sending them as there might have been with a letter, and no immediate repercussions as there might have been with a phone call. In her heart, she knew that the accusation last spring was connected to the e-mail she'd sent Noah: *I've never stopped loving you.* Someone must have seen her with him in Cape May and begun to wonder. One of the residents had family in Cape May, didn't he? And that little girl who was in the hospital last year, waiting for a heart—wasn't she from Cape May? It wasn't that far. It could have been anyone. All Grace knew was that she had been okay until she e-mailed Noah. Like someone terrified of heights who is fine until she looks down and sees how high up she is. Grace had done that with her life, glanced back last February and realized how distant she was from who she had once been, who she had wanted to be, and she had panicked and grabbed hold of Noah, as if he could save her from falling.

If you had a jar filled with anything except money or food, what it would it be? Time, she thought. More time.

"Not questions!" Max laughed.

"Medicine," Jenn replied. "Cures."

If you could return to the best day of your life, what day would you return to? Grace sipped her coffee, its warmth spreading a small ache through her chest. *If you could somehow swallow a pill that would stop one thing of your choice from happening, what would that pill stop?* She glanced around the table, everyone's face illuminated in the candlelight, and it was as if the sound had disappeared and she was watching this scene from somewhere else, staring into her future from the other side of the window, and it struck her with the force of a blow that this was how it would look after Jack was gone.

TWENTY-FOUR

*G*race borrowed her mother's suit again for the hearing. It fit differently now, loose. Her father, also in a suit, drove. Stephen would meet them at the courthouse. Rebecca was on duty and would watch Jack. Her mother was taking the kids to a movie. Grace didn't want them anywhere CPS could find them. Logistics. She couldn't think beyond this simple plotting of who would be where and when. She stared out the window, her hands in her lap, her mouth dry. Bennett had warned her not to pin her hopes on the evidentiary hearing. It was a formality, he said. All CPS had to do was show a preponderance of evidence *suggesting* abuse.

At a red light, the woman in the car next to them was putting on lipstick in the rearview mirror. Someone honked. *Unless there's a compelling reason not to, the court will err on the side of the child.* They passed a McDonald's, car dealerships with colorful flags gusting in the wind. Planes lifted off from Philadelphia International Airport. The sky seemed transparent.

"If we can't get full custody reinstated, and it's not likely, Grace, we'll push to have the dispositional hearing moved up. The standard is thirty days, but we'll shoot for ten with liberal visitation."

The courtroom was on the second floor, a dingy space with dirty beige curtains closed over the high windows, straight-backed wooden chairs at scratched wooden desks, black-and-white tile floors. Bennett shook her father's hand, then led Grace and an exhausted-looking Stephen to a table up front. It wasn't a jury trial. Aside from the social worker and the county lawyer, there was only Jenn, dressed in nurse's scrubs and running shoes, and Stephen's brother, Jeff, along with his girlfriend, Mandy. Anju hurried in a few minutes later with Brian Steckler, the head of cardiology.

Grace didn't know what to do with her eyes, her hands. She focused on the judge, an attractive woman with coffee-colored skin and curly hair pulled from her face by a thick headband. A lilac-colored turtleneck showed above her black robe.

Are you a mother? Grace wanted to ask. Nothing else seemed relevant.

"Now tell me again why the county is recommending visiting restrictions for *all* family members?" the judge asked. "The father's stayed in the hospital with the child the last two days, has he not?"

"Yes, Your Honor, he has," Bennett said.

"And the child's doing well?"

"Yes, he is."

The judge smiled, her white teeth seeming to glow in the dark oval of her face. She directed her gaze to Kate. "Well, Ms. Halverson?"

Kate stood. She was wearing an ill-fitting beige suit with boxy shoulders and a frilly white blouse. A girl trying to look older than she was. "We believe that the child remains in danger." Her voice quavered. For a moment, Grace almost felt sorry for her. She couldn't have been more than twenty-five. And she didn't wear a wedding band, so in all likelihood she wasn't married and didn't have children. How could she possibly be an expert in assessing families at risk? What did she have to go on, really, besides the horrifying statistics that been drilled into her?

Child fatalities have risen by 30 percent in the last decade.

About 35–55 percent of those kids had already come under the CPS radar.

Every eleven minutes a child is reported abused or neglected.

"Several experts on Munchausen by Proxy Syndrome have noted that attempts on the mother's part to prove that her child really *is* ill typically escalate when the child is hospitalized." Kate was saying. "My—

the county's—concern is that Mrs. Connolly will try to orchestrate some sort of relapse in the child through the father."

Bennett only smiled at this and stood, buttoning his suit jacket calmly as he did. "This is pure conjecture, Your Honor," he said.

"I agree, Mr. Marsh, so why don't you go ahead? The sooner we clear this up, the sooner you can all return to your lives and to ensuring the health of the child."

Grace jerked her head up, the force of her longing for just that, to *return to your lives,* like an electric shock.

And then Bennett was speaking, his tone measured and sure. He talked about the mercurial and often confusing nature of mitochondrial disease. He read statements attesting to Grace's character from half a dozen doctors and nurses. His voice was steady and lulling. "Many of the county's concerns," he said, "appear to be based on something my client either said or didn't say." He casually picked up the report. "If I can just quote a few of the things that CPS apparently found alarming?" He glanced over the edges of his eyeglasses at the judge, who made a motion with her hand to hurry it along.

Bennett adjusted his glasses "First example," he said, and began to read: " 'Following a routine catheterization, mother-perpetrator expressed displeasure when son was dismissed from the hospital before mother felt he was ready.'" Bennett paused. "Second example: 'Mom refers to hospital as "home away from home." Third, 'Mother expressed relief upon learning of child's diagnosis.' " Bennett glanced up, arms spread as if to suggest how at a loss he was. "*Relief,* Your Honor."

"My hearing is just fine, Mr. Marsh."

"My point is that feeling relief is not a crime and, in fact—" He picked up a xeroxed article. "I quote: Relief is a normal reaction in parents of sick children when given a diagnosis, no matter how bad, for what was previously an unknown or unnamed condition." He set the paper down, and picked up the CPS report again. "My fourth example," he continued. " 'Mother seems to enjoy hospital atmosphere, *befriending* several nurses and *going so far* as to ask about their personal lives.' " His tone turned angry, and Grace wondered if he was really upset or if this was just for effect. She found herself again watching the judge, whose eyes met hers, briefly, before shifting back to Bennett. "Fifth: 'Mom enjoys peppering conversations with medical vocabulary.' " He looked up. "She has a master's degree in epidemiology, for God's sake!" He tossed the report onto the desk and took off his glasses. "I could go on. And on. But the bottom line is that none of these statements suggests that Grace is a danger to her child or that her child is at risk or even that she is a less-than-adequate parent. Not one of them! And the last time I checked, this was not Iran or Chile or some other country where people are penalized for what they say."

The judge turned to Kate, and raised her eyebrows. "Do you want to respond, Ms. Helverson?"

"Yes. We . . . the . . ." She looked down at her notes, then said. "The fact that Mr. Marsh refuses to accept the legitimacy of this disease concerns the state—"

"*What?*" Bennett laughed. "Am *I* now on trial for what I've said?" he asked Kate.

Kate's neck and ears turned pink. "This kind of unwillingness to even *acknowledge* the disease is a hallmark of the pathology, Your Honor."

"Ahh," Bennett interrupted. "So now trusting someone is part of the disease?"

Kate ignored him. "The mother *fits* the Munchausen's profile," she said to the judge and rattled off the warning signs that applied to Grace. "This *so-called* disease has a mortality rate of nine percent," she added when she had finished.

Bennett stood, pushing himself up wearily this time, as if he were bored. "I'm sorry," he said. "But this accusation borders on silly. Yes, Grace has medical knowledge, and yes, she knows a lot about her son's disease, maybe more than many doctors, and yes, she has 'doctor-shopped' as the so-called experts want to call it, though others might say this is just being smart. We shop around when looking for houses and cars and washing machines, don't we?" He sighed. "None of the claims made by Child Protective Services suggest a psychiatric illness much less a crime, Your Honor. If anything, these characteristics—intelligence, medical knowledge—only make my client and other women like her that much stronger, that much more willing to ask questions, and yes, that much more willing to complain, and my take, quite frankly"—he tossed his pencil onto the desk—"is that someone just doesn't like this."

"Your Honor," Kate said. "All the county is asking for is more time to review the evidence. Statistics from Health and Human Services show that forty-six percent of children who die from abuse have been reported at least once to Child Protective Services, but nothing was done because the evidence wasn't found to be adequate. It is in this case, however. Mrs. Connolly scores high on half of the indices indicating that the child is at high risk of further abuse." She ticked them off on her fingers: history of depression, previous reports of abuse, a multitude of stresses in dealing with the child's illness, large periods of time when Grace was alone with the child, the child's age—under five—which put him in the group of children who accounted for seventy-eight percent of all deaths due to abuse and neglect in the last year for which there were statistics. "In light of this—"

"Objection." Bennett stood.

"That's fine, Mr. Marsh," the judge said evenly, gesturing for him to sit. "I object as well. I object, in fact, to this entire hearing." Again, her eyes briefly met Grace's before she turned to the county attorney and social worker. Vaguely, Grace was aware of Stephen squeezing her hand, but she was afraid to look at him. She was afraid to hope, afraid to breathe almost, as if to move at all might somehow change the judge's mind. She focused on a scuff mark on the floor just in front of her. Was it possible that this really would be no more than the misunderstanding everyone said it was?

"I'm not one bit pleased that this case is in front of me," the judge was saying. "The information is conflicting, it *is* based on circumstance"—she nodded at Bennett—"and I'm holding a sheaf of letters" —she held them up—"from friends and family, not to mention doctors and nurses from a *number* of renowned institutions, Ms. Helverson, who not only attest to the severity and unpredictability of the child's illness, but also to Mrs. Connolly's attributes as a devoted mother." The judge paused. "I am considering this case at all *only* because of the fact that two accusations were made independently of one another within a short time frame."

Grace glanced hesitantly at Kate, who was leaning towards the county attorney, her cheeks flushed, nodding her head, and in that second, Grace felt a prickling sensation in her chest, and knew something was wrong. It was not going to be *a misunderstanding*. The judge paused to take a breath, and somehow, in that space, the interval between heartbeats, everything changed. The county lawyer, not Kate, was standing, saying that he had hoped he could have avoided this, and the judge, looking irritated, was nodding.

"This *supposedly* devoted mother," the lawyer was saying, and there was something in the way he said it: *supposedly*. The rest of the words came in waves, crashing forward, then retreating, pulling her life out from under her. "Might not seem relevant . . ." and "surely the state has no intention . . ." and "clearly established pattern of deception," and Bennett was interjecting that this had nothing to with the case and Stephen's hand in hers was freezing, and Grace felt as if her bones had dissolved, as if nothing was holding her intact.

Adultery. The word echoed.

"Nobody denies that the child has a serious illness, so serious, in fact, that for all his mother knew, it was to be his last Christmas. And yet . . . and yet . . . this *supposedly* devoted mother—" If he said it again, Grace thought, she would scream. "Chose to spend Christmas Eve sneaking off with her lover rather than . . ."

The room went still. She felt Stephen turn to her. *Christmas Eve?* Stop looking at me, she wanted to sob.

"Clearly, this woman is quite adept at appearing to be one thing when she is actually another."

The words were like shiny marbles on which she tried to run, but there was nothing to hold on to, nothing to keep her from falling, even though Stephen was still squeezing her hand so hard that her fingers felt bruised.

This isn't my life, Grace was thinking, and nearly choked on the bitter realization that every parent who had ever sat in this room and faced the possibility of losing their child had probably thought the same thing. How quickly it all spins away from you. But when had that really happened? With the first e-mail to Noah—*Is that you?* Or the second or the fourth or the fifteenth—*I've never stopped*—or was it before that, the day they found out about Jack's illness or the summer twenty years ago when she met Noah or the autumn she stopped returning his calls?

She stared at her shoes, her face burning with shame. She was going to lose Jack for the reason she'd known all along that she would: punishment for having been with Noah. A *lover.* How dare she?

It didn't make sense to me either, she wanted to protest.

She listened to the judge and the court attorney and Bennett talking around her. She was desperate to remember that day at the beach, the surf pounding in her chest now, the roar of wind making it difficult to breathe. She heard how it sounded, the words like a fast-moving river overflowing its banks, flooding everything: *sneaking off, lover, Christmas Eve.* The phrases floated before her face. All she knew was that a year ago, had she been hearing this story about someone else, she too would have questioned just how devoted this mother really was.

It wasn't how it sounded. But it never was, was it? A walk on the beach. *What the hell are you doing here?* Laughter, coffee.

The judge was asking her something and Grace looked up, begging with her eyes, *please understand*. She was asked if the relationship was over and she nodded. "Yes." She was asked when she had last spoken to Noah. The sound in the room disappeared, and she reached for the edge of the table. The force of her answer was like a blow to her chest. The judge repeated the question.

"The night before last," Grace said. It was a whisper. But everyone heard.

The court would reconvene in two weeks, at which time a dispositional hearing would be held to determine a further course of action. The child would remain in the hospital in state custody. Mother was

to be evaluated by a court-appointed psychologist specializing in ficti-
tious disorders. Parents were to be granted four supervised visits per
week lasting no more than one hour per visit.

Stephen's face like an abandoned building set on fire and crumpling in upon itself.

"We will take the very best care of him," Anju assured her.

Jenn hugged Grace. She started to cry. "I can't believe they're
doing this to you."

"Why don't you leave Max and Erin with us for the night?" her
dad said.

Jeff and Mandy gave her a hug.

Nobody looked her in the eye.

They drove in silence through the city. Eyes closed, Grace was aware
only of the shifting light and heat on her face and neck as they moved
under the shadows of high-rises, then back into sunshine, under an
overpass—rumbling echoes overhead—back to open road. And then
the thrum of bridge struts vibrating under the wheels, the dark beneath her closed eyes turning orange with light. She opened them to
green water the color of bottle glass. "Can you close the window?"
she asked, shivering.

"I need the air," he said. "Just—here." He started shrugging off his
sport coat. She held the wheel for him, then took his jacket and
wrapped it over her legs like a blanket.

"Stephen?" she said after a few minutes. Her voice sounded hollow. "Please talk to me."

"And say what, Grace?"

"I don't know. Just, where are you?"

"In the hospital with Jack, in the courtroom." His voice tightened.
"Sitting in bed with you on Christmas Eve, joking about how you got
windburn walking across the mall parking lot."

Her face burned. "I know what you're thinking, but I *was* walking
outside."

"I don't want to hear it, Grace."

"I know there's nothing I can say—"

"Then don't, okay?" The gentleness in his tone undid her.

She began crying. "I am so *so* sorry."

"I know." He reached to cover her hand with his. "I really do."

They drove again in silence. An airplane cut like a scalpel through the layers of pale clouds, and she thought for some reason of that TWA flight that had crashed off Long Island Sound the summer before Erin was born, of the newspaper photos she'd seen nearly a year later of the pieced-together airplane. Over a million pieces of wreckage retrieved from the debris field: a burned seat belt, a Timberland boot, an engagement ring, a child's stuffed Tweety Bird. Now, she wondered, what is the debris field of a life, of a marriage? How many miles, how many years, how many pieces of wreckage?

In the end, the crash detectives determined that the explosion that sent the plane spinning into the Atlantic was caused not by a bomb or an errant government test missile, not by some gross mechanical or human failure, but by a spark no bigger than that needed to light a cigarette. Something *that* small. But what caused the spark, for none of the plane's 150 miles' worth of wiring was frayed or worn. The experts explained how sometimes, in the space between two wires that run parallel to each other, not touching, neither of them damaged, electricity will arc outward, migrating. That was the word they used: *migrating*. It was how she often thought of her love for Noah, a migration to a place she remembered beneath the level of consciousness almost, in her bones and cells, and she knew that no matter what she said to Stephen and no matter how many times in the coming days and weeks she would try to explain what happened, it all began just that simply, just that easily, one tiny negative spark—*hey you*—migrating into tragedy.

They passed an adult bookstore with a battered-looking sedan parked out front, a pawn shop with a neon LOTTERY barely visible in its sun-drenched window, a row of gas stations, a 7-Eleven. She glanced again at Stephen. "Can I tell you one thing?" she said.

He flicked his eyes in her direction. His eyelashes were damp with tears.

"That phone call two nights ago, I was panicked and I couldn't—" She squeezed shut her eyes. "But I ended the affair the *minute* I found out about the report."

"I don't want to know this, Grace."

"I wouldn't have jeopardized the kids, Stephen."

"But you did." His voice was gentle. He shook his head. "Look, I'm not trying to punish you because I know you'll beat yourself up far more than I ever could, but I just don't care right now what you did or why or when you ended it or any of that. Maybe at some point, I will, but right now, the only thing I care about is Jack and that we, that I"—he jabbed a finger at himself—"lost custody of him." He glanced at her. "You having an affair isn't even on the radar screen next to that."

She felt like a fool. He was right.

"All I care about—*all*—is jumping through whatever hoops we have to to get Jack back. And beyond that?" His face tightened. "There is no beyond that."

As soon as they were home Grace walked upstairs to change out of her mother's suit. Her legs felt heavy, leaden, as if she were wading through water. On Jack's door was the yellow: WELCOME HOME JACK! poster that Erin had made only three days ago. The day Jack phoned her in the morning, laughing, all better. *Why you not here, Mama?* She flicked on the lights in his room, then stood for a moment in his doorway, inhaling the scent of talcum powder and floral room fresheners. She felt dead inside, absent from herself. A rocket-shaped sippy cup, half full with apple juice sat on Jack's dresser and it occurred to her that it had probably been sitting there for three days and she should take it downstairs, but she didn't have the energy to do even that.

Standing in her closet in her underwear a few minutes later, her arms goose-bumped, she couldn't decide what to wear. It was only midafternoon, bright sunlight crashing against the windows. But the day felt over. She pulled on the flannel pajamas the kids had given her for Christmas, and crawled into bed. She wanted to just get to tomorrow. Tomorrow, when she could visit Jack.

From the kitchen, she heard the rush of water in the sink and a few minutes later, the loud burping of the coffeemaker. Fractured snippets of TV. Nothing would be on but talk shows and soap operas: betrayal and more betrayal. She thought of Noah, but there was no longer any feeling attached to his name, not even the smallest flicker of desire. She didn't care. Whatever she'd felt for him was gone. All she wanted was for Jack to come home and Stephen to forgive her.

She couldn't sleep and finally gave up. In the bathroom, she pulled her hair into a tight ponytail, surprised by how wild her eyes looked, the pupils dilated as if she were in pain. A moon book of Jack's was on the counter. *When the Moon Broke Away,* about how the moon was made. She picked it up and hugged it to her chest, willing herself to cry.

Downstairs, Stephen was asleep on the couch, knees tucked to his chest, his suit jacket spread over his legs and feet. She moved around the kitchen quietly, glancing at the stack of mail without reading anything, then poured herself a cup of coffee and took it upstairs along with Jack's moon book, holding the mug against her breastbone as she sat in bed, not sleeping or trying to sleep, just thinking Jack's name over and over, as if by saying it she could keep him safe. Jenn and Rebecca and Anju would be with him tonight and she'd see him tomorrow. The song from *Annie* kept sounding stupidly in her head: *Tomorrow! Tomorrow! I love ya tomorrow! You're always a day away!* The colors in the room changed as the light fell, the sharp edges of the bureau and lampshade, the stack of books on the desk by the window growing indistinct, flattening into shape only, into color. Dark brown. Cream. Navy. Burgundy. And rectangle, circle, square. She'd been working on shapes with Jack lately. His favorite was a rocket shape, and she tried to show him how a rocket shape was really a rectangle with a triangle on top, but he had waved her away with disgust. "No, not rectangle and triangle. *Rocket.*"

The phone rang, startling her. She waited for the answering machine to pick up. "Oh, Grace," her mother said, then began to cry, her mangled sobs filling the bedroom, which was steeped in darkness now. Grace didn't move, just lay on the bed, mummy-like, her eyes dry, hugging Jack's moon book to her chest.

Eventually, she heard Stephen rustling around downstairs, then the hall light flipped on, and he came up, hair tousled, sleep lines etched into his face. "My head's killing me," he said as he walked into the bathroom and opened the medicine cabinet for the ibuprofin.

"You probably need to eat," she said.

"I don't think I could keep anything down." He sat on the edge of the bed, elbows to his knees, massaging his temples.

"How about toast?"

"Maybe." He didn't look at her. In the dark bedroom, with only the hall light on behind him, all she could see was his silhouette. "I thought I'd be prepared for when Jack died," he said huskily after a moment. "I knew it would hurt, but—" He looked at her, his eyes glistening. "I mean, we've known for two years now that he wasn't going to make it, so I just thought—" He started crying. "But now that he's not here, I just, I don't know how to do this, Grace. I don't know how I'm going to."

She sat forward, wrapping her arms around him. "Don't," she said. "Don't do this. He's okay, he's— we'll see him tomorrow."

"But this is what it'll be like," he cried. "Somebody or something just takes him away, and there's *nothing*—" the word stretched into a moan "—*nothing* we can do."

They ended up watching TV. The History Channel. It felt safe— battles already won, lives already lived. The phone rang twice more but each time they let the machine pick up. The first time it was Bennett, calling to confirm that their visitation with Jack was all set for ten in the morning. The second call was from Kempley: "Just wanted to find out how things went today. I'll try back later." At one point, Stephen went downstairs and returned with a pint of chocolate ice cream and two spoons. "Why are you being so nice to me?" she asked, her voice breaking.

"Shush," he said gently. "Let's just eat."

The phone rang again—Jenn this time. "Hey, you guys. Just wanted to tell you that Jack's doing great. Rebecca was with him all afternoon, and I've been here since five. The little bugger beat me in *three* games of Candy Land." She paused. "Are you there, Grace?"

Grace gestured for Stephen to hand her the phone. "Hey," she said quietly.

"I've been worried sick about you," Jenn said. "I don't even know what to say."

"I know. Me either." She swallowed hard. "Is he really okay, Jenn? Has he been asking where we are?"

"A few times, but he knows you're coming tomorrow, and everyone's keeping him pretty busy."

She started crying. "Oh, God, Jenn, how can he possibly understand?"

"He doesn't need to, Grace. He really is okay."

After Jenn hung up, Grace handed the receiver to Stephen. Tears were streaming down his face now too. She moved to hold him, and he let her, but only for a moment before he wordlessly rolled away from her into his own separate space.

PART IV

Fear

Everyone knows promises come from fear.

—Anne Michaels

TWENTY-FIVE

*O*nce the unimaginable has happened, how do you believe it won't again? *How do you ever stop being afraid? Or is it that after the unimaginable happens, there is nothing left to fear? What else is fear's purpose, after all, but to protect what we love? Language itself evolved from this fear of loss, the first human sound a cry of separation.*

Don't go.

Come back.

Stay.

Is a voice the opposite of fear, then? Is a word? A string of words? A story? Is silence synonymous with fright?

Think of how, in the immediate aftermath of September 11, when there were no survivors to be found, no more blood to give or supplies to donate, people wrote. On butcher paper and walls and the makeshift plywood boards surrounding Ground Zero. On the posters of the missing. Our "public diaries of grief," one reporter called them. Our "message boards to the dead."

A word. A name. Don't go.

Perhaps even darkness is just another kind of silence. Our innate fear of the dark, scientists say, reaches its peak by age two, then decreases. But I wonder: Is it that our fear lessens with age? Or do we have more words to name the shapes our fears have taken?

Even our laws are just a reflection of our fears. What is a law but a suit of armor composed of words into which we step each day so that we might be safe? The more fears a society has, the more laws. In ancient Greece, even grief was banned, the public lamentation of mourning mothers perceived as a direct threat to the order of the state. Don't go. *And in Ethiopia at the end of the twentieth century, the military junta declared it a crime for the mothers of disappeared sons to cry.* Come back.

The history of medicine is also a history of fear. Think of how in the twelfth century, lepers were so feared that its sufferers were taken to church to have a burial mass said over them as they knelt beneath a black cloth. Lepers were ordered to carry bells or strike wooden sticks together to warn people of their approach. They were forbidden to walk on narrow streets, to ever touch a child.

To speak above a whisper.

In Philadelphia in 1793, during the outbreak of yellow fever, people were afraid to shake hands; they walked in the middle of the streets to avoid contaminated houses; they shot guns indoors to "purify" the air. They feared westerly winds, and they feared the new moon. "It is not death that makes a plague," wrote the physician Benjamin Rush, "[but] the fear and helplessness in people."

In the midst of the influenza outbreak of 1918, people wore gauze masks, sterilized water fountains with blowtorches, put sulfur in their clothing, had their teeth pulled and their tonsils removed. During the polio epidemic, sick children were taken from their homes by police and put in isolation wards. Tuberculosis sufferers were forbidden to laugh.

We scoff at these things now. How naïve people once were, we think. How silly. But we laugh in direct proportion to our fear, for despite all our technology, our scientific and medical breakthroughs, despite our ability to peer inside another's brain or to hold someone's heart in our palm and place it into another man's chest, there is so much that we don't—and maybe can't—ever know.

And so we fear.

Ours is the generation descended from the one that learned the hard way how banal evil could be, how the ordinary, routine surface of everyday life could trick us into complacency, how the worst atrocities of the century could be—and were—committed under our own noses. And so we live now in a world where we fear everyone, where we trust no one: not the kindergarten teacher who lives alone or the neighbor we barely know or even the ordinary woman in St. Louis or Memphis or the Pine Barrens of New Jersey whose youngest son is so terribly sick. Is she a heroic mother, fighting to save her child, or a monster glorying in this drama? The question terrifies us because we can't ever know the answer for sure.

People think the opposite of fear is courage.

It is actually faith.

TWENTY-SIX

Grace sat cross-legged on the floor in her robe and PJs, the coffee table scattered with ransacked photo albums and shoeboxes filled with unsorted pictures. It was not yet four in the morning, but she couldn't sleep. At ten they could visit Jack. Six hours still.

"*A* is for Astronaut," she wrote, the marker squeaking across the shiny paper. Above the words, she glued a photo of Jack in his astronaut pajamas. "*A* is also for Aunt Jenn," she added. She cut Jenn's face from last year's Christmas photo of her and the boys, then started sifting through the photos again, looking for something to go with *B*. Birthdays, she thought. And beach. She held up a photo of Jack playing in the sand the summer before, wearing a sopping wet, sand-crusted T-shirt that hung below his knees, and huge surfer boy mirrored sunglasses that were twice as big as his little bird face.

She turned the picture over, then drew the glue stick across its back. The house was dark, quiet but for the click of scissors or the squeak of the marker. She was making Jack a book for the nurses to read to him when she wasn't with him during these next fourteen days. *Fourteen*. The number was impossible. "*D* is for Daddy," she wrote next to a picture of Jack grabbing Stephen's nose. A game they played: "I got your nose, Daddy!"

"Oh yeah? Well, I got your ear."

"Well I got your other ear!"

She pressed the picture into place. She thought of how Stephen had continued to squeeze her hand even as those words—*affair, adultery*—reverberated around the courtroom.

"*E* is for Erin," she started to write, but her eyes blurred with tears, and she set the marker down, hands in her lap. He was *so* good, she thought, staring again at the picture of Stephen and Jack. And he always had been.

"*G* is for Goose," she wrote. *And good.*

"*H* is for Hospital. And Heart."

"*J* is for Jack."

"*M* is for Mama and Max and Moon." *Munchausen's. Mitochondrial disease.*

She heard the beep of Stephen's alarm upstairs, though outside it was still dark, not yet five. The flush of the toilet, water running through the pipes. So he was still going to the Y. Despite herself, she felt a surge of anger that he could just do the same old things, that even now nothing changed for him. Nothing. He'd probably go swimming the day Jack died, she thought bitterly, then immediately regretted it. Why shouldn't he? What was wrong with her?

"What are you doing?" he asked sleepily from the kitchen doorway a few minutes later, his gym bag slung over his shoulder.

"Making a book for Jack. You want to see?"

He stood behind her and glanced through the letters she'd done so far. "It's great," he said when he finished. "I like the *D* page."

"You're a good dad, Stephen," she said. "I know I don't tell you that enough."

"We're both good parents, Grace." He sighed. "I know that, okay?"

She turned to look up at him, but he wouldn't meet her eyes.

"I'm going to make this up to you," she said thickly.

"You can't." His voice was hard. "I'll be back by eight."

As soon as they walked into the hospital lobby, Kate stood up from a bench near the information booth, her camel-colored coat folded neatly over her arms. "Mr. and Mrs. Connolly," she said, glancing at her watch. "I appreciate your being on time."

Grace couldn't even begin to respond. Nothing *except* being here, *on time,* had mattered since yesterday afternoon. Not even Max and Erin, if the truth be told, not even Stephen. Grace regarded her icily.

He is my *child*, she wanted to scream. My *child*. Do you have any idea what that means. Do you have a clue?

"I'm sorry," Kate stammered. "I didn't mean that to sound . . ."

Grace interrupted. "Can we please just see Jack?"

Before Kate could answer, the guard who had escorted Grace from the hospital three days before stepped out of the glass-fronted security office near the service elevators. "If you'll just step over here with me, folks," he said. He lifted his eyes to Grace's. "It's policy," he said quietly. "I'm real sorry."

Inside the office, the guard asked Grace to set her purse on the table by the door. He quickly rifled through it while they watched, lifting out the picture book she'd made for Jack. "Ms. Helverson?" He held it up to her. "This okay?"

"You have a problem with a *book*!" Grace said, whirling to face Kate.

Kate nodded to the guard, who replaced the book in Grace's purse. "Man, I hate doing this," he mumbled under his breath. He sighed, then asked Grace to stand, arms outstretched at her sides, feet planted apart.

Stephen strode from the room, nearly shoving Kate aside.

"This'll take just a minute," the guard said softly as he moved a security wand over Grace's arms, down her sides to her legs. Grace stared straight ahead at the wall in front of her, at the smudge where a picture must have hung. She was aware of Kate, shifting uncomfortably in the doorway, staring at her feet like a guilty little girl, but to look at her, even in anger or hate—both of which Grace felt—would have been a response and to give Kate even that much would have cost more than Grace could afford.

Jack was sitting up in bed, staring at the TV. Bright January sunlight slanted across his sheets, crowded with stuffed animals, books, and Matchbox cars. His nose was running and dried tears had left salty streaks on his cheeks. Grace stepped back when she saw him. "They *promised*," she wailed in a low whisper to Stephen. "They *promised* they wouldn't leave him alone." They: Jenn, Rebecca, Anju.

"Mama!" Jack said, pulling himself up by the metal bed rails, his Ronald McDonald hospital gown hanging off one shoulder. "Why you not stay me?"

She was across the room in a minute. "Well, I wanted to, you silly goose." She hitched up his gown and held his little face in her hands. "I couldn't *wait* to see you!"

"Daddy too?" He squinted up at her. The left side of his face, which he must have slept on, was puffy with fluid. "Why you come, Daddy?" he asked over her shoulder.

"What do you mean?" Stephen growled. "You got a problem with that, Mister?" He tousled Jack's hair as Grace lifted him carefully over the side of the bed. He was warm and cuddly and he smelled of baby powder and bananas, and Grace wanted to just stand there in the sunlight, nose pressed against his cheek, forever. "Oh Jack," she whispered into his skin. "Mama missed you so much." She nuzzled her face into his neck. "I was so excited I couldn't even go to sleep," she whispered in his ear, and he put his hands on her cheeks and put his forehead to hers and whispered, "Me *either*, Mama!"

"Really?" she laughed. And then, "Uh-oh." She squinted at him suspiciously. "Were you up all night with Mr. Moon again?"

He laughed. "Yeah, I was!"

"*What?*" Stephen said, "I thought I told you to stop hanging around that guy!"

"But, Daddy, he comes to see me," Jack said. "He comes right in my window."

"Your *window?*" Stephen bellowed, hands on his hips. "Let me see!" He stalked across the room and yanked up the already opened blinds. More light, bright, pure yellow—the exact color of her child's laughter, Grace thought—spilled into the room.

"Well, I don't see that Moon guy anywhere!" Stephen turned from the window back to Jack and Grace. He pointed at Jack. "Are you *sure* he comes in the window?"

"Daddy!" Jack said. "Mr. Moon isn't outside in daytime! He only comes see me in night time!" He laughed again, and one of the monitors started beeping. Rebecca hurried in. "Hey guys!" she said, pushing the reset button. She wagged her finger at Jack. "What are you up to, buddy?" then hurried out, calling "I'll be back." Laughter increased the heart rate, Grace knew and abruptly remembered accusing Stephen once of hastening Jack's death by making him laugh so much. Regret spiraled through her.

They lowered the bars on Jack's bed so that they could both sit with him, both touch him. Grace watched his chest rise and fall as he and Stephen zoomed his cars across his blankets. Despite the oxygen he was still getting, his nostrils flared with each breath, which meant he was still working too hard to breathe. Why hadn't Rebecca or Anju noticed? Grace wondered. But they wouldn't unless they'd actually spent time interacting with him, getting him to talk and laugh. And mornings on this floor—any floor in a children's hospital, she imagined—were crazy, and Jack *was* doing better. Still, it seemed another failure of her's and Anju's, of the hospital's and the whole child protection system's, because nothing about this situation was really protecting Jack, which was the only way any of it could have somehow made sense. She thought of the outcomes-study she'd read years ago and which she'd thought of every time she chose to stay in the hospital with Jack no matter what he was in for: hospital deaths were typically the result not of any single catastrophic error—the wrong surgery or wrong medicine or even negligence—but were the consequence of a series of seemingly trivial errors. Something as simple as Jack's oxygen being not quite high enough . . . She thought of that airplane crash again: one small spark.

"Hey, Goose," she interrupted his game. "Did you see Dr. Mehta today?"

He nodded. "I was crying," he said.

"I see that." She traced the line of a tear down his cheek. "I think a tear went right here," she said. She angled his face in the light and pretended to study his other cheek. "And another went this way." She took a breath. "So why were you crying?" she asked after a minute. Please don't let it be because of me, she thought. Because I wasn't here.

"I didn't want Dr. Mehta listen to my heart today," Jack said, zooming a police car over the mountain he'd made with his knee. He looked at her.

Grace made a sad face. "Oh, poor Dr. Mehta," she said. "Why didn't you want her to listen today?"

"I just didn't."

"So what you want to play with me now?" he asked after they'd played Candy Land and cars and read through half a dozen books. The hour was up.

"Well, Mama and Daddy have to go soon," Grace told him in an artificial voice that felt like yet another betrayal. Of them both. She didn't care that he was only three. He shouldn't think, even for a second, that leaving him was somehow *okay* for her, a choice. Except wasn't this what she'd done on Christmas Eve? *This supposedly devoted mother.* Hadn't she chosen to leave him to be with Noah? The thought made her heart quicken. Did it matter that he'd been napping most of the time that she was gone, that she was home by the time he awoke?

"You can't go," Jack was whining now.

"But Rebecca's going to come play with you," Grace persisted.

"No," he whimpered. "Not Becca, Mama. I want *you* to stay me."

"Oh, honey-bunny, I can't, but I'm going to come back in two days." She held up two fingers. "Only two!" She smiled so brightly, it hurt. "Look! One. Two."

His chin quivered and two huge tears spilled from his eyes.

"And you know what else," she rushed on. "Mama made you a special book." She opened to the first page. "See, *A* is for Astronaut. Who wants to be an astronaut?"

"I don't know," he said, hanging his head.

"*What*?" Stephen started to tickle him.

"No, Daddy, don't!" Jack swatted the book onto the floor, crying now. "I want Mama to stay me."

"Oh sweetie, Mama wants to stay with you more than anything, but I can't. That's why I made you a special book." She pulled him to her. "And Aunt Jenn is going to read it to you and Rebecca." She looked at Stephen helplessly.

"Mr. and Mrs. Connolly?" Kate said from the doorway. "It's time."

"Hey Jack-attack," Stephen said, "How about if I read you your new book?"

"No!" Jack sobbed. "I don't want you to read me, Daddy. I want Mama to stay me!" His monitor started beeping.

"Please, Jack." Grace begged. "Oh Goose, please, please don't cry, it's not good for your heart." Would Kate blame her for this too? "Will you please leave?" she said frantically to Kate. "Can't you see that we're doing our best?"

"Two minutes," Kate said and walked away.

The minute she did, Grace turned back to Jack. "Oh sweetie, you're going to have lots of fun with all your friends and maybe Becca will take you down to the playroom and let you do the computers. What do you think about that?"

"But you have to stay me," he sobbed.

"I want to, baby, Mama loves you so much." Tears streamed from her eyes. "Can't you do something?" she hissed to Stephen over his head. "I'm not just going to—"

"Hey buddy." It was Rebecca. "Did I hear someone say something about computers?" Grace hadn't heard her come in, and smiled gratefully. Wordlessly, Rebecca handed Grace a Kleenex to dry her eyes, then sat on the opposite side of the bed, stroking Jack's arm. "I've got a present for you," Rebecca teased gently, and pulled a video out from behind her back, then quickly hid it when Jack turned to look at her. This was horrible, Grace thought. They were all bribing him, tricking him, betraying him.

Kate had returned with the security guard. "I really need you to go now."

"No," Jack started crying again. "You can't."

The security guard met her eyes, the expression in his own, compassionate. She imagined he was a father himself, and she understood then that the world really was divided into two kinds of people, and it wasn't rich and poor or educated versus uneducated or black against white, but something so much simpler, so much more important:

those who were parents and those who weren't. She knew it was un-
fair, unjustified—she had enough friends without children who
would have been devastated by such a judgment. And yet, she
couldn't have rescinded the thought either. Nothing in life, *nothing*,
was more important than loving a child, and nothing was more important in her life—than loving her children. Never had she suspected that her e-mail to Noah last January, her stupid adolescent
e-mail, would result in this kind of damage.

"Shush, baby, it's okay," she whispered to Jack. "We can't just leave
him like this," she sobbed to Stephen.

"Well, we have to!" he snapped, prying Jack's fingers from her
sweater. Jack started screaming. "Goddamnit," Stephen said, "would
you go? You aren't helping."

She pushed herself out of his room, coatless, her breathing harsh,
her ribs feeling as if they were broken. "Stay me," she heard Jack
scream as the door shut, and she literally sank, crouched against the
wall by the elevator, forehead to her knees, holding her elbows, afraid
she was going to be sick. She saw Kate, a blur of brown shoes and tan
coat.

"I'm sorry, Mrs. Connolly." It was Kate. "You may not believe me,
but—"

"You're right," Grace practically spat, lifting her head. "I don't believe you. Just get away from me."

Kate took a step back.

"You're heartless," Grace continued, forcing herself up. "You are a
horrible—" The elevator doors pinged open and she backed into
Jenn, who was just stepping out.

"Grace, my God, what the hell happened?"

"What *happened*?" Grace sobbed. "He was alone, Jenn, that's what
happened. And you promised! You *promised* you'd stay with him."

"I did," Jenn cried. "I was just—"

The elevator doors closed.

TWENTY-SEVEN

They didn't speak on the ride home. They didn't look at each other. At the house, Stephen pulled into the drive, but kept the engine running. "You aren't coming in?" Grace asked.

"I've got to get back to work." He was staring ahead, hands on the steering wheel, as if the car were still moving. She followed his gaze and tried to imagine what he was seeing, what he was thinking. The unseasonably warm winter had caused some of the tulips they'd planted last fall to bloom—blue, purple, and yellow. She stared at the bulbs, thinking of how all that life and energy was pushing up only ten feet from where, right now, her marriage was ending.

Still not looking at her, his voice directionless, he asked, "When are you getting the kids from your mother's?"

"In a little bit."

He nodded. "They need to go back to school." He sounded beat, and she didn't have the heart to argue. The silence between them lengthened, the shadow of their words was elongated and out of proportion, as if what they weren't saying had more substance than what they were. She wanted to ask, to say it out loud, *we're done, aren't we?* But she was afraid. Certain questions were like comets, asteroids with the long tail of unknowing, and sometimes they extinguished themselves without answer, and sometimes they exploded into the world so powerfully that everything before that question would become extinct.

Like the first time after hearing the words *mitochondrial disease* that she asked about his prognosis. She'd had that feeling then that if she could have just *not* asked, the answer itself wouldn't have existed. Heisenberg: *The questions we ask change the world we see.*

"Will you be home for dinner?" she said as she got out of the car.

It was gorgeous out. A brilliant blue sky. Her entire life felt like that color, she thought, which wasn't really a color at all but just a distortion of light through specific ions in the atmosphere.

"I'll be home," he said, as if he couldn't promise anything beyond just that much. Overhead, a line of birds stitched a seam across the open wound of sky.

Max and Erin were subdued at dinner. Stephen explained as best as he could what had happened. Grace listened numbly. Erin started crying and Grace pulled her onto her lap and held her close.

All afternoon, Grace had had moments of glancing around her home, taking in the most ordinary objects: the Question Jar, a white coffee mug with the name of her hair salon on it, potholders Erin had made, Max's hockey schedule on the fridge, a scribble of Jack's, the green and purple UMDF magnet. Her home, these *things*. She thought of how a victim of Post-Tramautic Stress Disorder often needed to touch objects—concrete, ordinary objects, as a reminder: that he was *not* trapped in some rain-soaked jungle in Vietnam; she was *not* in the midst of whatever moment was the absolute worst of her life.

Outside the day faded, like a Polaroid reversing itself, clarity coming undone. The edges of the lake blurred, trees leaving smears of color across the broken bone of the horizon.

After dinner, Grace gave Erin a bath and read to her, then curled on her side in Erin's bed, stroking her hair, watching her fall asleep. Butterscotch-scented bubble bath tonight. Strawberry-scented shampoo. "You smell like an ice-cream sundae," Grace whispered.

Just as she was rising to leave, Erin opened her eyes. "Mama?"

"I thought you were asleep," Grace said. "What is it, lovey?"

"Do you think Jack's afraid?"

"Oh, Erin, no, honey. He *likes* the hospital, you know that. He gets to watch movies and have the remote control to himself and he can eat dinner in bed."

"But . . ." Her voice wobbled. "He's used to you being with him."

"I know, and you are a wonderful, *wonderful,* big sister to worry about Jack, but I really think he's okay. Becca's with him tonight, and Aunt Jenn was there all day." She kissed Erin on the side of the head. "Why don't you draw some pictures for his room tomorrow? I bet that would cheer him up."

"Okay," Erin said, turning on her side and snuggling into the pillow. As Grace was leaving though, she asked. "Can you leave my closet light on tonight?"

"Of course," Grace said, her throat scratchy with sadness. Erin had never before been afraid of the dark.

She knocked on Max's door, then pushed it open. He was lying on his bed, staring at the poster of Wayne Gretzky taped to his ceiling. "You okay?" she asked.

He didn't look at her. "What's going to happen to Jack?"

"What Dad said. Hopefully, he'll be home in thirteen days."

Max nodded. "Do you really think they'll try to take us?"

"No, honey, I don't." She stepped over his book bag and a pile of sports magazines to get to the bed, then sat next to him. "We just want to be careful," she said.

He didn't answer, just continued to stare up at the ceiling.

"Hey," she said quietly. "Do you believe me?"

He shrugged. "What if you're wrong?"

She sighed. "I don't think I am, Max."

"Well, I'd just run away if they tried to take me."

"Oh, God, Max, that would be the absolute worst thing you could do." She stared at her hands, her heart pounding, panicked even at the thought of him running.

"*Why?* They're the ones who—"

"Shush. Listen to me." She laid her hand on his chest.

"I'm not going with them, Mom." Tears welled in his eyes.

"And I don't think you'll have to, sweetie, but *if*—and it's a big if, Max, but *if* Child Protective Services took you, running away would only make things even worse." But what could be worse than some stranger dropping you off with a family you didn't know, or worse, leaving you in a group home? How had this happened, she wondered thickly. Four months ago they had been arguing because she didn't know the names of any of the Flyers' players.

"If," she began again, "*if* anything were to happen, I would need you to watch out for Erin." Surely they would be kept together, she thought, but she didn't know this either. Her hands were shaking. Stephen was right, she thought. She had jeopardized her children, and it didn't matter if it was intentional or not. She looked at Max. "I am so sorry. I am so so sorry that we even have to talk about this."

Stephen had left the metro section of the *Inquirer* opened to the page with the article about her on her side of the bed.

"What's this?" She picked it up.

"Your fifteen minutes of fame." He didn't look up from his laptop.

And there it was. "Mother Charged with Rare Disorder Loses Custody of Child."

Her mouth fell open. "Who—How did they—" She looked at him, then at the paper. Today's date in the corner.

"I don't know, Grace," Stephen said. "I assume these things are public record. Sheila brought it to me this afternoon." Sheila. His assistant.

Philadelphia prosecutors may soon find themselves in court trying to prove the existence of a rare psychological disorder. Munchausen Syndrome by Proxy is an illness whereby the seemingly ideal mother of a sick child actually induces the illness herself, solely to get fame and attention. It won't be the first time the city has seen such a case . . .

She read it through once but couldn't focus, the words jumping out at her. She saw Marie Noe's name, then her own, then Jack's. It was like reading a foreign language, trying to piece together meaning from the few translatable words. "Disorder," "killing," "further investigation," "state custody." She looked at Stephen, uncomprehending, then sat on the edge of the bed and tried again.

In 1999 the story of Marie Noe, the Philadelphia woman accused of this same disorder, received national coverage when Noe confessed to killing eight of

*her ten children, all of whom had died between 1949 and 1968. At the time of
their deaths, the cause was attributed to SIDs. Noe was even featured under a
pseudonym in a 1963* Life *magazine article that called her "America's most famous bereaved mother."*

*Although the parallels between the Noe case and this most recent one are
markedly different, they have one chilling similarity: in both, the life of an innocent child hangs in the balance. Which is why, according to a spokesperson for
Philadelphia Child Protective Services, the state took immediate custody of
three-year-old Jack Connolly.*

Grace paused without looking up, aware of Stephen's eyes on her,
the heat of his anger. She let the paper drop. "Fifteen minutes of
fame?" Her arms were shaking. "You really think—"

"No." Stephen's face reddened. "That was shitty. I'm sorry."

She nodded, lifted the paper again, and continued reading.

*The child's mother, 37-year-old Grace Connolly, insists that her son is suffer-
ing from mitochondrial disease, a genetic disorder in which the body cannot convert
food into energy. "But," says one of the many people who comprise Jack's medical
team (consisting of a cardiologist, nephrologists, palliative care expert, and scores of
therapists, specialized nurses, and respiratory technicians), "anyone who knows
this child would be hard-pressed to believe he's as sick as his mother insists."*

The words were like the jagged boulders in the middle of a rapids:
everything that didn't find its way around them—her name, her family, her marriage, her *life*—would be smashed into pieces.

Everyone she knew read the *Inquirer*: her neighbors, her parents'
friends, the kids' teachers probably, people at the hospital, Stephen's
colleagues. Everyone.

She started reading the article again, trying to focus. Her eyes kept
jumping to that one phrase: *"But, says one of the many people who comprise Jack's medical team . . ."*

Who? She wondered. Who?

The psychiatrist approved by the court worked in a nondescript office
building a few blocks from Family Court. Industrial gray carpet and
mismatched chairs filled the waiting area, along with an overflowing

chest of battered toys and books. Only nine in the morning, and already the room was crowded with sullen-looking parents and kids.

The psychologist, after listening to Grace tell her story, asked if Grace was obsessed with Jack's illness. And okay, maybe she was, Grace thought, though she hated that word. *Obsessed*. It implied something dark and inappropriate, something with an ulterior motive. "What could I possibly have to gain by this so-called *obsessive* behavior, other than the obvious?" she asked Dr. Lee. "I want my child to be well. I want him to live." Dr. Lee nodded, dark bangs obscuring her eyes. She seemed to be waiting. But for what? Because this was it. The whole story. Grace wanted Jack to live.

"Do you think this desire of yours is realistic?"

Grace looked at her. Did it matter? After a moment, she said, "Jack has lived far longer than any of the doctors thought he would." She felt as if she were talking through a long cardboard tube, her words disembodied and far away. "And in part maybe it's because I *was* unrealistic, because I *was* consumed. But I had to be. The experts didn't just show up at our door. *I* found *them*. *I* contacted *them*." She raised her eyes to the doctor's, angry tears blurring her vision. "Are you suggesting I shouldn't have?"

Dr. Lee didn't respond directly. "Would it be fair to say that you saw yourself as a hero, of sorts?"

"Hero?" Grace repeated, feeling dizzy. "Is that—" She stopped. *"Hero?"* The word slammed into her, and she felt its impact but couldn't make sense of it. She couldn't connect it to herself. She couldn't begin to understand what Dr. Lee was talking about. Unless Grace hadn't heard her correctly? But no, she had echoed that word, *hero,* back to Dr. Lee twice and Dr. Lee hadn't corrected her.

Grace leaned forward in the chair. Her child was dying, and he was alone in the hospital and so *hero*, whatever that meant—because Grace could not grasp its meaning—was a preposterous, stupid word.

"You look surprised," Dr. Lee said.

"Hero?" Grace practically spat the word. She didn't care if she was supposed to be calm or agreeable or whatever Bennett had advised. *Hero?*

"Is it really that shocking to you, Grace? Your friends and family and even some of the doctors and nurses have used similar terms to describe you." Dr. Lee glanced at the manila file folder in her lap. "Let's see, you're 'incredible,' 'amazing,' 'strongest person they know,' and yes, here, 'hero.' " She glanced up. "Isn't it at least possible, Grace, that Jack's illness made you feel important in a way you never had before?"

The days had no shape. Stephen went to the Y, then to work; the kids went to school. They were like a family in a play. A pretend family. An intact family. Stay-at-home mother, hardworking father, older brother, younger sister. They attended a hockey game of Max's one night, played Monopoly another. Stephen brought work home and stayed up at the kitchen table, a martini next to him. Grace sat in bed with the TV on, trying to organize boxes full of loose photos into albums. She kept finding the pictures that she'd cut to make Jack's book. In some of them Stephen was missing, in some of them she was missing, in some, Jack. These were the photos that came the closest, she thought, to revealing the truth.

Twelve days.
    And then ten.
    Eight.
    She went to the bookstore in the new mall and sat in the café for an entire morning. Weak wintry light spilled over the bleached wooden tables. She chose one near the wall, away from the counter and the noise of the espresso machines. She forced herself to take a sip of her coffee. She couldn't think about touching the cranberry scone she had purchased. She wasn't sure why she had even bought it. Instinct, not desire. Evolution's lesson of survival: eat when you can, for you never know when in the future there will be a war or a famine or a drought. It occurred to her that maybe this was, in part, what she'd done with Noah: tried to stockpile love, more than she

needed, against the time when Jack was gone and she would not have enough.

After a while, she left the café and browsed, ending up in the true crime section. *What kind of person reads these books?* she wondered. *And why?* She stared at the titles. *Special Delivery:* "A family slaughtered and a baby born by murder." *Sleep, My Child, Forever:* "The mesmerizing crime story of a mother whose double life hid the dark heart of a murderer." *Mother's Day:* "The shocking tale of a mother who murdered her daughters with the help of her sons."

Small Sacrifices.

A Mother's Betrayal.

And then *Cradle of Death.* The Marie Noe Story.

Grace pulled it from the shelf, a hard knot in her stomach, and opened to the insert—*eight pages of photos!* They were black-and-white. In one, the Noes stood in front of a window, shadows from the Venetian blinds casting dark bars across their faces. They looked like the stern Iowa farm couple in Grant Wood's *American Gothic*. The same gaunt faces and stoic expressions. In another photo, the Noes stood in New Cathedral Cemetery, at one of the children's graves. On the next page a photograph of St. Hugh's, the church "around the corner from their home," that the Noes "regularly attended."

Abruptly, she closed the book, and set it on the shelf, not bothering to put it back in the right place. This is not your life, she told herself. And these horrible stories have nothing to do with you.

In the children's section, she pulled *The Child's Everything About the Moon Book* from the shelf. There was a cartoon picture on the cover of a red-haired boy in a space suit. She took it to one of the overstuffed armchairs to glance through, thinking maybe she'd get it for Jack.

"There's no sound on the moon," she read. "So you can shout as loud as you want or play drums all night, and the grownups won't tell you to 'Be Quiet!'

"Your alarm clock can't wake you up on the moon, because you won't be able to hear it, and it doesn't matter if you sing out of tune because nobody will hear you!"

She smiled. Jack would love this!

But a few pages later, she read: "If you weigh forty pounds on earth, on the moon you will weigh only seven. On the moon it seems you would hardly be there at all." She closed the book and left it on the table next to her.

You would hardly be there at all.

TWENTY-EIGHT

S even days.
Six.

She walked around the lake, her hands in the pockets of her sweatshirt. It was so silent. Nothing but the crunch of her footsteps, the crack of a branch, the rustle of an animal she didn't see or a bird whose name, a year ago she wouldn't have known. *Chimney swift, Northern mockingbird, Eastern bluebird.* She thought of Noah, of John James Audubon. The irony of his killing the birds he loved and wanted to save. Even that seemed related now to Munchausen's. Everything did.

"How do you know he wasn't the one who accused you?" Stephen stood at the counter making a martini. She knew immediately who he meant.

"I just know," she said.

"You know," he mocked. "You questioned *me*, but with him you *know*."

"I didn't say I didn't question him too. But he wouldn't have done this. He had no reason."

"How do you know he's not lying? Maybe he wanted to punish you for dumping him all those years ago."

"Please, Stephen. I don't want to defend him to you. He just wouldn't."

"Does he know that you've lost your child because of him?"

She watched him peel a lemon rind into a long curl and drop it into the chilled glass. "I haven't spoken to him, if that's what you're asking."

He glanced at her over his shoulder, eyebrows raised, then turned back around. "So you're still protecting him."

"Protecting him from what?"

Stephen glanced at her, the muscles around his eyes tensed with anger. "Protecting him from *what*?" he said as he turned all the way around to face her. "How about from the fact that he's single-handedly *fucked* up our lives for starters? How about the fact that he single-handedly cost me, *me*"—he jabbed his finger at his chest— "custody of my child?" He whirled back around, picked up the lemon and threw it against the sink, knocking his martini over, the glass shattering, vodka everywhere. "Goddamnit!"

Grace sat at the table, head bowed, hands over her ears. When she looked up, Stephen was crouched on the floor, angrily picking up broken glass.

On the opposite side of the lake, the land sloped towards the water, then back up. Through the bars of the trees, she saw a bright spot of color. Marriott Nielsen out jogging. A car passed and she looked up, waving out of habit. Demetra Schoch. It was a small neighborhood, and though they didn't often socialize, the neighbors all knew the basics of each other's lives. They knew that Grace was Ellen and Paul Martin's daughter, Stephen Connolly's wife, the mother of three children. They knew her youngest had some sort of terminal disease—a strange name, something rare. They might have said that Grace was a smart woman, that she had a master's degree. University of Pennsylvania, something related to medicine. Not a doctor or nurse, though. Something academic. And Stephen worked with one of the Center City banks. A great guy, they might have said. Would give you the shirt off his back. A swimmer. You could set your watch by him at the Y. Six o'clock every morning.

Or at least that was what they might have said a week ago. Now all she was was the woman who had lost custody of her child, the woman so desperate for attention she had made her child sick just to get it. She stared across the lake, too small for boats, but perfect for ice-skating, for playing hockey, for swimming. The branches of the pines looked dislocated and broken. The sky was a pale sling, holding the world in place.

V is for Visit. Mama and Daddy love to Visit Jack.
And Very. Mama loves Jack Very Very much.

"Are we going to talk about this?" Grace asked, rolling over to face Stephen. He was sitting in bed, staring at the TV, arms crossed over his bare chest.

"Not at eleven thirty at night." He flicked the remote. Reruns of *Gunsmoke*, Doc and Miss Kitty leaning on the bar of the Long Branch, talking to Matt Dillon.

"I didn't necessarily mean tonight. Just sometime?"

He flicked the channels again. *Larry King Live*, an interview with the guy from *America's Most Wanted*. Back to *Gunsmoke* again.

Grace turned back onto her side, eyes closed. She heard Stephen lift the snifter of Grand Marnier from the bedside table and drain it in a gulp. "Look," he sighed. "I'm pretty confused about things. I don't know what I think right now . . . about anything."

She sat up, chilled suddenly. "You're not suggesting that I might have hurt—that—"

He wouldn't look at her.

"Oh, Stephen, don't," she said. "Please. I know you're angry, but you can't— You don't believe for a minute that I would—"

"Didn't, Grace. I *didn't* believe."

"What are you saying?" Her voice sounded high and far away, as if she were speaking in a place where the air was too thin. "You *know* that I would never harm Jack, Stephen." She looked at him, begging with her eyes, which he refused to meet. "How dare you," she said after a minute. Her voice broke. "How dare you."

He sighed. "You're right, okay? You're right. I'm just so goddamn angry."

"Do you hate me *that* much?"

He looked at her sadly. "Sometimes." He flicked off the TV, then turned onto his side.

The days were like the chalked squares in a game of hopscotch. Every other one she leaped over, landing on one foot, unbalanced. Jack's name was like the white pebble tossed across the grid and that she must try to retrieve without falling.

Five days.

Four.

Then three.

She handed Erin the pack of yellow construction paper. Jack's favorite color. The color of Mr. Moon. They'd shopped at the craft store after school. "You want to work at the table while I make dinner?" Grace asked as she pulled a package of hamburger rolls from the grocery bag. From Max's room upstairs, rock music throbbed full blast.

"But what if I don't finish and it's time to eat?"

"We'll just have dinner in the family room. How would that be?"

Erin nodded, smiling. This was how it had been every night: takeout pizza, Chinese food, tonight sloppy joes in front of the TV. As if they couldn't bear to be a real family until Jack came home.

It had been twelve days. Two to go. Grace would see him tomorrow, bring more drawings from Erin. His room was crammed. Balloons from the nurses, a *Blue's Clues* balloon from Kempley, stuffed animals, a remote-control car that he could race in the bed from Becca, cards, drawings, even an orange-and-black Flyers' poster from Max.

"Hey, duckey, before you start, would you do me a favor and go tell your brother to turn down that music?" Grace said

"Mom," Erin whined.

"Oh, come on. And tell him we bought scones."

Two more days. It seemed impossible that they'd done it. Only two more. She reached beneath the cabinet for the electric skillet. Anju had phoned the judge after that first awful morning and arranged to lengthen the visits so that they had more transition time before leaving. It had been better. Not good, but better. Jack understood at least. "Two days," he'd say as they were leaving. He'd hold up two fingers. "You come visit me again in two days, right Mama?"

Outside the sky was still faintly light, though it was close to six. Shadows stretched from the pines towards the lake, the sun reflected in its center like a heart. Although it was only February, she pushed up the window over the sink, and a balmy pine-scented breeze drifted in, rustling the pile of drawings, homework papers, and permission slips stacked on the counter. Grace inhaled sharply, wanting to cry almost, though she wasn't sure why. Not sadness, but the opposite maybe. Happiness? It seemed perverse, but there it was. *Two days*. They would get through this. She smiled, moving purposefully through the rest of the house, opening windows, letting in the air. And then upstairs, where Erin and Max were laughing in his bedroom. "Hey guys, help me get some of these windows open," she called down the hallway.

"Hello? Like, it's winter, Mom," Max called to her from his room.

"But it's nice out. Come on." Max was trying to get Erin to squeeze a fake rubber eyeball. His room was filthy, not a single area of carpet showing beneath the dirty clothes and books and hockey equipment. "How can you stand this?" Grace said from the door. How about opening at least one window?" She turned to go. "Did Erin tell you we bought scones?"

"No!" He started to push by her, but Grace stopped him, her arm across the doorway. "Window first," she said, pointing.

"So what kind of scones?" Max followed Grace down the stairs, Erin in tow. Four steps from the bottom, he leaped over the banister, landing on the floor with a huge thud.

"Max!" Grace said. "I've told you not to do that a thousand times. You're going to yank the banister right out of the wall one day."

But the phone was ringing and Max was sliding across the waxed floor in his sock feet as if on a boogie board at the beach.

Grace winked at Erin. "What are we going to do with that boy?"

But then Max was shouting, "Mom!" and his face was white and his eyes were scared and he was thrusting the receiver at her like it was burning. "I think it's Aunt Jenn."

She was already across the room. "You *think*?"

"I don't know, she's really crying."

Her father drove. Her mom came to stay with Max and Erin. Rush hour, the traffic going in the opposite direction, away from the city, was bumper-to-bumper. Like an emergency evacuation, she thought. As if all these people were trying to escape something horrible that she was rushing toward.

They didn't listen to the radio, didn't talk. The road narrowed for construction. Men in hard hats and T-shirts were finishing up for the afternoon, the thick smell of tar in the air. Was this the day Jack would die? She had tried to imagine before what it would be like, but it had been nothing like this: the sky feverish with sunset, the ragged red fibers of the clouds. Every now and then, her dad laid his hand over hers and squeezed. "He's a survivor, Grace. He's pulled through worse."

But I was with him, she thought. And then horribly—at least they can't blame me.

"Mama's here, Goose. It's okay. Mama's here. Mama's got you." He'd already coded twice. Twice they had resuscitated him. She understood that he would not live, vital organs already shutting down.

He squeezed her fingers. "Ma-ma," he croaked. "You. Stay. Me?"

"I'm never letting go," she whispered into his ear. "Daddy either." Jack nodded. He kept reaching to itch his nose, a reaction to the morphine, but he'd nod off halfway, arm dropping to his chest. And then he'd stop breathing, the monitor would beep, and he'd jerk awake. "Ma-ma?"

"I'm here, Goose. Daddy too."

How do you memorize a face, a skill so crucial to survival that there is a specific region of the brain that is responsible for this and only this?

His reddish rooster hair. His long eyelashes. His fierce little eyebrows.

People moved in and out, but she didn't take her eyes off him. She thought of how damaged hearts are usually larger than healthy ones, sometimes two times as large, and she knew that her own was huge and that after this night, it would be filled with scars that for the rest of her life would force it to work harder and harder just to keep beating. She thought too of how, when she was giving birth to Jack, she had told Stephen, and even the doctor, at one point, "Don't touch me," not because of the pain or even irritation, but from concentration. Never had she been more focused on a single act, more aware of her body. She understood now that Jack's dying was similar, that she would become untouchable again, every cell, every pore, every muscle and bone turned towards letting him go.

"His S4s are getting worse," someone said. "He's Cheyne-Stoking." She and Stephen sat on either side of him, holding his hands, watching his chest, his breathing starting and stopping, growing more shallow, raspier. Anju came in to intubate him, securing the respirator tube to his cheek with adhesive tape. Later still, Grace heard someone mention the ECMO. Extra Corporeal Membrance Oxygenator, followed by Anju's "Absolutely not."

"What did they just ask?" Stephen said.

Grace explained. "The ECMO's basically a pump that takes all the blood from the body, reoxygenates it, then forces it to circulate."

"So why—"

"The mortality rates are awful."

"But isn't it better—"

She met his eyes. "No," she said gently. "No."

The sense of hearing is the last sense to go, and so they read him his moon books. *"Look! There's a new moon tonight,"* said Bobby. *"I wonder what they did with the old one,"* said Betty. There was an ocean in Grace's chest, her breath like waves pulling her under. *"Well, it just so happens that my birthday's tomorrow,"* said Bear. *"Well, it just so happens that my birthday's tomorrow, said Moon.* She thought as she had so often these past three years of how there are no muscles to help push air from lungs, how breathing out is simply a relaxing of the muscles used to breathe in. A matter of letting go.

"Goodnight stars. Goodnight air. Goodnight noises everywhere."

Kate was in the hallway, wearing jeans and a Villanova sweatshirt, her eyes swollen, skin blotchy from crying. As soon as Grace saw her, she faltered, turning back to Stephen and burying her face into his shoulder. "Make her go," she whispered. Her throat hurt from the hours of talking and reading to Jack nonstop. At one point, someone had brought coffee but she had forgotten it until it was too cold.

"I'm not here for Child Protective Services." Kate started crying. "I am so so sorry."

"This isn't the time," Stephen said.

"I know, I just . . . I never meant . . . ."

Grace started crying and Stephen's arm tightened across her shoulders. "Please go," she sobbed into his shoulder, though she was talking to Kate. "If you have a heart at all—at *all*, don't make us have to look at *you* or feel sorry for *you*."

"Grace," Stephen said.

"No!" Grace wailed. "Hasn't she done enough? Hasn't she—" She couldn't finish.

She heard Kate walking away, the squeak of tennis shoes over the tile floor, the ping of the elevator. When she looked up, the hallway was empty. In the playroom, early morning sunlight was just starting to fall over the bright yellow playhouse with the plastic flowers in the window box and the bright red shutters.

A child's funeral. An oxymoron. *Child's. Funeral.* And yet ten million children in the world die every year. Every 3.6 seconds someone dies of hunger, three-fourths of them children. In the United States alone, 145,000 children and teens die each year. A baby dies every nineteen minutes. One out of every 139 children never makes it until his or her first birthday.

Still.

A child's funeral.

Stephen wore his Eeyore tie, and they served Jack's favorite foods: grilled cheese sandwiches with the crusts cut off and graham crackers and grapes. Chocolate milk. J candy. They played Elton John's "Rocket Man," and Frank Sinatra's "Fly Me to the Moon." It seemed the entire cardiology floor was there. Rebecca and Colin, Anju, the nurses, even one of the cleaning women. Kempley flew in from Charlotte. Jenn and Diane and all three boys were there. Bennett. Jeff and Mandy, Grace's grandfather. The security guard from the hospital. The judge.

PART V
Grief

Every story is a story about death. But perhaps, if we are lucky, our story about death is also a story about love.

—Helen Humphreys, *Lost Garden*

I honestly believe that people who never have children or who never love a child are doomed to a sort of foolishness because it can't be described or explained, that love. I didn't know anything before I had him, and I haven't learned anything since I lost him. Everything that isn't loving a child is just for show.

—Haven Kimmel, *The Solace of Leaving Early*

TWENTY-NINE

*P*erhaps grief enters our lives like a virus, most deadly when first encountered. After a while we become resistant; we adapt. And perhaps too, as it was with the mitochondria, we find that this grief has become a part of who we are.

"We die with the dying," the poet T. S. Eliot wrote. A part of us is forever lost. Amputated. So we will learn to write with our left hand instead of our right, to move from a wheelchair to a car without the use of our legs. We will learn to laugh again, though the sound will be altered, and we will learn to love again, though never in the same way.

When Mount Pinatubo erupted in the Philippines in 1991, a stratospheric cloud of sulfur dioxide circled the Earth within three weeks, leaving in its wake unusually brilliant sunsets and clouds the color of fire. Grief is like this, mythic and terrible, sorrow undoing the world so completely that even the clouds on the opposite ends of the Earth are altered.

No wonder incidents of agoraphobia arise after bereavements. Nothing holds us, nothing remains—not even the familiar sky—to anchor us to the lives we once led. The emptiness is unbearable, and every open space reminds us of what is gone. Is this also why we invent new ways to describe our grief, as if qualifying it is the same as containing it? Accumulated grief and disenfranchised grief, anticipatory grief, delayed grief, chronic grief. Still, there aren't enough words. Every grief as singular as a snowflake, no two ever exactly alike.

And what of all those other terms—still unknown—that exist the way the future does, there and not there all at once? The English language has over 450,000 commonly used words, but none can describe even the most basic of things: A woman who has lost a spouse is a widow, a child who has lost her parents is an orphan. But what do we call a mother who has lost her child?

What do we call a child who has lost her sibling?

The death of a child, wrote Dostoyevsky, is the greatest reason to doubt the existence of God.

THIRTY

The opened suitcase lay across the bed like a metal heart. Stephen pulled a stack of T-shirts from the dresser drawer and set them into it. He had changed into a loose pair of khakis and a UMDF T-shirt. It had been his first day back to work. Only five days since . . . *Five* days. They felt like years.

Grace sat on the bed, a chalky taste in her mouth. She'd just finished tucking Erin in, rubbing her back for what seemed like hours while she cried herself to sleep, missing Jack. "I don't know how to even begin to understand this," Grace said to Stephen.

Stephen moved into the bathroom and began putting vitamin bottles into his shaving kit. "I don't want to pretend that things will be okay, and that eventually, we'll all get back to normal, and then wham! two or three months down the road, just when the kids are starting to heal a little, hit them with my leaving." He came to stand in the doorway. She thought of how, in earthquakes, this was the supposedly the safest place to be. "It just seems cruel, Grace."

"And this isn't?"

"I don't mean it to be."

She looked at him incredulously. "We just . . . five days ago . . . we just . . . ." She couldn't say it, couldn't get the words out. "Erin is terrified that they're going to take her, you know. The last thing she needs is for you to disappear now too."

"I won't disappear," he said gently. "And I know how this looks, and I'm sure it probably seems like the cruelest thing I could do right now, but I honestly—" His voice quavered, and he came and sat next to her on the bed. "I don't know how else to do it, Grace." His eyes were red-rimmed, bloodshot with tiredness and grief.

"Why do you have to do it at all?"

At first, he didn't answer. They sat, side by side, hands useless in their laps. And then, "I can't forgive you," he said.

She nodded. She wanted to feel shocked or devastated, but she had known that he would never forgive her, and if she had let herself think about it, she might have known he would move out too—that he would have to.

"I'll come for dinner a couple of times a week, if that's okay," he said. "And I'll take the kids on weekends. I found a place near the office. It's already furnished." His words landed soundlessly around her. The way snow falls, she thought, accumulating into something treacherous before you even realize it. "I know they say you shouldn't make any major decisions for a while, but this isn't rash, Grace."

"When did you do this then? Start looking?"

"The day after court."

She stared at him. "And you don't think your feelings will change? Eventually?"

He held her eyes for a long moment, then shook his head. "I don't think so."

She nodded. Again. When she spoke, her voice was flat, something squashed deep inside her. "They say that eighty-five percent of couples whose children die don't make it." She inhaled slowly. "I wanted us to be different, Stephen, I thought we would be."

His face hardened. So did his voice. "We both know I'm not leaving because of Jack."

She looked at him bleakly. "It's all connected, though."

"Is it?" he asked. "I mean, what percentage of couples stay together after an affair?"

Plenty, she wanted to tell him. *People forgive one another.* But she didn't answer, just stared helplessly past the open bathroom door. She felt as she had the night Jack died—knowing exactly what was happening and yet not really believing it either. "I know I screwed up," she said finally, looking at Stephen. "And I will never *ever* stop being sorry for what I did to you or to—to—" *To Jack*, she wanted to say, but her voice only squeaked. She turned away from him, not wanting him to see her cry, not wanting to make it worse.

"Oh, Grace." His voice softened. "This isn't a punishment."

She turned back to look at him. "Why can't you just give me a chance then?" Her throat ached. "Please, Stephen. I'll go to counseling or we could both go, or—or, *I'll* leave, I'll stay at my mom's and—"

He put his hand on her knee. "Don't, baby."

THIRTY-ONE

race sat with Erin at the round children's table in the fourth-grade science classroom where they met twice a week for sibling grief counseling. The room was filled with the sound of the kids coloring, their mothers or fathers or both sitting beside them, knees pressed to their chests in the small wooden chairs. The parents all had the same dark circles beneath their eyes, and they had all either lost weight—their clothes loose and billowy—or they'd gained weight, everything tight and constricting. Like people who lived in extreme environments of heat or cold—the Eskimos whose compact bodies were designed to conserve warmth; the Tutsi of Africa whose elongated body-type released heat to the surface more quickly—their physical shape was evidence of the struggle to adapt in a world that might otherwise have been intolerable.

Rarely did the parents look at one another. They couldn't. It was all they could do to acknowledge their children's grief, which was why they came here every Monday and Thursday afternoon. They'd all lost a child in the past year. It seemed impossible that any of them would recover. And so, like immigrant parents newly arrived in a foreign land, they placed their hopes in the children who survived.

Erin was drawing a picture of Jack racing a red car through the clouds. Below him, in a field full of flowers, she drew herself, huge blue tears dripping from her eyes.

Grace felt lost.

Leanne, the children's grief expert, squatted next to Erin, one arm around the back of her chair. "You still get really sad when you think about Jack, don't you?."

Erin nodded without looking up from her picture.

"Jack looks pretty happy, though." Leanne pointed to the red car.

"I really like—" but before she could finish, Erin grabbed her blue crayon and scribbled over Jack.

"Erin, honey—" Grace leaned forward, then stopped herself. Their children had to go through this, Leanne had told the parents. The parents couldn't protect them. It went against everything that Grace believed being a mother was.

"What's wrong, Erin?" Leanne asked. "I thought that was a pretty neat picture."

"Don't say that!" Erin yelled.

"Hey, there," Grace said. She combed Erin's dark tangled hair with her fingers.

After a minute, Leanne said, "You're pretty mad at Jack, huh?"

Erin shrugged. "It's just a stupid picture. I didn't like it."

"Why not?" Leanne asked.

Erin squeezed her eyes closed and shook her head, tears slipping down her face. Grace tucked a strand of her daughter's hair behind her ear. "Try to talk to Leanne, honey-bunny," she said.

"I just want to go home," Erin cried.

"I know, lovey, but we need to talk to Leanne first, so she can help us."

Erin started sobbing, choking on her words. "He shouldn't be happy," she said. "I don't know why I made him like that." She laid her head on the table and sobbed.

"But I love that you made Jack happy," Grace said. "I bet he probably is."

"No!" Erin wailed, lifting her head. "He's not. He can't be."

"Why not, Erin?" Leanne asked gently.

"If I—if I died I—I wouldn't be happy. I would miss my bro-ther." The word was a small frozen twig; it broke in half beneath the weight of Erin's grief.

Grace pulled her daughter against her. "Just because Jack is happy doesn't mean he doesn't miss us." Her own voice faltered. "Of course he does."

But she stared at Leanne helplessly. She understood how Erin felt. How was it possible for someone we love to be happy without us?

She held her child tight against her chest and kissed the back of her head and told her, "Jack thought you were the best sister in the world. Remember how he used to cheer when he saw you coming out of school?"

Erin nodded, sniffling.

Neither adult said anything for a minute. And then, "How about we go over to the anger circle?" Leanne asked. The anger circle was a space at the front of the room where the kids went to express their anger. They ripped up old magazines and crumpled the pages into tight little balls. They drew mad faces on balloons, then popped them. Sometimes they did mad dances or Leanne lined them up and let them take turns making their angriest noises into a tape recorder, which they then played back to their parents. Before long, the kids were laughing, and impossibly, miraculously, so were their parents.

All the kids were in the anger circle now, lying on the carpet. Leanne sat on the floor with the kids, her silver-threaded Indian-print skirt gathered around her legs. "Who can tell me about some of the people or things we get angry at?" she asked.

"I got mad at the doctors," Josh whispered.

"Yeah, me too," Todd said.

"Was it fair to get mad at them?" Leanne asked.

Todd shook his head no.

"But isn't it the doctor's job to make us better when we're sick?" She glanced at Erin, who was staring at her shoes, then at Josh. "What do you think, bud?"

"My mom said the doctors tried their best," he whispered.

"That's what my mom said," Seth explained. "But sometimes even when the doctors try as hard at they can, the person still dies. That's what happened to my sister."

"That's right," Leanne said. She glanced at the other kids. "What about the rest of you guys?" she said. "Did anyone else get mad?"

"I was mad at the driver who hit my brother," Julie said.

"I was mad at God."

"You can't get mad at God!" Todd yelled.

"Well, I did!" Megan shouted. "I'm still mad!"

"I was mad at cancer," another little girl interrupted. They were going around the circle now, taking turns.

"I was mad at my mom for not making my sister better." Tears streamed down McKensie's face.

Grace watched Erin, wondering what she would say. She was picking at the rubber sole of her shoe, her hair hanging over her face so that Grace couldn't see her. "I didn't get mad at anybody," she said quietly when it was her turn. She looked up. "But my dad got really angry at my mom and said that it was her fault my brother died and he didn't love her anymore. That's why he moved out."

THIRTY-TWO

$\mathcal{G}$race spoke softly: "My son, Jack—he was three, he died of a genetic disease thirty days ago tonight. The state had custody, and I—" She focused on her hands. "I wasn't there until the very end." Even as she took her turn, awkwardly introducing herself to the six women and four men who comprised the Mother's Against Munchausen Accusations Support Group, Grace wasn't sure why she had come.

Thirty days. One month. She couldn't think of it like that. A month. It seemed too whole, too complete. She thought of how children's ages were often measured in smaller increments—twelve months instead of one year, twenty-four months instead of two years, and she wondered if this came from the time when children often died at a young age and so their parents chose the larger number, the number with more weight—not *two* months but *eight* weeks—as if this could help anchor the child to the earth. Grace measured the time since Jack's death in a similar way. It was incomprehensible that she would *not* mark each day, like one of those white crosses at Normandy. When you saw them all stretched out, row after endless row, the magnitude of the loss was impossible to ignore.

Her days were like those crosses now.

She stared numbly at the worn beige carpet of this living room in some stranger's house. "You think any school or church in the state would let *us* hold a support meeting on their premises?" Martha, the woman who was hosting the group had asked her over the phone when Grace called to find out where the meetings were held. That the location might be a problem hadn't occurred to her, though of course, it made perfect sense. It didn't matter if these women had been falsely accused. Why would *anyone* want to be associated with them?

The mental state of the Munchausen Mom is very much akin to the socio-pathic mind-set. The only difference is that instead of killing for financial gain, the Munchausen Mom injures or kills for no real reason at all.

The man seated next to her was talking now, his voice barely audible, his eyes brimming. "My daughter, Lindsay, was taken by CPS two months ago," he said, "and unless we admit to this thing . . ." He squeezed the hand of the round-faced woman sitting next to him, who was staring at her lap, twisting a Kleenex into shreds.

Without looking up, she said, "We thought that if we got a legal separation, the state would give Hal custody, but our lawyer thinks they might use that against me."

"Oh, Candy," Martha said.

Earlier, Grace had sat in her car a few houses away, trying to force herself to actually get out and walk up the flagstone path to the door of this small modular home, its tiny porch crowded with tricycles and plastic toys. In the side yard was a bright yellow slide and jungle gym, swings that moved ghostlike in the March breeze.

Across the street, a car door had slammed, and a man in a suit exited a black Mercedes, dropping his cell phone on the asphalt, the back breaking off, the battery flying beneath the tires. It was early evening, the sun just sinking below the tree line, bathing everything in a harsh pink light. A woman arrived, wearing running shorts despite the cold, ace bandages around both her knees. A few minutes later, an overweight woman with a run in the back of her pale stockings carried a tinfoil-covered plate of something up the path and handed it to whoever opened the door. Watching them, Grace felt a stab of recognition. The subconscious need to break things, to make the damage in their lives somehow visible: torn stockings, bandaged legs, broken cell phones. Like those indigenous cultures where people literally cut themselves to mark the loss of a child, the idea of remaining whole unbearable.

Thirty days.

Since Jack died, Grace too had become error-prone and clumsy, some part of her needing, perhaps, this outward proof that the world had been damaged. She shattered a glass while clearing the table, slipped last week getting out of the tub. She found herself tripping over rugs, stubbing her toe, bumping into furniture she had moved effortlessly around for years. Like Alice in Wonderland, she was suddenly too big or too small in this altered world. Nothing fit, nothing was the right size, the right shape, the right distance.

A couple pulled up in a beat-up station wagon with an empty child seat in the back and a "baby on board" sticker in the window. Grace felt her stomach tighten with recognition.

Jack's child seat was still in Grace's car.

Inside the cramped house, Grace immediately noticed the empty IV stand in the corner of the living room. She felt the blood drain from face. But then Martha—it must have been Martha—was walking towards her, hand outstretched. "Grace?" she asked. "I'm so glad you came." She led Grace into the living room, already jammed with people chatting in groups of twos and threes. A green lawn chair, a white rocking chair that looked as if it belonged in a baby's room, and two mismatched ladder-back chairs were mixed in with the rest of the living room furniture to form a tight circle. On the coffee table were stacks of papers listing Web sites of defense lawyers, names and addresses of congressmen and legislators involved in child abuse laws, the address for the Department of Health and Human Services, sample letters asking for congressional inquiries into child protection agencies. A fan of pastel-colored fact sheets listed *Key Risks of Having Your Child Removed by the State,* and *The Social Worker at Your Door: Ten Hints to Help You Protect Your Children.* Brochures from VOCAL: Victims of Child Abuse Laws, and the National Child Abuse Defense and Resource Center.

Except for Grace and another woman, a young girl with bad skin in ripped jeans and a sweatshirt, the other members already knew one another. The young woman hadn't been formally accused, she said, but her child's doctor had been acting hostile and twice had suggested that she was the one needing help, not her son. Grace thought of John Bartholomew suggesting something similar when she wanted to bring Jack to his clinic in San Diego, of Eric Markind's belief that a child's family *aggravated* his pain.

"You're right to be concerned," the man who had dropped his cell phone said. He mentioned something about his own child's feeding tube, which the young woman's son also had. The man shook his head. "We hear our son is totally off tube feedings now, which is just more proof to the state that my wife was the one keeping him on it unnecessarily, but ask anyone who saw us try to feed him. It was heartbreaking how much pain he was in. It was at the point where he would just refuse to eat at all."

Grace wondered where his wife was now and what had happened to his son. It sounded as if they hadn't seen him in a long time. As if he'd read her mind, the man looked at her, his eyes unbearably sad, and said, "My wife decided two weeks ago to just admit that she'd been faking Jake's problems. It was the only way she thought we had a prayer of ever getting him back."

For a moment, they were silent, the man staring down and twisting his wedding band. Grace's shirt felt plastered to her back despite the cool temperatures outside. The room was too crowded for this many people. For a moment, she felt such an overwhelming sense of despair that it seemed she was drowning, her heart bobbing in her chest like an empty life preserver. After a moment, she said to the man, "I would have done the same thing as your wife, if it meant that I could have been with my son." She glanced at Martha. "This probably isn't the right thing to be saying, but—"

The woman with the ace bandages on her knees, who was sitting next to Grace, touched her arm. "Don't worry about right or wrong. I read your story in the papers, and . . . after what you've been through . . . it's unconscionable."

A few of the others were nodding, but Grace could barely meet their eyes. She felt shattered inside, the pain unspooling inside her. It had been three weeks since Stephen had left, three weeks since anyone aside from her kids had touched her, three weeks since anyone—including her parents, who were too locked into their own confusion and grief—had spoken to her with such kindness.

• • •

She left Martha's with a sheaf of papers and brochures. It was cold now, the sun gone. Down the street, where she had parked, an American flag fluttered from the porch of a single-story house that had obviously just been built, the ground around it still dirt, a huge metal Dumpster at the end of the drive. The night was quiet but for the flapping sound of that cloth against the darkened sky. Such a different night from the frigid gray of the one, not even three months ago, when Stephen came home, his fist bruised, and told her of the accusation. It seemed another life, another woman who had been sitting in bed, laughing almost, at the absurdity that anyone would accuse *her*.

"What are you working on?" she asked Max. She was still wearing her coat.

"History." He didn't look up.

"Well, how about a break? I was thinking of having some ice cream."

"No thanks."

Wearily, she sat on his bed, watching him move a highlighter over his history text. Orange light from the lava lamp on his dresser undulated over the walls. His fourteenth birthday was in two weeks. In the fall, he'd start high school.

After a while, she joked, "Hey, I'm getting kind of scared by all this studying," but it wasn't as much of a joke as she wanted it to be. Ever since Jack had died, this was all he did. And his room was immaculate, his desk was organized, his textbooks neatly lined up in front of him between metal bookends.

He still didn't answer.

"Well. I'll let you be then." She stood, reaching to tousle his hair as she left the room. At the door, she glanced down and saw in the overflowing trashcan a crumpled paper with a red A+ and "Great report, Max!" scrawled along the margin. "Sweetie?" she asked. "What's this?" She stooped to retrieve it. "Can I see?"

He shrugged. "It's old," he said by way of explanation.

It was the report on mitochondrial disease that he'd done for his biology class in January. Two months ago. Two months ago Jack had still been home, and they'd taken him and Erin to see the Muppets on Ice. *"My brother Jack has mitochondrial disease,"* she read now. *"This means that he has lots of problems in his major organs that require a lot of energy."* Six weeks ago, she had finally sent in the Make-A-Wish Foundation request, her New Year's resolution, and the whole family sat around the table one night with the kids' school calendars and Max's sports schedule and tried to settle on a date for the trip. *"But sometimes I think Jack's biggest problem is that a lot of people don't even know what mitochondrial disease is. Even some doctors have never heard of it."* Grace looked up, tears stinging her eyes, then returned to the paper. *"So what exactly is mitochondrial disease?"*

"This is great, Max," she said when she finished. "Why did you throw it out?"

He glanced at her, then grinned. "Because," he said, "I *knew* you'd do *that*."

"But these are good tears," she protested.

So she still cries at the drop of a hat, huh?

You mean she was like that way back then too?

Max rolled his eyes, then returned to his book.

Downstairs, Grace stood in front of the open refrigerator, which was mostly empty. She shopped daily now, as if she lived in a foreign country, buying just what she needed each morning. She'd been cooking again, not because she was hungry, but because there was something reassuring in following a recipe. In not having to think. In completing simple directions, exact measurements.

Now, she pulled a container of Thai noodles and beef from the top shelf and picked out a chunk of beef with her fingers. She'd made it the night before. Stephen had come for dinner.

"This looks fantastic," he said, spooning some onto his plate. He didn't look at her. He never did. "But you don't have to go to all this trouble."

"I don't like it," Erin said tearfully, pushing her noodles around the plate.

"But it's all stuff you like, honey-bunny," Grace said. "Noodles and broccoli and pieces of steak. And look—"

"But I don't *like* it," she cried.

"Well, I do," Max said.

"I didn't ask you!" she screamed.

"Hey, hey." Stephen pushed back his chair and pulled Erin onto his lap. "What's going on here?"

Erin cried harder, shoulders heaving. "I just—I just—"

"Just what, lovey?" Grace asked. "Do you want me to make you some macaroni and cheese? Would that make you feel better?"

"Nooooo," she wailed, nose running, her face streaked with tears and dirt. "You don't understand!" She couldn't stop crying, nearly choking on her tears. "I don't—I don't want"—she hiccupped—"macaroni by *myself*. I want it for—everyone!" She started crying again. "Why can't we just have things like we used to?"

Grace closed the refrigerator, then glanced at the mail on the counter, a thick stack of cream-colored envelopes. Sympathy cards. Still. Half of them each day were from people she didn't even know who had heard about Jack through the United Mitochondrial Disease Foundation or M.A.M.A. or the article in the *Philadelphia Inquirer.* "Mother Accused of Munchausen by Proxy Exonerated." Grace knew the article by heart: *It shouldn't take the death of a child to open the public's eyes to the horrors of child abuse, but neither should it take the death of a child to open the public's eyes to the devastation wrought when children, under the auspices of Child Protective Services, are wrongly taken from their homes . . .* She glanced quickly through the cards, looking—though she didn't want to be—for Noah's handwriting. Did he even know that Jack had died? But how could he? she wondered. And how could he not?

Except for a letter from her grandfather, she didn't recognize any of the names on the return addresses. She set the envelopes aside, placed her grandfather's letter on the top of the pile—she would read them in the morning—and after turning off the lights and checking to make sure the door was locked, climbed the stairs.

Stephen's half of the bed was covered with library books about grief, as if this too were a subject she could study, the way she had with mitochondrial disease and pediatric heart failure and Munchausen's. *Finding Hope When a Child Dies; When the Bough Breaks; Ended Beginnings*. It was what she had always done, how she had always coped, as if answers always came packaged in words.

Most of the advice seemed disingenuous—all that crap about finding something positive in her child's death. "Am I grieving normally?" one of the books had asked, followed by a questionnaire to be filled out at three months, six months, and again at one year, as if grief were no different from taking a car in for an oil change every three thousand miles. *Have I learned to laugh again? Do I take pride in my personal appearance?* The rest of the books were too clinical, written by some PhD in psychology or some "expert" in thanatology. If it hadn't been written by someone who knew what grief felt like at two in the morning or what it tasted like or the way it made even the air feel thick so that taking a shower or actually walking down the stairs was exhausting, then Grace wasn't interested. All the facts in the world couldn't help her now, and all the ways grief was divvied up into stages and kinds and types— disenfranchised grief and detached grief and anticipatory grief and delayed grief—who did that really help? Not the people who were torn open with loss, not the people who were desperate to learn how to walk or sit or breathe with this gaping hole in the middle of their chests.

It didn't matter that Child Protective Services had immediately closed the case following Jack's death or that Kate had written a formal apology, enclosing with it a copy of her resignation letter. CPS would not expunge the accusation from their records. "I don't know if you remember Eliza's Law," Bennett said.

"I remember," Grace said. It was the law named after the six-year-old who was beaten to death despite the numerous reports to Child Protective Services.

Bennett looked surprised, or relieved perhaps, that he wouldn't have to explain again. "Then you know that it's also the law that forbids the destruction of abuse records for *any* reason for ten years after the accusation."

Or until the child turns eighteen.

It was the first time Grace and Stephen had been in Bennett's office since the previous January. It felt surreal to be here, Grace thought, sitting on the same couch, staring at those same black-and-white photographs of the bridges. If she squinted, made the room blurry, she could almost imagine it was December still, that Jack was still alive. All that bright sunlight outside was really the blinding white of snow.

"I don't understand," she said now. "Jack is—" She glanced at her hands folded primly in her lap. Every minute of every day she lived with this knowledge in her bones: Jack was dead. And yet, except for the night that she had attended the M.A.M.A. group, she hadn't ever said it out loud.

"After what they did," Stephen said, "You'd think they would be bending over backwards to clear Grace's name."

"They've done what they can, Stephen," Bennett said. "They closed the case; they made a formal apology."

"Well, it's not enough. It's a joke, in fact." Stephen stood, hands in his pockets, paced to the oak bookshelves, then turned. "So, what are our choices? Can we sue them?"

"No!" Grace gave him a withering look. "My God, Stephen." She turned to Bennett. "A lawsuit isn't an option."

Bennett glanced from her to Stephen, then back to her. "I think that's best." He sighed. "The problem is that too many children are slipping through the cracks still. Obviously, the agencies are loath to make exceptions."

"Even when they're flat-out wrong?" Stephen pushed. "Even when the child they were *supposedly* protecting is dead?"

"Stop it, Stephen, please," Grace pleaded. She glanced again at Bennett. "I'm sorry," she said. "This is just difficult to accept."

"I'm the one who's sorry," Bennett said. He rubbed his hand over his forehead, his eyes no longer meeting hers. "CPS can't expunge the file, Grace, not as long as you have other children in your care."

She nodded, as if she understood. She wouldn't fight, wouldn't argue. The accusation had taken this from her too.

She woke up, crying again. The same nightmare: She was trying to get to Jack, but he was on the other side of a busy downtown street, and there was too much traffic and no one would slow down, and every time a bus or a truck obscured her view of him even for a minute, he got farther and farther away until finally she couldn't see him at all. It was incomprehensible, even in her sleep, how easy it should have been to save him, and still she had failed. She woke then, her heart pounding, whimpering, her voice scratchy, as if she really had been screaming his name over the roar of traffic, and before she could even think, it's only a dream, she remembered that it wasn't.

THIRTY-THREE

Grace headed home after leaving the diner where she'd gone for breakfast. She had planned to go shopping, maybe even treat herself to a manicure. She used to dream about having time to do things like this, and the kids were with Stephen for the weekend, so she could, but all she really wanted was to go home, get back into bed, and sleep.

She stopped behind a green Volkswagen Beetle waiting to turn left. A bumper sticker on the back: CAPE MAY BIRD OBSERVATORY. The words detonated inside her, so that for a moment, all she knew, all she felt, all she could think was *Noah*. She pictured him standing on the beach in an orange windbreaker, arm outstretched towards a chrome-colored sky, telling her how young albatrosses spend their first five years alone over the ocean. Or sitting in the Drift In and Sea Café with her and Max, eating French fries like a starving man, telling them how passenger pigeons all laid their eggs on the exact same day and how nestlings placed their bills in the mother's to be fed, and if the nestling died, the mother became desperate to get rid of the milk, which literally killed her if she didn't.

He had told them that Huron Indians believed the souls of the dead came back as passenger pigeons, and that at one time, over a fourth of all land birds in the United States were passenger pigeons, so many of them that Audubon himself once watched a flock pass overhead, the sky turning black with wings for three straight days.

The Volkswagen turned just as the traffic light changed to red. Something broke loose in her. Waves of longing smashed against the bones of her ribs. She missed him. It had been three months since she had spoken to him. He didn't know that Jack had died. She closed her eyes, the heat blasting through the windshield like a drug.

I would have traded your life for Jack's in an instant, she told Noah in her mind. She pictured them walking along the nature trail at Higbie's Beach, holding hands. He was telling her how only half of all song-birds that leave the coast ever see it again, 50 percent of them dying; how a pair of Canadian geese lived together for forty-two years. Once, on a rainy afternoon, lying in his bed, he told her how Ameri-can goldfinches weave nests so tightly that they are waterproof, and that the nestlings often drowned inside if there was a drenching rain and the parents were away.

The kids in the SUV behind her honked, their car pulsing with music. It seemed impossible to lift her foot from the brake and move it to the accelerator. She tried to steer her thoughts back to what she should do—she *would* go shopping, she would splurge—but his hand was on her rib cage and he was telling her that a bird's heart in pro-portion to a man's was larger and beat three times as fast. His fingers were on her sternum: *Here, this is where your flight muscles would be.* Angry tears blurred her vision as she turned toward her house. It was unconscionable to think about Noah, to miss him in the same breath in which she thought about Jack. There was no comparison. Noah didn't die, and even if he had, the loss of him from her life should have been minor, she told herself, should have been nothing, incon-sequential, compared to losing her child, her husband.

Should have been.

"Are you sure about this, Grace?" Over the phone, Grace heard Jenn take a sip of coffee. "I thought you wanted to work things out with Stephen."

Grace laid her head against the rocking chair, staring at the bars of shadow cast onto the opposite wall by Jack's crib. "I miss him, Jenn." *Noah.* "I had so much energy when I was with him. I was happy." *Happy.* The word was like one of those fantastic animals—galloping crocodiles, dinosaurs the size of sparrows—that long ago became ex-tinct. "And I know how that sounds, okay? The idea that I even *could* be happy with Jack so sick." She paused. "But I was."

"Look, I'm worried about you," Jenn said. "Seeing Noah again is the last thing—"

"It's not over, Jenn. A *bumper sticker*, a stupid bumper sticker and it was like . . . I just wanted to see him, listen to him talk about birds."

"Here." He handed her a perfect conch shell, pure salt white, the size of a locket.

"How did you—God!" She swatted him. "I walk this beach for miles and all I find are fragments and you . . ." She smiled. "Thank you."

"That's what I want to be to you, Grace, what I want us to be: whole and intact even if everything around us is broken."

"Wait till I get off the phone," she heard Jenn tell one of the boys in the background, and then to Grace, she said: "Why can't you just e-mail him, Grace? Or call? Why do you have to go there? It's only going to confuse things."

The sky was dark, without stars, the windows open. Grace often thought of this—opening windows—as the last normal thing she did on the day he died. It was an act that filled her with regret each time she thought about it. Because when she returned to the house the next morning and climbed the stairs to his room, it no longer smelled like him. She had aired his room out too, like a fool, a goddamn fool, never considering—but why would she have—that he would die that very night, that even as she had stood in Max's room with her kids, laughing, saying to Max—*did Erin tell you we bought scones*—Jack had already coded. Later, on the morning of his funeral, she had sat in his rocking chair, crying inconsolably, not even for him, but for his baby smells, which were forever gone. She undersood then why Andy Warhol had once tried to have a "smell museum," saving the perfumes of everyone he loved.

Grace came into Jack's room often now, sat in this chair, wrapped herself in one of his blankets, read his books. Now on the phone, she told Jenn, "Things are already confused with Stephen. I thought I wanted to work things out with him, but . . ."

"You're playing with fire," Jenn said. "Whether you admit it or not." In the background came the clinking of silverware. Whenever Jenn was upset she cleaned, threw clothes in the washing machine, took apart the stovetop to scrub the burners.

Grace smiled. "Let me guess. Emptying the dishwasher?"

"Let's just say, for the sake of argument," Jenn continued, "that you *do* feel the same way about Noah as you did a year ago. What happens to wanting Stephen back? And what do you tell Max and Erin? Are you prepared to bring Noah into *their* lives?" She sighed. "I think you need time, Grace." Her voice softened. "And yes, I'm emptying the stupid dishwasher."

Grace stood and walked across the room to the window and leaned her forehead against the glass.

"Don't get me wrong: I think Stephen's a jerk for walking out," Jenn continued, "but you guys have been through the most god-awful thing, and I don't know . . . I'd hate to see you give up."

"I'm not the one who gave up."

A long silence. And then, "What about when you were with Noah?"

Grace sighed. "Okay," she said. "Fair enough." She paced back to Jack's bed, which looked the same as it had the last morning she'd taken him from it. Books, stuffed animals, cars. "I'm lonely," she said quietly. Her voice splintered with shame. "And it sounds pathetic, and I *feel* pathetic, but I—I want to be touched, Jenn, I want—" Her voice cracked. "I want to be held, I want someone to look at me and actually see *me,* not the mother whose child died, not the woman accused of Munchausen's or—or—" She stared at the dark sky, a bright moon darting in and out of the pale clouds.

Look, Jack, Mr. Moon came to see you.

Scientists said that it was moving away from the Earth an inch and a half a year.

Jenn stayed silent, and Grace could picture her, divvying up the silverware: forks, knives, spoons, and shaking her head in frustration.

"I'm not sure *I* can even see who I am anymore," Grace said. Jack's death had hardened her, made her unrecognizable even to herself. There were days when she couldn't even stand to be around Erin or Max, days when she was driving and imagined just letting the car veer off the road into a tree, days when she felt so much rage that she wanted to smash something. And just yesterday, waiting for Erin to finish swim lessons at the Y, one of the other mothers started going on about how tragic it was that funding for the National Endowment for the Arts had been cut, and Grace commented that she thought the NEA should be abolished altogether and that what was really tragic was a government that could afford to spend millions of dollars on folk singers and poets no one had ever heard of while a quarter of the nation's children were living in poverty. Of course, no one responded. Who was going to argue with the mother of a child who had just died? Who was going to tell *her* that she was full of shit? Everyone just nodded politely, and averted their eyes, until someone changed the subject. Sometimes Grace felt as if she were barely a person anymore. "I feel like I'm drowning, that if Max and Erin didn't need me, I'd simply float away, and a part of me even resents them for that, for keeping me here."

"Oh Grace," Jenn said. "Haven't you lost enough?"

Grace was crying.

"I just hope he's worth it," Jenn said finally.

THIRTY-FOUR

*A*t any given moment, three percent of the Earth is covered in the frothy white foam of waves. Fourteen thousand waves break upon a single patch of beach each day. The seventh wave is always slightly larger than the others. Grace couldn't remember where she'd learned this or why anyone would bother trying to figure it out. It was like attempting to understand grief, she thought, thinking of the stack of books still sitting by her bed: *A Grief Observed, The Dynamics of Grief, The Grief Recovery Plan.* Maybe she hoped that the words in those books would become like the waves, crashing upon the shore—what was it? every five seconds—each time taking a few grains of sand. In a year's time, as much as nine inches of the Cape May shoreline would have eroded. Maybe, she thought, sadness was like sand. Can loss be washed away a grain at a time?

She stood at the water's edge, her shoes dangling from her hand. Her sundress, damp with sweat, stuck to her back. Noah had been on the Hawk Watch platform with a group of birders when she arrived, the parking lot packed with cars. She'd go back up in a little while, she told herself, though a part of her wanted to stand right where she was, unmoving, forever.

Fragments of conversations floated by as people strolled: A couple arguing. *I thought you said . . . why are we . . .* Women gossiping. *I don't know what he sees in . . . Are you kidding?* They called after their kids: *Stop running, you're kicking up sand! I told you . . .* From behind her came the whack of paddleballs and the shrieks of kids. Sweat trickled down her nose and collarbone. A few feet away, a cluster of teenage girls laughed, squealing with hilarity. *Oh my God . . . No way! Wait . . . Tell me again . . .*

Grace stood still, half listening, her face tilted toward the sun, her eyes closed.

What did you do? But you don't mean . . . No!

More laughter. A lifeguard's whistle pierced the air. Another wave crashed forward, soaking the bottom of her dress.

Do you think you'll . . . But what about . . .

The sunlight glowed bright orange beneath her eyelids. She thought of all the choices these girls would make, all the choices she had made before even graduating from high school, without fully understanding that every choice eliminated hundreds—thousands—of others. And all the choices not made, all the chances not taken, maybe these were the things that actually determined the shape each life held.

"Grace!"

She spun to face him, her heart pounding so forcefully she could feel it in her throat. It took a moment for her eyes to adjust to the shimmering brightness.

He was leaning over, hands on his knees, trying to catch his breath. Sweat dripped from his chin and forehead. "Do you . . ." He inhaled sharply. "Have any . . ." He took another breath. ". . . idea . . . what you . . . just did to me?"

"Oh God, I'm sorry." She shaded her eyes with one hand. He looked heavier and tanned. His nose was peeling.

"I don't think I've run that fast in twenty years," he panted. "I couldn't believe it when I saw your car." He wiped his face with the bottom edge of his T-shirt and straightened. "And then when I saw Jack's car seat, God, I was relieved." He took another breath. "I had called Children's the day after that hearing you were supposed to have, and when they said there was no Jack Connolly on the patient list—Jesus, I was relieved."

She felt the corners of her mouth go numb, her smile frozen. She couldn't look at him.

"Grace? You took him home right? You got him back, didn't you?"

She couldn't speak, couldn't look at him, couldn't bear to say it.

"Grace? Everything's—I mean, his seat's still there, so . . . ?"

Her mouth quivered. She pretended to focus on something up the beach. "I'm not ready to take his car seat out yet," she said. Her voice was flat. She kept staring past him. "He—he—" She still couldn't say it. *He died before we could take him home. I wasn't with my child for most of the last two weeks of his life.* If she looked at Noah she would break into a million pieces.

But she didn't need to speak. A low wail erupted out of him. "No," he cried. "No." And then, "Can I hold you for a minute?" he asked.

She nodded, still without looking at him, still without moving.

He held her so tightly, it hurt to breathe. She could feel his heart. The back of his T-shirt was damp with sweat, and the skin of his neck smelled of the beach, salty and clean. "I missed you so much," she whispered, and he squeezed her even tighter. Minutes passed before he let her go and stepped back, his hands on either side of her face, seemingly memorizing her. "You're beautiful in gray," he said.

She glanced down at her pale blue dress, then realized he was talking about her hair. She lifted her hand to it. "I just haven't . . . I don't know. I think I'm just going to let it grow out this way."

They walked, weaving in out of the Memorial Day crowds, to the sunken concrete ship and back. She told him about the last four months: about the book she made for Jack and being frisked by the hospital security guard, and about that first god-awful visit. And then Jack's dying, the funeral, Stephen's leaving. Her voice was flat.

"Five days after you bury your child and he walks out? Jesus."

"Don't," Grace said. "He lost his child too. You don't know what he feels." They were sitting in the sand now, shadows from the dunes encroaching farther down the beach as the sun began to set. Low tide, the waves and wet sand shimmering gold as if someone had poured glitter into the ocean. A bird lifted off and she pointed. "What kind was that?"

"Forster's tern."

"And that?" She pointed again.

He glanced at her. "How's Max?"

"He's unreachable." She shook her head. "Getting perfect grades. His room is immaculate. I feel like I've lost him too."

"Did he know about us?"

"I don't think so." She clasped her arms around her knees and rested her chin on them. "I love you," she said quietly, and in that moment she did, though it wasn't at all what she had thought she would say. But all she'd had to do was show up on the beach, and there he was, stampeding towards her, arms outstretched, energy and joy buzzing around him like an electrical field. She didn't have to do anything; she didn't have to be anything.

Loss on top of loss toppled inside her. Jack had made her feel this way. The center of his world. The minute she opened his door in the mornings or after his nap, he was madly scrambling to his feet in his crib, arms outstretched, calling out with delight as if she were the best surprise in the world. "Mama! You come to get me!" That wild rooster hair, his PJs all bedraggled.

Noah bent to kiss her, brushing a strand of her hair out of the way. His fingers were callused—she'd forgotten this—and his lips were salty. "I love you too," he said.

They sat for a while without talking, Noah leaning back on his elbows, feet stretched in front of him. She closed her eyes, nearly falling asleep, her head on her knees, the sun like a warm hand at the back of her neck. At seven, the lifeguards up and down the beach stood on their chairs and blew their whistles, signaling that they were now off duty. The sun fell back toward the dunes.

"Would you be here if Stephen hadn't left you?" he asked after a while, and she knew he'd been waiting to ask this all afternoon.

She glanced at him without lifting her head. "Probably not."

He was staring up at the sky, eyes squinted, a muscle jumping along his jaw. It was such a familiar posture, she thought. Always, he would look up when he stepped outside or stood in front of a window. A kind of waiting. And it occurred to her that this was the posture of loss, and that it was familiar in part because it was a posture she herself had adopted, always glancing up at night, trying to locate the moon.

"Would you have at least gotten in touch with me?" His voice was edged with hurt, uncertainty, confusion maybe.

She shook her head. "I'm not sure."

He nodded, his jaw clenched.

She picked up a broken shell, its inside the bluish-pink of a dying heart, and using it like a shovel lifted a small pile of sand, then poured it over her ankles. Again and again, the sand cool against her feet. How was it that she had never understood until now how much the ocean was a landscape of loss: constantly breaking waves, emptied shells, land carried out to sea a little bit each year. She glanced up at Noah, but he looked far away. She touched his arm. "Hey."

"Why didn't you tell me about Jack's—about Jack before now?" he asked, still staring ahead. She followed his gaze to the pale outline of a ship along the horizon line, and thought of how the horizon wasn't a real place, wasn't somewhere you could ever truly reach because it didn't exist except in the imagination.

She kept her hand on his arm, fingertips at his pulse. "I just couldn't."

"Not even an e-mail?" He looked at her, hurt coloring his eyes a darker blue. "I'm just trying to—did you simply not think to tell me or did you want to and I don't know, it was some kind of guilt thing or—or—I don't understand."

How could she tell him, *I didn't think of you at all*. Her shoulders dropped. "Oh Noah, I was just getting through the days, starting over, getting through another." She paused. "I wasn't trying to hurt you." It was a phrase she had repeated over and over in the past few months. To Stephen and her parents and Max and Erin. And to Jack. Especially to Jack. Every night. *I'm sorry, Goose*. Staring up at the moon.

"So what made you decide to come here now?"

"I missed you." The words were like waves, rushing forward onto the sand, then pulling themselves back.

"Just like that?" His voice was gentle. "After four months?"

She dropped her hand from his arm, told him about the bumper sticker.

"So if you hadn't been behind that car . . ."

"But I was." She looked at him. "I don't know what you want me to say."

"I'm just trying to—it all seems so . . . so . . . random."

Tears filled her eyes. It was. He was right. And she understood that no matter how much she loved this man—and she did—it wasn't enough to make her want to do all the things she would have to if she truly wanted a life with him.

"You came to say good-bye, didn't you?" He held her gaze.

Words lifted in her—denials, equivocations, *I'm not sure; maybe.* Words like bright fish leaping to the surface of a silver pond, then slipping away. There were so many things she wanted to explain—*I wasn't planning this, I didn't know*—but in the end, she just nodded.

Wordlessly, he got up and walked the fifty feet or so to the water, where he stood, arms on his hips, head bowed. Orange sunlight hammered the ocean into a flat glossy surface. Down the beach, a group of guys had set up a volleyball net. Grace focused on the whack of the ball going back and forth. She was playing with the sand again, lifting it onto a shell, pouring it back out. When she looked up, she expected Noah to be gone, but instead, he was walking back towards her.

"Hey, you."

Hey, you. The first words he'd ever spoken to her.

Now, he held out a hand and she took it and he pulled her up. All he said was, "Do you have to rush back tonight or can you stay a while?"

She told him she could stay.

They sat on plastic deck chairs on Noah's balcony, the dark bay like an upside-down sky, lights from the various boats scattered like stars. He'd made a pitcher of rum daiquiris and they passed a can of honey-roasted cashews back and forth, their clothes growing damp in the moisture-filled air.

"Tell me about Jack," he said during a lull in the conversation.

Grace set down her drink without taking a sip. "What do you want to know?"

"Anything." He shrugged. "Just some little thing you remember."

But she remembered everything. It's what mothers did. Hoarded every detail they could about their child: the colored balls of his socks in the top drawer of his dresser; the yeasty smell of his skin after a nap; the first time he said "Mama," or went out in the snow or saw the ocean, toddling straight into the crashing waves before Grace could grab him back. She thought of Jack constantly, anything—everything—a reminder: a box of graham crackers, a child with reddish or curly hair. Passing a truck on the interstate—*Honk him, Mama!* Making a salad for dinner . . .

Noah laid his palm on her bare knee. "I didn't mean to upset you."

She lifted his hand and laced her fingers through his. "Jack was a little scientist," she said quietly. "Fifty percent of his conversation was the word *why*." Her voice was scratchy. "He'd ask where Stephen was, and I'd say, 'at the gym,' and Jack would ask why. So I'd say, 'because he goes swimming there,' and Jack would ask why he went swimming." The wind lifted her words, flinging them up like the scraps of stale bread she and Stephen and a toddling Max had once tossed to the gulls. She glanced at Noah. "So, I'd tell him Stephen liked swimming and *of course*, Jack wanted to know *why* he liked it. Once, I was tired or distracted and I told Jack, 'If you say *why* one more time, I'm going to scream,' and of course—" She laughed.

"—he asked why," Noah finished.

She nodded, grateful. Even her parents were hesitant to talk about Jack anymore, to say his name. She thought of how *Y* had been Jack's favorite letter, how he used to stand with his feet together and his arms pointed up and out and announce, "Look! I'm a *Y*!" He liked to stick black olives on the ends of his fingers and pretend they were fingernails; he used to call Max "Ax."

Noah nudged her leg with his foot. "I wish you could see your face when you talk about Jack," he said. "It's beautiful."

"Really?" She smiled. "That's what I want," she said. "I'm always afraid that I'll be sad when I talk about him, which is so opposite of how he was." She pictured him shrieking and hobbling naked down the hall and away from her after his bath or clomping around in Erin's white snow boots and an old football helmet of Max's and telling them, "I'm an astronut." Astro-*nut*. Or sitting on her lap as she read to him, *Happy Birthday, Moon*. Memories tumbled forward like bright toys bobbing in the waves. Jack in his crib on his third—

"I could watch you all night." Noah leaned back in his chair, his arms crossed behind his head. Waves slapped against the docks below. A breeze carried with it the fishy smell of the bay. "What were you just smiling at?"

"Oh, Jack's third birthday." She leaned back in her own chair, her head against the sliding glass door just behind them, and stared up at the sky. "He had no idea what a birthday was, so all week we'd been telling him that when he was three, he would be a big boy." She rolled her eyes. "*Huge* mistake. I go into his room that morning, and he's standing in his crib, looking at his legs, and he asks if he's three yet, and before I can say yes, Jack *throws* himself onto the mattress and starts shouting at me, 'No! Not today! Not today! I can't! I can't!' "

Noah was laughing.

"God, he was mad," Grace said. "Apparently, he thought his legs were going to just shoot up when he was three, like the beanstalk in *Jack and the Beanstalk*." She reached for her frozen daiquiri and took a sip. "I think of him all the time," she said. "It's so stupid, but every day, at three o'clock, I think, 'Oh good, time to wake Jack up from his nap,' except, of course . . ." Her voice trailed off and she took another sip of her drink. Moonlight shone on the water below, a sheenless black taffeta, and she thought of the mourning dresses women had once worn to signal their grief to the world. It made so much sense to her. Why had people stopped?

"Nah, nah, ha ha! You can't find me!"

"Did you hear something, Mama?" Erin asked.

"It sounded like a goose," Grace said.

Erin giggled. They could hear Jack's loud breathing in the hall closet, the doorknob rattling as he pulled himself up. "I think he might be in the closet," she whispered.

They heard rustling and the squeak of coat hangers, and then on the whispered count of three, Grace and Erin yanked open the door.

Jack stumbled out, swatting at coat sleeves, his head thrown back in laughter. "You finded me!"

"Hey," Noah inched his chair closer to hers. "Where'd you go?"

"Up there." She stared at the quarter moon, only a thin sliver, like a cupped hand, she thought, or a cradle. *Her absence is like the sky*, C. S. Lewis had written after the death of his wife. It was how Grace felt about Jack.

"Did you know that the light the moon shines on Earth is one thousand times greater than the light shone by all the stars put together?"

She smiled sadly. Noah had collected these facts about the moon for her the way someone else might collect beautiful shells or rare coins or stamps from faraway places. *The moon's power over the tides is more than two times stronger than the sun's.*

From the street came the squeal of brakes and the raucous shouts of drunken teenagers. After a moment, Grace said, "I read somewhere that researchers studying parent-child attachment have found that what matters most isn't how much the parent loves the baby or how good the parent is, so much as the fact that the parent consistently returns to the child after periods of separation." She was still staring up. "Apparently, a part of what the child is doing by playing hide-and-seek is making sure that the parent can always find him." A tear slid down her cheek, and she swiped it away.

"Sometimes I hate the whole idea of heaven," she continued after a moment. "What if it really exists—" Another tear. She didn't bother trying to wipe it. "What if Jack's up there—" her voice caught. "What if he's up there waiting for me to find him?"

Noah pulled her to him, arms tight around her shoulders, his mouth against her ear. "If heaven's real," he whispered, "then Jack also knows that you're looking up at him right now."

From the moment she decided to drive to Cape May, Grace had suspected that she and Noah would make love. That was the easy part, though maybe it shouldn't have been. All she knew was that when she thought of Noah, it was the feel of his arms, his mouth, his fingers tracing the arc of her collarbone, the curve of her thigh that she thought of. It was how, whenever she first peeled off her clothes, he'd suck in his breath and say "Goddamnit, Grace. Come here." Or lying in bed, how he'd tell her, "I haven't paid enough attention to your ankles" or "this part of your back, right here."

In the morning, she found Noah at the table, reading *The New Yorker* and eating a slice of peach pie.

"Now there's a healthy breakfast." She sat down opposite him, already dressed in the clothes she'd worn yesterday, and reached for his arm.

He pushed his plate away, the pie half-eaten. "I don't know why I'm eating this. I'm not even hungry." He glanced at her hand on his arm. "Do you realize that you always put your fingers right on my pulse?"

"I like listening to your heart."

He didn't say anything, just gently extricated himself from her. "You need coffee." He stood to pour her a mug, and she glanced around his kitchen with its clean countertops and magnet-free refrigerator, so unlike her own. A pile of magazines was stacked on one side of the table: *Smithsonian, Wilson Quarterly, Audubon, The New Yorker*. She pictured him eating here alone each night, reading while he ate.

Wordlessly, he set the steaming mug in front of her, then stood at the window, his back to her. The sky was the color of driftwood, swirls of gray cloud moving across it like the waves on a sonogram.

She took a sip of her coffee, turning the mug to read the quote on its side: Leonardo da Vinci. *Once you have flown, you will walk the earth / with your eyes turned skyward / for there you have been / there you long to return.*

"I was just reading about these ornithologists from Cornell . . ." Noah turned and nodded at the opened magazine on the table. "They're in Louisiana searching for the long-lost Ivory-Billed, *Compephilus principalis,* which has been extinct for over fifty years. It was a beautiful bird, apparently, two feet long, bill to tail. The 'Lord God bird,' people called it." He rubbed his face with both hands, as if still struggling to wake up. "Anyway, a couple of experienced ornithologists, on separate occasions, say they've sighted it, but no one can find it. A ghost bird. There and not there all at once." He glanced at her over his shoulder, his eyes bereft, then continued. "It hit me that that's what I've been doing, Grace. Searching for something that probably doesn't even exist, and maybe hasn't for a long time." She couldn't see his face. "It's ironic, I guess. My *entire* life: trying to understand a species that's always leaving."

She set down her mug, stood up and went around the table to stand behind him, arms around his chest, her face pressed to his back. "If I was seventeen again or twenty or twenty-three, I'd do so much differently," she whispered thickly. "I'd fight for you. I wouldn't let twenty years go by."

"I know." He turned in her arms to face her. And then quietly, holding her gaze, he said, "I don't want to hear from you after this. I need you out of my life for good." His voice was gentle, and she thought of how it's not the heart that is the strongest muscle in the body, but the tongue, as if words mattered more than blood, the struggle to shape and form them, then let them go.

She nodded, feeling stunned, though she knew he was right. She focused on a small square in his plaid flannel shirt, studying each thread and struggling not to cry, to just breathe. Behind him, the gray sky was as enormous as loss. A line of birds moved like dark type across the blank pages of cloud. Indecipherable. A sentence trailing off into pale ellipses like an unfinished thought.

The farther two quarks move away from each other the more fiercely they are pulled back together.

At the door he gave her a hug. Not the usual bear hug, though, but something gentle, quiet almost, a hug like a crocheted shawl full of space and air.

"You got a lot of sun." Stephen took the plate she handed him and carried it across the kitchen to the table.

"It was a gorgeous weekend." Grace turned to fill another plate.

"Were you at the beach?"

She froze for a moment, her heart racing, then resumed filling the plate with the store-bought chicken salad she'd picked up on the way home that morning. "Would it matter?" she asked. She handed him another plate.

He dropped his eyes. "I'm sorry. I had no right . . ." He set the plates down on the counter behind him.

"I needed to clean things up, Stephen." She met his eyes. "So, yes I did go to the beach. And it is finished."

He looked away, hands in his khaki pockets, jingling change, something he did when he was anxious. "Look, Grace," he said. "I— I went on a date last week."

Her stomach dropped. "A date?"

"Sort of. A friend of Sheila's. We just had dinner. Her daughter died of leukemia a year ago, and I guess Sheila thought . . ."

She turned back to the counter, holding onto the edge of it, tears burning her eyes. "How convenient," she said. Her voice caught, and she paused, took a sharp breath before continuing. "You can share stories of your dead children." Despite herself, she started to weep.

"Grace—"

"No," she sobbed, turning to look at him. "Do you have any idea how much *I've* needed to talk to you about him? Goddamn you, Stephen. You are the only person in this whole world who has a clue about how I feel, and you're talking to some—"

"I am not! Listen to me!" He put his hands on her shoulders, the first time he'd touched her in months, which only made her cry harder. "Come on, Grace." He blew out a ragged breath. "I'm not talking to anyone about Jack. I can't. I just— Here." He reached across the counter for a tissue, and handed it to her.

She pressed it to her eyes and turned back to the chicken salad, still sniffling. "Do you think you'll ever be able to talk with me about him?" she said sadly.

"I hope so."

She nodded, then handed him another plate. He was still standing there, jiggling the change in his pocket. "What?"

"We need to try to move on."

"No, *you* need to, Stephen, or you *think* you do, but we, Max and Erin and me, we need you *here*." Her eyes filled again. "Have you seen Max's room?" He'd taken down all the Flyers posters from his walls. "Has he told you that he's not playing hockey this fall?"

"What?" He rubbed his hand across his face, massaging his temples. "Look, I'll talk with him."

"You think it's that easy, you'll just talk to him. He needs you *here*, Stephen, *I* need you—"

"Don't push me, Grace. I'm glad you cleared things up for yourself, but nothing's changed for me."

THIRTY-FIVE

Why can't you at least try it?" Grace asked. *It*: Counseling. "What are you so afraid of?" They'd been on the phone for over an hour. Arguing. Again.

"We're going in circles, Grace. I know how you feel; you know how I feel, and there's really nothing else—"

"*Why* are you doing this?"

"Doing *what*?" he shouted. "Disagreeing with you, God forbid? You don't get everything just because you want it!"

"You think I don't know that?" she asked incredulously. "My child is dead, Stephen. *Our* child. I can write a goddamned book on not getting what I want."

"This *isn't* about Jack. You're using him, Grace, and it makes me sick."

"Everything is about Jack, Stephen. Every detail of my life is about him."

"Really? Because it didn't seem that way last Christmas Eve."

"Why—" She squeezed her eyes shut.

"Look, I'm hanging up," he told her.

"No, please don't," she cried. "Please, we can—"

But he did.

She couldn't find the car keys. They weren't in her purse or in the metal bowl on the kitchen counter where she usually kept them.

"Max, check the car and stop arguing with Erin," Grace said as she hurried upstairs to look in her bedroom. They were going to the Aquarium, Max already complaining, but she was worried about him. All he did lately was lie on his bed, staring at the empty ceiling.

Ever since Jack died she kept losing things: keys, earrings, her cell phone, street names, dates. She would read a couple pages of a book and a half hour later forget what she'd read; when she picked up the book again, she was confused by what had taken place. Or she drove to the grocery store for something specific and came home with everything but the one item she had absolutely needed. She left the house again and again some mornings, forgetting: her purse, keys, coffee, money.

People in mourning did this, she'd read. The searching mimics the feeling of grief itself. Like phantom pain, a part of them would always return to what is gone. Grace had thought then of people who collected things—Japanese tin toys from their childhood or sea shells or life lists of birds—and wondered if collecting too was simply another way to grieve, to hold on.

"So do you ever find the ones you've banded?" she asked as Noah handed her his Styrofoam coffee cup and gently pulled the struggling bird from the mist net.

"We find *maybe* two a year, but that's out of the four or five thousand we collect and band." Noah flicked on the meager battery-operated light and slid the harrier into an empty Pringles can, air holes punched into the end, the bird's legs protruding from the other. "Of the million birds banded in the country every year only about sixty thousand are ever found again, half of them dead."

She watched him fasten the aluminum alloy band over the bird's right leg, measure its beak and talons, set him on the balance scale, then record the numbers in the logbook. "So is it worth it then, all this?"

"Are you kidding?" He looked at her. "When one comes back it is."

She watched as he carried the bird back outside and set it free, the hawk's white underwings flashing against the dark sky, a thin trail of moonlight glinting on the metal band attached permanently now to the bird's leg.

• • •

She walked through her bedroom for the third time, lifting up books and towels and checking the night table drawers—*again*.

"The keys aren't in the car, Mom!" Max yelled up the stairs.

"You probably didn't even look that good," Erin taunted.

"You probably didn't even look that good," Max mimicked.

"If you two do not stop—" Grace started to yell from the top of the stairs.

"We won't go?" Max said hopefully.

The keys were in Jack's room. On the floor by the rocking chair.

"It amazes me how little this place has changed," Jenn commented as they wandered from one dusty exhibit to the next. They were at the Franklin Institute with Erin and her friend, Samantha.

Faded signs directed kids to use the old-fashioned pulleys, levers, and cranks to build friction between two arcs of metal or generate enough electricity to power a light bulb. At another display, they used Mohs' scale of hardness to determine which minerals were stronger than others. Kids scratched pennies against glass or glass against quartz. At yet another table, they created static electricity by rubbing silk on various materials. Grace thought of Noah, of the blue sparks that had seemed to jump from his skin to hers the first time she'd touched him.

The rooms were chaotic as children darted from one experiment to the next, shouting, *Look at this!* or *Let me try!* or *You already had a turn!* They pushed and shoved, parents hurrying after them, the children's names rising up like helium balloons: *Zachary, you have to wait! Jenna, stay with Aubrey! Come on, Abby! No, Jack, this way.*

Jack.

The name slammed into her. Her eyes met Jenn's.

In the Heart Room, the forty-five-year-old two-story papier-mâché heart dominated the exhibit, kids scrambling through the corridors of the right atrium where they heard the recorded thump of blood entering the heart, then descending the stairs into the left ventricle, the hallway a narrow constricted artery that they had to squeeze through. A woman ducked backwards out of the entrance with a screaming toddler and Grace remembered the time she and Stephen took Max here when he was about that age, two or three maybe. He too had howled in fear as if it were a haunted house they'd entered. For a year or so after that, he thought hearts were scary dark places, full of frightening things. Now it occurred to Grace that maybe he had been right.

While Erin and Samantha stood in line, holding hands, to go through the heart, Grace moved around the room, reading the various information panels:

Did you know that the heart is 5,000 times more electromagnetically powerful than the brain?

Did you know that if the blood vessels in the human body were laid end to end, they would stretch for more than 60,000 miles, enough to circle the earth at least twice?

Beyond the high windows of the museum, flags of nearly a hundred nations fluttered along the Benjamin Franklin Parkway. The sky was so bright that the trees stretching along the boulevard towards the Art Museum looked more blue than green, as if they had absorbed some of its color. Farther away, though she could not see it from here, was Children's Hospital. She hadn't been back yet, but she wanted to say hello to Anju and Rebecca, thank some of the nurses who were with Jack those last two weeks, perhaps donate some of his books to the sixth-floor playroom. Her stomach clenched at the idea. Maybe for his birthday, she told herself. August 8. It was still three weeks away, but the thought of it was like an explosion inside her. *Birthday*. The word itself, the whole idea of it, hurt. And yet there was no choice but to keep moving towards it.

Did you know that the heart contracts 100,000 times a day, 40 million times a year, two and a half billion times in a lifetime?

Did you know that in an average lifetime a person will breathe about 75 million gallons of air?

"Look at me, Mama!"

She turned to see Erin and Samantha waving gaily from the balcony just off the left atrium. Grace waved as Erin ducked back inside the heart.

In the display case in front of her was an AbioCor, the first self-contained mechanical heart. It looked like a plastic yo-yo. She read the accompanying words without really taking them in. *The AbioCor heart weighs about two pounds and consists of a chamber filled with hydraulic fluid in the middle. A battery-operated centrifugal pump* . . . At the next panel, there were headphones and she listened first to Ravel's *Mother Goose Suite*, then pushed a button and heard the second movement of Bach's Brandenburg Concerto No. 4. *Did you know that musical scores that approximate the rhythm of a resting heart can actually slow one that is beating too fast?*

Erin ran up to her, hugging Grace around the legs.

"Where's Samantha?" Grace asked.

"She's with Aunt Jenn over there." Erin pointed and Grace spotted them at the display where you could listen to the different sounds the heart made. "Aunt Jenn said we had to ask you if we could go through the heart again."

Grace cupped her hand to Erin's chin. "Is that what you want to do?"

Erin nodded eagerly, bouncing on her toes. She was a mess, socks falling down, hair all over the place, chocolate milkshake stains on her shirt, but she looked happy, and for a moment, Grace was too. "You having a good time, lovey?" she asked.

"This is my favorite place!" Erin said. "And I'm so glad Max didn't come!"

"Hey, now," Grace cautioned, but she was smiling. How did it happen, life pivoting back towards normal, happiness spiraling through the most ordinary moments? She kissed the top of Erin's head. "Go on, you silly girl, I'll wave to you again when you get to the top of the heart." She watched her run off— "Mom says we can go again!"—Jenn turning to meet her eyes over the throng of kids, shaking her head with a familiar, "where-the-hell-do-they-get-their-energy?" look.

Did you know that during the first winter of the Siege of Leningrad in World War II, the city's radio station remained on the air to reassure people that they were not alone, and when the radio announcers were too weak or too cold to play music or recite news, they turned on a metronome that monotonously clicked back and forth, like a heartbeat, letting it echo through loudspeakers in the streets to reassure people that they were not alone.

"She's doing great," Jenn said, coming up beside Grace.

"She is, isn't she?" Grace nodded to the metronome inside the glass case. "Did you know this?"

"Yeah, I'd heard it somewhere." They both turned to watch for the girls. "Does all this make you think about Jack?"

"Everything makes me think about Jack," Grace said. "But it's okay. I mean, there are still these horrible times—I'm *dreading* his birthday—but we also have these times when we're actually happy. The other night Max and I were watching this stupid—and I can't stress that word enough—Austin Powers movie, and we were just having the best time. To hear him laugh at all . . ." She sighed. "It's weird too, though, the whole notion that we really are moving on. Sometimes it feels like I'm losing him all over again."

THIRTY-SIX

Grace and Stephen stood in the laundry room, talking over the rattling of the washer as it gyrated through its spin cycle. Grace forgot how or when this had become a habit, coming into this room when they needed to discuss something important.

"So we're all set then?" Already Stephen's hand was on the door-knob.

Grace pulled one of Max's T-shirts from the dryer, the colors faded from the heat, and held it to her face for a moment, inhaling the warmth. *I can't do this*, she thought. *I can't.* Tomorrow was Jack's birthday. He would have been four.

"Grace?"

"Please stay here tonight," she said. "I haven't asked you for much since . . ." She shook her head. "Just please, Stephen." There were no windows in this room, but she could hear rain lashing against the side of the house.

"Come on, Grace, Max and I will be back first thing in the morning." They were going to a Phillies game. "We're going to get through this." The washer shuddered and clanked as it finished the spin cycle, and he waited for it to stop. "I just don't want to confuse the kids."

"It's his birthday," she pleaded. "The kids will understand that your staying is special."

"Damn it, Grace, you agreed to this. *Weeks* ago." He sighed. "The stadium is ten minutes from my apartment. It doesn't make sense to drive back here tonight."

She didn't answer, only nodded miserably as she pulled a pink T-shirt from the dryer. She folded it and set it on the ironing board, her eyes welling, her nose running. She wiped it on the sleeve of her shirt, an old one of Stephen's actually, then squatted to pull another tangle of warm clothes from the dryer.

"I should get going," Stephen said again.

Max was in the family room, watching cartoons and eating Cocoa Puffs straight from the box. The windows were dark with rain that blew in sudden sheets against the glass. He'd been crying, Grace knew. She glanced at Stephen to see if he'd noticed, but he was staring forlornly at the string of birthday cards she had hung from the mantel, and that she would take to his grave tomorrow.

I'm sorry, she wanted to tell Stephen. *I wasn't sure.* She'd put the cards up and taken them down half a dozen times last night, rereading each one. They were addressed to her, really: *We know this day will be difficult. You will be in our thoughts.* There had to be two dozen.

Abruptly, Max pushed himself up from the couch and walked out of the room.

"Sweetie, do you want to talk?" Grace called.

"About what? This stupid birthday for my *dead* brother?"

Stephen started to follow him. "Watch the tone of voice you use with your—" but Grace put a hand on his arm, stopping him.

"It's okay. Let him be."

She followed them out to the porch a few minutes later to wave good-bye. Erin would be home from Brownies any minute. The rain had stopped, though silver needles of water dripped from the trees and porch railings, and the sky remained overcast. The light hurt her eyes. She pulled the cotton cardigan she had grabbed on her way out the door tight across her chest and hugged herself against the unseasonable chill. The Nielsens from next door drove past, the luggage rack of their white station wagon loaded with suitcases for their annual vacation on Long Beach Island. They beeped the horn and waved. Stephen and Grace simultaneously lifted their arms to wave in return, and in the clear ordinariness of that moment Grace imagined her own life was ordinary again, that she was still the woman she had been only a year ago—energized and happy, harried with Jack's birthday preparations as she followed Stephen out to the porch with last-minute reminders: *You have the list, right? Don't forget the piñata. They've got it all ready to go at Party World. And we probably need more Scotch tape. I don't think I wrote it down.* But she would never be that woman again, she knew. In one of the bereavement magazines at the grief center where Erin was still going, she had read that somewhere in the world a child dies every two seconds, twenty-four hours a day. Every two seconds. Less than the time it took to inhale and exhale a single breath. How was it possible, she wondered, that the world had ever felt ordinary to begin with?

Stephen was halfway to the car when he tossed Max his keys. "I'll be right there," he called, trudging back to the porch. His face was contorted with the effort not to cry.

"What is it?" Grace asked.

His shoes squished in the rain-soaked lawn. He didn't look up until he was standing at the bottom of the porch, and when he did, she was surprised to see how awful he looked, haggard and unshaven, his skin sallow-looking in the anemic light. Rain beaded on his T-shirt, in his hair. He swallowed hard, and she took a step down, the cement cold and damp against her bare feet.

"Don't," he gulped. "I just, I wanted—" He shook his head and turned to stare down the street. "We'll come back tonight," he said. "I'll—I'll sleep in Erin's room."

Tears sprang to her eyes. "Thank you."

He shook his head. "The birthday decorations," he choked. "I'm so glad you did that. And you were right. We should celebrate. I wasn't sure, but—"

"Me either." Her voice cracked. "It was worse *not* to do anything. It seemed so empty." Her throat closed over the word *empty*, and now she was the one glancing away to the sky behind Stephen. A chevron of geese moved over the trees as effortlessly as regret.

● ● ●

"You're not even going to try?" Kempley asked.

"How? The names are blacked out." She pulled her hair free of its ponytail. "They made the accusations in *good faith*, remember?" She hated the bitterness in her voice, the sneer in "good faith."

"And you have no idea who it could have been?"

She turned to lower the stream of water into the tub. "That's the thing, Kempley. It could have been anyone. There are days when I think maybe it was my mom or my friend Jenn or Stephen's brother or God, even Noah, though I *know* that's ridiculous." Grace balanced the phone between her ear and shoulder as she slid off her jeans. "When was it over in Salem?" she asked. "I mean, what did people do?" She poured the vanilla body wash into the tub, then shut the door behind her while it filled. Martha had phoned earlier to tell Grace about another woman in the area who had been accused of Munchausen's. Her daughter had mitochondrial disease.

"When was it *over*?" Kempley said. "I'm not sure it ever was."

Grace walked into Jack's room and leaned her head against the windowpane. Sunday afternoon. Stephen would be back with the kids in an hour. "Come on, it's not still happening," she said. "It had to end sometime."

"Well, the government declared a day of atonement in 1697," Kempley said. "So I guess you could say that the effects lingered for a good five years."

"What do you mean, 'day of atonement?' " Grace closed her eyes against the onslaught of light. "Maybe that helped the accusers, but how did the ones who were accused ever get beyond it? I am so god-damn afraid still, and I don't want to be one of those awful clingy mothers who suffocate their kids to death." She panicked if Max was five minutes late, if Erin was at a friend's house for more than an hour. She'd bought them both cell phones so that she could reach them.

"It's a good question," Kempley was saying now. "But truthfully, it wasn't even until nineteen fifty-seven that the Massachusetts General Court finally proclaimed that 'more civilized laws had superseded those under which the accused had been tried.' "

"Nineteen fifty-seven," Grace repeated. "So it wasn't ever over for the people who lived it."

In the bathroom, she turned off the water and unbuttoned her cotton shirt. She was more tanned than she'd been since the summer she met Noah, thinner too. *Noah.* An ache beneath her ribs. She thought of the woman Martha had phoned to tell her about, the one whose little girl had mito. Only a little over three months since Jack had died—182 days—and already, *already*, it was happening again. She wondered if the same person who had initially accused her had accused this woman too. "I keep wanting to believe that things are different from they were back then," she had said to Kempley. "But maybe that's as crazy as believing in witches."

"Ahh, 'Let not the reader argue, from any of these evidences of iniquity, that the times of the Puritans were more vicious than our own . . .' "

"Is that *The Crucible?* I don't remember it."

"Hawthorne, The opening of *Endicott and the Red Cross.*

Now Grace stared for a moment at her face in the mirror, surprised anew by the gray in her hair, the hollowness in her face. She liked it, though. That she looked different now, that everything, even her hair color, the shape of her face, had been altered. Like a map of a country that no longer exists.

"Hi, honey bunny!" She scooped Erin up in a hug, then held out an arm for Max, even as her eyes focused on Stephen. "Did you guys have a good weekend?" she asked after the kids went inside. His arms were bigger from working out more and he too was more tanned than he'd been since the summer Jack was born, their last in the beach house. It was as if they were both, literally, trying to burn the grief from their lives.

"The weekend wasn't bad," he said now. "How about yours?"

"It was okay."

"Well you look great."

She smiled. "You too." And then, quietly, "I can't believe the summer's almost over." Labor Day was a week away.

"I try not to think about it." The muscle in his jaw jumped. "I'm dreading this whole fall. Our anniversary, the holidays."

"I know."

He shook his head, still staring off. "Jack attack," he said softly.

"Astro-*nut*," she said.

Stephen smiled. "Some woman was yelling at her son yesterday at the pool and his name was Jack, and I swear I wanted to walk over and kiss the woman, I was so grateful just to hear someone say his name. I didn't even care that she was browbeating the poor kid."

"Are you sure we're doing the right thing, Stephen?"

He looked at her. "I'm not sure of anything anymore, Grace."

THIRTY-SEVEN

S eptember 11. Exactly seven months from the day Jack died; one-hundred eighty-nine days. Grace sat in the Starbucks at her usual table by the large plate glass window, sunlight throwing into sharp relief the shadows cast by the metal bistro tables on the side-walk outside. *Relief.* Later, it would strike her as an odd word to use about anything connected to that day.

She'd left her cell phone at home, not wanting to talk to anyone. She nursed her cappuccino for a while, chin on her palm, staring out the window at the gorgeous autumn morning. There was nothing much to look at—the parking lot stretching to the highway, people coming and going at the gym next door. Conversation drifted around her: something about an airplane crash, and as always, Grace thought of her dad, though he hadn't piloted in years. Two women hugged at their cars, one comforting the other, and Grace wondered idly what was wrong. Mostly she just thought of Jack, missing him so much more than she had ever thought possible.

Seven months.

Was this why she didn't notice the unnatural quiet of the now emptied Starbucks? Why she wasn't cognizant of how absence—of voices and laughter—had already taken hold? Or was it, as she would think later, that she did notice, but for her, especially on that morn-ing—*seven months*—it felt right that a sense of emptiness permeated everything.

She drove with the windows open on the way to the cemetery, the radio off. An autumn blue sky, the kind of sky that pilots called "severe clear," her father had once told her, meaning there was infi-nite visibility. The perfect day for flying. She couldn't know, of course, that an airplane had already crashed into the North Tower of the World Trade Center, followed twenty-one minutes later by a second one that crashed into the South Tower. She couldn't have imagined that people were jumping from the 110-story buildings in an effort to escape, that another airplane was headed for the Pentagon, and another—which wouldn't make it—to the White House.

In the cemetery, birds wheeled overhead as she sat by Jack's grave and read *Cosmo's Moon* out loud. She knew it by heart: *You've been following me, said Cosmo. And the moon seemed to blush.* Grace imagined she would always know it by heart—*I guess never saying good-bye means you never get to say hello, said the moon.* And she understood that these sentences were the details of her life that she would remember even when other seemingly more important ones were gone: the frigid feel of Lake Erie even in July; her mother sitting on the kitchen floor in her pajamas, crying because her batch of fudge hadn't turned out; Noah that first day at the church picnic: *Hey you, how about a little help, here?* Kissing Stephen in the rain one night after a party; reading the phrase "mitochondrial myopathy" on the Internet for first time on an October afternoon.

When she finished reading, she set the book down and just thought about Jack, which meant the day wasn't so different from any other day. It was still impossible to go for more than half an hour or so before the realization of Jack's death was pressed to her face like a chloroform-soaked handkerchief, obliterating everything else. Four months ago, she couldn't go more than a minute or two.

As she was leaving, she noticed that already some of the leaves in the maple trees had turned yellow. She thought of how the word *apoptosis* meaning "cell death," came from the Greek word for "falling leaves."

The minute Grace entered the kitchen, she heard the beeping of her cell phone, which meant she had messages. The answering machine was blinking as well. She set her purse on the counter, kicked off her sandals, and hit the play button. The first call was from Stephen: "It's me. I'm at work. Call me as soon as you get this." The next message was Stephen as well: "I'm in the car now. Call my cell." She imagined it was about Jack and wondered if he'd changed his mind at the last minute. She had asked him to come with her to the cemetery, but he told her no, he'd go alone after work.

She picked up the kids' cereal bowls from the table and carried them to the sink as she listened through a number of hang-ups—Stephen again? But it was her mother's voice next. "Stephen just phoned. He's on his way to the cemetery." Grace jerked her head up. "Your dad's picking up Max," her mother continued, "and I'm on my way to get Erin."

Grace glanced at her watch, confused. Was Erin sick? But then why was her dad getting Max and why was Stephen—? And then it—*Munchausen's*—slammed into her with the force of a punch, and she was across the room, hands shaking as she grabbed her cell phone from the table and scrolled through the list of "received calls." Stephen, Stephen, Stephen, her mother, Stephen again, Kempley, her mother—all in the last hour. She felt as if the air had been siphoned from the room, her fingers thick and uncoordinated as she punched in Stephen's cell phone number, trying to remind herself to take deep breaths, to calm down, but even as she was thinking this, tears sprang to her eyes, and her heart felt as if it would break in half. On the second ring, she was switched into Stephen's voice mail, which meant he was on the phone with someone else. Bennett? "Goddamn it," she cried out loud, trying her mom's phone, panicked now, because it had to be Munchausen's, it had to be. Why else would they be acting like this, pulling the kids out of school, Stephen on his way over?

The answering machine was still playing and now Kempley was on it, barely coherent, sobbing. "Oh God, Grace, I—I can't believe this," and the kitchen was dissolving, the walls turning to liquid, and it didn't matter that it made no sense that Kempley would know of another accusation before even Grace did. Grace's cell phone rang then, Stephen phoning her back, and she grabbed it, crying herself now. "What happened?"

"Turn on the TV," he said.

• • •

On the drive to her parents' house, she saw neighbors who were usually at work getting their kids out of the car and ushering them inside. Charlotte McCann was on the driveway, crying and hugging her husband, his car door still flung open.

Erin stayed in the kitchen with Grace's mom, while Grace, her father, Stephen, and Max stared numbly at the TV, as they watched those ordinary silver jetliners arc almost gracefully across that perfect blue sky. Again and again, they watched the towers fall. They didn't implode in a riot of Hollywood special effects; they didn't topple over or slam dramatically into even more buildings so much as they seemed simply to slip from view. Like a drowning man silently letting go after struggling to stay above water far longer than anyone believed was possible. Again and again. And still, no matter how many times they saw it, it didn't seem real. None of them cried; Grace could barely feel.

The news anchors struggled to find something, anything to say— *Firemen, typically carrying equipment weighing anywhere from eighty to a hundred pounds, advanced up the stairs of a burning building at the rate of one floor per minute. Steel loses half its strength at 1022 degrees Fahrenheit and melts at 2500*—but there were no words, there would never be enough words, to fill the gaping hole in the sky where the towers had been. All afternoon, this desperate listing of facts: *The towers contained four hundred thousand tons of structural steel, six acres of marble, 12,000 miles of electrical cable . . .* as if the magnitude of the loss could be measured and quantified. It seemed so utterly beside the point that it verged on ridiculous, and yet Grace understood that this relentless insistence on numbers and measurements—*191 miles of heating ducts, enough concrete to build a sidewalk from New York to D.C.*—wasn't so different from her own attention to the technical, quantifiable aspects of Jack's illness. Both were an attempt to offset all the things for which there were no numbers: the weight of a life or the value of a laugh.

Max sat on the floor, leaning against the couch where Grace sat with Stephen. On TV, a witness, his business suit covered in dust and ashes, described how just before the impact of the first plane, hundreds of pigeons lifted off at once; seconds later, when the man saw the explosion in the North Tower, he realized the birds must have felt the collision before the sound waves carried. At the mention of the birds, Grace thought of Noah, a dull ache reverberating though her.

"It was the worst thing I've ever seen. They were actually jumping—" a woman was sobbing, "and my little girl kept asking what they were, and what do you say," the woman wailed, "how do you answer something like that?"

"What did you say?" the reporter asked.

"I just kept telling her they were birds."

Stephen leaned forward and put his hand on Max's shoulder. "You okay?" he asked. Max shrugged. What did "okay" even mean? Grace smiled sadly at Stephen. "I'm glad you're here," she whispered, and he took her hand in his and said, "Me too."

And then back to the anchors, grim-faced and disbelieving, the litany of facts: *ten thousand gallons of fuel were being carried on the two Boeing 767s. If the energy of the Oklahoma City bomb was converted into fuel, it would equal only fifty-one gallons.*

It took ten seconds to collapse what took eight years to build.

The explosive energy of the two planes was over nine trillion joules.

Joules. The same unit measurement used in defibrillators. Fifty joules to recalibrate a man's heart. Twenty-five for a child's.

They had dinner with Grace's parents, then went back to their house. Max immediately turned CNN on in the family room. Stephen tucked Erin in, then, looking beat, came into the kitchen to make a drink. "It seems strange that it's still light out," Grace said. It was still summer, although the newscasters and reporters were already referring to it as autumn: *The autumn the world changed, the autumn we'll never forget,* as if even the season had been sabotaged by the terrorists.

Stephen didn't say anything, just carried the empty ice tray to the sink to fill it. Grace watched his eyes fall on the bone-colored conch shell she'd set on the windowsill two months ago. *That's what I want to be to you, Grace: whole and intact, even when everything around us is broken.* The thought seemed only sad tonight. What was the cost, she wondered, of remaining intact in the midst of so much wreckage? She stared again at the sky, faded to pale blue, the horizon bruised with purple.

"I keep thinking about what those families are going through," Stephen said. He leaned against the counter, drink in hand.

What Grace kept thinking about was Rudy Giuliani, the mayor of New York City, speaking of "unbearable losses" and the news anchors talking about living in a "transfigured world" and about how there was no such thing as normal anymore, and the unimaginable had become imaginable and how it all made perfect sense because this is what she had been feeling since the night Jack died.

The sky was dark now. From the living room came the murmur of a newscaster. "I thought I'd been accused of Munchausen's again this morning," she said now. "All those frantic messages, and my parents going to get the kids." She wasn't sure why she was telling him this.

"Oh, Grace, I didn't even think of that." He set his drink on the counter behind him. "God, I'm sorry."

She didn't say anything, just nodded.

"You want to know what I thought when I saw the news this morning?"

She waited.

"I thought, 'Thank God, I'm finally going to be able to cry.' "

"Have you yet?"

"About today?"

"About any of it. Jack, us . . ."

He shook his head. "I think if I ever start, Grace, I won't be able to stop."

After Stephen left, Grace watched TV with Max until nearly midnight. The networks had stopped showing the footage of the second plane and the Towers' collapse. The focus now was on the families of the victims, holding up the handmade posters and leaflets of the missing, their eyes blazing with grief and determination:

He's always been a survivor . . .

If anyone can make it, she will.

I know he's out there . . .

All the things they said about Jack every time he had a relapse.

On the way up to bed, Grace took the shell from the kitchen windowsill and set it on her night table. *This one intact thing.* But even it was so fragile, tossed about in the surf, each five-foot wave exerting over five hundred pounds of pressure against every square inch of shoreline it struck. It made no sense what survived and what didn't—and tonight, more than ever, she wanted it to.

She held the phone on her lap for what seemed a long time. The TV was still on, footage of colored emergency lights swirling through the debris of dust and ash of what was already being called Ground Zero.

"Were you asleep?" she asked when Stephen answered.

"Is that possible?"

She heard the clink of ice against a glass. "I don't know why I called."

"I was just thinking of how, when that second plane hit, my first, my *only*, reaction was to get the kids and to get a hold of you. It was instinctual, gut-level. *Get the kids.*"

"Me too."

"I know. God, the minute you walked into your mom's kitchen and just held onto Max, didn't say anything, didn't cry, just held him. All day that's what I wanted to do: hold you." His voice sounded distant, blurry, from the wind maybe or from the drinks. "I should probably wait until I have less alcohol in me to have this conversation, but there it is, for what it's worth."

She closed her eyes. She didn't want to get her hopes up.

"We clung to each other as if we ourselves were falling," wrote John Updike in *The New Yorker.*

"We're living through an eclipse of normality, a twilight landscape. The sun isn't quite right. It's a little darker than it should be when you look at it," author Edward Linenthal would say in *Time.*

"It was like watching the moon fall," actor Robert DeNiro would say in *Esquire*.

She leaned over the counter, scanning the newspaper, waiting for her coffee to heat up in the microwave. She read that from the space station two-hundred forty miles above earth, astronauts had seen the dark plume of smoke and ash that day. "Tears flow differently in space," she read, and thought of Jack, somewhere far away from her.

On October 11, the nation marked the one-month anniversary of the attacks. They were fighting a war now in Afghanistan. Reagan National Airport remained closed. The newspapers reported huge increases in the sales of American flags, crosses, Bibles, and engagement rings; in dating services, and pregnancies. The National Infertility Association had a fifty percent jump in their Web site traffic. Emptiness was intolerable.

Sitting in a Starbucks after dropping Erin off at school, Grace often found herself reading the *Philadelphia Inquirer* someone had left on a table, phrases coming into focus, then falling away through the scrim of tears that was constant. "Mechanics of Failure," she read. "Archeology of Grief." The towers had fallen in ten seconds, each floor collapsing onto the floor below, then slamming into the next floor, then the next, the cumulative weight and speed catastrophic. An entire floor compacted into six inches. Grace couldn't comprehend it. Sixty feet of building compressed into three. A geologic stratum of loss. It was how her life had felt in the weeks before Jack died, she thought, staring blankly out the window, coffee mug clutched in her hands. The weight of the Munchausen's accusation had slammed through her, buckling one support after the other from her life, building its own tragic momentum. Now, without Jack, and with Noah gone from her life, her world too felt pulverized, compressed into something unrecognizable and otherworldly.

She would sip her coffee, the bitter liquid churning in her stomach, the grinding of the espresso machine momentarily drowning the sound of conversations. That a four-hundred-thousand-pound airplane could crash into a building at over five hundred miles an hour, releasing the equivalent of seventeen hundred *tons'* worth of TNT, and people in their offices would go about returning phone calls, checking files, e-mailing coworkers and friends seemed incomprehensible. Why didn't they run the minute they felt the building's tremor, smelled the smoke, saw the bits of paper fluttering past their windows? How could they have waited? And yet how could they have possibly known what was happening?

On Halloween, Erin dressed up as an angel. Max didn't trick or treat this year. The papers were full of pictures, little kids dressed as firefighters and policemen. "Terror has a whole new meaning," the papers declared, and "Horror is no longer the stuff of haunted houses or scary costumes." On November 11, the nation marked the two-month anniversary of the attacks, and Grace marked the nine-month anniversary of Jack's death. Nine months. The amount of time she had carried him inside her.

Every day now there were more stories: about the little boy who used to fall asleep by counting the windows of the Twin Towers—his stars, which he used to be able to see from his bed. Now he couldn't sleep; there was nothing left to count. Or the florist whose shop was located near Ground Zero. In the aftermath of the attacks, she had been forced to stock different kinds of flowers, hardier ones that could survive without the shade once cast by the towers' shadow. And calla lilies, whose strong smell helped diffuse the acrid stench that had become a part of the sky itself.

And then Thanksgiving. "Everyone is a pilgrim now," Grace read in *Time,* "stripped down to bare essentials. . . ." Stephen and Grace and the kids went to Grace's parents as they always had. Jenn and Diane and their three boys came, so the house was loud and crowded, and there were pale slivers of time when Jack's absence didn't cut through her. Just after dinner, though, when everyone was crowded in the kitchen helping with dishes, Stephen found her alone in the den, hugging herself and staring out at the lake. He came up behind her, hands on her shoulders, chin on her neck. "Why don't I come home?" he said quietly.

THIRTY-EIGHT

She heard Erin's door creak open, and then she was standing in the doorway, crying.

"Honey-bunny, what's wrong?" Grace set down her book and held out her arms. "Did you have a bad dream?"

Erin only cried louder. "I—I don't want to—to go to the doctor's," she sobbed. She had her annual checkup with Dr. Morris in the morning. He had been all of the kids' pediatrician.

"Hey, what's up, sweet pea?" Stephen had lowered the paper. "I thought you liked Dr. Morris."

"But what if—what if—he takes me away?"

"Well, I just won't let him," Stephen said. "How about that?"

"No!" she wailed. "You can't! You couldn't with Jack and they—they—"

"Oh God," Grace said under her breath. "I didn't even think." She was across the room, arms around her daughter, whose nightgown was soaked.

Erin was sobbing so hard, it sounded as if she were choking. "I—I—I wet the bed."

"Oh honey-bunny." Grace took Erin's hand. "Let's go get you some clean jammies, okay? And then if you want, you can come sleep with Daddy and me. How would that be?"

"But I still don't want to go to-tomorrow," she hiccupped.

"Shush, baby, you don't have to. I'll call Dr. Morris and tell him you're as good as new." Which she wasn't at all, Grace thought as she turned on the small ballerina lamp in Erin's room.

"I dreamed that they took me and I couldn't see you anymore and then I died." She spoke in jerks, shoulders still heaving.

Grace tugged the soaked nightie over Erin's upraised arms. Sadness looped itself through her. "I will never let that happen," she whispered as she sat back on her heels and pulled a fresh T-shirt over Erin's head. But she knew even as she said it that Erin didn't believe her. And how could she?

Grace stared at Erin, asleep between them, snoring loudly. "*I* thought about the accusation, of course, but it just never occurred to me that she would be making those associations." She stroked her daughter's hair. "I feel like an idiot."

"You can't know everything, Grace." Stephen said. The TV was on mute, bluish light flickering over them. "That she doesn't believe that her parents can protect her, though. Jesus."

When she searched Google for his name, over a hundred and twenty references came up. Dr. John Bartholomew. He was on the board of numerous medical and charitable foundations. He'd authored dozens of articles, had had dozens more written about him. Profiles. Interviews. And he was involved in a number of accusations of Munchausen's, Had John Bartholomew been the one, then, to accuse her? Apparently he had accused a number of women he'd never met, women like Grace, who had written to and e-mailed doctors, randomly at times, and desperately perhaps, because they didn't know what else to do or where else to go because their own doctors kept insisting it was nothing, that the mothers were overreacting, *they* were making things worse, *they* were making mountains out of molehills, *they* needed to just relax and *stop thinking so much*. "Diagnosis by Immaculate Perception," the mothers on the M.A.M.A. site called it.

She kept thinking it had to be him and if she could know this for sure, she could stop being so afraid. What did she have to lose? Her name had been cleared publicly, CPS had written a formal letter of apology. And Jack was gone.

It took her over an hour to get up the nerve. If it had been him, would he accuse her again? She stood in Jack's room for a long time, holding onto his crib, thnking, wondering. She wondered if John Bartholomew had children and if any of them had ever been as sick as Jack, though she knew the answer, knew that if he'd had a sick child of his own, he never could have accused as many mothers as the women on the M.A.M.A. site said he had. She knew that if he had a sick child, he would have understood that when your child is ill, it is impossible— ridiculous even—to talk or think or write about anything else, impossible to care, and because of that, yes, you might seem—and maybe you even are—self-righteous because you can't imagine, you simply can't, that anything else matters. *MSBP mothers are notorious for documenting, in diary form, the course of the child's illness*, the experts wrote, and *The MSBP mother never has enough time to tell her story,* the experts said, but if any of these experts—if John Bartholomew—had a child with a terminal illness, they would have known this too: that these mothers wrote because they were terrified of forgetting something important, something someone said, some clue, some small detail that might help. They wrote out of panic, struggling to give coherence to a story that made no sense; they wrote for the same reason that Scheherazade told her stories, a thousand and one of them, in *Tales of the Arabian Nights*: they wrote to forestall the time when there was no story left to tell—when their child was gone.

She picked up one of Jack's Matchbox cars and ran it along the rails of his crib. Did John Bartholomew know that women with children had significantly fewer heart attacks than those who stayed childless or that in every language the word for mother carries an "m" sound, the first consonant babies learn, or that a blindfolded woman can identify her child by smell within minutes of its being born, even if she's delivered her child by cesarean.

She dialed twice before she let the call go through to the hospital. She was transferred to his department, to his assistant, who took her name and asked what her call was in reference to. She explained that Dr. Bartholomew had reviewed her child's records a year and a half before. She gave them Jack's name.

She recognized his voice immediately, his tone was chilly. "I'm not sure what I can do," he told her brusquely.

She carried the phone with her to the living room and sat in the dark on the couch they rarely used. Light from the kitchen illuminated the pale upholstered chairs and oriental rugs and Waterford vases filled with long-stemmed silk flowers. This wasn't a room they'd used more than a few times since Jack was born—a Christmas dinner maybe, a retirement event for Stephen's former boss. It wasn't a room to be comfortable in, a room for laughter or children. It was a room for show, for appearances. The perfect room, she thought, to talk to the man who had probably accused her of Munchausen's.

When she explained that Jack had died, biting her lip to keep from crying, Bartholomew apologized perfunctorily and, sounding exasperated, asked again what he could do. She told him then that she'd been accused of Munchausen's shortly after her interaction with him, that it had cost her the last ten days of her child's life. "I know that whoever accused me did so in good faith," she lied. She was shaking, fingers sweaty on the phone receiver. "I thought it might have been you and if it was . . ." Her voice cracked. "I just need to know." She squeezed shut her eyes, determined not to weep. "Please, I'm not angry, I understand, I just, I can't move on, I'm so afraid, and my other kids . . ."

"I'm sorry, but I can't help you," he interrupted.

"I am begging you." She was nearly whispering.

"This conversation is inappropriate, Mrs. Connolly." His voice was hard. "And to continue is to put us both in a position I'm sure neither of us wants to be in. But for the record, no, I did not accuse you." A hint of something, compassion maybe? crept into his voice. "Please do not phone my office again."

"I thought you'd be pleased that it wasn't him." Stephen handed her a serving bowl. They were doing the dishes.

"But now I'll never know." She set the bowl on the counter, and held out her dishcloth for another. "I guess I hoped that if it was him I could put it behind me finally."

THIRTY-NINE

She was just finishing putting up the last of the Christmas garlands along the bookcases in the family room when she heard the rumble of the garage door. Stephen and his brother had been out Christmas shopping for the women.

"So?" Grace asked as Stephen came in through the laundry room. "What's the deal with your brother and Mandy?" They hadn't seen Jeff since before Thanksgiving, which he'd spent with Mandy's family.

"He bought her a ring," Stephen said, taking off his coat and glancing around the room. "It looks great in here, honey." He stood in front of the fireplace, holding his hands to the flames.

"A ring? As in diamond? Are you kidding me?" Grace climbed down from the stepladder. "What did you— God, she's so young."

"Yeah, but it sounds like they're both really happy." He shook his head. "The way he talks about her . . . hell, the way he talks about himself. I've never heard him sound this upbeat and excited. They want to start having kids right away."

Grace sat on the couch behind him, warmth from the fire spreading over her legs. Stephen glanced at her over his shoulder. "Actually, there's more."

"Oh for the love of God, Stephen. You are *not* going to tell me she's . . ."

"Pregnant? No." Stephen came over to the couch and sat next to Grace "I wish it was that." He regarded her with a look in his eyes that she couldn't quite read. Worry mostly, and she felt the muscles in her stomach knot in fear.

"No." She started to push herself up. "No," she repeated. "Not again. There's nothing—"

"Wait a minute." He tugged at her to sit back down. "It's not another accusation."

"Then what?" Her voice was shrill.

He exhaled a long breath. "Mandy was the one who reported you the first time, Grace, the March before we found out."

She shrugged his arm from hers. *"What?"*

"Apparently it was something *I* said about the hospital being your social life. It was when Jack was in for those two weeks, and I can't remember the context. I imagine I was just trying to joke, play down the seriousness of what was happening to Jack, but shit." He leaned forward, elbows to knees, raking his hands through his hair. "I guess CPS took the accusation more seriously because she's a social worker." He looked at her, his eyes bleak. "I don't know what to say."

"It's not your fault." She was surprised by how calm she sounded. Or was she numb? "I just—Jeff's marrying her?" Where was the rage she'd been feeling for the past few months every time she thought about this, every time she went on the M.A.M.A. site and read another story of another accused woman?

"He doesn't want to lose us, Grace." He looked at her. It was a question.

It would have been easier had it been Bartholomew. Doctors against powerless mothers who dared to question them. A tidier plot. Clear-cut good guys and bad guys. But Mandy was an inexperienced girl who had overreacted, as Kate perhaps had. And their intentions hadn't been bad. They thought they were doing their jobs. "He's not going to lose us," she said slowly. The words felt automatic, without meaning. What was she supposed to say? And yet, what other answer was there? Jeff was his brother. And they'd lost enough.

"I guess she realized at some point that she was off base, and she tried to retract it, but she was so involved with Jeff that everyone just assumed she was backing off because of him. It's why she had Jeff warn us about the accusation. Apparently she even talked to the judge on our behalf."

Grace stood and walked to the fire, the heat searing. She'd hung Jack's stocking, of course, and she idly reached up and touched its toe. She felt emptied out, the rage gone, leaked out of her like air from a balloon. It was over. There wasn't hate or regret or anything except a dull ache of sadness that a mistake so tiny, a *misunderstanding*, as Bennett had said all along, could have caused this much damage.

"How long has your brother known about this?" Grace asked without turning around to look at him. As soon as she said the words though, she realized it didn't matter. She realized she didn't care. She realized that it was over. Finally.

FORTY

Grace sat at the kitchen table with a stack of mail and a plate of Christmas cookies. Stephen and Max were shoveling the front porch, and Erin had just come in from making a snowman, her nose bright red. Grace set a cup of hot chocolate in front of her. "Do you want to help me open these?" She gestured to the stack of Christmas cards."

"Maybe after I get warm." Her teeth were chattering. "Do you think Daddy can make us a fire when he comes in?"

"I think Daddy would love to make us a fire," Grace said, as she slid her fingernail beneath the seal of the first envelope.

It was a card with a picture of a child in a manger. "Peace on Earth," it read in pale blue script. The room went still. How was it possible that people—her *friends*—didn't understand that cards like these with their pictures of infants, even if that infant was supposed to represent Jesus, shredded her to pieces inside? She forced herself to look up, but it was like hearing her name called in a strange place and glancing around to find nothing and no one she recognized. It seemed impossible that this was the same kitchen where a year ago she had stood making salads with Jack while he sat on the counter and helped her rip the lettuce. It was his job to turn the handle on the salad spinner, and she'd pretend the lettuce was inside screaming for him to stop. "We're getting dizzy! Cut it out!" she'd say in a squeaky voice, and Jack would laugh, and turn the handle harder.

She set the Christmas card down. Outside, a gust of wind tore a branch from its tree. What was appropriate when a child had died? she wondered numbly as she regarded the stack of envelopes. Did you still send pictures of your own kids dressed in their matching Christmas outfits? Did you still include the yearly newsletter with its breezy accounts of the family's trials and tribulations of the past twelve months?

She glanced down again, wanting to lay her head on her arms as Erin was doing. Her hands, loosely cupped around the steaming coffee mug, were dry, old-looking. The entire surface of a person's skin was replaced every month. An idle thought, but even this seized her with a grief so sharp that she nearly gasped. This too was gone, she realized, the part of her that literally, physically had held Jack's hand or slapped him five or combed his sweaty hair from his forehead the last time she saw him.

She recognized her grandfather's spidery scrawl on one of the envelopes and pulled his card from the pile. For fifty-nine years, sending the Christmas cards had been Grace's grandmother's job. She kept track of addresses on index cards that she stored in a tin recipe box and that she brought with her when she and Grace's grandfather flew to New Jersey from Michigan for Thanksgiving. Her grandmother had been so proud of how many cards she sent out—nearly four hundred one year; of how she always wrote a personal note on each one. She had died of lung cancer two years ago. After fifty-nine years of marriage.

"We love you, honey, and are glad you and Stephen have worked things out," her grandfather had written in his loose script. The *we* caught in her throat. She stared at his carefully printed letters, their bottoms flattened by the ruler he used to keep the lines straight. "*We* know our little Jack is watching over you."

She gripped her coffee mug with both hands, heat searing the tips of her fingers. After Jack died, Grace's grandfather wrote her a letter and told her that he still talked to her grandmother every day. He meant this as comfort, but it seemed only sad. It reminded Grace of the time she and Stephen came home from a party to find a message on their answering machine, a man sobbing, "Please, oh God, please call me, Wendy." Obviously, the man had dialed the wrong number and was too distraught to know it, and there was no way to let him know that whoever Wendy was, she hadn't gotten his message.

Funny, how that man's voice became a part of her history with

Stephen. They wondered about him on and off for years. Out having a drink, one or the other would ask, "Do you think Wendy ever called?" They tried to imagine what had so devastated the man. What had he done to her or she to him? Eventually, mentioning Wendy evolved into a sort of shorthand way to describe being ignored or worse, maybe, made invisible. Stephen once used it to explain the months shortly before his dad left his mother. "It was a total Wendy." Or if one of them was lost in thought, the other might call out, "Wendy, oh Wendy, are you there?" Grace had said it last winter. "You're a goddamned Wendy," she sobbed. "I am begging you to listen to me, and you don't have a clue!"

Outside, the world looked swollen with snow, the white edges of the trees disappearing into the white sky. Jenn had told her once about a patient she'd cared for who had damaged his right visual cortex in a bike accident, which meant that he couldn't see the entire left half of the world. He saw trees with branches on only one side of a trunk, arm chairs with one arm, only one half of a person's face. It was how Grace felt with Jack gone from her life: part of the world had disappeared.

She picked up her grandfather's card again, silvery trees etched against a white background. He had been a nightclub singer, dreaming of making it big like Perry Como or Bing Crosby; her grandmother was a dancer, a red-haired Ginger Rogers. Both of them were nineteen years old when they met in a dance hall in Minneapolis on an ordinary Wednesday night in 1940. He'd been filling in for a buddy who had come down with the flu or he wouldn't have been there at all, would never have met Grace's grandmother. A week later they married. *One week.* And they stayed that way, still holding hands in their seventies, going dancing every Thursday night. He still called her "sweetheart," whistled a catcall when she entered a room "dressed to the nines." She still blushed: "Oh, Wayne, for goodness sake." Fifty-nine years. After *one* week. Destiny. Fate. Words she had used about Noah.

Her grandfather quit singing to raise his family. He became a salesman for General Mills. Her grandmother gave up her dancing to become a wife and mother. And not once ever asked, as far as Grace knew, if that had really been enough. Everyone assumed it was, herself included, until Noah returned to her life and she began wondering about her own decisions, and about the shadow life of choices *not* made that trailed behind the life she lived now. Had there really been no resentment in her grandparents' lives, she wondered, no regret, no yearning for the lives and the dreams they had relinquished? Grace held her coffee mug to her chin and blew on it. Tears scalded her eyes. Was it really so simple to pack away the life not led like a wedding dress or a once-worn ball gown, beautiful but so impractical?

Erin, still lying on her arm, was lazily filling in the lines of a coloring book. "You getting tired, lovey?" Grace asked, tugging lightly on one of Erin's braids. Erin nodded without lifting her head. In the bright kitchen light, her dark braids held a reddish cast, as Jack's hair had, inherited from Grace's grandmother. Grace smiled, remembering the two-thousand-page *Mendelian Inheritance in Man* she and her classmates had taken turns lugging to Advanced Genetics. The book listed every known heritable characteristic: the ability to move one's ears; to curl one's tongue. The inability to smell freesia flowers or cyanide. Red hair; blue eyes. And diseases: Klinefelter Syndrome, Gaucher disease, mitochondrial myopathy. It all seemed so random, though, the traits that survived, the ones that didn't. Why red hair? Why mitochondrial disease? And why *not* something like fidelity or perseverance? The ability to stay married for *fifty-nine* years. This, more than anything, was what Grace wanted now.

Erin had fallen asleep, her crayon slipping from her hand. Grace pushed back her chair and squatted next to her daughter. "Come on, lovey." She stroked Erin's arm. "Let's go up, baby." Erin groaned and turned her face away. Grace tried again, managing to tug her child into her arms so that she could lift her. She carried Erin to the couch, and tucked a wool blanket around her shoulders and feet.

She turned on the tree for when Erin awoke, then sat in the rocking chair by the sliding glass door that faced the lake. Her parents' house was just across it on the opposite side. The snow drifted lazily down. She imagined the sight of it would always bring her back to

Jack, to the three Christmases they'd had together, stark against all the others she would have without him.

The smoke rising from someone's chimney looked like a double helix. She smiled. She could practically hear Max groaning and telling her, "You are *such* a geek, Mom." Max from last year, maybe. This Max didn't laugh much. This Max took everything so seriously. And how could he not? The world as he knew it kept ending, over and over, and he blamed himself.

It was *his* bird report that brought Noah into her life, he apparently thought, which made it *his* fault that Jack died, *his* fault that his dad had left. And yes, it helped that Stephen was back, but they were still so wary, so aware of how fragile everything was. She wasn't sure when any of them would truly feel safe, when little things like Stephen being late to pick Erin up from Brownies or Grace taking one of them to the doctor for something utterly ordinary wouldn't throw them into a tailspin.

Grace hadn't realized that Max knew Noah was connected to the accusation until right before Thanksgiving when, cleaning out his desk, he found his report on Audubon. Grace was in bed reading and looked up to see him in the doorway, sobbing so violently his entire body was shuddering. "Oh, honey, what?" she had asked, and he handed her the report, something broken and horrible in his eyes. She had thought of the night Stephen had first walked into their bedroom after learning of the accusation from his brother, and she felt the same sense of foreboding and fear. She opened her arms to Max and he came to her as he hadn't since he was a little boy. "If it wasn't for me, none of this would have happened," he choked, and then over and over, "I'm sorry, Mom, I'm sorry, I'm sorry," even though she never stopped telling him, "No, sweetie, no, you have nothing to be sorry for, *nothing*." He cried until his voice grew hoarse and he drifted off to sleep, and even then, in the midst of whatever dream he was in, he'd begin to whimper, tears leaking from his eyes. She lay awake for hours, stroking his hair, watching him, and whispering, "It's not your fault, Max. None of this is your fault."

She herself had lain awake half the night, filled with loathing for herself, for what she'd done to her family, in the name of *destiny, fate.* The words *she'd* wanted to use. Grace had stared at her son, this giant boy, his eyelashes wet with tears, and knew that her affair with Noah hadn't been about destiny at all, but about desperation and a smallness of spirit and a bone-deep selfishness.

What kind of woman, what kind of mother, *leaves her children—her dying child—on Christmas Eve?*

On the couch, Erin stirred, kicking her blanket to the side. Grace leaned forward and tucked it back around her feet. She heard Max and Stephen in the garage, stomping the snow from their boots. She swallowed hard. There were so many ways to make mistakes, she had wanted Max to understand, and there were so many choices and in one of them was some minuscule, barely perceptible detail that would end up forever altering your life. She'd learned in graduate school the ways tragedy arrives in such ridiculously small occurrences. African sleeping sickness, caused by a single bite from a tsetse fly, which is attracted to bright hues so that something as innocuous as your choice of wardrobe—the color of your shirt—could be the difference between sickness and health.

Or a shift of temperature somewhere far below the equator and ocean currents were affected halfway around the world, causing the southwestern United States to endure a warmer, rainier spring. The piñon trees in that area consequently produce a bumper crop of nuts, and this, in turn, led to an explosion in the population of deer mice, and more deer mice equaled more contact with humans—which often equaled a greater chance that a rare and deadly form of the hanta virus would be spread. Or somewhere in Seattle, hamburgers cooked not quite long enough, a few seconds maybe, and four children die. This was what was truly horrific, Grace knew. It wasn't only the tragedy itself but how preventable it all could have been. An airline flying into a building: if the weather had only been less perfect, the sky not quite so blue, the sun not as bright. The very beauty of the morning contributing to all the horror that followed.

The list was endless: The 1976 outbreak of Legionnaires' disease in the Philadelphia Bellevue Stratford, where the bacterium was carried through the hotel's air conditioning system so that those who congregated in the lobby, where there were more ducts, were more likely to become infected. And why had they congregated there? Perhaps they were more gregarious. Or perhaps they didn't know the city well and so lingered in the lobby, reading brochures and talking to the bellhops. Maybe they were lonely. Maybe they didn't want to return to their room. Something that simple. Or people sleep together once and a deadly virus is passed on. Every encounter, every breath, every choice, is enough to alter your life.

It was as random, she thought, as genetics itself, the plot of anyone's life written not so much in the genes but in their mutations, the mistakes and accidents that never should have been. A switch of the 46th base of chromosome 5 and a person was more susceptible to asthma, something as fundamental as their *breathing* forever altered. Or the deletion of one specific base, the 6,174th, on one specific gene in one specific chromosome, the 13th, and breast cancer became more likely. With mitochondrial disease, all it took was a single mutation in any one of the over 16,000 base pairs that comprised its DNA. It seemed wrong, *was* wrong. One mutation out of thousands, a spelling error, for God's sake, a *typo*. She stared at the tree and imagined a string of Christmas bulbs, how if one light is burned out, the entire string remains dark. It should have been more complicated, she thought wearily, as if complexity somehow mitigated the damage or at least made it more understandable. It didn't.

And in the end, that single minuscule accident wasn't so different, was it, from a boy, whose name even her grandfather no longer remembered, getting the flu sixty-one years before, which meant that his buddy covered for him at work and consequently met a red-headed dancer with whom he fell in love. A fluke. A boy gets the flu or maybe just a bad cold, and a week later his buddy is married, and that one impossibly tiny week spirals into the fifty-nine years of marriage and four children and then grandchildren. Entire generations.

Or a boy gets a homework assignment, one of the thousands of similar assignments he'll get all through school, and he decides, for no particular reason, to write about birds.

A woman wakes in the night and sends an e-mail she never should have written.

A girl, barely out of college, makes a phone call to Child Protective Services.

The air we breathe is a mistake, she thought, caused by ancient bacteria: a random mutation somewhere down the evolutionary line and the whole process of photosynthesis began.

FORTY-ONE

*T*he four of them had almost finished the puzzle by late afternoon on New Year's Eve. Max had found a company on the Internet that turned photos into high-quality jigsaws. And so the family puzzle was Jack as a baby in a little red-and-green plaid sport coat and bow-tie, bald as a peanut.

"I don't know about reading last year's resolutions," Grace had said earlier to Stephen. She was in the kitchen slicing pumpkin bread, then placing it into a cloth-lined basket. "Maybe we should just start fresh."

Stephen nodded. "Do you remember Jack's resolution?"

She smiled without turning around. Already the snow that had fallen a few days before had melted. The late afternoon sun bled through the low clouds and spilled across the horizon, coloring the lake a bright fiery pink. From upstairs came the squeak and groan of Erin playing "Let's see" in the tub. Grace rested the edge of the bread knife against the counter. "He was resolved to get a *Shrek* video and, to quote, 'let Mama give me two cookies for dessert instead of one,' *and* to go to the rocket place—"

"Cape Canaveral," Stephen said. "I tell myself that he did go there, in a way."

Grace stared wistfully across the lake. "I tell myself the same thing."

Max slapped the second-to-last puzzle piece into place, then Erin put in the final one. The room smelled of pine and wood smoke, of cranberry-scented candles.

"I can't believe you actually dressed Jack like this," Max said, grabbing another square of pumpkin bread.

Stephen cocked an eyebrow at his son "You ever see some of the outfits your mother had for you?"

"Oh, but Max was adorable!" Grace protested.

"Yeah, those little-boy-blue shorts did wonders for my image, Mom!"

"You were a toddler." She smiled at him. "You didn't have an image." She glanced at his face in the flickering light, grateful for the sound of his laughter.

"A toddler." He rolled his eyes. "I was in junior high."

"You were?" Erin squealed.

"No," Grace laughed. "He was not." She shook her head at the memory. When she looked up, Stephen was watching her. He held her gaze. Light from the Christmas candles that lined the edge of the mantel elongated his face and shadowed his eyes. Her children's father, she thought. Her husband. The phrase pulsed inside her, and for a moment, she couldn't speak, could barely swallow.

And then Max said, "What about the time he mooned us at the dinner table?"

"Oh my God," Grace said, "Why did he anyway? I can't believe I told the M.A.M.A. group about that."

"What?" Stephen laughed. "You're kidding?"

Grace shrugged. "It just seemed so, so *Jack*."

"It was," Stephen said. "But the real question, *Max*, is who taught him that to begin with?"

"I didn't! I swear!" But Max couldn't even get out the words without laughing.

Erin giggled. "That was so funny."

"It was not!" Grace said. "It was disgusting. We were in the middle of dinner."

"Remember how he thought candy canes were Js?" Erin said.

"Well, they are," Grace said. "*J*-candy."

"He used to get so mad when we hung them on the tree 'cause he said they were upside-down."

"What about when he was jumping in his crib and he jumped over the edge?"

"Or how he used to say he wanted to be an astro-*nut*?"

"Oh, he was an astro-*nut,* all right."

After the kids went to bed, Grace and Stephen stayed up for a while, staring at the festivities on TV in Times Square. It seemed sad. How it just went on—life and routine—no matter what occurred in the world: terrorist attacks and wars and people dying every day. A ball dropping. A countdown. Another year pitching toward its end, sliding down the steep incline of all that had happened.

Outside, it began to rain, and Grace dozed off, her head back, leaning against Stephen's shoulder, his arm around her. Even in her sleep, his heartbeat sounded in her ear, a steady unwavering cadence that went on and on.

EPILOGUE

What Survives

Speaking of marvels, I am alive
together with you, when I might have been
alive with anyone under the sun. . . .
. . . .
the odds against us are endless,
our chances of being alive together
statistically nonexistent;
still we have made it . . .

—Lisel Mueller, "Alive Together,"
New and Selected Poems

WHAT SURVIVES

What will survive of us is love.

Philip Larkin

E *ven at the biological level of cells, the dominant story of our lives is one of loss and rebuilding. By the time we are born, 90 percent of our cells have already been killed off, and in the first few years of our lives, connections between the synapses in the brain will be forever lost, replaced with new ones. For as long as we are alive, our cells will continue to divide—four million times every second—so that by the time we die, every cell in our body will have been replaced hundreds, thousands, of times. Nothing about us is permanent, each of us, as naturalist Loren Eisley writes, a "statistical possibility around which hover a million other lives never destined to be born."*

What, then, survives?

Nothing.

And everything.

Think of how, before an embryo ever implants itself in the uterus, the probability of its surviving to birth is no more than 30 percent. Out of all conceptions 10 to 15 percent have a chromosomal abnormality, and of these fetuses, more than two-thirds never survive to term. And yet every day and against all odds, children are born with devastating illnesses. And every day and against all odds, these children survive, even flourish. They dream of going to the moon or becoming a Power Ranger, a chess champion, a ballerina.

Nothing.

And everything.

Heat left over from the Big Bang is still aglow in the universe, and dinosaur eggs that eighty million years ago were close to hatching, are found fully fossilized and intact. Buried beneath layers of Greenland ice is volcanic ash from

Krakatau and lead pollution from ancient Roman smelters. At 138 feet down is snow dating from the Civil War; 2,500 feet down, snow from the days of Plato. Plants grow from rocks or volcanic soil. A willow tree can grow from just a cutting. The surface of Mars still carries traces of liquid water now gone, enough water to have filled two Lake Eries, the very lake where millions of years into the future a seventeen-year-old girl would fall in love. "Hey you."

What survives? Everything you ever heard or saw or felt or dreamed: *the expression on Stephen's face the first time he held Erin. A daughter.* Certain words or facts: semipalmated; Munchausen's. *The farther two quarks move away from each other, the more fiercely they are pulled back together The final words, intaglio'd into stone at the Witch's Memorial, of those women who were hanged over three hundred years ago in a small New England town.* But he bid me tell you that you might look to unnatural things for the cause of it. *The sound of your son's laughter. Mitochondria, those ancient bacteria. Or red hair, blue eyes.*

Whenever you read a book or scan your e-mail or watch on TV as buildings topple endlessly to the ground, the experience causes physical changes in your brain. New memories are formed that will forever alter how you see the world, and though we may forget the old memories, nothing is ever lost.

The smell of pumpkin bread on New Year's Eve.

Your name is my flight song.

A child crying: Stay me!

Noah, is that you?

The taste of butter-pecan ice cream and the smell of mint in the kitchen of a yellow beach house in a seaside town in Delaware and a glass jar full of questions printed on bright scraps of paper: If you could eliminate one color from the spectrum, what would it be? If you could give rain a scent, of what would it smell?

What survives? By placing special electrodes into the parts of the brain that control memory, physicians can now stimulate recall in an 85-year-old so specifically that he can quote verbatim a newspaper article read half a century earlier. Think of birds flying thousands of miles to a home they've known only in memory, of heliotropic plants, whose leaves unfurl and close in conjunction with the rising and setting of the sun even when those plants are kept in darkness. Oysters, taken from the ocean and set in a pan of seawater, still open and close their shells in time with tides they no longer feel. And cells of the heart, alone in a petri dish, continue to beat.

What survives? Glance up at a red-throated loon, a species nearly twenty million years old, as it stitches together the brilliant blue sky of a perfect autumn morning. Is anything ever really lost? Exactly 2,800 words, spoken by the fire-fighters climbing into the South Tower, still exist on a dispatcher's tape. And business cards, broken sculptures, the bent stairwell sign from the 102nd floor. A tin of melted coins. Four autographed baseballs. Shoes, wedding rings, voices on cell phones and answering machines.

What survives? And who and why? How is it that a 110-story building can collapse in on itself, pulverizing fire trucks, cement stairwells, and people, and yet workers, in the aftermath, will find a pane of glass perfectly intact? Or bread dough sitting on a cutting board, still bearing the imprint of someone's fingers? A menu from the dining hall of Deutsche Bank listing the breakfast specials for that morning: smoked-salmon omelets, chocolate-filled pancakes. A yo-yo, a tube of pink lipstick, a half-eaten doughnut. The beaded party dress that had hung in one of the Plaza's boutique windows. Someone's résumé, a lottery ticket. Watches—still telling time.

And children. In the months following that horrible morning, over fifty children would be born to widows of September 11, the first one only two days later. In his name, Farqad, *which means "star," does his father live on, watching from above? Another father survives in his daughter's cleft chin, another in his son's big feet, another in the name,* Alexis, *that he chose months before she was born, and months before he died.*

What survives? Names on the toys donated to hospital playrooms—in memory of—or on walls or quilts or in the "Portraits of Grief" that the nation read that autumn. On a wall in Washington, D.C. The color yellow and French fries served in a red beach bucket. A Wednesday night in 1941 and the fifty-nine-year marriage that blazed cometlike through the generations. A conch shell found along the shoreline, perfectly intact.

Nothing.

And everything.

Did you know that except for hydrogen, all the atoms that make us up—the calcium in our bones and iron in our blood, the carbon in our brains—were manufactured in red giant stars thousands of light years away in time and space? Did you know that water created billions of years ago still exists? That perhaps this very water is in our blood now, and that one day it will form a cloud, or that years before we were born, it lived within a glacier? Did you know that memories are forms of energy and so can never be destroyed, and that grief will one day become love and that love will eventually become hope?

Did you know?

ACKNOWLEDGMENTS

My wonderful nieces and nephews have changed my life, changed me, in myriad ways. My writing too is deeper and more multifaceted because of the person these four children have allowed me to become. To them more thanks than I know how to express.

To the many women who have been falsely accused of Munchausen Syndrome by Proxy and who so generously, albeit guardedly, shared their stories with me in letters, e-mails, and phone calls. I could not have written this book without your help.

To those who suffer from mitochondrial disease and/or those who love someone who suffers from it, there are no words to express what you have taught me about resilience and hope and the importance of telling even the most painful stories. Behind them lie innumerable moments of beauty, courage, and grace.

To the writers and editors who have donated their time, energy and talent to the annual "Writers at the Beach: Pure Sea Glass" writing conference in an effort to raise both money for and awareness of mitochondrial disease, thank you for reminding me that stories really do change lives. I have watched it happen. In just two years, there is more awareness of this disease in my little state of Delaware than I could have imagined.

To the staff at Booksandcoffee in Dewey Beach, Delaware, especially Terry Lake and Debby Creasy, who not only gave me a wonderful setting in which to write *The Life You Longed For*, but who also offered me plenty of coffee, encouragement, and enthusiasm—all equally necessary.

To the participants of the Rehoboth Beach Writers' Guild Free

Writes! You have taught me anew what first brought me to writing over twenty years ago: there is so much joy in the small moments of success, so much joy simply in showing up each day, pen in hand, ready to take the leap.

To my friends Gail Comorat and Anne Colwell, I don't know where to begin. Your own talent as writers is so much a part of *The Life You Longed For*. Your insights into the characters, your astute questions, your numerous comments on draft after draft have been invaluable. As has your friendship, which I truly cherish.

To my amazing agent Candice Fuhrmann who, even in the midst of arguing with me about certain issues in *The Life You Longed For* (and the book is exponentially better for the arguments she won), never stopped believing in my writing, in this book, in me—and so fought hard to find it the best home she could.

Which brings me to my editor at Touchstone Fireside, Cherise Davis: You have trusted me, respected my ideas, worked hard to make *The Life You Longed For* the book I dreamed it could be. Thank you.

Reading Group Guide
for

The Life You Longed For

by Maribeth Fischer

THE LIFE YOU LONGED FOR

by Maribeth Fischer

"She began wondering about her own decisions, and about the shadow life of choices not made that trailed behind the life she lived now."

Grace, an epidemiologist, wife, and mother of three, spends most of her time fighting for the life of her youngest son, Jack, who suffers from mitochondrial disease—a chronic genetic disorder that occurs when the mitochondria of the cell fail to produce enough energy for cell or organ function. Adored by family and friends for her courage and commitment, Grace, however, is not a saint. She is having an affair with a man she abandoned twenty years ago, a man who offers her a glimpse into the life she didn't choose.

Just when Jack needs his mother the most, a new enemy confronts the family. Grace is accused of Munchausen syndrome by proxy, a form of child abuse in which the mother makes her own child sick in order to gain attention. Afraid she is the victim of a modern-day witch hunt, Grace arms herself with knowledge and wages war against the two medical mysteries—all the while trying to shield a secret that could destroy her family.

"A strong new voice in women's fiction" (*Publishers Weekly*), Maribeth Fischer has crafted both a suspenseful medical drama and a thoughtful piece on the true meaning of survival.

1. Prior to reading this novel, were you aware of Munchausen syndrome by proxy? If so, how has your opinion changed, if at all?

2. "But you hold on to what you have to, she knew, thinking of how certain desert cacti can hoard a single drop of rainwater for decades . . . And people with their secrets? They were no different, she believed, preserving them at enormous costs because sometimes, like water or instinct, their secrets were all that allowed them to survive" (p. 4). How does Grace's secret allow her to survive?

3. "The farther two quarks move away from each other, the more fiercely they're pulled back together" (p. 15). Does this statement hold true for all of Grace's relationships or just her relationship with Noah?

4. This book is broken up into sections titled "Desire," "Belief," "Betrayal," "Fear," "Grief," and "What Survives." What meaning did you find in the introductions to each section?

5. "No one who knew her would ever guess, not just *where* she had been, but *who.* Someone else" (p. 18). How is Grace different with Noah than she is with her family and friends?

6. Do you think Grace is a good mother? Why or why not?

7. "In most stories about the moon, someone was always trying to catch it, to pull it back down to Earth: the man who sees it reflected in the water and tries to pick it up, only to have it slip from his grasp just when he thought he'd had it" (p. 94). What does the moon symbolize in *The Life You Longed For*?

8. When accusations are made against her, Grace compares them to a modern-day witch hunt. Do you think this is a fair comparison?

9. "To find the right answer, one must ask the right question" (p. 227). What question do you think Grace needs to ask herself?

10. "How was it that she had never understood until now how much the ocean was a landscape of loss: constantly breaking waves, emptied shells, land carried out to sea a little bit each year" (p. 270). What role does nature play in this story?

11. Discuss the book's central theme—survival—and how it applies to each of the main characters. Which character is best equipped to deal with his or her own struggles?

12. Are you satisfied with the outcome of the love triangle in this novel? Why or why not?

ENHANCE YOUR BOOK CLUB

1. Watch the film version of *The Crucible* at your book club meeting and discuss the parallels to *The Life You Longed For*.

2. Ask each of your book club members to bring a children's book to donate to your local children's hospital. (For a children's hospital near you, go to www.childrenshospitals.net.) Or collect funds and donate them to United Mitochondrial Disease Foundation (8085 Saltsburg Road, Suite 201, Pittsburgh, PA 15239; www.umdf.org/about_umdf/donate.aspx).

3. Take your book club to a local Audubon center. (For locations, go to www.audubon.org/states/index.php.)

AUTHOR QUESTIONS AND ANSWERS

Throughout the story you refer to several songs, authors, and novels, such as Dostoyevsky and *Alice in Wonderland*. Do these references have special meaning to you, or did they simply fit with the story?

I keep notebooks with quotes or lines from songs that I especially like or that ring true. The one by Dostoyevsky—about the death of a child being the greatest reason not to believe in the existence of God—rang so true the first time I read it that I immediately copied it and have never forgotten it. The quote (p. 241) from Haven Kimmel's The Solace of Leaving Early *is another one that just hit me in the gut with its truth when I read it. Some things are so hard to express. Expressing the love one feels for a child, or the loss of a child—I'll never stop looking for a way to express this because they are feelings that are so important to who I am. When I find a writer who captures something of these hard-to-express truths, then I save those words.*

Your first novel, *The Language of Good-bye*, addresses the issue of infidelity. Why did you return to this subject in *The Life You Longed For*?

Infidelity interests me as a writer because in some ways it is the worst betrayal I can imagine—to lie to and cheat on the person you love—to the person who loves you. At the same time, though, infidelity seems so human, in that the infidelity itself is also about love (or at least the kind of infidelity I am interested in writing of). It's about wanting love, about wanting to be seen in ways that the adulterer feels he or she isn't being seen. I don't think there is anything about infidelity that is okay, and yet I can understand the temptation. Very little is more important in our lives than being understood, listened to, and recognized.

In a reading group guide for your last novel, you talked about your work on this novel, at that time titled *What Survives*: "The main characters are a woman whose youngest child has a terminal illness, a man who works in a community development corporation to improve impoverished inner-city neighborhoods, and an ornithologist whose task, in part, is to save endangered species of birds. Through the intersection of these characters, each of whom is dealing with a survival issue, I want to explore what exactly it means to survive." It sounds as if originally you were going to tell the story from three different perspectives. Is that true? If so, what transformed this book into Grace's story? What other elements, other than the title, evolved throughout your writing process to create what is now *The Life You Longed For*?

Survival is still very much the issue in **The Life You Longed For,** *but rather than what survival means, I became more interested in what it is that survives of our lives, our loves, our dreams. And I could explore this through Grace alone because the focus of her entire life is on survival—not just the literal issue of keeping Jack alive, but the issue of what would remain of him, of her love for him, of his for her, once he was gone. It was never really an issue of whether Jack would survive but in what ways his family, especially Grace, would find to hold on to him.*

As I wrote this book, I realized that maybe holding on to memories, loves, and dreams is how things survive and the big question, the real question for me, and therefore for Grace, is when we need to hold tight and when we need to let go.

The novel begins with Grace going to visit her lover on Christmas Eve instead of being home with her sick child. Were you worried readers would find this unbelievable or be turned off from the main character?

Yes, I was worried that people would be turned off by this, but hopefully, the reader quickly sees that Grace loves her children enormously, and I think too that most readers would agree that what Grace is dealing with—knowing her child will die—is one of the most awful things any parent would have to face. Grace is desperate and she's scared, and I believed that no matter how readers felt about her adultery, they would have a hard time being unsympathetic to her as a person.

September 11 is touched upon in your story. Why did you decide to include that day into the fabric of your novel, one that already has dark storylines such as mitochondrial disease, Munchausen syndrome by proxy, and the Salem witch trials?

I simply couldn't imagine how anyone could write a novel set in 2001 and not include that event. I had also started working—on September 10, 2001—as a volunteer at a grief counseling center, I lived ten minutes away from the Pentagon, and my uncle's first wife—my aunt, who was the mother of a college-age girl and a six-year-old boy—was on the plane that crashed into the Pentagon. It was never an option for me not to include it.

As an advocate for the United Mitochondrial Disease Foundation, a charitable organization that serves people with the disease as well as promotes awareness, what would you like the public to know about this disease?

I want the public to know that mitochondrial disease is implicated in hundreds of different diseases such as Alzheimer's, autism, hearing disorders, gastrointestinal issues, growth problems, heart defects—the list is endless. What happens, though, is that the heart disease will get diagnosed, or the hearing disorder, but the underlying cause, the mitochondrial disease, goes undiagnosed for years, with parents often going to numerous doctors looking for answers. Mitochondrial disease affects as many as 1 in 2,000 children, but without awareness of this disease it's hard to get funding for research and it's difficult to get researchers to study it; and for the families and parents, the lack of understanding of what the disease is only makes their burden that much greater. Too often the burden of educating people about the disease falls onto the parents, who already have too much to do for and with their children, and all too often have too little time.

Where did you get the idea to use the Salem witch trials in your novel? Do you believe, as Kempley does, that Munchausen's is a way to explain what no one can understand and that it "preys on a woman's worst fears about herself"?

My original idea actually was to write about a woman who had falsely accused her friend of being a witch during the Salem witch trials, of having to watch that friend get hung as a witch. I wondered what it would be like to have to live in Salem in the aftermath. How did one ever get over doing something like this to another? How would the accuser face the woman's husband, her children? When I started to write that story, though, I found the research I would need to do in order to write believably about life in the 1690s overwhelming. And what interested me was the emotions, the mind-sets of people, the why of people's behavior. That's when I began looking for a modern-day version of the trials and I happened to have seen a 20/20 show about Munchausen's . . . The parallels struck me immediately. And yes, I think Munchausen's, like the witch trials, offers an answer to what is frightening and unfathomable.

"It was what she had always done, how she had always coped, as if the answers always came packaged in words" (p. 258). "To find the right answer, one must ask the right question" (p. 291). Were you looking for answers while writing this book? Did you find them?

I think I wanted to understand how to hold on to someone who is gone or will be gone, and I hope I do have a better understanding of this. And the "anguished question," to use the writer Wallace Stegner's term, that seems to be at the heart of all that I write is the issue of what happens when a good woman does something awful, as you could say Grace did in this book. Does she deserve to have her whole life, her qualities as a mother, called into question? What survives of her in the end?

How long did it take you to write this book? What special research did you do in the areas of Munchausen's, the Salem witch trials, and ornithology?

From start to finish, **The Life You Longed For** *took me five years* to write. I read everything I could on Munchausen syndrome by proxy; I probably have every book written on it, as well as half a dozen binders filled with articles. I talked to women who had been falsely accused, and some of them allowed me to read their official trial transcripts. I read numerous books on child abuse and child abuse laws; I went to Salem and researched the witch trials—again, mostly through reading. I read about disease and the history of disease so that I could make Grace a credible epidemiologist, and of course I read numerous books on birds, gleaning from them the unusual details that someone who was truly passionate about ornithology, like Noah, would know. I read books on grief, even read some things about the Detroit Tigers and about hockey (since Max liked hockey). Throughout the past five years, I was constantly reading science-based books and articles, so that I would have a lot of scientific references that I could give to Grace. I absolutely love doing the research. One of the best aspects of being a writer is having an excuse to learn about things I never would have otherwise.